W9-CHC-955

WITHDRAWN FROM LIBRARY

Also by Sara Maitland

*A Big-Enough God: A Feminist's Search
for a Joyful Theology*

The Rushdie File

Virgin Territory

Telling Tales

*A Map of the New Country:
Women & Christianity*

Ancestral Truths

Three Times Table

Daughter of Jerusalem

Angel Maker

MONTGOMERY COLLEGE
ROCKVILLE CAMPUS LIBRARY
ROCKVILLE, MARYLAND

Angel Maker

the short stories of sara maitland

a john macrae book

henry holt and company

new york

ABF 4670

APR 0 7 1997

MONTGOMERY COLLEGE
ROCKVILLE CAMPUS LIBRARY
ROCKVILLE, MARYLAND

Henry Holt and Company, Inc.
Publishers since 1866
115 West 18th Street
New York, New York 10011

Henry Holt® is a registered
trademark of Henry Holt and Company, Inc.

Copyright © 1996 by Sara Maitland
All rights reserved.
Published in Canada by Fitzhenry & Whiteside Ltd.,
195 Allstate Parkway, Markham, Ontario L3R 4T8.

Library of Congress Cataloging-in-Publication Data
Maitland, Sara, 1950–
Angel maker : the short stories of
Sara Maitland / Sara Maitland. — 1st ed.
p. cm.
"A John Macrae book."
1. Women—Social life and customs—Fiction. I. Title.
PR6063.A355A6   1996   95-33667
823'.914—dc20   CIP

ISBN 0-8050-4412-4

Henry Holt books are available for special promotions
and premiums. For details contact: Director, Special Markets.

First Edition—1996

Designed by Betty Lew

Printed in the United States of America
All first editions are printed on acid-free paper. ∞

1   3   5   7   9   10   8   6   4   2

Contents

Angel Maker

Angel Maker

Gretel will come through the forest again this afternoon, as she has come so many times before, since that first time.

It is a golden October day; last night I smelled for the first time this year the distant savor of frost—it was still far away in the Northlands, but hunting southwards following the swallows and pushing before it nights of jewel-bright sharpness and days of astonishing radiance—the sky dazzling blue in contrast to the soft mysterious gold yellows and flame reds of the leaves and the ground-cover grass still green, a green that is deeper now than at any time of year—the frail yellow hues of spring and the dusty density of summer both gone, washed away by the September rain. It is quiet in the forest at this time of year, not silent but a gentle, rustly quiet, except when the winds blow. Today it is not windy nor will be before evening when, if I am not too tired by the events of the afternoon, I will call up a wind and dance, crazy, ancient and unseen, along with the dying leaves whose final flourishing will amuse both them and me.

But before that Gretel will come; discerning in her need the cryptic signs of the path through the forest and walking with a firm but cautious stride. Her laced canvas boots will be the same green as the grass and the tufts of her short hair will blend with the extreme oranges and purples of the autumn wood. She has grown into a beautiful woman, as I always knew she would, and though I think her foolish now, that is not my problem but hers. I do not choose, I never have chosen, to make other women's choices my problem; I do not judge and I do not take the consequences of my refusal to judge. That is my privilege and the price that they must pay for my services. She will regret it, or not regret it, as time alone will show, and her daughter one day perhaps will seek me out in some other forest, in some other time. And in the meantime she has grown into a beautiful woman, for those who have eyes to see it.

I am waiting for her in the bright morning, while my winter doves pick seeds around the gingerbread house. Some things do not change and the windows are all still made of spun sugar, as white and clear as glass, but melting sweet. But bubblegum has solved the old problem of keeping the place together and progress is something I have always believed in. She is a grown-up now but still she prefers, as I prefer, the sugar-candy gingerbread to the chromium and steel cleanliness that some others offer. It is warmth and comfort a woman needs at such times, not hard shiny edges—them as want that can go elsewhere and good riddance to bad rubbish I say.

She will come alone this time.

That is something; something gained in so many centuries.

Of course, the first time she came, all neat and pretty in her cotton skirts and tidy pinny, she was so young that she had to bring him with her—Hansel, I mean; they were not old enough to be separated, she could not go out and about without the boy-child. I saw them come through the forest and they seemed like any two little children to me then, tasty enough and milky sweet, and their eyes huge and round under those thick little fringes, lighting with joy at the sight of the sweety sticky house. But I did not recognize her, even though I could not but admire the abandoned greed with which she tucked into the sweet things on offer, licking at my window till the panes melted and ran down her chin in runnels of sweetness.

I called to her in a whisper,

Nibble, nibble, nibble mouse,
Who is nibbling at my little house?

I should have known her from her answer but I had been alone too long. She smiled and sang,

The wind, the wind,
The heaven-born wind.

Ah, but she was a lucky one then, she had not sought me out knowingly, though without needy desire I cannot be found; the desire was there—the need to be comforted for the loss of her mother, the desire to be comforted for the betrayal by her father. She needed no special magic that time, just showing. So I locked him up, and fattened him up, and let her see that she could be without him, that she was strong and wise and could decide for herself. It worked, though I scared her so badly that she thrust me into the oven and burned me to death and went home and told them that I ate little children.

Well, every sane witch fears fire, it would be folly not to. It was my fault, I thought she was so young that I could decide for her. But it is not permitted; she chose him over me and all I could do was help them find their way back to Daddy afterwards. Now I never choose on their behalf. I wait. I wait. As I wait for her now.

I waited that time ten years and several centuries. She came back when she needed to. She came through the forest, a long swirling skirt spreading its Indian patterns around her, her hair long, its tendrils twisting in and out of the sunlight and adorned with ribbons; her feet were bare on the grass; her breasts were full and her hips sinuous. Her lips looked like those of a woman fulfilled, but her eyes like those of a woman betrayed. Betrayed again.

She stood on the edge of the clearing, and that greed had disappeared under an anxiety. She did not even smile to see the ginger-bread and sugar cottage. She looked at me as though she hated me. I smiled a little, and said,

Nibble, nibble, nibble mouse.
Who is nibbling at my little house?

I thought it might remind her and comfort her.

She said, almost reluctantly, "They say you can help me."

"Love potions?" I reply. "Charms for safety at sea? For murrain among cows, and zits on your rival's nose? Eye of newt and toe of dog."

I know she has not come for these, but I never decide for my women; they must ask me. It is not my problem.

Slowly she leaves the protection of the tall trees and crosses into the sunlight of my clearing; the chickens cheep and the doves coo; I reach up and break a soft piece of gingerbread, sparkly with sugar, off the eave above my head, and hold it out to her. She takes it almost fiercely and chews. There is a pause and then she says, "I'm preg-nant."

"I know," I say, and we wait in a long silence while she masticates the cake in her mouth, her long beady earrings joggling about. I know she is waiting for me to offer, but I am an old witch woman and I say nothing. The silence lengthens, even the trees seem hushed and the scratching of the birds fades away. I cannot help her if she cannot ask. After a while, I shuffle inside and get on with things. I think what a tough and joyous child she was all those years ago, shrieking and complaining, and I am angry. I do the washing up, trying not to bang the pots too loudly. I heat the oven and spray on the foam oven-cleaner; when I look out through the sugar-spun win-dows she is still standing in the clearing, her outline wavery and out of focus from the impurities in the sugar.

At length, she comes to the doorway, and looks in.

"Remember?" I ask, but she shakes her head.

I think she does remember, though, because after only a tiny pause she says, "I want it got rid of."

"All right," I say.

"It's against the law," she mutters; I don't mind being checked out, it seems sensible to me.

"Not my law," I tell her. "Your law?"

Suddenly she becomes verbose, "It's like this, you see, it's not that I don't like babies, it's just that he . . ."

"No," I say, quite stern. "Don't tell me, I don't want to know. I won't blame and I won't praise. There is only one reason: you want it. Nothing else. I'm not interested."

Suddenly she smiles, shy and illuminated. "OK," she says, "let's do it."

I go to the back of the cottage and fetch the cauldron; I swing it up on to the hook over the fire. I tell her to lie down. I fill the cauldron and start the long spell.

"Will it hurt?" she asks. "Wait and see," I answer.

The smoke rises and swirls about the room, and I take her hand and we go together into another place, a dark and magical room where women go to take charge over destiny, over forests and grow-ing time and small birds and sugar-candy windows, because we choose to. It is a place of risk. It is not a good place, but we go, not because we must, but because we will.

Hours later, we come back and it is dark. It is cold and drafty, because the fire has melted the window panes and the night winds are coming in. I wrap her in a quilt stitched of all the good things in the forest and in the tales of childhood, and then although I am tired I melt more sugar and remake my windows.

In the morning I make her a nice cup of tea and give her a sugar bun plucked from beside the bathroom down-drain. While she gets dressed I sew the scarlet flowering pimpernels which have bloomed on her undersheet into the quilt for the next woman. When she comes down I think that she will leave in silence, but at the last moment she turns to me and says, "Will she be all right, my daughter?"

I should refuse to answer, I should keep my own rules, but it is she, it is Gretel, the little child who came to me in great loss and fear all those years ago, and I love her. So I answer, "They don't call me the Angel Maker for nothing."

It takes her a moment or two to work it out; it is, after all, very early in the morning. Suddenly she grins an enormous evil grin, full of dislike of me, of herself, of the world; also full of irony, and joy and freedom and knowledge. She bunches her fingers into a fist and without warning smashes into one of my newly set windows. She takes a huge chunk of sugar in her hand and sucks it voluptuously. Then she turns, crosses the clearing and goes back into the forest. I think I have seen the last of her, and stand recovering my energy from the gentle warmth of the morning sun, but after a few moments she reappears from behind a tree; she waves her sugar-candy shard at me and shouts, "Sod the bastards, just sod the lot of them. Including Him." And she goes away leaving me cackling in my clearing, with yet another window to cook. And another long wait.

I waited again. Understand, she came a thousand times; she came a thousand times as the little child with her brother who did not understand her mother's withdrawal, who did not understand her father's betrayal; she came a thousand times as the young woman with some man's child, with her own child in her belly. And yet I still waited for her to come again. I waited in almost perfect patience. I waited until last month, a wet morning after the turn of the moon, and she came again. I knew she would.

During the waiting time, business had changed. Little call now for love potions and cures for the murrain and kettle mending and fire tending and the little spells of yesteryear. They have Dating Agencies and Inoculations and Hire Purchase and Calor Gas: all of which I might say are strong magics, stronger than mine, and cheaper, and more secret. I have always favored progress. In the end they took even the deep magic; they changed their laws and called mine quackery. I still hold that a woman needs another woman's hand to clasp and a little sugar splinter to suck on when she goes into the dark place and takes control of the spinning of her own destiny; they say she needs hygiene and counseling and medical attention and I say I never lost one who could be saved, and when they were done with me they knew that they had chosen and were responsible for that. I never questioned that they sucked by the wind, the heaven-born wind, and that those who needed me could find me always. But there is always magic business for a self-respecting old witch to live off. I move with the times, I invested in an oxygen-cooled thermos-flask, and went out and charmed the men they needed, and I waited for her to come.

She was thirty-eight now and could not wait much longer. Stupid, though. In the end I had to go to the town and lay down clues. It was breaking my own rules, of course, and I knew it. It was a long time since I had walked on streets that had hard surfaces and bright neon lights; there were fireworks in every puddle, magic fireworks mothered by the brightness of the lights, golden and sparkly in the wind. But though I had gone with intent, when I saw the first of the children I was innocent and delighted. A darling little thing, wrapped not in a blanket but in a sensible progressive snow-suit, her dark eyes poking up over the edge of a red and green padded snowsuit, and bright with the joy of being a wanted child. Her mother, stiff with pride and tiredness, pushed her in a little open wheeled chair, more frail and fairy than any pumpkin carriage.

"Oh, the little angel," I cried, and fell upon her with an improper kiss. Perhaps we make rules only for the strange and painful pleasure of breaking them. Her mother recognized me, of course, and was appalled. I saw her stiffen with embarrassment and turn aside with a charm to ward off evil. " 'Aroint thee, witch,' " the rump-fed runnion cried (her girlfriend's to Aleppo gone, mistress of a Channel 4 documentary, but in a sieve I'll thither sail and like a rat without a tail I'll do, I'll do and I'll do)—does she take responsibility for what she does, despite my best efforts? I wonder. But I saw that Gretel was there and her eyes widened and her wonder deepened. I knew that she would come. And she did. And we talked women talk and agreed that today is the day that she must come. I will do for her what she cannot bring herself to do for herself. I ask no questions and make no judgments, that is not my task. I taught her so long ago that she had to find her own strength and draw upon it, so I can scarcely complain if she draws upon mine.

Last night it was cold; riding upon my broomstick I smelled for the first time this year the distant savor of frost—it was still far away in the Northlands, but hunting southwards following the swallows and pushing before it nights of jewel-bright sharpness and days of astonishing radiance—the moon, so round as to spin the whole cosmos, rode out the darkness anchored to the lee of a ragged cloud, frilled and furbelowed in reflected silver.

He is handsome, the miller's wife's dark son, and his father astute and sturdy; they do not take fever, those children, and they grow beside the weir wide-eyed and hopeful, the rushing water stirring something in them that this child of Gretel's will need. Five centuries ago I would have sent her to him in the gloaming time and given her a little magic potion just in the unlikely case that he was unwilling, but I have taught her to stand firmer to her dignity even than that. Five centuries ago I might have burned for it, but I do not think of that. I may be old and ugly, but he is young and beautiful, and flattery will get one anywhere. Just now he loves a handsome piper from the king's castle keep and loves himself enough to love his own sperm and rejoice that he can spread it here and there without having either effort or responsibility. He will do perfectly for Gretel, and he gives me the ingredient of my magic and feels flattered to do so. At home I spin the crawling fluid in my centrifuge: I make only girl babies, but that is my secret, my power, the one thing I do not let my women choose for themselves—I have some professional dignity. Then I return the fluid to the vial and place it in the refrigerating thermos. I boil the cauldron and wait. Gretel will come through the forest again this afternoon, as she has come so many times before, since that first time.

And she comes, discerning in her need the cryptic signs of the path through the forest and walking with a firm but cautious stride. Her laced canvas boots are the same green as the grass and the tufts of her short hair blend with the extreme oranges and purples of the autumn wood. She has grown into a beautiful woman, as I always knew she would, and though I think her foolish now, that is not my problem but hers. She barely greets me, intent on her own journey and needing. I take her hand and lead her inside the cottage; for the first time I do not bother to break off any titbit for her, knowing that she does not really desire anything except the vial and its magic potency.

I give it to her without further ado. The glass twinkles more clearly than my spun-sugar windows, but I pass no comment upon this. I say only, "Do you know what to do?" I watch as her square strong knuckles close around the magic potion. "Yes, alas," she says, and it is a new grin of self-knowing and a deep irony. "Go in there," I tell her, and point towards the door of the bedroom. "The quilt is on the bed. Make yourself at home." I swear I meant no joke, but she grinned again and said, "Do you trust me? Don't you want to come too?" Her irony dissolves and she says, like a little child, "Please come and help me." And I, clinging to my own rules like a woman who expects to be saved by good conduct, say, "No."

I go out of the house and into the clearing. The grass is green and bright; only a little way away the trees of the forest flaunt their autumn coloring; when, after the winter, the summer comes again, Gretel will have a little girl child nursing at her breast. It is what she wants and what I have given her. And though I think her foolish, that is not my problem but hers. I do not choose, I have never chosen, to make other women's choices my problem; I do not judge and I do not take the consequences of my refusal to judge. That is my privilege and the price that they must pay for my services. She will regret it, or not regret it, as time alone will show, and her daughter one day perhaps will seek me out in some other forest, in some other time. And in the meantime she has grown into a beautiful woman, for those who have eyes to see it.

I busy myself as best I may about the clearing, and watch my chickens and my doves busy about their autumn work of feeding and preening, content during this resting time to be sufficient unto themselves, neither mating nor brooding. After what seems like a long, long while, I hear a sudden noisy crash and a tinkling shattering noise. A moment later Gretel emerges; the magic vial now empty, the spell used, is crushed into fragments in her left hand, from which red blood drips gently downwards, but in her right hand she is holding a long sharp icicle of spun sugar which she is sucking greedily. From my apron pocket I take a kerchief, and gently enfold her left hand. I wipe away both the glass and the blood, which later I will sew into the quilt for the next woman. I bind up her wounds. There is a long pause.

"I can give you a spell against morning sickness," I say.

"Thank you," she replies. "I would appreciate that."

There is another long pause, and then she says, "Thank you. Goodbye."

I say, "You'll be back."

She considers this then asks, "Whatever for?"

"How should I know yet, but you will be back. Again and again, forever."

She looks at the splinter of sugar in her hand and sucks it voluptuously. Then she turns, crosses the clearing and goes back into the forest. I think I have seen the last of her and stand recovering my energy from the gentle warmth of the sun, but after a few moments she reappears from behind a tree; she waves her sugar-candy shard at me and calls out, quite gently, "Goodbye for now then, Angel Maker." And she goes away leaving me cackling in my clearing, with yet another window to cook. And another long wait.

Well, it has been a long story. I don't know even now if it has made clear the most important thing. I love her so much, now and always.

Siren Song

Come, sailor, I am your dreaming;
long voyaging on icy seas
leads to the white haven of my arms.

It is never silent on the sea coast. There is always, even in a flat calm, the whispered sound of the smallest waves licking the silvered sand of the beach, tonguing the face of the rocks, and the soft sigh of the sand as each wave retreats and a few grains are carried down with it, reluctantly, inexorably.

It is never silent on the sea coast, but sometimes, at night, in the summer months, there can be a fleeting moment of something sweeter than silence; a magical hush. The soft irregular rhythms of that continuous rise and fall, rise and fall, rise and fall, rise and fall, become so monotonous, so expected, and so gentle, that they fit perfectly to heartbeat and to breathing; out on the seaway there is a slow roll of water, a gentle heave, and a flowing gleam of phosphorescence, and we know a porpoise is passing on its long travels.

In that moment, just occasionally, but worth the long expectancy, the moon rises, full, round, silver, and lays her swathe of white light across the barely shifting waters, and the twin points of light on the facing slope of each slow lift of water dance in delight. The moon at her full puts out the stars around her, but in compensation lays these dancing stars on the sea itself. The air is balmy, heavy, scented with summer and with seaweed. And if on such nights as these, we lay our hands or bare arms so that the moon beams fall on them, we can feel—attenuated, fragile, delicate—the warmth of the sun, kissing his virgin sister, and letting the last reverberation of his power refracted from her across the wide spaces, caress us in the darkness of the night.

When the white lady rides her pathway on the sea, when all else is still, when the waves have sunk to this sparkling, dancing murmur, then we rise from our nest and preen ourselves, preparing ourselves as the young bride does for her beloved and with an excitement that is not altogether different although we wish that it were.

We wait.

It is our destiny to wait, but we chose that destiny and so our waiting is not the anxious wonderings of the sailor's beloved in the noisy harbors north of us. Will he come? will he come on this light breeze, bending his back to the drumbeat and pulling wearily? or on another, on the shoulder of a storm? or out of the sunset boldly with the sails set filled with a home wind and a golden light? Will he come today? Tomorrow? Will he ever come again?

Our waiting is not like that. It is a long calm waiting and we are always ready when he comes.

We wait.

And so, when those other three sisters, the Fates, have spun a sailor's life-thread so thin and taut that it can be spun no further, then far away a new rhythm begins, so gentle and distant, that it is hard to be certain, although we are certain. More a movement on the surface of the water than a sound, but the feathers, the hairs—both—on our necks rise sensitive to his coming and we smile a little at each other and preen.

And carried on the calm night the sound of his coming takes shape. The slow drumbeat counts out the strokes. The cry of the helmsman in the stern is borne across the surface of the water to our longing ears. "In," he cries, ". . . and out. In—two, three; out—two, three." The oars hit the surface together as he calls them; the drum and the oars and the strong rich voice of the helmsman. "In . . . out . . . In . . . out."

They are freemen who row such a ship, for we do not hear the harsh sound of the lash; a dark arrhythmic note, joyless and painful, with which we have no business, no concern. As soon as we hear the coming of the ship clearly we draw breath and we strike the chord and we sing, so that our singing runs out along the pathway that the moon is making, towards the approaching ship. And the sweetness of our singing in the moonlight is what all men dream of.

The sound of our music comes to them first so gentle and distant that it is hard to be certain. Perhaps it is just the wishes of tired men rowing southwards through a calm night. We sing and the sound of our music swelling in the darkness becomes unmistakable, mysterious, desirable. The sweetness of our singing makes it so that each man believes we sing to him, for him alone. He does not see the rapt face of his companion on the rowing bench; he does not notice that he too has raised his head from the low easy slouch of the practiced rower and has thrown it back, harkening to the music that is coming across the moonlight as his mother used to come when he cried in the night.

> *Come sailor, I am your dreaming,*
> *long voyaging on icy seas*
> *leads to the white haven of my arms.*
> *Come, sailor.*
> *At home your mother weeps for you;*
> *She begs Athene, lover of brave men,*
> *to bring her boy-child home to her.*
> *The candle she has lit for you*
> *dims in the twin flames of my eyes.*
> *Put out her candle, sailor,*
> *and I will give you a place for each strong limb.*

We sing to each man alone and what we sing is what he dreams.

If he dreams of his mother, he will hear her voice in our song, he will see her sad patient waiting and her joy at his coming.

If he dreams of power and glory, swords will flash in the moonlight, like hot day, and chariot wheels will throw up the spray of the sea like dust, and the crown of laurel will glimmer on his brow.

If he dreams of wealth Hera, Queen of Olympus, will descend and give him the jewels from her peacocks' tails and the golden apples from the islands beyond the uttermost west.

If he dreams of poetry, the moon herself, Artemis the pure, will offer to teach him the music of the spheres, and he will hear the roar of applause in the amphitheater, taste the pride of his city, and the immortality of his name.

If he dreams of the Gods, Poseidon will rise glorious on the wave crest and greet him as lover and as friend; the dark voice of the sibyl will speak of the great mysteries in the cave and he will understand her as though she were his own chattering child.

Mostly however their dreams are not so high. Mostly they dream, as most men dream, of long white thighs, and full breasts and the dark place between women's legs. Some dream of it soft and welcoming; some dream of it proud and to be fought for. Some dream pleasure for their beloved and some dream pain for their paid whore, for their defeated enemy, for their chaste neighbor. Some dream women too young with frail fine bodies, long legs like colts and high tight little breasts with icy, frightened nipples; and some dream women too high and noble who would not look at them save with scorn, and dream them humbled and begging.

And to each of them, our song is the promise of the fulfillment of their dream. Just beyond the bowsprit, just beyond the pale light of the moon, there, there, almost within reach, there waiting to be taken, there, here, now, at once and easily, here, here their dream is waiting and will be given to them.

Come, sailor; make me a bride gift of your soul
and I will give you the pearls
and salt blood of my mouth.

"Come, sailor." We sing and they come.

The drumbeat wavers. The drummer lets his palms go soft, they beat little, desperate, plaintive tattoos that cannot command the muscled backs. The helmsman whimpers; his "ins" and his "outs" are no longer orders to be obeyed, but the sobs of each man's longing. The rhythm of the oars breaks down into chaos, and the ship turning a little even in the calm begins to drift towards the shallows.

There is a sudden splash. One has dropped his oar and hurled himself over the gunwale; we hear his arms beating the water and the heavier breathing as he starts to swim. Now there are shouts from the ship. Not shouts of fear—except for those of course whose fear is the kernel of their lust—but shouts of desire, of longing, of greeting, of joy. There are more splashes, more heavy bodies entering the water, more shouts and anger and laughter and tears.

Most are so perplexed and foolish in their lust that they drown long before they reach our shore. Some are killed by their colleagues as each man fears that the next—who at sunset only a few hours ago was his brother on the rowing bench, his comrade in arms, his dearest friend—may steal the object of his lust, his chosen victim, from him. Those that do not drown, or die at their comrade's hand, come wet and panting to the rocks at our feet and when they have had time to realize the empty hollowness of all they have ever dreamed of, we rend them with our long talons, sear them with our sharp beaks, destroy them with our bright eyes and devour them for our amusement and nourishment.

Then, with the moon high above us, white and harsh on the jagged rocks, we laugh; and for a few moments our pain is softened, our grief is comforted, our anger is slaked, our desire is fulfilled.

This is how it is. This is what we do, because this is what Sirens do and we are Sirens. Sirens, by the deceptive sweetness of their voices, lure brave travelers to their doom.

Down southwards, along the coasts of Sicily, of Demeter's own island, there are many dangers and pitfalls to trap the unwary and unlucky, to snare the bold high-hearted men who bend to the oars and plow the seaway's furrow into the bright future. But of all the perils the peril of the Sirens is the most perilous, not just to life but to men's souls, because the Sirens break a man on the snares and delusions of his own heart. There is blood and death and malevolence lurking under all desire and the desire for women is the darkest. A woman will take a man from his noble path for her own amusement, for no better motive than spite, for no higher gain than the satisfaction of her own foul lusts and greeds. There is vicious malice always beneath those fair appearances and Sirens are monsters who prove the evil that comes always with female beauty.

They tell the stories of Sirens, so that men may be warned not just when heaving on the rowing bench, or running before a following wind along the rocky, lovely coast of Sicily; but everywhere and always to beware, to beware of sweetness and rest and dreams. To beware of women and of womanly doings.

They tell the end of the story, they do not tell the beginning. They do not tell why we sing and why men must die from our song. They do not tell why we seek for revenge, why we need it and take it and only in taking it can we find any peace.

We will tell you.

She was our duty and our joy. Persephone—our care and our delight. When she had hardly grown into the woman months, into the turnings of the moon, while her cheeks were still smooth and round and her eyes too big for the precious face that carried them, before she was fully grown her mother gave her into our keeping.

Her mother, Demeter, the mother of all living things, Goddess of hill and valley, of flower and fern, of root and bud, tree and leaf, giver of fertility and growth and grace. Just to walk behind Demeter, just to see even the passing of the hem of her skirt as she moved through the fields touching grain stalk and fruit blossom into ripeness, is to have known joy. To look full into her generous face as we did, to help her with her strong labor, to receive as gift the warm smile that makes all plants grow, as we did—we, her chosen nymphs—is to drink deep of the nectar of the earth, to know the music of the world's spiraled dancing, and to live in the richness of springtime.

She gave us her daughter, the most precious of the many things she loved; she gave us her daughter, the beautiful Persephone, daughter of the gods and heir to all loveliness. She gave us Persephone to play with and take care of, while she, Demeter, mother of growth, of seedtime and harvest, was busy about her world-task.

We danced the hills and shores, the bright meadows of Sicily, most pleasing of all the islands, place of vine and olive and corn and wild flowers. We taught the child the music of mountain streams and the song of slow rivers; we taught her the harmony of bird wing and bat flight and the tune the clouds make by day and the stars make by night as they journey across the sky. It is hard to find words for that time, for our joy and our industry. We left nothing undone that we ought to have done and the doing of it was always a pleasure. We loved Persephone, we loved her because we loved her mother and we loved her because she was lovable, loveworthy.

She was innocent and we were careful.

It made no difference.

He came sudden, dark, fierce. He did not speak. He did not try to woo her or charm her or comfort her. He came in the dark sullen cold of the dead lands where he is King; and she had never known anything but life and warmth. He came with power. With strength. He raped her. It was not enough that he violated her, that he broke her and her dark private blood flowed out on the grass staining it and her. He hurt her. She cried not with authority, but with weakness in a whimpering pain. He raped her and the sun shone unmoved.

We tried to defend her and there was nothing we could do.

Our little white hands beat his back uselessly, so we have grown talons.

Our slim white legs ran to seek help but not swiftly enough, so we have grown wings.

The cold wind of his coming carried our little weak voices into nothingness so we learned to sing.

His hand smashed against our complaining mouths, blood and saliva on our white little teeth and so now we have beaks of iron.

There is no pain in our drowning sailors that can compare with the pain he inflicted on her.

There is no sadness in men's faces when they see us that can compare with the sadness of Demeter when we told her.

There is no shock in their dying that can compare with the shock when we learned she had consented; had eaten, had taken the six black pomegranate seeds from their sticky luscious red nest. Now that we have watched enough men die we understand better, but then, in our naïvete, we thought that to consent, to eat, to live rather than to die, meant that she had chosen. Now we know that sometimes, when there is no choice, when there is nothing that will change how the humiliation is then it is sometimes necessary to consent because that is the one, the only, thing that you can do; that you must do to be other than victim, to be yourself. That is a real thing and the worst thing.

We searched for her, with her mother, high and low, in heaven and on earth, and Demeter never reproached us. She did not reproach us. Her sadness became madness; became long days of weeping and long nights of wailing. She left the buds to rot on the tree, the grapes to stay unripened on the vine, the standing corn un-eared un-loved. She howled the dark moors and cursed the birds on the wing, but she did not reproach us.

We asked Zeus himself to return her to us. We humbled ourselves to ask him, as a favor, to give us back what was ours in the first place. And he laughed.

He laughed and told us that he thought it did not matter. He told us that the Dark Lord, his brother, was an honorable mate for Persephone, was a fitting lover for that sweet child. He told us that Hell, the place of shadows, could be a fine home for someone born and brought up in the sunshine. He told her mother not to be so foolish. He said that now she was deflowered there was nothing better she could hope for. And he laughed.

In the end, irritated by Demeter's insistence rather than moved by her grief, he allowed Persephone to come home for half the year: he made a gift out of what was her right. He felt generous and thought we should be grateful.

We are teaching him gratitude now. Are the sailors who drown grateful? Does the flesh we eat give thanks? Our seductions are sweeter than His was, and we kill our lovers rather than make them drag out long years in the darkness.

Sometimes, at the moon's setting, we wonder; we wonder if our vengeance has hurt us as much as it hurts them. We cannot dance in the sunlit fields anymore, we cannot accompany Demeter on her joyful wandering. We cannot comb Persephone's hair or dance with her in the springtime. Instead we must wait here.

We wait; we wait, we sing, and we destroy.

This is what Sirens do. We wait for the coming of strong men and by the deceptive sweetness of our voices we lure them to their doom. We are Sirens, this is what we do.

We break a man on the snares and delusions of his own heart. For our own amusement, for no better motive than spite, for no higher gain than the satisfaction of our own foul lusts and greeds.

There is vicious malice always beneath those fair appearances and we are monsters who prove the evil that comes always with female beauty. But our malice is not without cause; our cruelty is small payment for men's lust.

She was defenseless and he raped her. He raped her and went unpunished.

When they die, the sailors, when they drown or kill each other or are eaten while the moon shines high above us, white and harsh on the jagged rocks, we laugh; and for a few moments our pain is softened, our grief is comforted, our anger is slaked, our desire is fulfilled.

It will not last forever, our waiting. The priestess of the oracle has spoken: when a man comes, a single man, who does not respond to our singing, who passes by unmoved, whose desires are pure, without greed, without lust, then our waiting will be over and we will be free again.

We know that one day he will come. Odysseus, the shrewd one, red-headed, limping, pitching his sly good sense against the power of all the songs: the one who looked on Helen and was not moved, the one whose desire is simply to be home with his own woman, so that we have nothing to offer him.

We know he will come. We do not know if we will be glad or sorry. We do not know if we will be able to rest; we do not know if she, her despairing cries, wild against the shock and pain, will let us rest; we do not know if we want to rest.

And until he comes, whenever there is, in the summer months, a fleeting moment of something sweeter than silence—a magical hush; whenever the soft irregular rhythms of the calm sea's rise and fall, rise and fall, rise and fall, rise and fall, become so monotonous, so expected, and so gentle, that they fit perfectly to heartbeat and to breathing; whenever out on the seaway there is a slow roll of water, a gentle heave, and a flowing gleam of phosphorescence, and we know a porpoise is passing on its long travels; whenever these nights are upon us, we will be waiting, waiting and singing.

In the name of all the gods, we are justified when we seek vengeance; for our malice is not without cause; our cruelty is small payment for men's lust.

Flower Garden

Elsa Schiaparelli as a small child "planted seeds in her throat, mouth and ears, in the hopes of transforming her ugly duckling self into a beautiful flower garden."

Observer, 24 November 1985

Yes indeed. It makes so much sense of what came later; that elegance of artifice pushed beyond all sense into a new realm of adornment, that amazing *trompe-l'oeil* knitware, those hats the shape of shoes.

Because of course the seeds would not grow there, would they? Even if their tiny determinations escaped the huge hands of mammas and nannies, ferreting them out and flushing them away, still they would not grow in so cold and barren an environment—ear wax and nasal mucus do not provide the dark damp secrecy that germination requires.

But.

But the desperateness of the infant female knows no bounds. Which of us did not desire it, that magical transformation into the desirable?

The beginning of my story is easy enough.

Ageratum, Alyssum and Alyssum saxatile, Anchusa Blue Angel, Antirrhinum. Aquilegia (Columbine), Aster, Aubretia, Begonia.

She had not anticipated the range of choices. She is too old, she realizes almost sadly, to be taken in by the profusion of color in the pictures; her father is a keen gardener, he is standing further inside the shop discussing bonemeal with his friend the shopkeeper, it will take him hours, but when he is finished he will want to leave immediately. From years of watching him at work she knows how great the difference between the illustration and the reality is—art wins over nature all along the line although she has not yet formulated the words for this. Also as a gardener's child she knows enough to know that the circumstances matter, the soil and the sunlight and the seeding ground. Begonias, for instance, will not do, they have tuber roots—she needs some simple hardy annuals, bright and glittery in color, fast-growing, summer-flowering, shallow-rooted. The brooms are beautiful and her father loves them dearly, his tiny garden has several: their long slender branches bearing a profusion of small flowers, bizarrely elaborate in their coloring; but they will not do any more than the Begonias—they take years to grow and they have rough scratchy branches. She has seen her father bring home small broom plants, their balled roots wrapped in strips of dustbin bag. But she passes by the ornamental cabbages without a qualm, they are definitely not what she has in mind; the same applies to the cacti, only more so, she almost giggles.

Calendula, Campanula, Candytuft, Canterbury Bell, Carnation, Chrysanthemum.

The Chrysanthemums distract her from her business, reminding her of school too much and of those words that are difficult to spell: she is irritated, the names of the flowers were pleasing in themselves and now she thinks with anger of her elder brother who can spell everything and on whose shoulder her father's hand rests gently when he comes in from work. She is twelve years old and terribly, terribly unhappy. She hates her new school. All that passionate intensity that only a far distant year ago she put into her friends and her games and the life of her secret imagination is now directly purely and miserably towards her school, where she is lonely and wretched and stupid. She has tried to tell her parents and they do not listen, or they listen but apparently do not hear. They said, "You'll get used to it," and when she didn't they said, "Come on lovey," and, "You only get out what you put in." They told her it was a very good school, which seemed entirely irrelevant to her, and that very nice girls went there, which seemed ignorant and untrue, and how the hell did they think they knew? Now they were getting angry with her; they said things like, "Pull yourself together," and, "Do you call that mess homework?" and, "Don't slouch," "Don't scowl," "Don't shout," "Don't go on and on about it." And, "If you want to make yourself that ugly, go upstairs and do it in the privacy of your own room; don't inflict it on the rest of the world."

She could not find words to tell them, to explain to them about the enormousness of the building and its ugliness; the vast barren acres of wall that scared her and muddled her and she was never on time, and how there was no time allotted for transit. How she was meant to be in one place at one moment and another immediately after but they were miles away and none of the other kids liked her, and her friend had been sent off to boarding school and why couldn't she go too? And the dread, the stomach-churning dread, of the bus ride in the morning when the huge boys from the senior school teased her and her brother sat and watched them with a smirk on his face and refused to be on her side. And she did not understand what they were saying but it was horrible.

And now. She used often to come with her father to the garden center, and had wandered about the nurseries and asked him about different plants and sometimes he even let her choose something, or would buy her packets of seed or ask her if she thought some new variety was pretty and she had thought that he did it because he wanted to be with her and because he liked her and would help her, but this morning coming down to breakfast she had heard him say to her mother, "All right then, if I have to I'll take her, I know you deserve a break, but honestly." She writhes now in misery and shame, wrapping her arms round her body and caressing her own ribs through the pink sweatshirt which her mother had bought for her last year. Then she'd said, "Isn't it funny, darling, this is probably the last time I'll be buying you children's clothes. It makes me feel old." But the shirt still fitted; it didn't really it was too short in the sleeves but it still, well, fitted in the sense that her mother meant. Her body was like a wooden log. There was something wrong with it. It was ugly. Ugly. Ugly.

But the names of the flowers were not. Beautiful, soothing, a magic spell. She returned to them, blotting it all out briefly, incanting down the list, inspecting each packet on the flimsy metal stand with determination.

Cockscomb, Convolvulus, Cornflower, Dahlia, Daisy, Delphinium. Euphorbia, which she called Snow on the Mountain. Felicia, Freesia, Gazania, Geranium, Globe Amaranth, Godetia, Gypsophila—Baby's Breath.

The names are magic, distant dreams of beauty and sweetness and safety. Her parents called her Rose, because she had blossomed pink and sweet on a golden summer morning, they had told her that over and over again. They had been going to call her Helen after her grandmother but when they had seen how lovely she was they wanted to name her after a flower. She had liked that story and now she did not believe a word of it.

"Rosie," called her father from up the shop where in the half dark he and the shop man were mixing together foul-smelling substances which would make the lawn grow sweet and green, "Rosie, I'm going out with Jack to look at some new fuchsia he's got in. Do you want to come?" He was lovely, her father, his moustache lay along his lip looking silky, but it wasn't it was rough and scratchy; when she had been tiny she had played a game with him when he would try and scratch her cheek while she snuggled in his lap attempting to crawl her head up the inside of his jumper. He was very good looking, she thought, and turned to go with him, remembering good times in the backyard with him and Jack, where the other customers weren't meant to go and had to wait outside and be helped by "the girl" who knew nothing about plants and could never work out the price of half a tray. Then she remembered that he didn't want her, that he had not wanted to bring her, that he was probably embarrassed to be seen with her now she had turned out so hideous. "No," she said, "I'm busy." And saw not a look of loss but a flicker of irritation. "OK then, don't get up to mischief."

Of course she would have to steal the seeds to make it work. She hadn't realized that until now. It had to be wicked. She was wicked and bad and ugly. She was a witch with secret powers. Now was her opportunity. But her nerve failed. She could not decide what she wanted.

Something poisonous and evil—Foxgloves full of dangerous drugs, Laburnum whose pods could kill you, Yew berries plucked from church yards at dead of night, Deadly Nightshade—she would like to grow deadly nightshade, like the witches in *Macbeth*. If there were butterfly-attracting plants, were there toad- and bat-attracting plants, too? That was what she wanted. She would teach them. She would grow Deadly Nightshade in that very secret garden and mix the red berries in her parents' drinks and that would teach them. Or perhaps it would poison her, the long heads of Foxglove, Digitalis, make her heart pound and beat until it split her open and then they would be sorry. That would teach them a lesson: they thought she was ugly and stupid and dull and sulky, but she had power. Her mother knew and was afraid of it.

"Rosie, if you want to play on that swing, I think you should wear trousers." Her father noticed too but he never said anything. Just the other day she had come downstairs with no knickers on and sat on the floor with her legs crossed, and he had noticed and he had not said anything. He had looked. Yes, he had looked. But not because of the power. Because, because her skin there was not like her mother's, foxy-furred, lush. Actually she looked like a badly plucked chicken, white and sickly. In the evil-smelling flower garden, though, she would grow her flowers and they would blossom forth wild with delight. Dark and damp, seeds at least liked that, and she would be a garden. But she had to choose. It was her secret.

Hollyhock, Jacaranda, Larkspur, Lavender (too sweet and old ladyish for her schemes), Linaria, Lobelia. Love-lies-bleeding.

Damn. No. That she did not want, cascading out of her. The roots of the flowers might stop it, that blood, she did not want that, ever, ever.

Lupins, which were hideous, her father would not have them in his garden, Marigolds, Mecanopsis—the beautiful blue poppies that she antici-pated finding in heaven in the old days when she had believed in heaven, Myosotis (forget-me-not), Nasturtium, Nicotiana, promisingly wicked that and smelling so sweetly. Pansies were babyish and Passion flowers not what they sounded, nothing to do with that but with Jesus and stupid old church. Phlox, Pink, Polyanthus, Primrose, Primula—like they had taken her mother when she went in the hospital just after she had begun at the horrid school and no one would tell her why, she was not having them inside her. Rudbeckia, Salvia, Scabious, Silene, Smilax, Stock.

She is beginning to panic. She must make her selection before her father comes back. If he sees her buy seeds he will want to help her plant them, he will be pleased with her and see her as cooperative and good, but she is planning something more powerful and strong than he can dream of. She will surprise him with her beauty and her sweetness, but she must do it, he must not help her, she does not want him to know, to help, to offer. No one must know. She has to crouch down now, she is getting near to the bottom of the seed display frame. If she cannot decide soon she will have to move on to the vegetables. That will not do.

Sunflower and Sweet Pea.

More varieties than she can cope with and they will have to be staked. She could not bear to drive in a stake right into her heart like a vampire. She wants no one's blood, not even her own. It is not blood she is seeking.

Sweet Sultan, Sweet William.

But he is not and only God knows how much she hates him, and that is why she does not believe in God anymore—he smirks in the bus when the other boys make remarks. Why has he not told her parents, why have they not noticed that she has to go all that way and be the only girl until they arrive in Brook Street and then

Stephanie gets on whose breasts are there and whose hair is in fat copper-colored curls and the boys still make remarks, but different, kindly, admiring, they do not run their hands down her back to laugh because she does not wear a bra, they do not pinch and flick at Stephanie who is beautiful and clever and lovely and sixteen. She loathes Stephanie and she wants to be like her, be her. She smiles, Stephanie does, at the boys, but she never smiles at her; sometimes she encourages them to mock at her they say hateful things, about how ugly and skimpy and unlovable she is and William sits there and smirks. Now she is hurrying, missing packets, and yet still unable to stop until she reaches the end.

Tagetes, Thunbergia, Verbena, Veronica, Viola, Viscara, Wallflower, Zinnia.

There is a Zinnia called Envy and it is chartreuse green. Her hand reaches out towards the packet, to grow green flowers, the flowers of the forest and the envy of the gardeners. She hears her father and Jack coming into the back of the shop and straightens up. Now she cannot reach the Zinnia and she is glad. Envy is not what she wants. In seconds it has all gone wrong. She wanted only to be beautiful, to be beautiful and beloved. She reaches out almost vaguely and takes the packet nearest to hand; she shoves it up front of her pink shirt and turns towards her father. She has never stolen anything in her life before. Her shirt feels transparent, both the seed packet and her flat button nipples tingle under his and Jack's eyes. She will not care. She summons a soft smile. When he sees her father's eyes crinkle with pleasure she knows how good a smile it was. Side by side they leave the shop together.

All day she smiles and is charming. She expresses a keen interest in the bonemeal fertilizer her father has purchased. She helps her mother in the kitchen, washing up with a rather sweet but willing ineptitude. She tells them a funny story about her history teacher at the school. She participates in a conversation about their summer holiday, even when William comes in and contradicts everything she has said. Her parents are relieved and then delighted. They have not had such an agreeable Saturday for months. They respond easily to her good will, they build on it, apparently lovingly. By early evening she has almost deceived herself as well as them, almost desires that it should be this way, that they have been right and all she has to do is make an effort. But upstairs in the drawer, tucked away under her hair ribbons, the little packet is waiting for her. She knows it is there and that her parents are foolish to be so easily deluded. They think she is their sweet little rose, growing in their tidy garden, a little bonemeal will keep her blooming; they do not know that she is jungle and desert, dangerous and wild. She is too ugly to live in the lovely and orderly garden that her father has made for her. She is too important and powerful to be pruned into his shapes. She senses her own confusion dimly, and senses it as excitement.

It is bedtime and she kisses them nicely and goes to her lair. She opens the drawer carefully and for the first time examines the packet.

She has chosen Candytuft *(Iberis),* Dwarf Fairy Mixed:

Easy to grow, colorful border plants producing pretty little clustered heads of flowers in summer. Regular in height, brilliant range of shades. Ht. approx 15 cm. Sow March—July where intended to bloom.

It couldn't be better. The hands of the gods were guiding her. She almost giggled to think that she might have snatched up some ornamental thistle.

She takes off all her clothes and stands in front of the mirror. Her body is flat shapeless bony. All the things the boys say on the bus. Ugly. Above the scrawny shoulders—"Darling, do drink your milk, you're too thin"—her hair hangs straight and strawlike. Her face is plain; her eyebrows too heavy, her skin yellowy and blotchy, her mouth too big, her nose too small. Ugly. She looks like a deranged chicken. Her tummy sticks out and she has no other curves. Her legs run straight down, skinny and shapeless. Ugly. Ugly. Ugly. She forces herself to look at her crotch, white and pallid, plucked chicken waiting for the oven. Ugly. Slowly she takes the seed packet and folds it so that only the picture shows; then she holds it up against her crotch and smiles. She will be exotic, lovely, lovable. She will be weird and wonderful, mysterious, powerful. She will be sexy. Her father will love her. He will come with her on the bus and shut the boys up. He will shout at William and wipe that smirk off his face. He will tell her mother . . . her fantasy fails her suddenly. She removes the packet and turns away from the mirror. She cannot quite decide what she wants her father to say to her mother. Time will tell, she thinks, mimicking her mother's own mimicry of the cliché.

Now she is decisive: she opens her bedroom door and listens; from below she can hear the television. She will be safe. She skips still naked along the corridor and into her parents' bedroom; she rummages through her mother's things with swift graceful hands, thorough but disturbing nothing. Briefly she considers a life career as a burglar. She extracts one of her mother's tampons from the box and then after a pause a second one. She wants to take the instruction sheet too but fears that her mother might miss it: surely it could not be that difficult to put in? Perhaps there was some use in those horrendous "personal hygiene" classes the school laid on for them. From the bathroom she collects a toothmug and fills it with water.

It turns out to be lucky that she had taken the two tampons. Her first idea had been to soak it in water before sprinkling the seeds on it, but when she extracts it from its wrapping and tube and puts it in the toothmug it fans out, rather beautiful but, she feels certain, uninsertable. Its limpness in her hand suddenly disgusts her and she breaks out of her room to flush it down the toilet.

But the seeds will need watering, will need dampness in order to sprout. She knows that. She knows too a way, her need making conscious something she has done all her childhood but without awareness. She does a new thing therefore when she lies down on the bed, face downwards, the packet of seeds beside her, and places her three middle fingers on her pubic bone, curling the tips inwards. So great is her sense of adventure and obsession that the whole thing works with extraordinary ease, not the soft bedtime comforter, replacing thumb and teddy unnoticed years ago, but power and will, and a belly deep mounting confidence in herself and her authority. She reaches with her spare hand for the packet of seeds and lays it flat against her stomach: it is its stiff cold shape against her own flesh that makes her come and she feels both sacred and scared.

And after that it is quite simple to lick her finger and dip it into the seed packet and then wipe the seeds off as far up her vagina as she can reach; it takes a number of finger loads before she is satisfied that there is enough. Then she takes the tampon and inserts that too, tamping it down carefully as her father would tamp down the earth over his planted seeds. She reminds herself that in the morning she must remove the seed packet and the tampon tube and throw them away at school on Monday; she thinks that after about ten days she will remove the tampon and the seeds should have germinated. She does not think any further than that because she falls asleep satisfied.

I said that the beginning of the story was easy—relatively easy at any rate. It is the end of my story that is hard, because I do not know what would happen next and no one seems able to tell me. Would seeds germinate in an adolescent vagina? Yeast grows well there, as too many of us know to our discomfort, but Candytuft seeds? In primary school biology I learned that germination requires darkness and wetness and warmth; certainly those conditions are fulfilled. But pH levels, the relative acidity of vaginal secretions versus plain water, the changes and fluctuations of conditions?

I do not think that even if they germinated the conditions would be suitable for full flowering, do you? "The only way to find out," said my friend Jill after we had worked our way through two evenings of speculation, "is to try it." It was her idea about the tampon incidentally, both as a moisture preserver and as a rooting substance—like the cotton wool she and I and doubtless many other children used to grow mustard and cress. But I cannot bring myself to do so. I do want to know the answer, for Rose, for myself and for what has become pure curiosity, but I cannot actually do the experiment. I consider it and am alarmed at the specter of infection, or at the very boldness and weirdness of wanting to know. Nor can I now, because it is too late, just guess and tell the story that way—not because it would be dishonest since this is after all a fiction, but because I would not be satisfied, emotionally. So I have written two endings.

1. Rose is still a little child. She cannot bring herself to wait the full ten days, in fact she cannot bring herself to wait even twenty-four hours. On Sunday evening she pulls out the tampon to see what is happening, even though the more mature part of her mind knows that nothing will have happened yet. Although she reinserts it some of the seeds have fallen out and she does not know accurately how many are left. She repeats this on Monday and Tuesday, nicking another tampon from her mother's drawer since the first one is getting somewhat grungy and increasingly difficult to reinsert. The discomfort and fidgetiness of all this is taking away from the sense of excitement and power that she had when she started. She also remembers the great delight of masturbation and further disrupts the potential germination process by exploring this now more interesting process. On Wednesday there is a new girl on the bus when she goes to school. Because she is new and the boys have as it happens something more interesting to talk about they ignore the two little girls who sit near the front and smile shyly at each other. When Stephanie gets on the bus the new girl leans over and whispers, boldly, but as it turns out she is a bold child, "Cor, get 'er, is she the school tart?" Rose and she then giggle all the way to school and all the way home again in the afternoon. By Thursday they are best friends. Now that she has a friend and no longer has to face the misery of the journey or the scariness of the long bleak passageways, Rose begins to enjoy herself. On Friday morning she extracts the tampon finally, notices that none of the seeds show the least signs of germinating and has a reasonably good try in the bath at washing herself out. She abandons the project, embarrassed to think she could have been so loony, turns her attention to the business of growing up in the real world, finds that her parents are not actually sadists, but decent well-meaning people who are, like all parents, a bit thick but still OK more or less. They had also been right in their handling of the whole situation, it had been "just a phase" their daughter had been going through. Rose lives happily ever after, or at least until she gets a desperate crush on her biology teacher.

2. Rose is a very stubborn adolescent who is deeply and truly unhappy. The sense of power and self-determination that the adventures of Saturday gave her are extraordinarily important to her; the
whole experience has the quality of obsession. Despite the mounting
discomfort, she does in fact rigorously and disciplinedly keep the
tampon in for ten days. By this time she has a stomachache, a constant violent itching and a discharge, which is yellowish, curdy, foul
smelling and ugly, ugly, ugly. On the tenth day she extracts the
tampon and finds that the seeds have indeed germinated, but, instead of beautiful green shoots, her vagina is full of what look like
rock worms, colorless, translucent wriggles. Her disgust at her body
mounts, it is hateful, ugly and incapable of producing anything of
worth. She throws up violently and flushes her vomit and her experiment down the loo. However, the discharge, the itching and the
stomach cramps do not diminish. Her mother, doing the family
laundry, eventually notices the discharge and tries to speak to Rose
about it. Her daughter however is in such a misery of pain and guilt
that she sulks, withdraws further and refuses even to speak to her
mother. The mother, not entirely unreasonably, panics now, notices
how unwell her daughter is looking and jumps to parental conclu-
sions. She drags Rose off to the family doctor, an action which, in
her anxiety, she manages to present as a punishment rather than an
attempt to get help. The elderly and not unkindly meaning doctor
manages to extract from Rose what has happened but with so little
tact and usable sympathy that far from feeling better she feels worse.
The doctor also feels duty-bound to tell the mother. She freaks out.
The father when he is told is so totally embarrassed and unable to
cope that he loses his temper and yells at Rose, who is now not only
suffering from severe pelvic inflammation but from suicidal impulses
as well. Her brother, whose problems I do not have time to go into
now, thus becomes privy to his sister's secret, and one evening in a
long misogynistic and beer-laden rap session with his friend tells the
story as a further proof of the utter weirdness, disgustingness and
dangerousness of women. Within a week all the senior school boys

know and within ten days so do all the girls. Within two weeks Rose, from remarks made on the bus, knows that they all know. She lives unhappily ever after, or at least until she finds a women's group where in sisterly solidarity she learns that she is not a total freak.

*B*ut there is another ending. A dream ending, as sweet and tender as so lovely and adventurous a young woman deserves.

3. The flowers grow; uncurling inside her, in an environment so perfectly safe and delightful that they sprout faster and stronger than usual. Rose tends to them lovingly; the weather is bright and sunny and she creeps off into the high hay field behind the house each afternoon after school and naked spreads her legs for the sun to bless her fruitfulness. The shoots grow green and leafy, tiny buds form on them and they spread themselves out exquisite and charming around her pubis. She takes great care of them, delicately trimming and pinching out the lead shoot to keep their firm bushy shape and taking great care not to crush them. Admittedly this means that she has to forge her mother's signature to get her out of school games for a whole month, but a little self-interested lying is not necessarily bad for a young woman growing up. Now she has something more interesting and precious to think about, she does not mind the taunts of the boys on the bus, and can secretly gloat over their ignorance and uncreativeness. At last the young plants flower, in all the promised shades of white and cream and pink and purple. They are beautiful. She is quite enchanted with her own body and with her own power. She is beautiful. With some skill she lures her father up to her bedroom; as she hears his footsteps on the stairs she whips off all her clothes and spreads herself out for him. He opens the door and stands there looking at her for a whole long minute, then he says, "Darling, how beautiful, how clever of you, you must have worked so hard." He grins affectionately and says, "Quick, quick, we must show Mummy, she'll be so proud." And he calls for his wife and she comes and stands beside him and looks too and says, "Oh

my love, what a beautiful surprise." And holding hands they walk across the room to inspect her flowering body more closely.

"Wow," says the mother, "I could never have kept such a secret; you are clever." "They're beautiful," says the father, "and you're beautiful." And without letting go of his wife's hand he leans down without touching her body and picks just one head of the flowering Candytuft and his wife pins it in his button hole. Then he grins at her cheerfully and says, "I'll tell you what, pop on a loose frock so they don't get squashed and we'll go and show Nan and Gramps." So later that evening, with their woman child in the middle, the three of them go hand in hand dancing down the road to visit her grandmother and show her the beautiful flowers.

The Lady Artemis

The note of the hounds' belling changes as they break out of the steep-sided valley and set off across the open moorland. Free from the trees, the sounds unmuffled by the noisy stream, their baying seems thinner but clearer. Amid the strong vibration of hounds on a hot sweet scent is mixed the occasional yap of distress. The instinct to hunt has taken them over and yet they know that something is not quite right.

The stag's head, face on, with the high spreading antlers resembles the inside of the woman he flees. Does the stag know this? Instinct takes him too, the panic of the hunted, the power and thrust of the long hind legs, the desperate pounding beneath the rough hair on the deep chest. And yet—the eyes are not the liquid dark eyes of a deer; they are the eyes of a terrorized man who does not understand what has happened, who knows that all the world is craziness and panic and fear.

When all is silent at the bottom of the valley the Lady Artemis turns again to her bathing. Her toes are splayed wide and firm on the rock, but now she lifts one foot and steps down into the pool. It is not deep; the water comes only slightly above her knees, making a second dark triangle of water, below the smaller dark triangle of hair. The force of the water is considerable, making creamy foam garters on her lower thighs, but she does not look as though she is worried about slipping. She bends forward gracefully, untying the ribbon from her short black hair. The snake tattooed on her spine curves with her, as though alive. Her hands reach for the water and splash it up against her breasts. The light, filtered through the green leaves of the trees and soaked into the copper-colored floor of the glade, has a curious quality of stillness, almost eerie. It is high noon and hot above the valley, but down by the stream there is no time. The waterfall behind her crashes noisily, continuously, spraying her buttocks with icy water; nonetheless the effect is of complete stillness, stillness and silence.

When a small bird chirps above her in a tree there is something shocking in its noise. In the slowness of the moment of her bathing the leaves of the beech trees turn away from summer growth and incline towards the autumn, towards death and winter and retreat and rebirth. The sun continues to shine. Whether the Lady Artemis is aware that anything has happened is not clear.

Across the moor, miles away now, the ancient drama is played out. The hounds are good hounds; the love and enthusiasm of their owner has seen to that. They follow ever closer, the excitement of the kill urging them forward. They are baffled only because this stag does not turn at bay, but stumbling keeps on running, not towards the sea and sweet death by drowning, but towards the city.

Actaeon, rational thought destroyed by fear, and by the stag he is becoming, reduced to instincts and instincts divided against themselves, is seeking the arms of his mother. But it is too late. Alce, the lead hound, the beautiful bitch, his pride and darling, the sweet love of his life, snaps at his rear haunches. Her teeth find flesh. He does not feel so much pain as terror. The foam scudded along his flanks flies off as he turns at last. The stag turns, but the man cannot, for a brief second too long, bring himself to attack his own favorite bitch. She clings on, undaunted. The pack are upon him. He sinks to his knees, his noble head swaying despairingly. He falls. The hounds, hysterical, roll with him, tearing at his gut. Suddenly there is blood everywhere. There is no huntsman to call them off; they have never experienced the hotness of living meat. Alce, the lead bitch, so obedient, pauses, waiting for the loving sting of the thong that will call her off and will leave the stag edible and dignified in its death throes. When the instruction does not come she is frenzied. The whole pack goes berserk. The stag is dismembered, disemboweled, inaccurately, hotly, pieces are spread across the moorland. The blood is hot and sticky. There is hide, and entrails and gut and gore and gobs of foam. Beyond the pain and terror there is nothing. Somewhere in the maelstrom of blood, it all goes away. Actaeon is devoured by his bitch pack, while the dog pack in the kennels below howl dismally as they catch the savor of the killing on the hot midday air. His blood cousin Pentheus will be torn to pieces by a bitch pack too, in a similar bacchanal fury and the lead bitch will be his own mother. Actaeon is spared that at least. As if he cared. Actaeon. That graceful boy. For after he is dead it is easier to remember him as a boy, a charming child, than to allow that he had become a man, beautiful, strange, withdrawn and arrogant. A man fully grown and fully responsible. The gossip was kind to him afterwards, as it sometimes can be when the truth is too awful. Actaeon, the prince, son of a noble line. What had he done to deserve this? It seems unfair. But the Lady Artemis does not deal in justice. It is not a cause that interests her.

*B*ut Actaeon had loved the virgin goddess. He had dedicated himself to her. He ran from the gaudy palaces and sought her places. He hunted her forests and loved her wild things. Like many true hunters he loved the animals he killed; he knew and respected them. He would rise before dawn, moving shadowy through the deserted city, and climb towards the falling stars to shoot duck as they rose from their nestings on small high lakes in the hills. He would watch entranced by the creeping of the morning. Stare as the blacker shapes of the hills sucked in the substance of the night leaving the air grey. And later, the world fully lit but colorless in complex shadings and gradations of whites, through innumerable greys to the blacks. And the color coming in slowly, pale through creams and pinks to gold. He would crouch in the marshy places beside the lakes, delighted to shoot his arrows at the rising duck, and as delighted just to see them take sharp wing against the morning and fly away. He would walk on the beach in the afternoons, and squat for hours watching the minute, private life of a single rock pool, its busy secret comings and goings, while the waves crashed in his ears and he forgot the greater fish he had come to spear swimming brave and weightless in the deep water world off the point. He would walk the forests at night just to watch the fox-cubs, Her furred children, bundle out of their holes and frolic in the pastel light of the moon, Her moon. He had despised the bright evenings of Thebes, the noisy, laughing, chatting, singing city; he thought himself too wise, too pure, too free. He dedicated himself to the Lady Artemis.

He thought he worshiped her, and never knew until the end that he worshipped his own fear and enthroned it as a goddess and called it chastity.

And he had good cause to fear, poor child. He had seen his own mother's sister, Semele, the loveliest of them all, burst into flames and be consumed by her own passion. Burning, burning there in the courtyard of the most civilized palace in Greece, burning until there was just a small pile of dry ashes, and farewell to the lovely Semele. He had seen Dionysius, the child she bore at such cost, grow up in debauchery and glory; outshine them all, those beautiful sons of beautiful mothers, grow wild and corrupt and, damn him, joyful; nourished by the fires that had devoured his mother, destroying her to sustain himself, and rejoicing drunken, delirious, uncontrolled, dangerous and godly. Actaeon aspired to no such splendid frenzy; he sought the cool of the night and refused to hear the keening of the wind and the wildness of his own lusts. He and his cousin Pentheus clinging together, the last bastions of sanity, they were sure, of order and decorum and safety—had not their grandfather Cadmus, the founder of Thebes, brought the arts of writing to Greece and established himself and his family by wisdom and calm cunning.

But perhaps best not to think about Cadmus, the old king in his senile raving, who in his dreams and deliriums was still searching for his beautiful white sister Europa, stolen away across the sea. Searching, searching and never finding, so that there was nothing feminine, nothing sweet and light and lovely left in his life, and he could not look at his own wife without weeping. So what to remember instead, in that golden tangled court? The crazed jealousies of his uncle who had dashed his own son to death against the wall? Ino, his aunt, hurling herself and her other son into the sea and drowning to protect herself and him from her own abandoned, greedy, ambitious loveliness.

And something else. Sons do not tell how they come to pity their mothers. Sons must not say how they come to hate their fathers. Actaeon never told: following Eurydice through the green fields, playing in the grass, among the flowers. The child how small, how tender, how darkly curious, following his beloved, his adored father. Actaeon's father: a man as distant and proud and strong as his son was to become, bred in the southern deserts and always traveling on, a great hunter himself and something more, a keeper of bees, a singer of songs, a pauser, one who stops only to amuse himself. But Actaeon has always amused him before, he has liked taking his son out hunting and teaching him the ways of a man—the little boy, his mouth still damp and sweet, to be taught that women are weak and need not be accounted to, worth only a laugh. And his beautiful mother Autone, so fraily lovely and sweetly loving, and his father choosing instead to hunt the full-blown blousy Eurydice. And in the green field, among the flowers, his father's clothes abandoned beside her clothes, like brighter heavier flowers shot with gold and giddy perfume, and his father leaning over slowly, so slowly, and the child watching crouched in green grasses which tickled his nose and he must not sneeze, and the white legs reaching up to encircle his father's hips, and his father's buttocks plunging, and the two-backed beast alive and writhing in the green field, among the flowers. His father's hard buttocks and Orpheus forgotten strumming his lyre at home; his father's buttocks leaping uncontrolled and his lovely mother paling, saying nothing, and a small child with a secret, for it is as evil and secret for a child to see as it is for a child to act. And now he does not remember that he remembers.

No matter. He thought he was chaste, he thought he was pure. He built a small shrine in the woods, and the Lady was worshipped there, smooth and white and cold, a little gentle smile and kind white hands, and her proud long-legged dogs at her feet. Should he have remembered other things? The screaming in the women's place, the dark opening, the space between pink and stretched wide, and the emerging head damp, dark, mysterious, and the birthing. That she, the Lady Artemis, was there and singing with the women then. She brought the women her fierce virgin self, and the power to birth their children in; she brought her space, her un-heldness, her freedom, her wild energy to their heavy work under the dark archway where a man can never stand. Should he have remembered, when he worshipped his pale silent goddess, the young girls coming back from the forest, laughing, turning away from the boys who only days before had been their playmates, and now they contained within themselves a secret knowledge and their faces were smeared with brown blood, and they were proud, and excited, and embarrassed, and wild, and secretive. They came back from their rite of the Lady Artemis changed and empowered with the strong ritual of blood letting and no man could go with them and see what they had seen. And should he have known that when her moon careened wild and untamed across the winter sky, and the young bitch wolves not yet come to their first season, would howl and growl and come down onto the sheep folds in an orgy of random bloodthirstiness and killings without sense or hunger, that this too was the work of his double-dealing white lady.

Should he have sensed that there were better and safer goddesses for fearful and frightened young men; goddesses who would be tender to such mothers' sons, but that she was huge and free and bloody and not interested at all in the plight of any young man? But he did not acknowledge his own fear; he was foolish and brave and arrogant like many fathers' sons.

*H*e did not know, but he should have known. So he was neither innocent nor guilty when he sought her. Innocence and guilt are no concern to the Lady Artemis. Justice is not a cause that interests her.

It is hard to know what happened. It is a secret between them. She will not stay to tell and he is gone, shredded and strewn across the moor by his own bitch pack. He went out early, full of joy, five pairs of hounds lolloping happily round his heels—lean, lovely and loved, carefully bred, crossed Spartan and Cretan hounds, their mixed ancestry showing in their oddly brindled coats, the advantages of the cross not showing until they started running on a strong scent; then their tirelessness, graceful speed and full throated cry reveal the finest hunting dogs in Greece. And when he sets them to run and runs with them, graceful, strong, as tireless as they, people are delighted and say that he grows more and more like his father every day. And when he hears this a coldness comes over him, though he does not remember why, and he turns his dogs to the hillsides and runs away from everybody.

He hunted hare that morning for the simple pleasure of it. The dogs break the hare and it runs, small but fast, round and about and in and out, while he stands on the shoulder of a higher hill and watches his dogs with delight as they stream out, Alce always at the lead, and their sterns straight behind them as though blown on the wind. As the morning heightens and the heat builds up they catch the pungent scent of fox and are off. He could have called them in, kept their noses to the duller savor of hare, but he does not, he runs with them, despite the sun and away over the moorland, up and down. Sometimes they check and he can come up with them, sometimes his knowledge of the terrain and the ways of foxes spare him miles of running. Always he can hear their sweet song breaking the silence of the wild places as they run further from home and he with them rejoicing. The fox is no fool, it leads the way and the dogs follow and he follows the dogs. The fox plunges off the open ground and into a steep wooded valley and the hounds follow over the edge and into the ravine and he leaps down the side after them, laughing aloud for the great delight of it all. And when the fox goes to earth he leaves it be and calls in the hounds, and they come, their pink mouths open for his caresses. Their flanks heave happily from the long run and he thinks they will all descend to the bottom of the gorge so that he can water them.

It is magical as they go down. The trees are tall, mixed hardwoods and scrub, and under the shade of the trees it is very, very quiet. Apart from the river at the bottom whose shouting they can hear, it is almost silent. The sides of the valley are so steep that he has to slither down and the dogs pick their way with their absurd hindquarters well above their heads. At the bottom is the river. A wonderful active stream, jumping and laughing over rocks, with eddies and spurts, cutting down hard and miniature rapids and dark gold pools, falling swiftly, foamily downwards. The dogs lap greedily and he sits down to watch them. Languorously almost he stands up again and man and dogs together they make their way dreamily down the valley. Once the dogs stiffen, and seeing it, he listens; inside the noise of the stream there is another grunting sound. He casts around, and to his delight finds a boar sow laying her litter. The dogs are aquiver, but he holds them with his eyes and watches. The piglets as they are born are wet and pink, the sow is heavy and open, grunting with her work. He would like to help her through this magic moment, but she does not need him. There are five little damp piglets at her dugs and another born as he watches, neatly in its little package of mucous membrane. Her snout is busy at it, her tail bent back awkwardly. When he fears that the dogs' excitement will disturb her he gets up as quietly as possible and leaves her to her work. He is in a time of perfect happiness, and contentment. There is nothing more that he would like.

He picks his way round some boulders and finds himself on the edge of a stand of beech trees; nothing grows under them but there is a carpet of fallen leaves and masts, a rich copper-colored flooring. The light in that clear space under the trees, filtered through the pale green of the beech leaves and reflecting the copper of the ground, has a curious quality of stillness. The hounds seem strangely still and peaceful. He is at the upper end of the glade, and at his feet the stream drops abruptly down a sharp waterfall to a pool deeper and calmer than those above the fall, though still neither large nor filled with tranquil water. Beside the pool there is a pile of rocks, carried down by some earlier flooding. There is a patch of grass too, bright lurid green and scattered with white flowers. Standing alone on this patch of grass is the Lady Artemis preparing peacefully to take her bath. He knows absolutely that it is she, and he watches awestruck. She has already laid aside her quiver and bow; he can see them tidily stacked against a tree beyond the patch of green grass. Her hair which is darker and shorter than he had imagined is tied back from her face with a simple blue ribbon. Her feet, which he had dreamed of as long and slender, are smaller and sturdier than that, but even from his odd foreshortening perspective he can see that her legs, as they run up to the hem of her tunic, and beyond, are brown and fine and lovely. She is not white and cool, but creamy and warm. She is tall and her arms, naked to the shoulder, are muscled and strong. She loosens the knot of her plain linen cincture, which is wound three times round her waist, and she unwinds it with careful precision. She folds it neatly and throws it behind her, so that it lies white on the green grass. Then she bends forward slightly, takes her tunic in both hands a few inches above the hem and pulls it up over her head. For a brief moment therefore Actaeon sees her naked body, but cannot see her face. The horror comes, the sweat-wringing fear. Her body is not long and white and boylike as his imagination had drawn it; it is rounded and full-bodied. From the point of each nipple her breasts are tattooed outwards in scarlet spirals; her belly is more curved than the flat tautness of his dreams, and just below her slightly protrudant navel is a scarlet cross; the triangle of her pubic hair is dyed red and into it is carved and stained a redder lozenge. She is the grunting birthing sow, she is the wide pink mouths and stained fangs of his bitches, she is the power he feared always, dark and untamed, unpossessed, undefeated, unknown. The power that is broken and bent in the women of Thebes, here free and flowing, devouring and uncaring. Uncaring—neither good nor evil, neither secret nor open, neither gentle nor fierce. Indifferent. She does not care.

And his fear is palpable so that she knows she is observed. The hounds whine at his feet as she pulls off her tunic and looks up. The bitches, ignoring him, leap down the waterfall, all ten of them, a glorious single pounce like the water. They fawn against her body, leaning up, hiding the triangle and the lozenge, licking the belly and breasts. She looks at him, straight, and his panic rises. She looks him in the eyes. The hounds, trembling, are stilled, remaining close to her, deserting him. The beech trees do not stir, there is no wind, no noon-time, no sunlight; there is only her, looking at him. His panic surges. He cannot, he cannot bear it; the fear is sick in his mouth and shit on his legs. In its shriveling he notices, unnoticing, that watching her unseen had given him an erection. He is animal, he is filth, he is a lie and a poison. He has seen her naked and there is no escape. He falls to his hands and knees. He pushes his head forward and moans. It is more like a roar, the roar of a rutting stag, but filled with desolation. She looks away, something else attracting her bland attention, and her hand drops down to caress Alce, his bitch, whose soft ear now lies over her wrist. She pets the hounds, not looking at him. He roars again and feels a new weight on his head. She is hunting her prey he thinks, I am her prey he thinks although she is not hunting but fondling the hounds just as he does. I am her prey. I am an animal. I am devoured. He turns to flee, to hide from the utterness of her, his legs have new strength, they are long and hairy. His head entangles in the branches. He does not rise from his hands and knees, because now his arms have hooves and they too are long and strong. The antlers are pulling his head downwards, stretching his neck. He has to get away. She will turn the dogs on him, because he has seen her naked. The hair on his face bristles, the hair on his back stands up in fear. He breaks across the glade. The stilled dogs can no longer stand it; they look to her for guidance and receive none. One of them whines. The whine restores their instinct. They turn from her, Alce leading. The first note of her hunting song breaks from her mouth as she leaps across the golden clearing. The stag is running now, beating his way up the almost vertical sides of the valley; the terror of the man at the sight of true virginity quickly replaced by the terror of the hunted animal. He knows, even as he hears the belling sound behind him that they will hunt to the death and there will be no escape. But the knowledge is wordless; he is stag now. He comes out of the valley and sniffs the upland air. He can hear the busy hounds singing joyfully at their work as they labor up the hill behind him.

He pauses, taking a great breath of air, and then he starts to run. He knows there will be no escape. He feels the bloody ending, inevitable and horrible for over an hour of hard, heart-and-lung-breaking running. For over an hour before he feels Alce's fangs sink into his hindquarters, he knows that he will feel them.

When all is silent in the bottom of the valley, the Lady Artemis continues with her bathing. Whether she is aware that anything has happened is uncertain. But remember it was his fear and not her malice that destroyed him, for Endymion, the shepherd prince of Latmos, saw the same thing and lay in the moonlight rejoicing and contented.

Lullaby for My Dyke and Her Cat

The immediate problem is to think of some way to explain it to the boys; for their sake as much as mine—though I can't cope with them peering at me lovingly for the next few weeks and suggesting that perhaps I need a nice rest—which I do of course, but that is another story. And I'm not the sort of person who functions well on Valium, it doesn't suit my style and I think it would be dangerous for the baby. I can hardly use post-natal depression which I thought of at first, because my son is over a year now and having sailed through the whole thing so far I think it would lack credibility. I did consider telling them I had been experimenting with hallucinogenic drugs, but I doubt if they'd believe that either, and the consequences might prove even more complicated than the reality.

Reality is an odd word to use in this context. You see, I thought my son was turning into a cat. Only for a moment or two, and he wasn't anyway, so it doesn't really matter a lot.

When I tell Liz it will make her laugh. At least I hope to God it does. I think it probably will.

I'm not sure if I've ever told you about Liz; she's my best friend. We go back a long way together; as a matter of fact—although this is so corny that we don't often mention it—we met at an anti–Vietnam War demo in Grosvenor Square in 1968. Neither of us was being particularly heroic, I should say, but we were both with people who knew each other, and then of course it turned out that we were both at college together, so really we had met before though we just hadn't noticed. And if you remember how it was, one thing led to another, and then we were best friends, and before long there was feminism and we discovered that together and fought about it together—both against each other and together against others and we were better friends still. You know people put down the sixties now, it's become trendy to be blasé and dismissive about it, but I go on believing that there was really something there, something important and that those of us who failed to sustain the vision that we had then have something to answer for; and how to know this and hold on to it and still not succumb to the coziness of Liberal Guilt is a question well worth asking, but one doesn't too often because it is all a bit painful; and we have not been rewarded with the joyfulness and richness that we so optimistically believed in. Or perhaps all I want to say is that those were incredibly happy days for me and I look back on them with nostalgia and regret and the certain knowledge that I blew it and yet totally uncertain as to quite how or when. And a large part of that happiness was having Liz as my best friend and—to be crude—getting the benefit of her extraordinary acute and eccentric mind. And then to everyone's surprise except mine, and possibly Dr. Turner's (who was our tutor in our final year and knew damn well that mine was show-off and Liz's was solid) she got an incredibly fancy degree and a research fellowship and I went off to Devon to teach my aphasic children and we did not see each other so much: because she was hardly one to brave the countryside, of which she radically disapproved; and because I was so into hearing those silenced voices and playing with ideas about language and the social construction of the self that I never went away. And then, listening to them so hard, I couldn't take the right line on abortion and we squabbled about that; and she went off to the States for a year and you would have thought that our friendship had come to an end.

But it didn't. I started to write stuff and woke up one morning and realized that, for the moment, the kids didn't have anything more to teach me—I'd never thought that I'd had much to teach them and being them they never made guilt inducing demands for gratitude so I said goodbye and came to London. Then when I was finishing my second book I suddenly realized how much of it I owed to Liz as well as to the children and the school and I put that in the acknowledgments as a good feminist ought and the week *before* it was published the telephone rang and this unforgettable voice said, "How *dare* you bracket me with brain-damaged infants?"

And I laughed from pure joy. Then she said, "It's not bad at all and you always did have a way with words but . . ." and with concision and no indulgence she listed thirty-seven real problems with the text. Now it is always flattering to have that degree of attention paid to your work, and also she was enormously knowledgeable—and it wasn't even her subject—but if anyone else I hadn't seen for five years had done that to me I would probably have killed them. As it was, within twenty minutes I had leapt on my bike and was pedaling merrily off to Victoria Park where she was living and where we fell into each other's arms and we were best friends—still or again? I do not know and I do not care.

This is all narrative, it tells nothing, except narrative. And I'm not good at "the well-rounded character," that stand-by of Western prose literature. I don't know how, within the limits of a short story, to show the way our lives fitted into a much larger web or mesh of friendships and work connections: that is what I want to tell, and also I want to describe her—because I assure you all this does have a lot to do with my present dilemma about explaining to the men I live with how it was that I came to think that my son was turning into a cat. But narrative is not the answer—or not at least to the questions that I want to ask.

Apart from linear narrative there is also anecdote. (There is also analysis, of course, but I think that it is cheating to tell the reader what she has to think about something unless you also tell her the something she is meant to be thinking about: for instance, I can tell you that one of the most delightful things about Liz was that she was extremely witty—faster on her verbal toes than anyone I've ever met, and that at times she would sacrifice anything, truth, friendship, and innocent people's social comfort, for a good line—but unless I can give you concrete examples of this, which is difficult because all the best jokes come so totally out of context which is long and elaborate and often inaccessible to anyone else, it is not fair on you. You might, like many others, find her humor not charming at all but unnerving and sadistic and why should you have to take it from me?) Anyway anecdote:

*O*nce she and I were having supper with some people, one of whom was a friend of mine who dislikes Liz rather a lot; and the two of us—Liz and I—were showing off rather, and the friend said crossly, bad timing, suddenly heavy, "For God's sake, you two; stop being each other's *alter egos* and behave yourselves, the way you two go on isn't natural." Well, I would just have said yeah and let it go at that, but Liz launched into an elaborate though completely accurate description of the reproductive cycle of the *Coriantis,* the Bucket Orchid; and then another about the horsehair worm. (I don't know if you know about either of these natural phenomena, but they both have life-cycle patterns which are so far-fetched, arbitrary and ridiculous that they boggle the mind, make one wonder if Darwin can actually be right, or whether in fact and after all there isn't a delightfully humorous and whimsical old man with a beard up there running the whole show for the amusement of a bunch of angels. You can read about the horsehair worm, if you want, in a wonderful book which practically comes to this conclusion called *Pilgrim at Tinker's Creek,* which is written by a woman called Annie Dillard. But I'm getting off the point again.) Liz gave this lecture with great élan and brilliance, if somewhat excessive length. She didn't like this friend any more than the friend liked her. "Nothing in nature," she concluded, "is remotely natural. Why should our relationship be?"

Once when we were very much younger, I got into a terrible temper and smashed thirty-seven empty milk bottles against the wall of our kitchen. Liz swept up all the broken glass, gave me a hug and never mentioned it again until, over ten years later, when we were talking on the telephone as I described above and she finished her current list of criticisms of my book, she said, "You see, one for each milk bottle; I've been longing to punish you for that idiotic tantrum."

Once quite recently we were rather drunk at a large and noisy party; Liz was dancing on the other side of the room and some man—not a very nice one—asked me some question about Liz's early career, and Liz detached herself from the arms of her partner at once and crossed the room and touched his sleeve and said, "It's not fair to ask Meg those sorts of questions; she's the only woman around who knew me before I was invented." She went right back to her dancing and I said to the man, "That's the loveliest compliment I've ever been paid." And he clearly thought the pair of us were entirely mad.

Once when it was the middle of an extremely cold winter I went round to visit her and, despite several degrees of frost and a howling wind, her cat door was tied open with the lace from her tennis shoes. Shivering I asked her why and she told me that she was afraid that having to push on the icy glass would hurt the cat's nose.

Once. You see, it doesn't work. I've also just remembered that I've forgotten to mention something extremely important about Liz; or rather extremely important to the story that, despite all these digressions, I'm trying to tell you. Well, to be honest, I didn't really forget, I just was not sure at what point to put it in: either in terms of politics, or in terms of artistry. Now of course I've left it so late that it has far more force than I really wanted it to; I feel it to be a fact about her just as the color of her hair (pale mouse) or her stately bosom and tiny ankles. She's a lesbian. And once, a long time ago, when we were younger, we . . . well, that bit isn't very important. Now I often think that difference helps and sustains our friendship: once we were talking on the phone about whether or not we wanted to go into analysis and she said, "My problem is when I'm in a room on my own I don't know if I'm alive." And I said, "Whereas when I'm in a room on my own I can't understand why I'm not alone." And this made us laugh with considerable pleasure. I didn't go into analysis as it turned out, but she did: she's quite a lot braver than me in many ways. However, be this as it may, I'm not making very good progress with this story about thinking my son was turning into a cat.

Liz has a cat; her cat is black with a few grey hairs (not dissimilar from mine now I think about it), and quite small and is called Mog. Not directly from Moggie as you might think, but because there are these children's books about a witch called Meg and her cat Mog: they're rather fine books actually and are written in a children's lowercase script rather than proper print. So when I gave Liz a kitten when I first went to Devon and she to Essex and we stopped sharing a flat, she called her Mog because of my name being Meg. People come and go in Liz's domestic life, but Mog stays. She's got old of course and a bit arthritic, and less inclined to frolic; but if you go to Liz's there she will be, as often as not curled around Liz's shoulder and drooped across what we unkindly call "The Continental Shelf": a wide soft plain created by Liz's breasts.

Liz really loves Mog, in a very simple and pure relationship that I find inexhaustibly touching—a fact that I, like most of her friends, express by mockery and cynicism. When I was first pregnant I went to tell her about it—for some reason I felt extraordinarily nervous about doing so, though I have looked to her and received support in many far less promising ventures—and she looked faintly disgusted. (This did not altogether surprise me, she has the most bizarrely naive views about the facts of life; once when she wanted to find out what heterosexuality was about she asked if she could borrow my cap and was amazed when I told her [a] that this freaked me out and [b] that it wouldn't work.) Then she sighed thoughtfully and said, "God, another damn case of sublimation." "What?" I said, startled. "You know," she said. "Another poor heterosexual woman trying to substitute for the fact that she cannot achieve the one perfect relationship in this sad world: the relationship between a dyke and her cat. Haven't you noticed it? Here we all are pushing forty and having to settle for what we can get; and you're all getting babies because you know you can't have what we've got." Then she collapsed on the sofa in fits of giggles with Mog in her arms. Later she twanged my bra strap rather overenthusiastically—because I never wore one until I got pregnant when it hurt not to—and said that at least we now had something in common. Later still she bought some beautiful scarlet and black wool and knitted the most wonderful pram suit you have ever seen covered with cabbalistic designs and said if it was a girl would I please keep her in pristine purity until she was sixteen and then hand her over for the traditional *droit de seigneuresse?* After that she did not talk about the pregnancy very much, but the morning that Noah was born she came to visit us both with him still so new that he looked like a tiny interplanetary voyager trying to disguise himself as a human being. And, despite the forbidding notices all over the place, she picked him up and hugged him and said he was nearly as lovely as Mog. But when Paul arrived she swapped bawdy jokes with him about deliveries and knife-crazed surgeons until I felt quite pissed off with the pair of them.

So that is sort of the background; except that I've completely left Paul out of all this somehow. He is the bloke I live with; he and I share a slightly grotty little house with another good friend called David—and it is to them, and now Noah as well of course, that I am referring when I say "the boys." I feel a bit overwhelmed to be honest about the number of males there are in my habitation; I had sort of planned on having a daughter to even things out a bit but David and Paul are very old friends and it would be asking a bit much to suggest that David left and there isn't any room for anyone else so there you are. Or rather, there I am, and by and large pretty pleased with it.

So. Last night I had a panicked call from Liz. Mog was sick. Liz was in tears. I have not seen her cry for years; the last time was when I . . . well that would be another long anecdote and I really must get on with this, especially as the anecdotes don't seem to help much. So I chucked the supper-filled Noah at his dad, ignored both their whingeings about it and rode off as fast as I could to Liz's flat, pausing only at an off-license to buy a large bottle of brandy.

The vet had sent Mog home to die. She had had what seemed to be a twisted gut and the vet had opened her up and discovered that she was riddled with feline cancer. He had suggested putting her down and Liz had refused, refused point blank. The vet had got annoyed with her, said there was nothing more he could do and sent Liz and Mog home. There was nothing we could do either. We sat on Liz's bed with Mog laid out on her Continental Shelf with her eyes slitting up, and we drank the brandy steadily, while Liz petted the dankening fur and I periodically petted Liz. Sometime about two in the morning Mog died. A while later I said as gently as I knew how, "Liz, she's dead." And Liz said, "No, no," in a little kid's voice. So I took them both in my arms and we just sat there a whole lot longer, and Liz cried and cried and cried, and then she didn't cry anymore, she just sat in my arms and held on to Mog. Later still we finished what was left of the brandy, and at about five I said I would have to go because of getting home before Noah woke up and did she want to come? And she said that she didn't, so I said I would take the day off work and come back later with Noah and she said, "Thank you."

I admit that bicycling home I realized I was a bit smashed, but not that smashed and it was the darkest night I had been out in for some time and quite windy and spooky, and I'm not a great night person and it is rare to put it mildly that I am out and about at so late and weird an hour. When I arrived the house was silent and dark. I brought the bike in and locked up behind me and went upstairs, suddenly very tired and longing for my bed. At the top of the stairs is Noah's little room; it was more a reflex of tenderness and tiredness that made me go in to look at him than anything else. He sleeps with a night-light on, which gives the room a faint and sweet glow. I leaned over the cot as I often do, expecting to be reassured by his sound and total sleep. He was lying as usual on his front with his nappied bottom sticking up in the air and his paw in his mouth, and his whiskers slicked out elegantly; where his sleeper poppers had come undone a little of his soft ginger fur poked out. I thought vaguely that we must get him out of nappies before the summer because it would be too hot for his tail when I realized what was happening. My baby was turning into a cat. And I was so shit scared that I created the most amazing rumpus; screaming and screaming. And Noah woke up and joined in and Paul and David appeared shocked and sleep-hagged, and even in my panic I noticed that David was actually wearing the most preposterous pair of bright yellow silk pajamas that I had given him for his last birthday and for some reason this did not comfort me. As soon as I had Noah in my arms I realized that it was nothing, nothing at all, a trick of the light, or my tiredness, and he was just my little boy, nearly eighteen months old and only as softly furred as all small human beings are, his face warm and pink and whisker-free. The boys were both concerned and cross. Paul took Noah and settled him down again, and David offered to make some hot chocolate, and I just wanted to be in bed, alone.

You see, I wasn't scared because I thought that Noah was turning into a cat, but because I thought that if he was it meant I was becoming a lesbian and for a tiny moment I felt so relieved. It had been stupid, stupid, and there is no way I can explain it to Paul. I mean it was just a moment of madness, and drunkenness and lateness, wasn't it?

So why am I curled up alone in my bed with some lovely hot chocolate and a unique promise to do Noah's breakfast and crying and crying?

⁂

Conquistador

Power, he thought. Power and what to do with it. The flight from Spain useless, giving him only the power that previously other men had used against him. Finding no answers. How to turn power away from the act of commanding, mastering, dominating and yet lead these starving bastards, these loyal companions? They certainly had no desire for him to renounce power. They apologized to each other for him when he would not let them kill the native peoples.

Power, he thought. And then, food. Jesus Maria, he was hungry. They had, earlier in the journey, boiled their shoe leather for broth. Yet the Indians went shoeless and full. Food, and no more power. He wanted to get out of the boat, to go into the jungle and yield to it. The answer was there, in the jungle.

He had been filled with joy when they had left the icy mountains and the warm rain had embraced them: it rotted their equipment and blurred their vision, but the casting off of the old apparel and the steaming vagueness held a promise for him—the loss of the hard precision, the virile clarity that he had come to fear. The jungle was a new delight: the sun seldom penetrated the overhead roof of branches, but it was not needed. The profusion and fertility of the jungle generated a heat of its own: and they crawled through the humidity like a flea caught in the hairy chest of a man wearing a leather jacket. Around them they could hear but seldom see the signs of a dense animal life. Huge butterflies and flashes of parakeet moved across the green gloom. Used to forests where great stands of trees of a single variety created an orderly magnificence he was unprepared for this chaotic richness: palms and laurels and rubber trees and rosewood and mahogany and steelwood and bamboos and chocolate trees and silk-cottons and figs and acacias and purple-hearts and cow-trees and brazil-nut trees and garlic trees and cashews and balsa and more cedars than there were names for. Even, occasionally, the cinnamon trees for which they had come here, but never enough; never enough of anything to give a feeling of arrival. Occasionally giant hardwoods broke through the roof and towered away on their own, buttressed by flying roots like the great cathedrals of Europe, but living, growing, fighting for light. Not fighting, reaching: there was no competition. Even the dead trees stood upright, sustained by their comrades, and everything living supported something else. Creepers or great sprays of orchids six feet long burst flowering out of living wood sixty feet above his head. Richness and rottenness beyond imagining. In the evening the beauty was claustrophobic in its intensity; the sun slanting sideways broke up the monotony of green and revealed its variety, like a green fire. The heat and the safety and the darkness took him back to his childhood and when the hunger began he would turn in his sleep towards his nurse and there would be food and comfort, until he could not tell the warmth of his body from the warmth of hers and neither from the warmth of the jungle. Was that what he wanted? To cut back, with a machete of the mind, to somewhere before there was coldness and learning and authority, back to that warmth and unity.

But Pizarro, his leader, brought the words and the fires and the lusts of destruction, down into the jungle with him. They cut a swathe wide enough for the two thousand hogs to waddle through. When Francisco realized that Pizarro was ready and eager to kill, and worse than kill, to torture and maim every Indian he encountered, he knew that he would have to get away, escape, be free of this influence and noise. Volunteering to go ahead and forage was only an excuse. He and his companions had leapt into the small boat and fled deeper into the jungle.

He was in love again. A better, sweeter love than the pale shadow that had so driven him in his youth in Spain. He was in love now with the jungle which both freed and corrected him. He thought about power and hunger. He thought that they would all probably die here. They would anyway have to die somewhere. He loved the jungle and its peoples. Asked for no information they told no lies. Spoken to they replied, sometimes with a marvelous and wide generosity, sometimes with a kinship that he longed for. He could do no wrong: as he and the river became one all things became well; even his mistakes grew hilarious, tinged with the joyful fear of being tickled when a small boy. Once they landed in the realm of a strange feathered king, Aparia the Great, who had armies at his command, but also food and he had given them the latter. Francisco struggled to talk to him. Aparia asked who they were and he tried to explain: from Spain, from the land of the Emperor of all the world. A land where they worshiped one God. Christians: followers of a King without power who died for them. Servants of a King with all Power, who laid claim to all the world. Even while he was speaking he did not know what he was saying, what he believed; he could not understand his own thoughts. Aparia could not understand them either. Waiting, politely, until Francisco was finished he asked again, "Who are you?" and again Francisco had tried to explain. It was dark, sweaty, hot, humid. His brain was rotting like the jungle, he had no control over his tongue or his mind. Again the King listened, again was baffled and again asked "Who are you?" Explosively, Francisco lost his temper. There in the jungle, beside his river he could stand it no longer. The hills of Quito, the highlands he thought he had left behind him forever, seemed bright and clear and strong and manly against the steaming confusion of the river and the excessive piles of food. He threw up his hands in a gesture of pride and cried, "We are the Children of the Sun." Immediately he repented. What was there to boast of? Of killing curious and beautiful people, like these, of raping women and desecrating holy places. But the river, his mother and loving corrected all things. Aparia was delighted, "Brothers, brothers," he laughed, "We too are children of the Sun, children of the Great one, infants of the Sun."

As they passed on down the river, fed by the generosity of Aparia and for a while at least not hungry, Francisco was both amused and ashamed. The river went on and on and did not change, and perhaps it went on forever and would never bring them to the sea. And beside it the jungle went on too, but not only downwards beside them, but outwards, away from them also. And no one could know how far, perhaps it too went on forever and he did not know whether to be joyful or afraid. Was this what he had come for?

The high hill country at Quito he had hated. The wind had made his empty eye socket ache and the immensity of the sky had made him feel blind. He had seen other men newly come up from the coastal plain stretch their eyes and take in the enormity of the space, but no matter how swiftly he had swiveled his neck he had been fully aware that he was only seeing half of what the others saw. Waiting up there for Pizzarro to prepare the expedition he had taken to wearing an eye-patch which made him look rakish and remembering his boyhood, which made him feel cold. Much as he hated his cousin and commander he could hardly wait for the man to be ready. His desire to go into the jungle mounted and his anxiety increased with every delay. He asked himself if he was running away and knew that the answer was yes and that that was a good and brave thing. But of the wanting itself he was suspicious. He had wanted love once, very young, in Spain. She had been beautiful and good and witty—but he had persuaded her to become his mistress and after pleasuring himself on her caught for one moment, once only, a look of fear and disgust in her face so strong that he had put the whole ocean between them. He knew that pleasing himself he had hurt her, and that she would not blame him, that she was grateful to him for loving her. Not that power then, not that desire. In San Juan de Guayaquil he had raped an Indian woman. He had not known it would be rape, he had paid her and thought her willing, but when he raised his face from her shoulder he had seen again that same look of pain and loss. He had wanted to be a conqueror: but recovering from the wound which cost him his eye and discovering how much he minded even that partial blindness and disfiguring, he thought of the death he had dealt out and felt ashamed. He had won a captaincy and lost his ambition. He did not know what to seek now except a loss of power, and a turning into himself to explore and use the power there. Men turned to religion he knew, but not that God, that barren violent God whose name he had learned at his nurse's knee but whose violence and power and cruelty he had learned out here in the New World from the Holy Fathers. Not that God, not that way. But something. The jungle called him, there was something to be sought in the jungle.

He knew well enough the dangers of penetrating a strange cruel land under the command of strange and equally cruel man. The jungle to the East of the great mountains and Pizzarro to the West of them had swallowed men up, killed them or worse. He knew, but also he had to go. He was restless at Quito all the time, impoverished and cold. He loathed the place.

He was happy when they rode out of the East gates of Quito on that bright February morning. Ah, a splendid sight: a Spanish army larger than the force that defeated the noble Incas, lavishly equipped, and handsomely led. Gonzalo Pizzarro the finest horseman in Peru, the most fearless and bold of all those fierce bold Pizzarro brothers, who could lead men to hell and bring back the few that he found worthy. His dashing kinsman and lieutenant, Francisco da Orellana, who had lost an eye but won a province in the war against the Golden Indians. Two hundred and forty mounted Spaniards, the courage and promise of the New World. Four thousand bound Indians, and as many hogs and llamas, and then the great snarling pack of killer hounds, two thousand strong. Pizzarro swore by the hounds, "Best provision we can have. Cheaper to feed than Indians and available for all purposes conceivable: hunting, fighting and even, if the worse comes to the worst, eating." He did not need to add that they were handy also for his favorite activity, torture. Dogging wild Indians was the sport of the Spaniards; Pizzarro also did not mind dogging his own men if all else failed. His private motto was, "If they have to die why shouldn't they amuse me in the process?" They had to die because he was Gonzalo Pizzarro. And knowing all this Francisco was still glad when they marched out of Quito and began the long descent into the jungle.

And now they floated down the river and he thought about power and food. Too much of the former and not enough of the latter. How to lose one and obtain the other. Desire simplified into something to fill the stomach. But that was not desire, that was need. Desire rose above that like a citadel and it kept them all alive. One night, trapped in the boat by the hostility of the local tribe whom he would not let them kill, without sleep or food for days, pinioned by the high cradle sides of the boat which were meant for protection against the poisoned arrows of the enemy but which served the mind as prison bars, the Companions had started talking. Who had started it he did not know, lost in his confusion between the sweet dreams of his good eye and the nightmares of his other hollow place; he heard only the vague beginnings, attending only when it became a game. It had of course to do with food—that humiliating and delightful obsession of them all.

". . . and right now I would like roast fowl in French royal sauce."

"No, no, wine from the valleys of Italy."

"Seriously, what would you like best in all the world, not now, just now, but really. What is your great desire?" That must have been the friar, not the scribbling one who kept the account of the journey in the pretense that they would ever come out of the jungle, to the end of the river, alive; but the other who spoke seldom and then always of his God.

They went round the boat, cramped together in the darkness, too close to lie; a moment of the night lit only by the phosphorescence on the water, a moment of intimacy and honesty forced on them by the long river and the daily knowledge of death.

"Women."

"Gold."

"The thanks of the King Emperor, and his grant of land."

"My mother."

"A child."

"Home."

"The beatific vision."

"To be able to read."

"Captain?"

He had known his turn would come. His great desire? He could not name it because he did not know. To escape from all power, to float thus on the river for eternity. These were not answers.

"The Kingdom of Eldorado," he said and the Companions cheered. Distant as dawn dreams and beyond imagining, that was why they were all here. The land where the Lord Prince covered his beautiful body only with a coating of gold dust and washed each evening in a pool of clear water which no one ever panned or sifted.

The friar said, "I do not believe in the Kingdom of Eldorado. It's just a puny and worldly description of heaven; only a weak way of trying to say God and Salvation."

They were silent in the boat; disappointed, disbelieving, shaken for a moment in the faith which had brought them all from Spain to Hell and now closed them in the boat, in the prison on their infant-cradle. But Francisco shook off his thoughts and asked, "Brother, why are you here then?"

"There are souls to be won. A great conquest to be made for the Lord God."

So it was just power again, power and mastery. "They say," he said carefully, "I have heard there is a man in Spain, wounded in the service of the Emperor, who had turned to religion and has a way of prayer that is for the man himself. Goes inward to the heart, not outward for more souls. A way of penance and self-discipline, weeding out the desires, freeing a man to seek only God."

"Yes. Yes, I have heard that too. A nobleman. Probably a Holy Man, but I cannot think it can be right—to seek something for the self, when there are so many lost souls, here and in the Islands. Not everyone can turn inwards, however great the treasure. I think it not so much a penance as an indulgence when there is so much paganism and idolatry to be conquered. These, all these, have to be saved. To the uttermost ends of the earth. Without elaborate retreats and mortifications I am safe in the arms of Mother Church, but all these savages are damned, eternally and forever damned unless we come to them and make them understand."

"Oh, it is you who have not understood anyway." The other Friar, Carvajal, spoke. "This man he's from the Basque region. The family of Loyola. I've read some of his writings. He's no man for turning inwards—he's a fighting man, he wants to form an army, a Godly army. His way of prayer is just exercises, drilling, military discipline, for the winning of souls. Don't you worry, he wants to exchange one sword for another, not hang up the sword of the Lord."

Francisco lost interest. Not that way. The way of the sword. He had come to the end of that road. There had to be another way, a way of letting go, taking in not giving out; receiving, acquiescing, consenting. Seven hundred miles they had covered in the first eight days of their journey, when they had left Pizzarro and the main expeditionary force. He had thought then, I have let go, the river has taken me. Not a Conquistador now, but a twig on the river, giddy, dashed, powerless before the flow. I have let go, he had thought and he had been frightened. He had halted the wild enthusiastic rush of their first descent. He had wanted to assert himself against this mighty river trimmed with this immense jungle. He had needed to challenge the river, to prove himself a man, a noble man, Hidalgo, the conqueror of the Incas, the master of the river. "Row back upstream," he had ordered the Companions—though then they had still been his men and he their master—"row back upstream, force the boat against the river, defeat her." He would row back upstream, rejoin his Commander-in-Chief, return to his power and authority, lieutenant to Gonzalo Pizzarro, the fiercest of the Pizzarro clan, the King Emperor's own Governor of the whole province of Quito, the slayer of pigs and idolators. Francisco thought he had rejected all that and escaped it, but before the power of the river he wanted to go back to what he knew. His courage failed him.

His darling Companions, the men he now loved and cherished and was loved by, had refused. Too aware of their own weakness they could not bear the thought that the river might defeat them. Aware too that they were better led now than if they returned to Pizzarro. They had a leader, a man of cool and established courage, a man of authority who at the same time was not likely to have them shot on a whim, or in a fit of temper, or with calculation to demonstrate his power. He was and he knew it not the common type of leader. And there was something else, frightened by the strength of the river and the darkness of the jungle, they turned their faces towards Spain, towards the ultimate source of authority and power, towards the motherland. Desperate, hungry and scared they groped Eastwards towards the morning, towards home. They refused to attempt to travel backwards up the river. Pizzarro would have shot them all; would have been willing to die alone and mad in the depths of the jungle rather than waive his right to command. Lost in his private struggle, Francisco had consented. They had gone on downstream.

And now he was not sorry. But joyous. His thoughts grew vaguer and faded away, except of course the thought of food. Around food and sleep the day revolved and they drifted down the endless river, rocked by its smooth movements, at one with its gentle force. Each bend revealed only another bend, and the jungle clung beside them like a mother holding her child by the hand. There were no orders to be given, none to be taken. He was happy and unafraid. The silence surged into his head and his bare toes curled joyfully as though tickled. He stopped even wearing his eye-patch, convinced that the empty socket could feel the damp warmth and the dark abundance like sight.

And so they came at last to the land of which Aparia the Great had warned them, for which the rumors and stories of their journey had prepared them. The land of the Great Mistress, the country of the Women Warriors. And here, for no apparent cause and with no hope of escape, they were mercilessly attacked by the local population. For seven days they could not sleep, they could not eat, they were driven and harried and killed and oppressed. Francisco was taken by surprise. He had come to believe that he alone was the oppressor, the only wielder of power, the rapist, the killer, the torturer. He had learned that they, the Spaniards, were the Conquerors:

if they ceased to conquer, ceased to oppress, there would be no more violence. And that itself had been an assumption of power, a generosity dealt out to a weaker people. Now they were the victims and it made him furious. He had never been a victim before. He was angry and bitter and very much afraid. The old defenses came back. Kill. Kill whatever threatens you, destroy whatever is different. If you turn the other cheek that too will be wounded.

Their boat was driven into a gully, against an island. He wanted to live, not die. The dream was ending. He was waking from a long dream and reality was returning. He saw the bright and polished courts of Spain, a civilized people, a people who must live and teach others. A people of great value, beloved of God, people who knew, who had a right, a duty to survive. He drew his sword and smiled at its preserved brightness. He yelled to his men, rallying them as they dithered like cowards. He was not afraid, his mind dazzling him with its great brightness. He organized the charge. It was the Feast Day of John the Baptist. "Gloria in excelsis" he shouted and plunged in his sword. He felt it penetrate the naked flesh and he plunged and plunged and plunged.

It was the body of a woman. What he had sworn he would never do again, he had done. And on her face was the same look of disgusted surprise that he had seen on the face of his mistress in Spain, in the eyes of the prostitute in Guayaquil. The blood seeped out of her as out of them and what did it matter if the orifice was different. In his strength and fury he had practically hacked off her breast. In her spread out hand still her bow and at her otherwise naked thigh the belt that held her arrows. He had killed her.

After they had escaped and the Companions had calmed down he said, "Who was she? Who was she?" They had taken captive an Indian trumpeter. "Who was she?" he asked. And the man told him the tale of the Sisters: the women who lived in the dark interior and many provinces were subject to them. Their villages were built all of white stone and only women lived there. They could fight, but chose mainly not to: they took men as captives to have children by and if they were sons they returned them and the men to their own people, paying them for their services with green stones, precious and rare.

They were beautiful strong and creative. They had much fine-worked gold and worshiped the Great Mistress, the Mother.

He had killed her. He had killed an Indian and a woman, because he had been afraid. He knew suddenly that he had killed his guide. Just as Pizzarro did, he had killed the one who could have led him to his own desire, led him through the dark interior and shown him the other God, the one who was not himself, like him grown large, but Other. And now there was no way.

The river carried them downwards—but now it was carrying him away and not towards. For a moment of sunshine and pride he had wasted his chance. He had known from the beginning that this was Their river, it was They for whom he had been seeking. And when the moment had come at last, after so long and sweet a preparation, he had thrown it away—he had driven himself into the body of a woman. That was not the right way. He was lost. Lost.

A short while after all this they noticed that the waters were becoming tidal. They were approaching the sea. They were emerging from the jungle and coming back to the bright openness of the ocean. They began to clean their faces, polish their armor and construct clothing for themselves. They started having to fight with the river. It had carried them generously for over four thousand miles: now the tide began to assert itself and they had to struggle against it—create sails and anchors and drag lines, the stuff of the ocean, the bright place which the white man had truly conquered.

His time had passed. Francisco led the activity, organized, ordered, accepted congratulations. He watched the tide coming in and going out as he wrestled with it with ingenuity and intelligence. He was heartbroken but not without hope. Each time the tide went out, he thought, live, conquer, survive. And each time it poured back in he thought, return, I will come back, I will return.

But not this time. Not this time.

Francisco da Orellana, from Trujillo in Spain, was born about 1511. Nothing is known of his early life, but he must have left Europe as a very young man, for he had seen service in Nicaragua before he joined the Peruvian campaign under the Pizzarro brothers. He fought with distinction in the war, lost an eye and was rewarded with the Captaincy of the district of la Culata where he founded the city of San Juan de Guayaquil. In 1541 he set out under the command of Gonzalo Pizzarro on an expedition to search for the "Land of Cinnamon," which was supposed to exist on the Eastern slopes of the Andes, and for the fabulous Kingdom of Eldorado. In the head waters of the Amazon the expedition became stranded for lack of food and a small expeditionary force under Orellana went downstream seeking for friendly Indians who were supposed to live there. Circumstances, about which there remains some confusion, prevented the return of this force and instead the small group in one open boat rowed on down the entire length of the Amazon River (previously undiscovered): an expedition that took well over a year.

Orellana was an imaginative and creative leader, with a number of qualities unusual for his time—not the least of which was his willingness to accept the advice and desires of his men. This factor may well have contributed to the comparatively low loss of life on the expedition. More distinctive still was his attitude to the native peoples whom he encountered: he had a remarkable gift of languages and proceeded always on the theory that live friends were better than dead enemies. This policy, until near the end of the journey, was successful, and he was not only fed but fêted and befriended by Amazonian tribal peoples.

After leaving the river and sailing round into the Caribbean Orellana returned to Spain and immediately attempted to finance a new expedition to the land of his Amazon women warriors—after whom the river was named although they have never been seen by Europeans since then. Orellana's last expedition was a disaster from start to finish: shortage of money, rotten ships and virulent plague in Tenerife were just a few of his problems. Once arrived in the New World he failed even to find the main channel of the Amazon River and died in the delta in 1545.

The Burning Times

All witchcraft comes from carnal lust which is in women insatiable.

Kramer and Sprenger, Malleus Malificarum, 1486

In the long evenings of winter the house becomes intolerable. It is too close, too smoky and too full of them, my men, my husband and my sons. Their limbs seem immense; once I looked at one of the boys' legs, spreading out it seemed suddenly half across the room, and I thought that they were once folded up and inside me, and I felt sick. When I start having thoughts like this I have to go out.

Usually I walk to the church. Tonight it is cold going through the village, with evil little winds that turn and bite at my ankles. But the cold makes precise every surface of my skin, so I can feel the edges, the limits of my body and so be alone.

Inside the church it is still. The huge rood, the suffering, broken Jesus suspended high over the chancel steps is lost in the dark, his agony mercifully not visible. There are, though, two sources of light. Far away, high on the altar the light in front of the tabernacle flickers; he is always there, watching, waiting, listening, and we cannot get away from him. Down here, much nearer, is the Virgin, the lady crowned with the sun, aglow with the light from the candles lit by women like me. I kneel beneath her feet. "Mother, mother, Holy Mary Mother of God, help me, please, mother." But as I say the words the tears come, and when I look up at her through the tears and through the candle flames, she seems to be on fire, the flames licking round her bare feet. She is burning, smiling, burning and I scream.

Aloud. Dear mother, let no one have heard. But she will not listen to my prayers, because I burned my own mother. I betrayed her and they burned her and I danced around her pyre. She saw me and she understood and she forgave me. So I cannot forgive myself.

And I cannot confess this sin, because they will burn me too. They will torture and break me as they did her. Then they will burn me.

The church is empty, this time. There are only her and me here. Mother and daughter. Like before.

The statue of the Virgin is in painted wood. She holds her son somewhat clumsily I feel, having held three of my own. A chance lurch of that serene head and he will fall out of her arms; she should bring him lower so that he straddles her hip, as my mother-in-law showed me, as every mother learns. I try to concentrate on that, on the dangerous way in which she is holding the Son of God; and how easy it is for a child to fall out of even the most loving arms. But the scream does not go away, and while apparently locked in prayer I am crying and remembering.

It was a long way south of here, in an altogether pleasanter valley. Afterwards I came north. My old parish priest helped me find a new place; at first I worked for his friend who is priest here. It seemed like a sensible idea. Of course no one knew what I had done, but probably they would have been pleased even if they had. But our parish priest wanted me to come away because the daughter of a witch is always in danger. In a small village they remember well. The next time it can be you.

I do not want to remember these things; nor do I want to remember the smoke-filled cottage, those enormous and demanding men, and the sense of being always a stranger in a strange land.

There is very little in my life that I want to remember, but though I concentrate on the precariously balanced child and the repeated chain of prayers I cannot forget that I thought she was burning, I thought I saw the flames of the bonfire and I thought that her eyes were my mother's eyes.

I used sometimes to try and justify what I did to her. What she did was an abomination to the Lord God. It was the final sin—so dreadful that it was not even named in church where every sin imaginable and unimaginable was named. So grave a sin that I did not even know it was a sin. God would have wanted her burned. But I do not justify myself anymore, because even if that were true, it was not why I did it, not for the greater glory of God. No, not at all.

I blot it out you see, but it comes back. It comes back when I least expect it, when I think I am safe, like here praying in church, most piously, and I look up and I see the flames and my own mother burning.

She often seemed on fire, my mother. There was something wild in her. She laughed at everyone and at herself. Her hair was a great mass of tangled curls, and she would not smooth them down. She was a widow woman, they said, though as a child I heard other things as children will. She did not come from that village, but from another further west, towards the mountains. She never spoke of her childhood, or of what and where she had been before. She was a lacemaker; a very skillful lace-maker, and she loved the work. Our cottage was not kept very clean, she was not interested in that, my mother—not like me who wrestles with the smoke and the long muddy legs and the tight cluttered space to keep my home clean, who stays up through the night, despite my husband's calling me to bed, to shine and polish and scrub. I need the house to be clean and orderly, but not my mother, who picked up pretty things like a child and left them around to grow dusty and muddled. There was just one corner of the room that was clean and that was where her work was kept; her lace pillow with its hundreds of tiny pins bright as jewels and around them the flax threads bleached white and tied into knots that were spiders' webs and flowers and wreaths and pictures that grew magically out of nowhere; hanging down from the pillow were the bright nuts and shining stones and polished bone bobbins. A beautiful thing, a well used lace-pillow is, and she was far the best lace-maker I have ever known. Up here they do not make much lace; one of the few things I brought with me, because I knew she would hate it to be lost, was the veil she made me for my first communion. It was the envy of the village, with the sacred host and roses and apple blossom and little violets. Perhaps it was the beginning of our troubles, for it was then that people began to say that it was not right that a poor widow woman, if she was a widow woman indeed, should flaunt her daughter in lace like a lady's in front of the whole village. The women did not like her because she did not care what they said and seldom gossiped with them. Some evenings men would come round to our cottage, wanting either to kiss her or to marry her and take her lovely lace-pillow and the money she earned home to their own houses. But she would have none of that, but would laugh at them to their faces. The men did not like her either, because she laughed at them and did not care.

To make lace you have to have very good light; so that she did not work for many hours of the day though there was spinning and washing and flax gathering of course, but as I grew older I did much of that. But when she was not working, in the early morning and the dusks, we would go out singing through the fields, and the people thought that wanton, because they had to work those fields daily. Now I know what hard work it is to be a farming family, but then of course I did not, I knew only that we went singing and laughing while others worked and grumbled.

She could tell stories, my mother. I remember that. When I tried to tell them to my sons they came out lumpish and heavy. I do not know where I went wrong, except that for her they were a joy to tell. She told them for her own joy and for mine if I wanted to share hers, whereas I told them to hush the boys when I could stand their bawling no longer; it is probably different to tell them in joyful love. Sometimes when I was small and she was telling stories, the other children would come and listen too, and on sunny evenings between hay-making and harvest even the grown-up folk would come and she would sing and tell stories. They would even forget for a while that they did not like her, because they liked her stories so well.

Perhaps I make her sound like a soft and easy woman. She was not. She was all I have said, but hard and fierce too. By the time I was about eight I was spinning for her and she would not tolerate even the tiniest flaw in the threads; she said it was an insult to her, to the work and to me myself. Spinning flax hurts your fingers, not like spinning wool which I do now easily and without thought, as I go about my work. I have never spun flax since she . . . died.

In my own head I come to it with such reluctance, so slowly. Only the thought of how close and loud it will be in the cottage, and how one of them will be wanting something of me, keeps me here at all. They cannot interrupt prayer. It is the only place for peace. But here, beneath the feet of the Mother, I cannot help remembering and all the memories pull towards the same point, the leaping of the flames and me dancing. "Dance, for God's sake dance" said the old parish priest, who I think meant well by us always, "dance and smile or they will burn you too." He did not know what I had done, but I think that he held my mother in true respect; protecting me as best he could was for her. And "dance" he urged me with his eyes and his hand, the one on the furthest side from them. I looked at my mother and all the heat and hate was gone and I knew that she knew and understood and wanted me to dance and smile and not be burned.

I was coming to woman-years. When we swam in the pools of the stream my mother would tease my new body, not harshly, with affection, but children of that age should not be teased. Even my sons I protected from their father's teasing and from each other's at that age. My mother and I were together all the time. Because the village was unsure about her, because she did not belong to them, they were unsure of me too. So I was cut off a little, slightly distant and did not have a friend. But I did not think this either a need or a loss because I had her, my mother, and she made me happy.

Then Margaret came. She trudged into the village along the road from the West, carrying a sack over her shoulder. They say she paused in the village square and sniffed the air like a dog. They say she turned three circles and marked the ground with her left foot. They say she stared at old Simon with her right eye closed. But this was afterwards when they would have said anything. And, after all, she went to the priest's house and knocked politely on the door, and he came out to her and spoke civilly with her, everyone agrees. So directed, it seems fair to assume by him and not by any other power, she walked back across the square, right through the shadow of the church tower and came down the lane to our home. It was a warm late summer afternoon, and my mother sat at the doorway to work in the soft sunshine, and her hands were like butterflies on her lace-pillow. I was beside the cottage turning the drying flax and we were singing together as we so often did. And quite suddenly my mother's singing stopped and she gave a little shriek. When I turned round there was her lace-pillow rolling in the earth, the threads unwinding, the bobbins tangling with each other and the pins bent crooked in the dirty soiled lace. My mother was running up the lane and embracing a strange woman.

They came back to the cottage together, their arms around each other, and together they went into the house. Silenced I gathered up the lace-pillow, tried to sort out the muddle and then, slowly, I followed them into the cottage. They were standing there, quite quiet, not talking, their hands on each other's shoulders and smiling. I was forgotten.

I stood in the doorway, uneasy. They turned at last, my mother with her eyes all wild and shiny and Margaret, a friend they said from my mother's homeplace and childhood. Margaret pulled back her hood and the curious reddish curls that grew quite short on her forehead sprang up uncontrolled, as they always did. She smiled at me with a sweetness like sunshine, and my confusion began.

Here in the hushed church, the cold and quiet of it, I truly cannot remember the wildness of those few months. It is this cold stillness that I want now, not that mad, fevered, triumphant, terrible time. My mother made no lace, but was up at dawn and singing, singing. She made me do my work, but never paid me any attention. Or so it seemed to me. The harvest time came and I, as every year, went out as hired help in exchange for the grain we did not grow ourselves. I hated to go out in the pale light of the morning leaving them together, but I did not know what it was I hated. I wanted my mother back, but that was not all because Margaret . . . oh Margaret, Margaret. The joy, the delight of her for me then. She had high round breasts and between them a valley deep and filled with promises I did not even guess at. She was not like my mother and I, small quick women; she was tall, big, but not heavy with it; when she walked, and especially when she used a broom I would watch the rhythm of her whole body and not know what it was that seemed so perfectly pleasing. She would sing with my mother and my own singing seemed childish squeaking. She would pick up the little pretty things that my mother would bring into the house, flowers, stones, old feathers, and just by her calm looking would transform them from pretty into beautiful. I wanted her to go away and leave us in our old closeness and comfort. I wanted her to stay, to stay near me. During the day I would follow her like a puppy-dog and she treated me like one too with casual pats and tender gestures, but laughing and happy to have me amuse her. At night the big bed seemed too small for the three of us; if my leg touched hers, or even her rucked night shift, I would be instantly awake and aware of every inch of my skin; and yet I did not know why this was or if it was something I liked or hated. I stopped sleeping in the big bed, creeping out to lie by the hearth, but I slept no better there, straining through the night to hear her every movement, fearful and excited. She and my mother shared a secret joke that made them laugh and it drove me crazy that I did not know what it was.

So I ached and dozed and giggled and sulked and longed with longings that I had no name for. I thought they treated me like a child when I was not one. I yearned to be a child, to climb into their laps, either or both their laps, and be fondled and patted and stroked as children are. When we swam together I would watch my mother covertly, wanting her not to touch Margaret's wet, smooth body. Wanting Margaret not to follow my mother's fishlike swiftness with her eyes, wanting them both to look at me. But if they did I was ashamed of my own body which seemed ugly, gawky, childish, but which was disturbing my sleep and confusing my heart. But it was not a sad time, it was golden and laughing and joyful and I was confused.

After the harvest the lace-man came as always. He would buy my mother's lace, and look at the work of other lace-makers in the district. The prices were agreed between her and the lace-man in the presence of the parish priest, and usually my mother would come home with a glow of pride and pleasure. The lace-man would bring with him news from the world outside the village and my mother would be full of new stories and good humor. But this time my mother came back from the selling looking anxious. I thought it was because she had not done much work since Margaret came, but it was not that. She had got a good price for what she had done and had been asked for more. I pretended to sleep because I knew that my mother and Margaret would talk; I shut my eyes and lay and listened.

The Inquisitors were coming again.

They had not been to our village in my lifetime. I thought like a child that it sounded exciting, with bonfires and savage hunting, to the glory of Jesus Christ. I peeked through slitted eyes, waiting for more.

But my mother and Margaret looked like old women, hunched over the fire muttering, made small by the darkness and shadows, diminished by fear.

"We can go," said Margaret.

"Not again," said my mother, "not again, I can't bear it."

"I'll go," said Margaret, and I wanted to cry out and stop her. "You'll be alright if I go."

"I don't know, I don't know."

I shut my eyes. I did not want to see. My mother plaintive, defeated, afraid.

The days afterwards seemed darkened. Margaret did not go. She did not speak of going again, but some light had gone out of them both, and out of me. I wanted them to tell me what was happening. I wanted them to notice how their shadow had fallen on me, but they looked always at each other and with stricken eyes. I wanted to make them safe and smiling again and I could not.

The Inquisitors came. We were all summoned to Mass and a beautiful man with a white and passionate face preached to us of the dangers of hell and the perils of witchcraft, pleading with us to give up our witches, purify our community, glorify the Lord Jesus, and give the angels new tongues of praise. I remember thinking that I wished I knew a witch so that I could hand her over to him and be blessed with his smile and God's joy. And after the Mass we had a feast for our Lord Bishop's Inquisitors, who gave up their safe city lives for our protection, and who took to the dangerous highways in order to drive out the forces of Satan. It was a good feast and when Margaret and my mother went home I stayed in the square.

There was a small bonfire, and we danced around it, the young people of the village, excited by the sermon we had heard, and by the presence of strangers. At first I did not notice that something was different. Then I felt it; when I went to speak to groups of chatting people, people I had known all my life, they moved away. There was a silence where I came and it alarmed me. Then the parish priest came and took my hand and talked with me, and I thought the whole village was listening to us, and the rich clerics on their dais as well. The priest talked strangely, loudly, and with unusual affection. And suddenly I was very afraid.

When he let me go, I turned to leave the square because I wanted now to be home. The people parted for me to walk past, and when I reached the corner where our lane came out into the square I heard a disembodied voice, no one's voice, call out "Devil's brat," and I ran.

I ran down the lane, frightened. I ran down the lane as fast as I could because I wanted my mother. I ran into the house seeking her arms. My mother was lying on our bed with Margaret and they had no clothes on and their legs, bodies, arms, faces were entangled with each other in movement, intense and intensely beautiful. When I saw Margaret's buttocks in the light from the doorway, saw them lift and plunge, saw my mother's strong small butterfly hand reach across them, spread out, holding her, then I knew what I had longed for. When I heard my mother moan softly I knew what I had wanted. I wanted to touch Margaret like that. I wanted to moan like that. I had wanted and known for months without knowing what I wanted. I crouched down clasping my own stomach in a craziness of desire. I watched them to the glorious end, Margaret triumphant kneeling over my mother, and my mother moaning and laughing, legs kicking free and abandoned, and her arms reaching up round Margaret's neck to pull her proud head down onto the breasts where I thought only I had ever lain. They had stolen this from me. Margaret had stolen my mother from me, my mother had stolen Margaret from me. Under my very eyes, laughing at me, in the face of my longing which they had laughed at. Or had not laughed at because they had not noticed in the heat of their love for each other. On hands and knees I crept away from the door out into the lane, and they, wrapped in their own beauty and passion, did not even hear my coming and going.

I lay for a while curled up, reaching with my own fingers as they had reached for each other, not sure what I was looking for and finding it and hating it and loving it and hating them and hating them and hating them.

Then I got up, hating myself for that lust, hating them for raising it in me, and I smoothed down my skirts and arranged my snarling hatred into a modest smile, and I walked back up the lane, burning, burning with the sight of their excitement and my exclusion from it. I walked across the square and the fiddler stopped playing and then in the silence, before all the people, I denounced my mother for a witch.

The white-faced Inquisitor said I was a good girl.

When they went to hunt them up out of the cottage Margaret was gone. So they had to make do with just my mother.

They burned her.

They tortured her too and raped her and broke her. Through the next two nights we could hear her screaming. And I was afraid. I was afraid that she would denounce me, and I would burn. I was afraid that she would not and I would have to live. When they brought her out at last you could see what they had done to her. She told them that she and Margaret flew out the window at night and fucked with the Devil. She said that she and Margaret kissed the Devil's anus, and that they used his excrement to make men impotent. She said that Margaret had been made invisible by spells to escape her just punishment. She even said that the Devil made her lace for her, a web to catch Christian souls and that she transfixed the souls with her pins and weighted them down with her bobbins, the souls of babies who had just been baptized, that all her lacemaking was a glamour and illusion. At the end she could not stand up, but she would not denounce me though they wanted her to. She said I was innocent. And when they lit the fire and flames leapt up and our parish priest told me to dance and I danced, she smiled at me. She kept smiling at me until she started screaming. Only two people were smiling though the village square was full: my mother and the chief Inquisitor, whose pale face was glowing with a radiant joy.

That time they burned three other women too, from the district. I did not know them, I did not smile. I had betrayed my mother, because my evil desires had betrayed me. But on the bed, my mother's hand on Margaret's buttock, reaching across, fingers spread out, that had not been evil. It had been beautiful.

Nothing else in my life has been beautiful. The parish priest arranged for me to come here. Afterwards I had a strange time and I could not look at fires. He was worried that they would come back for me. So I came here and I worked for his friend until my husband wanted to marry me. He is a good straightforward man, well respected. It seemed the safest thing to do, it seemed like a safe place, as far as possible from all flames. He does not worry about my occasional nightmares. He never asks any questions. So long as I do all my duties I do not think he cares.

I have three sons, but I am glad I have no daughters. I might have loved a daughter.

They say it is better to marry than to burn, but only just I think, only just.

An Edwardian Tableau

True to their word, the Suffragists marched on the House of Commons yesterday, and the scenes witnessed exceeded in violence the utmost excesses of which even these militant women had previously been guilty.

It was an unending picture of shameful recklessness. Never before have otherwise sensible women gone so far in forgetting their womanhood.

Daily Sketch. Saturday, 19th November 1910

Dinner seemed interminable, and yet Caroline was not sure that she wanted it to end. Afterwards there were two things to be faced; she was so tired that they seemed the same, equally important, equally unimportant, it did not seem to matter. Richard would propose to her, and her mother would lecture her about coming down to dinner without stays. She knew the first from her father's heartiness; Richard and he had been in the library together before the other guests had arrived; also her mother at the last, the very last, moment had changed the seating so that Caroline and Richard were sitting next to each other. And would she accept him? His face moved backwards and forwards, in and out of focus, she was so tired that she did not know what she would do, what she wanted. He would be a bishop one day they all said, he was a canon already, he was too old for her, she was too young for him, she would be a bishop's wife perhaps, perhaps not; how could she not know? How could she not care? She had known about the lecture from her mother from the very moment she had come downstairs. How could she have thought that her mother, who noticed everything, would not notice? Her mother's standards were liberal but fixed, like her father's politics, and Caroline knew every shade of them. She was allowed to smoke when there were no guests in the house: she was allowed to hunt escorted by only the groom if Graham was away, but not if he was home and did not want to go out himself; and she could leave off stays in the daytime, but not in town and not for dinner. The lecture would cover these and other points and would include her mother's favorite little joke, "Impropriety is one thing, Indecency is another." She should not have risked it, she could not face it, the pain would have been better; no it wouldn't; even without the stays she could feel the pain, the bruise where only yesterday one of her whalebones had been snapped and driven into her side. Hunting falls never hurt like this, but people were gentle over hunting falls and they were your own fault or bad luck, not inflicted, deliberately laughingly inflicted, the way Graham had hurt her when they had both been very small— run to nurse and she would make it better—but now there was no nurse and no one she could tell. She was going to fall asleep, during dinner, at the table, no please not, please not God. They, they out there, her mother, her father, stout Lady Corson, the They outside her pain and tiredness were talking, listen to them, don't fall asleep, not Here, not Here.

They were discussing some minor corruption, some political corruption, something mildly bad, mildly important, Caroline could not remember the details. Sir George Corson kept saying how dreadful it was, how very dreadful, how it just went to show, how monstrous it was. Caroline's mother laughed her silvery laugh—and had her laugh always been like that or had she read somewhere of a silvery laugh and set out to procure one, just as she procured good cooks and beautiful dresses?—she laughed her beautiful, silvery laugh and said, "Of course, Sir George, these things wouldn't happen if you gave women the Vote, that would purify politics," because of course Caroline's mother believed in the vote in her beautiful, decorous way. Sir George responded, "Come now, Mrs. Allenby, women purify in the Home, you make the politicians of the future and it's far too important a job for us to give you time off to go running in and out of polling booths. You wouldn't like it if you had to do it, you wouldn't be in a position to purify anything then, you know. No, no, women don't need the vote, they have the sons of England to look after, and they have husbands to do the sordid things like voting for them." "What about the unmarried women?" asked someone down the other end of the table; the conversation was going to become general, it always did when the Vote came up: there were subjects, the Vote, the Hysterical Militants, the Impossible Irish, the Ridiculous Workers, the Poor Peers, subjects that no one could resist. Sir George looked swiftly round the table, all the women except Caroline were married and he could guess what was meant by the odd seating easily enough, so he laughed and said, "The unmarried women? Dear Madam, there shouldn't be any, and in any case we don't want to be ruled by the failures, that's not democracy to my way of thinking. Remember a *Saturday Review* article that hit the nail on the head, said that a woman who failed to marry had failed in business and nothing can be done about that. I agree; it seems a little harsh at first, but think about it, think about it." There was a little silence and then Richard raised his head and started speaking slowly and gently. Dear Richard, Caroline thought as his profile swum into focus and, yes, they would make him a bishop and she would be a bishop's wife. "It seems to me," he was saying, "that all this unrest is a symptom of a massive breakdown in trust. Everyone seems to be frightened, frightened and too proud, women don't trust their men anymore and the working people don't trust us. But it does seem to me that it must in some way be our fault, and if they can't trust us then we can't be worthy of the trust and must allow them something they do trust, the Vote or Unions or Home Rule or whatever it is. I think they're wrong, I think they would do better to trust people than institutions, but they don't and they must somehow be freed from their fear. There's too much fear and not enough trust and love."

Caroline's father laughed, "Come now, Souesby, where there are separate interests there's going to be distrust. We don't trust the workers come to that, and I for one don't trust the Irish, neither lot of them, and I don't trust those screaming women, and I don't see my way to doing so. Universal love indeed, you sound like one of those Russian Anarchist fellows."

But Richard was not daunted; he's brave, she thought, gentle and brave, just as he was out hunting. He went on, "That's not fair, Sir, and you won't scare me from my truth with an anarchist bogey. I'm not an anarchist, as you know perfectly well, but I will say that I have read a lot of their literature and I think they have some pretty sound ideas. Just building up more and more institutions is not going to help any of us; we must have more trust in each other, more of a common interest, and stop pinning our faith on all these organizations, and institutions, or at any rate look at them more closely and see if they deserve to continue."

Someone said, "That's a fine way for a good churchman to talk," but he smiled and replied in his politest voice, "If you knew my record, Madam, as a lunatic ritualist, practically an idolatrous Papist, I assure you, you probably wouldn't think of me as a good churchman at all. I don't think I care so much about being a good churchman as I do about being a good man, and I still say that we all, all of us, on every side, need more love and more trust. Speaking as a churchman I could say simply that Perfect love casteth out fear." And even as she thought how superb he was, how her mother herself could not have done it better, could not have been more firm, more silencing, more politely rude, Caroline heard her own voice, in the distance, far away, out there, say, "So does hate," and even then it might have been all right. She had said it very quietly, almost to herself, but Richard, attentive and loving, turned round and asked quite clearly what she had said and there was no escape. For a time-less moment her eyes seemed fixed on her mother's beautiful chest, her pure white shoulders rising up from the exquisitely ruched chiffon and the line of her neck running up past her pearls and into her lovely, lovely hair, and why thought Caroline, or half thought into the endless gap in time, why don't I look like that so that I could say things like this and no one would mind? Then she said rather loudly, "I said, 'so does hate.' Perfect hate casteth out fear." And in the silence, the astonished silence, that followed she could hear her head tapping out thoughts. That will teach them, that will teach them to sit here, so pompous and liberal and benign and intelligent and talk about purity and trust and love, when outside there is anger and meanness and hate, beautiful hate which made you feel six feet tall, which made you feel as you felt when you knew that your mare was going to take a fence that other people were refusing at, was going to take it perfectly, take it in her stride. That will teach you Canon Richard Souesby to keep your white hands clean and turn the other cheek and trust them all while they beat you and throw you about and laugh in your face. And then Lady Corson, kind, well meaning, stout Lady Corson, said loudly and carefully, "That reminds me of the most peculiar book I was reading, young women are so much more imaginative I think than we ever were. I wonder if you've heard of it, Mr. Allenby? It's called *Dreams,* by an Olive Schreiner. It was lent to me by. . . ." And they went on talking and gradually everyone else joined in, but not Richard; he sat silent beside her, did not look at her, looked at his food, and Caroline was afraid, afraid for herself, afraid of herself, and now he would not marry her and what would she do? How would she manage without him? How could she have thought that she did not care, that it did not matter whether she accepted him? And now he would not ask her and she loved him, she loved him, she loved him. But he did not turn round, did not smile, just sat looking at his food, eating his food. And her mother's chilly white shoulders were waiting, waiting till afterwards, till all the people had gone, and the fact that she was not wearing stays had ceased to matter compared to what she had done, she had silenced a whole dinner party, she had embarrassed everybody. The white, cold shoulders and the tiredness and the dreadful, dreadful pain in her side all became one cold blur and Richard would not ask her to marry him and she was getting colder and colder and farther away and then Emma was beside her and

"Would Miss Caroline like a drink of water?" Emma, so quiet and discreet, pouring water quietly, discreetly, and she drinking it and feeling better and gradually the dining room coming back towards her and she back into it, all so quietly and discreetly that no one noticed; no one except Richard and he turned towards her looking concerned and asked almost soundlessly if she were all right. He smiled sweetly, lovingly, and she thought that after all he would ask her to marry him and she would accept and he would look after her always, and she felt well and strong again and started listening to the conversation.

By now it had moved on to the awful Incident the day before, when hundreds of women had fought with the police for six hours, trying to get to the House of Commons. Well, she thought, it was bound to come up, it was bound to; she felt strong enough for it, she need not say anything, they need never know, she need only listen, even the pain seemed bearable. Sir George Corson was speaking again, "I don't often find myself agreeing with that dreadful *Mirror*. This time I did, they hit the nail on the head, *The Times* was far too soft on them. *The Mirror* said those women were the disgrace of the Empire and a source of shame to all womanhood. I couldn't agree more. Glad they left the word 'ladies' out. I wouldn't even call them 'women,' female, that's what they are, females. Disgusting." And no, she couldn't keep quiet, could not listen and say nothing, could not hear her friends spoken of like that, because they were her friends, her real friends, so she said, "I was there." She saw the ruching of her mother's dress move as her mother's shoulders tightened a little, disapproving. Then one of the ladies down the table said, "Caroline dear, I didn't know you were a militant," and there was perhaps a hint, a slight tone, of admiration, envy. It was not clear but it was enough for Caroline to go on, "Oh no, I wasn't. I mean I'm not a member of the Union or anything. I was there by mistake, but I got involved, because of the crowd and separated from Emma, there was this enormous crowd, watching them you see." How could she be so cool? Her mother's shoulders had relaxed again, she could go on, there would be no trouble, no trouble so long as she kept calm. "I didn't understand the newspapers this morning, it didn't seem like that then, the police were very brutal." Sir George interrupted, "Now, now, Miss Allenby, they were only doing their duty." "I thought," she said as carefully as possible, "that it was their duty to arrest anyone who assaulted them. They wouldn't arrest us." The shoulders tightened again. Was her whole life to be governed by the rise and fall of a pair of perfect, beautiful shoulders? "You see," she hurried on, "I got involved." Involved. There must be a better word: committed, converted. She had been standing, pushed about by the crowd, trying to see Emma, when suddenly a funny old, no not old, middle-aged lady had fallen to the ground at her feet. She had bent down to help and asked, "Are you all right?" But the woman was hysterical, she lay on the ground and sobbed, "They won't arrest us, they won't arrest us, they won't arrest us" over and over again. How could she explain to these safe people how nothing had made sense, how the police were refusing to arrest them; them, us, me? "Sir George, you don't understand, the crowd was all around pushing in; if one tried to get out, and at first I tried very hard, I did not want to be there, I don't believe that militancy will work, I didn't see the point of it, I wanted to get out, but if you tried then the horrible men in the crowd pushed you back in again, back to the police and they would not arrest you whatever you did. There was an old lady there in a wheelchair, perhaps she was as mad as anything, perhaps she should have stayed at home, but she was there, and the police pulled her out of the chair and threw her on the ground and then they shoved the chair away; I saw them do that. It was very frightening; if the ladies there did foolish things it was because they were so frightened." The panic had been the worst thing, she had been so frightened, so lost, so confused, turning in circles, pushing against other women, pushing them down, knocking them over herself in her desperate efforts to escape. Finally she had run into a policeman and had grabbed him thinking that here was safety, that he would help her, "Get me out of here, please get me out of here." He had seized her in his arms, crushing her so tightly that she could hardly breathe, tearing her blouse on his buttons and he had tried to kiss her and when she had protested he had laughed and said, "That's what you really want; that's what you're here for, isn't it, sweetie?"

She had started to struggle, to kick, even to bite. The policeman, suddenly angry, no longer smiling, had literally thrown her to the ground and as she landed she had felt one of her stays snap and ram itself up under her ribs. The pain and the shock had been too much and she had lain there with a red film running over her eyes for a moment, and then she had opened her eyes and seen the policeman standing there smiling, pointing her out to another of himself who was also smiling, but who looked almost frightened. A great wave of hatred, the sort she had not felt since she had been a little girl, filled her up, lifted her to her feet and she had realized that she was not frightened anymore. She was a fighting force, she was Deborah, and Joan of Arc, and Boadicea and there was no fear but only waves of beautiful hatred which made her feel six feet tall and insuperable. Hitting and shoving and insulting policemen had felt like Mafeking Night, only the bonfires were all inside her and hotter and brighter and better. But these things she could not explain, and she said, still quite calmly, to the dinner party, "You cannot imagine how horrible it was, how frightening; some of the members of Parliament came out on the steps to watch, they were smiling and laughing. One of them had a little child with him, she cannot have been more than ten, and he kept pointing us out to her and trying to make her laugh and she just stood there and looked amazed. He is probably a good honest man who would not go himself, let alone take his daughter to a fight, a match, whatever it is that men go to, Father, what's the word? I know, a 'mill,' but he still thought that seeing a thousand ladies abused by the police, English ladies by their own police, was a suitable amusement for her. And all those ladies were trying to do was to present a petition, asking for what they believe to be their rights. Apart from the vote, surely they have the right to petition Parliament? I hated that member of Parliament so much at that moment that even if they had been fighting for something that I thought bad, thought totally wrong, I would not have left those ladies then, I would not have wanted to, even if I'd been able to." She was getting excited, she knew it was a mistake, that it might spoil everything, that it would do the suffrage cause no good; but her excitement was not for the cause, it was for herself, because she had discovered that she need not be afraid, that she could be strong, that she need not be tied down in awe of her mother, that beauty was unimportant compared to the strength of her feelings, that militancy might not do much good for its cause but it did wonderful things for the militants. They knew what she knew, how good it was to be angry, to be really angry and show it, that when you were really angry nothing else mattered, that there was no pain, no fear, no restraint, no anything but an enormous space that you could fill up with yourself and see how huge and strong you really were. She knew how good it was to have an enemy and know that he hated and feared you, because the police had been frightened of the women and of what they had found in themselves, but that you only hated him and were not frightened so that you would win really even when he appeared to have won. And so she finished up almost panting, "Sir George, I have told you how dreadful it was, how humiliating and disgusting, how shameful to the government that let it happen. I haven't told you, I cannot tell you, how fine it was, how good I felt hating and fighting with the police, how good it was to abuse members of Parliament at the top of my voice, how fine and beautiful and lovely those muddy women on the ground were, how much I loved those 'Females,' as you call them when we helped each other. They have been waiting, all women have been waiting for fifty years for the Vote, waiting patiently to accept it as a pretty present from the men who laugh at them, who abuse them mentally and physically. I tell you that after yesterday I am beginning to believe that after thirty years of patience and waiting and teaching calmly, Our Lord must really have enjoyed hurling over the tables of the money lenders in the temple."

"Caroline! That is quite enough!" That was her father, his good-natured face red with embarrassment. Her mother was calmer and far colder, "I think we have heard quite enough about the hysterical conduct of some unhappy, unbalanced women for one evening. Emma, please offer Mrs. Lettering some more of the fruit shape. Tell me, Sir George, have you seen the Martins since they got back from Dresden? So strange to come back at this time of year, one can't help wondering why they've returned."

Caroline sat at her place and the warmth she had felt died away, but she wasn't sorry, she could not be sorry, neither for what she'd done nor for what she'd said. She would be sorry in the morning when she had to listen to her mother and watch the beautiful neck take on its curve of disdain; she would be sorry if Richard did not ask her to marry him, and sorrier still when he married someone else, but it would not be the right kind of sorry, not the kind they would expect. That kind was out of the question now she knew how strong she could be, how it felt to be free of fear, how it felt to be totally herself. Then she looked at Richard and he was smiling, not pityingly, not even kindly, but with open admiration. For a moment she was tempted into humility, into wondering what she had done to deserve this wonderful man, but her courage was high and with a final rush of bravery she thought, "Of course I have deserved it, of course I deserve this man, of course."

An Un-Romance

I am the Ice Queen, so they say.

I am the Belle Dame sans mercy, the divinely beautiful but wicked enchantress who comes upon young men alone and palely loitering and binds them in thrall.

I am the Ice Queen and I live in the Ice Palace, high up upon a crystal mountain. The Ice Palace glitters when the pale sunshine falls upon it; glitters like diamonds, like glass, like frost in the morning. Everything that comes within the chilly orbit of the Ice Palace freezes, and my translucent walls of blue ice are hung with the frozen corpses of butterflies. I have pierced each of them with a steel pin through the heart, and pinned it to my wall and their now stilled wings, petrified suddenly in mid-flight by blasts of cold, provide the only color in my ice-bound realm.

I am the Ice Queen and, when not transfixing butterflies, I sit holding my ice-mirror in my white hand and silently contemplate my perfect profile in a chilly orgy of narcissism.

There are several problems with this scenario: not least of which is that I would not have the first idea of how to go about admiring my perfect profile, even if I happened to own one which I do not, in an ice-mirror. It seems to me that if one tried to look at one's own profile in a hand-mirror—ice, glass or otherwise—one would, at best, see only wildly squinting, rolling eyes, and a half-focused view of one's chin. Moreover "Flat 3, 11 Bellingham Rd., London, E8" does not seem to me a remotely suitable postal address for an Ice Palace and Hackney is not commonly famed for the quantities of jewel-bright butterflies it generates.

Nevertheless I am the Ice Queen, so they say, and I live in the Ice Palace and even to approach my abode you must step over the rigid torsos of those who have been slain by the glass splinters from my heart. So, by and large, women regard me with a mixture of fear and jealousy and men with a mixture of malevolence and ambition. Were it not for an unfortunate element of self-mockery, of sardonic humor even, in my make-up I would find my life lonely, and might even end up believing all this guff myself. As it is, I am solitary, which I do not mind too much, and irritated, because the whole thing is so silly and boring. And deeply unfair.

Shall I tell you how I ended up in this position? I am guilty of The Great Sin. I am that dangerous woman, that villainess of every romance for the last five hundred years, that frigid but challenging bitch.

He loved me and I didn't love him.

Even that is too simple, I did love him actually, at least a bit, at least at the beginning. I just didn't love him enough. The earth did not move for me. I was still in Kansas. Despite having natural curls I turned down the job of Princess.

He was The Prince of course. He claimed the role boldly and made good his claim.

He was The Prince: for him the Sleeping Beauty, the sweet child, turned from her century of dreams, was expelled from the dark recesses of her own half-consciousness and growing self-knowledge, stirred at his kiss, came back to this world when he touched her and lived happily ever after. For him Snow White's pallor retreated like the winter and roses flowered again on her soft cheeks; for him the seven dwarves gave up their mother, sister, comrade, friend and were happy to do so, for it was fitting. For him Rapunzel stayed awake all night, plaiting that glorious red hair, over-and-under, over-and-under, strands of gold and copper, with the rich shine of new conkers, while the stars sparkled above her pointed tower and the witch snored in a lower room. For him Rapunzel endured the exquisite pain of having an eleven stone weight drag out the small fine hair on the back of her neck, and raised her head from the pillow and smiled when he climbed, at length, over her windowsill.

He was the younger son too; the innocent, cheeky one whose kind heart wins him fair lady.

He was the romantic in the garret; Shelley in his despising of the conventions; Keats in his courage in the face of disaster; Coleridge in the wild incoherence of his dreams; and Byron in the irresistible authority of his sexuality.

I really don't know to this day quite how he pulled it off, except that he was quite astonishingly good-looking. Dear God, but he was beautiful. He really was. I mean stop-in-the-street-and-stare beautiful. He was not blind to his own attractions, but then, why should he be? I've known vainer men with less justification. It wasn't his vanity that got us into this mess. He had huge dark bedroom eyes, with wonderful lashes, so heavy and feathery that sometimes when he was asleep you could not help wondering whether he would ever be able to lift them when he woke up. And he had an unexpectedly muscly body to go with it. But it wasn't that, there was something extraordinary about him; a kind of febrile intensity, vulnerability, openness. It wasn't just that he could talk, with fluency and charm and wit; in his presence you would have talked too—you would have talked as you had only dreamed you could talk. You would have become articulate and charming and generous and witty. And honest as you would not have thought you wanted to be: you would have told him the secrets of your heart, and given away the keys to your soul; and woken up too early the next morning expecting to feel embarrassed and experiencing only delight at yourself for your courage and at him for his tender interest.

I have been told that he was also a terrific lover and I can imagine only too easily that this was true, although I personally never got to find out. Not surprisingly, then, he was much loved by women, and, frankly, spoiled rotten.

Not surprisingly, also, I was delighted, no enchanted, when he turned those expressive eyes in my direction. Unlike him I am not particularly beautiful—though I'd like to make it clear I am not stunningly hideous either: simply all right, you know, along with most people. The point is that I was not a shy and blushing maiden plucked from some secret corner and drawn into the sunlight by his kindly attentions. Nor, by the way, was I some frigid, neurotic, castrating virgin who cast her vengeful eyes upon him. Three years ago I was just a young professional woman, more interested in her job than in any immediate plans for domestic and eternal bliss, but open to most of the pleasures of life. I earned and spent a reasonable sum of money. I had fun. I had a circle of people whom I thought of as my friends, and it overlapped here and there with other circles of not dissimilar people and so it was that his path and mine, regrettably, crossed.

We met at a dinner party and enjoyed each other; he invited me to some vaguely work-related drinks thing, and I reciprocated by inviting him to come to the private view of a rather smart artist the gallery I worked for was exhibiting. Our styles conferred credit on each other; of course I was pleased to be seen with so lovely and talented a young man, and as he also had good manners and charm it did me no harm. But the reverse was just as true: although, as I said, I'm not stunningly beautiful, I had style—rather extravagantly bizarre clothes and, then, a certain high confidence and enthusiasm for life—and, he was a painter and I worked for a rising and definitely chic gallery; certainly I did him no harm either. It made good sense.

Later we went to the theater together, and then talked for hours over supper, and by the end of the evening I was thinking that not only had I found a new friend, but one who was great fun and also pretty sexy. I liked him a lot. But I was off to Paris the next morning and so nothing came of it then.

While I was in Paris something very sad happened to another, quite different friend, of mine; so when I saw him again I wasn't concentrating on him. In addition to which I was premenstrual, tired and overworked. When he asked me to go to bed with him *I didn't notice.* What I should have done, of course, was either to say "no" very clearly and absolutely, or to say "yes" and get on with it. But I was not paying attention, it had been a bad day.

I knew it would be better soon; I fancied him anyway. Perhaps more than that; because the way one talked to him left one feeling naked and delicate and eroticized in a way I wasn't used to, I felt both excited and tremulous. In short I didn't want to say "no" very clearly; but I didn't particularly want to have sex with *anyone* that evening. I just didn't feel like it right then. Perhaps I should have made all this clearer, but my mind was elsewhere. In the following months he often accused me of "leading him on." He did not seem to understand that people had other things in their lives, obligations which predated him, things more interesting, more important than his lusts, even than his love. I was not paying attention to him. It wasn't planned; I just wasn't concentrating.

What I had not grasped was that no one had said "no" to him for years, at least certainly not off-handedly like that. He was too surprised to be angry. Instead he fell in love: it was the best way of salving his own pride though he would never have acknowledged that. He fell in love. It may have begun as an advanced technique for getting me into bed, but it accelerated rapidly into a mania.

He brought me flowers. Or rather he left them on my doorstep each night. I would get up in the morning, lurch to the door to collect the milk and there would be a bunch of roses. No card, just a bunch of roses. Well, who wouldn't be pleased and flattered? I was. The first morning; and the second, third and fourth mornings actually, but after that the flat began to look like a funeral parlor and the whole thing became embarrassing.

He wrote me poems. They were rather good poems, and that too was quite exciting and flattering, but he sent them to my office on the fax machine. Again the first time this was quite funny and charming and my colleagues were rather impressed, but three or four times a day week-in and week-out? It became an office joke. Everyone teased me, and I don't blame them. People would rush to the machine to read his latest offering, aloud and raucously. It took up time on the line; it was distracting and unprofessional. One of my bosses got annoyed and the other assumed that I was deeply in love, likely to get married at any moment and therefore unsuitable for promotion.

The next bit is harder to explain. I'm told that some people can only fancy people who don't fancy them, but I tend to be the other way around. For me at least, there is no aphrodisiac in the world so potent as being desired. I found, at the center of all this idiocy, an enormous pool of lust. I didn't want him to love me forever, I just wanted to fuck him. So while he was overflowing with great spiritual passion I was panting with a rather less elevated sort; and perhaps it is not altogether surprising that we ended up on a sofa one night, after several glasses of wine, with our tongues wrapped round each other's tonsils. He was a good kisser too; but . . . I have thought about this a lot since, and blamed myself, and fretted about it, and in the end have to fall back on the simple statement that a woman is allowed to change her mind. Suddenly it was all too much; yes I wanted some sex with him, but the price tag was too high; the price tag was romantic love and the world well lost. I remember thinking with great clarity that no sex was worth the simple and friendly world in which I liked living. That to sleep with him was to consent to his view of the universe in which we were soulmates designed for each other; which was that he was the Prince and I was the lucky maiden. He was the Knight and I was the Holy Grail. I tried to tell myself that I stopped because it would not be fair on him; but it wasn't that, not really, it was that he was not fair on me. He had claimed the only good role and was now casting the supporting parts. It was not me he loved, it was the idea of himself as the Lover.

I said the sexual equivalent of "thanks, but no thanks" and went home to bed. When I woke up in the morning I was a bit embarrassed really, but remember thinking that at least this should have cut his devotion off at the source. I was wrong. His conclusion was that I was a guilt-ridden, unhappy woman, who needed his love to cure me. He believed this unshakably.

He suborned my friends. They started pleading his cause for him. "He's so sweet," they said, "he loves you so; he's so unhappy; how can you resist him?" and later, "How can you be so mean?"

"I don't love him," I'd say desperately, "What can I do?"

"I don't love you," I told him. "Honestly, I don't love you."

"You will," he said sublimely.

Shakespeare has a lot to answer for. Those speeches of Viola's in *Twelfth Night,* for example. Persistence will break down resistance. A good woman is powerless before the force of a real man's love. So next thing he did was build himself a metaphorical willow cabin at my gate and called upon my soul within the house—mainly by telephone. It became nearly impossible for anyone else to get hold of me because the line was always engaged. He would call at all hours of the night and day. Eventually I got rid of the answering machine and took the phone off the hook, although it destroyed my social life. But this did no good because then he would take up a stand underneath the window and serenade me. At three o'clock in the morning this did not go down well with the neighbors.

"You will not rest between the elements of earth and air but you will pity me," he told me with one of his usual theatrical flourishes.

I did pity him, which was why, in the end, I asked the psychiatric social services rather than the police to remove him.

This turned out to be a bad move. People thought it was cruel of me. I felt I was being harassed. I felt I deserved the support and sympathy of my friends. But they did not see it in this way. For the first time in my life I encountered two terrible myths of our time.

Myth One: If I really wanted him to stop he would. If he didn't it was because *subconsciously*—oh subtle let-out clause—I didn't really want him to. I was encouraging him, and it was therefore all my fault. The more I protested the more people seemed to believe this. One evening I suggested that perhaps the two women I was talking to were *subconsciously* jealous, and would like red roses and constant attention from so beautiful a young man themselves. By midnight I had two fewer friends; they were both round at his flat reassuring him that of course underneath I really did love him, but I was afraid of intimacy, afraid of passion. I had always been a cold fish.

He reported all this garbage to me in a long passionate letter, bravely assuring me that he at least understood. He did not mind and could wait forever until I was ready for a love as large as his.

Myth Two: Love will conquer all. Not only will but should. To resist the onward sweep of love was to do an evil deed; was wicked and callous and probably neurotic. This means, apparently, that the lover has rights, but the beloved does not.

"Please stop it. Please go away," I said to him, trying to be kind.

"I can't help it," he said. "Love is like that. You wouldn't know, but I can tell you. You can't control love. You want to control everything because you're scared of passion and intimacy, but you can't control love. You can't choose. Love is blind, its arrows strike where they will."

"If you can't help loving me, then I can't help *not* loving you," I said wearily, "do be fair."

"Love isn't fair," he said, "it is bigger than fairness, it is more true than truth. You will learn that one day. Let me teach you."

If he had been an ugly little nerd everyone would have forgiven me. But he was Prince Charming; Cinderella had to kick off her slipper. It was because he was so lovely. That was not fair either.

And this went on and on. I was weary and fed-up. I was angry and put upon and I saw that he had won all the sympathy and I was looked at askance; women were nervous of me when their men were around; and men were angry on his behalf, angry at an uppity woman who had turned down so splendid an example of their sex. They also fancied me as I had never been fancied before but I could not enjoy it under the circumstances.

I didn't know, I swear that I didn't know he was listening. He shouldn't have been listening. I was eating a Chinese meal with one of the few people who were still neutral if not sympathetic. I hadn't noticed that he had come into the restaurant and was sitting at the table behind me. My friend said, "The poor thing. Can't you either be nice to him or call it off? He's suffering so."

And I said, with a mean little laugh, "There's no evidence that he's suffering. I think he enjoys it. If he was really suffering it might be different." My friend did not ask, "Different in what way?" which was lucky because I couldn't have told her.

He shaved off his eyebrows, he shaved off all his hair, and—oh insult to all the gods—he cut off his wonderful eyelashes. He presented himself to me, at a party the following evening, in front of fifty people, grinning with pride as though he had swum the deepest ocean, traveled the darkest forest, climbed the highest mountain and brought me treasure from the nest of the heavenly dove.

"I *am* suffering," he said.

He looked so damn silly that I giggled.

He fled the room and was never seen again.

As a matter of crude fact he went to live in Manchester and about ten months later married someone quite different, and settled down to a life of suburban respectability. But although this was fairly common knowledge it didn't change anyone's mind. He was forever the romantic hero, the *parfait gentil knight,* the Prince of all fairy tales.

And I am the Ice Queen, so they say.

No one else giggled when I did.

I am the Belle Dame sans mercy, the divinely beautiful but wicked enchantress who comes upon young men alone and palely loitering and binds them in thrall.

The old stories do not lie; that is their rule. Perhaps I am an Ice Queen; it is hard to know. But although they do not lie, they omit. They tell us about the frog turned into a Prince, but they never tell us about the Prince turned into a frog; though the divorce statistics uphold the frequency of this version. They do not tell us about the women who prefer dragons to knights; nor about the ones who prefer cottages to palaces, honest independent work to silk gowns. They do not mention the women who wish a slightly different Prince had turned up in their hour of need. And they never, never let on that there are those of us who prefer jam doughnuts to orgasms, an interesting day's work to grand passion, a Sainsbury's supermarket trolley to a pumpkin coach.

He loved me and I didn't love him.

Even that is too simple, I did love him actually, at least a bit, at least at the beginning. I just didn't love him enough. Despite having natural curls I turned down the job of Princess. I did not want the love of the typecast hero. And regardless of all the modern icing on the old cake, all the high-minded talk about equal rights and women's freedom, you still have to play one role or another in the romantic drama. If you refuse to be the Princess, beloved and beautiful, then you'll just have to be someone else: jealous stepmother, ugly sister, wicked witch, fairy godmother. And I am the Ice Queen, so they say, and I live in the Ice Palace. Pretty boring it is too. And very unfair.

Next time you hear a piteous tale of unrequited love, and its heroic courage, just spare a thought for the real victims of romance: the unrequiting lovers.

Forceps Delivery

None may presume her faith to prove
He proffers death that proffers love.
Edmund Waller, "On the Marriage of the Dwarfs"

Date: 1670

Place: Paris, the Salle St-Joseph, the lying-in ward of the Hotel Dieu, the Parisian charity hospital founded in A.D. 641 by St. Landry, Bishop of Paris; and the adjoining delivery room, the Chauffroy, so called because a fire was kept burning there to warm the mothers and neonatal children.

Cast: *Dr. Hugh Chamberlen*—a member of an eminent and hugely successful family of obstetricians. His grandfather and great-uncle, Huguenot refugees to England in the late sixteenth century, had invented the obstetric forceps, and the family had kept this as their well-advertised family "secret" for a century, to their immense profit and prestige, despite their own explicit recognition that a more general knowledge would save the lives of thousands of mothers and children during this period—before the discovery of asepsis and safer Caesarian section. (Without the forceps, in the event of a fully obstructed labor the choice was to let the mother labor until her uterus ruptured and she died, or to chop up the child *in utero,* smashing its skull and then removing it piecemeal with hooks; this often entailed very serious damage to the mother, particularly as modesty and the law demanded that the obstetrician should keep the woman's body covered, and so invisible, at all times.) In 1670, aged forty, Dr. Chamberlen went to France and offered his family secret for sale to *Dr. François Mariceau,* who although only thirty-three was recognized as the leading obstetrician in Europe. In 1668 he had published his *Observations sur le Grossesse et l'Accouchement* which became the authoritative textbook on the subject for many years. (Dr. Hugh Chamberlen, after his return from France, published the English translation of this work.) Dr. Mariceau was not eager to pay the fabulous sum proposed for an unspecified product and proposed a test case. He had in his care a *severely deformed rachitic dwarf primipara* aged twenty-eight and nameless. After examining her he concluded that the case was impossible; if Dr. Chamberlen could deliver her the secret would be worth paying for.

Now read on.

There are too many rhythms. Too many rhythms. I cannot settle into the pattern of a rhythm because of the others. Now I am gone into the place of infinite darkness, the place of impossible slavery, the labor for the child who cannot be born, I find too many rhythms.

Four days ago my waters broke. But the pains did not come. They walked me. They walked and jolted and jumped and shook me for three days and three nights. They came, the nurses came. They broke into my silence. They said, "Put your arms around our shoulders and we will walk you. Up and down. Up and down." Up and down. So that is the first rhythm. The rhythm of the walking. One two, one two, one two. Left right, left right. Up. Down. It is not easy to walk a dwarf. I know that. But it is not easy to be a dwarf. They walked me in shifts. Some were kind. Some were efficient, which is better than kind, for me. But some, when their shoulders ached, or their backs were tired and lopsided, they would straighten a little and then my feet do not reach the ground. My feet would trail, dragged behind. They would hang down, heavy feet on ugly bent legs, toes scuffling along the floor as I try to walk. Up and down. Up and down. One two. One two. Heavy, implacable, useless. The Princess had to sort the seeds, all the mixed seeds had to be sorted. Impossible task. Impossible useless task. But the birds came. The birds helped her. Nature came to her aid. But not to mine. Because I am unnatural. There is only the beat of the impossible walking. Stomp. Stomp. Stomp. It does not go away, even now, even at the end.

After three days of that stomping they changed their minds. They gave me a massive dose of senna and laid me down. And at first it seemed a sweet relief. To lie there on the bed alone and let go. Let it all go, rich and warm and stinking, flowing and farting, letting go as though the baby could be born that way, just letting go and sliding out. But then afterwards the pains came and I had not known. And that is the second rhythm, the rhythm of the pains. They come, they come from outside and from inside, in waves almost elegant, so total, so demanding, so absolute. They start far away, low and musical, and the flow upwards rising, rising higher and higher above my head and they sweep up and up to a crest that will finally swallow me altogether and there will be no other place and then, there, high above the world in a moment of perfected purity, perfected intensity, there at the moment of annihilation there is the turning, the retreat, the long harsh undertow of defeat. There at the riding point, there in the promise that everything will be simplified down into pure bright colors—red, green, yellow—there is the turning, the declining, the moving away. And down in the trough in the quiet space which the pain has created there is the moment of perfect repose, the knowledge of eternity and the fear of hell and the sight of heaven. There is a sense that the pain is pushing, pushing me down further down and lower on the bed; and I am longing, longing for someone to come, longing that they will come and lift me up, strong hands under my armpits to lift me up to a position where I can meet the pain in all its power, meet it fair and square. Exhausted by the flawless pain, pinned by it, flattened, swept away into its depth, I desire that someone else should be here, someone else to come and lift me up, up, up against that rhythm, so as to greet it as a friend, and no one comes. And struggling to find someone, some place, some space, some height, some elevation in the calm moment at the bottom of the trough of pain, the great wave comes again too soon, just too soon, just as I know I could find a way to be ready and eager, it comes too soon. And that rhythm goes on and on, like at the seashore, where you can watch all day and there is change but no ending, no break, no moment of stillness, but only the rising and falling, rising and falling, rising and falling of the waves that come from far away, from beyond the horizon. Out there, beyond where the sun sinks, is where the waves come from and there is hypnotic movement, where one longs for stillness and longs not to have one's longing met. And I know that the waves are not my own, not mine alone, but like the waves of the sea are universal and belong to all the women who come to this place, to this beaching point and stand looking out towards the New World, where nothing will ever be the same again. And at this point I can, almost, almost, enter into and enjoy the rhythm of it, because it joins me to all the women, all the mothers, whom I am not like and whom I can never be like, except here in the grip of the waves of pain. Almost. But also there is no escaping from the pain, so it must be lived with.

These things I learn here, flattened on this bed. I learn them and know them in the great swelling and ebbing of the rhythm of the pain. I know them and I tell them to myself and there is no comfort. But I do not complain, I do not cry out, I do not ask for any relief, because it is not consonant with my dignity to do so, and I have so little dignity. I have come to a place, the end of a nine-month journey, where I will abide in silence; where I will curl up in the silence of my pain and endure, endure, endure, for the victim of achondroplasia is a silent bear. I retreat, I retreat deep, deep into my lair, hibernating myself from it all, and I seek in silence the depths of the cave of pain, the belly of it where the child that is me and the child that is in me, both, still, against the impossible odds, struggle for survival.

But they will not leave me in my lair. They will not let me be.

There is another movement, a different rhythm and it is none of my making and it is intruded upon me. I search for a poised place, a balance, a harmony between the rhythm of the stomping and the rhythm of the pain, contrapuntal, like singing a round, both parts, oneself. And as I glimpse, pursue the idea of a pattern here, it is broken in upon, shattered, fragmented, by the comings and goings of the two doctors, and the game they are playing together.

Dr. Hugh Chamberlen is forty years old. He is a large and flamboyant man, with red hair and huge hands. He is famous. He is a famous obstetrician. He has, they say, astonishing success in a large number of difficult cases in his native London. He is obstetrician to the royal court, but his fame is not based on this alone. His family have been famous obstetricians for a century. They have a secret, they are not secret about this, it is well known and much vaunted. But no one knows what it is. His family are called in when all goes awry at the labors of the richest in the land. They arrive with a huge strange chest. It is carried into the room where the woman is in labor. Everyone else is sent out. The woman herself is blindfolded. Dr. Chamberlen's hands reach under the sheet. He smiles with confidence. His strong and hearty voice tells her all will be well. She can hear him muttering, feel him digging into her, and then she can feel the child moving. Where it had refused to move, it moves, it moves down the birth canal and is born.

When he came first I was encouraged. He seemed so full of confidence, this flashy and fashionable man. No problem, he says, no problem. The secret enables me to deliver in a matter of minutes the most difficult of cases. Fifteen mins max in your case, he says with a smile. Suddenly I do not trust him. He cares not about my pain, but about his triumph. And his triumph is not over the difficult delivery, it is over Dr. François Mariceau. Dr. Mariceau. I thought he was a lovely man, Dr. Mariceau. He seemed interested in me. He is thirty-three. He is tiny. He has tiny soft hands. He is the doctor here. They call him "the Oracle" because he knows so much about the delivery of babies and writes wise books. So. I liked his gentle hands. But I see the two of them smile at each other. They are playing a game and it has nothing to do with me. Over the hours the game is intruded into me, like the secret. Dr. Chamberlen wants to sell his secret to Dr. Mariceau. He wants a lot of money, ten thousand *livres* they say. Dr. Mariceau is canny. He does not want to spend all this money on a duff deal, he wants an authentic demonstration. He examines me, with his students. I will do nicely. The fetal head, they mutter, is too high, disengaged—and am I disengaged from this conversation, I am supposed to be. The baby has its face pressed to my belly. I did not know until then that it should not have, it should be backwards, pressed towards my buttocks; I wonder if the effects of the senna repelled it, made it turn around. There are things you do not ask doctors. Clearly, they agreed, the case was impossible. Let Dr. Chamberlen try his secret; if it works on me it's worth the price.

You see their rhythm imposes itself on mine. I too become rational, worldly, slightly jaundiced, hearing them. I cannot fly back into my silence and my weighted waiting. Not in their presence.

They like each other, these two. I realize that. It is a game they are playing, a game with some pride and some money invested, but a game nonetheless and played between friends who respect each other. I would like to play too, I would. I think I could hold a strong hand in this game, but then it would not be between friends. It does not matter who wins this expensive game. It will not be me. It will not be me.

So they walk me and dose me and walk me and the pains move me and lift me, and they ignore the pains and do not wait for the rhythm of them. They prod me and feel me. Their game is graceful and fun for them, and I am not part of it. They take me into the Chauffroy and it is warm and I would like to sleep there, but there is no resting among the conflicting, tugging rhythms. Dr. Mariceau is laughing, smiling, as he leaves; should he go to the bank, he asks, to get the ten thousand *livres;* and Dr. Chamberlen laughs too and says there will not be time because he will in minutes deliver me of a fine son. I want to tell him that I will die, I will not have a child at all, but that if I do I want a daughter, but then I will have broken my silence and will have no more defenses against them. Silence is hard earned, hard bought, it cannot be sold as cheaply as this big man's secret. I have fought for mine and won it, and it does not matter if he wants to deliver me of a fine son.

He is jovial, this English doctor. He cannot even talk to me in my own language, he does not even try. There is no one in the room but him and me, so that the secret can be preserved. His hands are too big. They have no respect for the other rhythms. They are too huge. He feels me. His fingers seek out my dark and secret places. His hands plunge in. And I know, suddenly and with agony, that first he wants to make a lot of money; but secondly his power and my deformity, his power over my body, which he cannot see because it is covered, his hands reaching and groping; he cannot forgive me for his curiosity; he cannot forgive me for making him curious, making him excited, even making him rich. I have experienced this before, the power of excitement that my strange, ugly, hated body has, and the power of the guilt and anger and unforgiveness. But before I could always walk away. And now I cannot walk away.

His hands withdraw. He will be without mercy now, only full of pride and determination. From his bag he takes the secret. He knows of his own failure now because he does not blindfold me. He makes no attempt to keep the secret from me. Or perhaps because I am silent, always silent, silent and deformed, he thinks I cannot talk, thinks I am stupid and ignorant. He puts his secret claws into my flesh; reaching in; hard, cold and going in.

I do not think of the child.

I never think of the child in there.

I will not think about the child that is trapped in there.

Trapped in my body as I am trapped in my body.

I refuse to think of the child, for fear that I might love it.

I never think of the child in there.

For three hours he works on me. It is arrhythmic.

Dr. Mariceau admires his efforts. Once he pauses to regain his breath. The tugging and the pushing. Getting the baby out is like getting the baby in. So much effort for the poor man. Ha. He is sweating. I am sweating too but that is different. With the sheet covering the secret, covering me too, though that seems not so important to him, he lets Mariceau enter.

The head is engaged now, he says, but the pubic bones are seriously deformed.

So, you admit defeat? smiles Dr. Mariceau.

Yes, yes, yes, I cry. But I do not say a word. I want them to leave me, to leave me alone to the impossibility of my own deliverance. They claimed to be saviors, the doctors, but now the game is between them. I have had enough.

Enough. Enough.

No, no, says the older doctor smiling. I have every faith in the secret, though I could use the patient's cooperation. But he never asked for it. This too cannot be my fault. Everything is my fault. My wicked and punished body is at fault.

And the other rhythm, the darkest, most inward rhythm, lifts itself, swells, surfaces, which until now I did not notice because I have always lived with it. I thought that in labor it might go away. It does not go away. It is the rhythm of the Dwarf. The rhythm of the freak, of the monster, of the nightmare. It is the rhythm of the dreams and fears of all whose legs are straight, whose height is normal, whose shoulders carry their heads with floating poise.

The rhythm of the Dwarf is a hammer beat in the inmost cave where the Dwarf prowls for treasure in the dark. The Dwarf taps, taps, taps at the rock of security.

This is the time of the Dwarf. The Dwarf is malevolent and heavy. The Dwarf is the sullen weight. The Dwarf does not speak. It is no good asking the Dwarf to speak. The Dwarf does not like either words or silence. The Dwarf is the heavy weight of unspoken anger. The Dwarf goes down into the dark, stomp, stomp, stomp. The Dwarf lives in the dark so that they do not have to see the misshapen.

Oh yes, I thought in the great crashing waves of labor, in the sweetness of giddiness of the intolerable pain, that I could leave the Dwarf behind. For twenty-eight years I have been the Dwarf, I have been carrying the Dwarf. I am the Dwarf. I thought that pregnancy would move it, that the new life swelling the body differently, making it a new shape, was bringing me to a new place where I could be woman, mother, something, anything that was not Dwarf. But now my labia are spread back, cut into, torn apart and the doctor's deep claws are inside me, grasping, tugging, struggling. Ripping. Inside in the dark cave is the child that the Dwarf has stolen away and kept prisoner. All children are taught to fear the Dwarf and rightly, rightly. Once there was a little girl who did not know she was a Dwarf, that little girl was me. But I learned, I learned. I learned that I am Dwarf, to be showpiece or to be terror. In this new world there is no place for the Dwarf. No one wants the shadow, wants the dark magic that is as old as the caves in the hills where we delve. Eight years ago the last official dwarf at the court of France died. I went to his funeral. To say goodbye to a hope. We have descended now from gods and the holders of dark power, when the High Pharaoh would dance in our honor, imitating our bodies, singing our songs by the hot Nile. We are reduced to this bed of pure pain, where for profit and showmanship this man with large hands opens up my body and pulls and pulls until it is broken.

So this is the time of the Dwarf now. A heavy time where words must be hewn out. Words can float in silence like bubbles, joyful and colored. But first they must be hewn out. Hacked painfully, heavily, out of the mine of noise which is the Dwarf's place. The Dwarf hates the baby inside me and will not let the baby be born. It is the Dwarf that has bent and deformed my pubic bones so that the baby cannot escape from the cave. The Dwarf hates all children, because once someone laughed, and in the laughter the Dwarf was born.

What I saw in his eyes was perhaps not there. After I knew he saw me as Dwarf and saw it salaciously. But for one sweet moment I saw only affection and desire. It seemed worth the risk, for a few hours not to be Dwarf but to be lover. That moment of escape, of hope, was signing my own death warrant and I knew it. He proffered death who proffered love, because there is no life for the deformed, no hope, no way out. When the roots go down, wriggling like a baby's toes, joyfully down into the warm wet earth, what happens when they hit the deep unmovable rock of the mountain of the Dwarf? They cannot go down or round. I know that now as I push and push and push on this baby, trying to push it down, push it through, push it out into the light, and I cannot. He cannot for all his large hands and bluff optimism. The Dwarf stomps on each little root of hope.

There is too much pain. There is too much pain. There are too many rhythms and they do not work together. They have walked me for three days and three nights. The pain has assaulted me for over seventy hours. The claws of the clever English doctor have dragged at my flesh for three hours; for three hours the body that he cannot see because it is under the sheet has been cut and shamed and broken. And the twenty-eight-year weight of the Dwarf, the twenty-eight-year rhythm of the darkness. It is too much.

Finally I am defeated. I break the silence. I say, "Please, leave me alone."

They take me back to the Salle St-Joseph. I feel the colder air on my broken body. I feel the explosion inside and the child drown in my blood. The other rhythms go. Only the low chuckle of the Dwarf remains. The belly-laugh of the dark place where the freaks must go. Welcomes. Welcomes me home forever.

Fag Hags: A Field Guide

Part I—Introduction

Fag hag is a derogatory term, and like most derogatory terms, especially those referring to women, it is somewhat loosely used. This is most unfortunate for all sorts of reasons, a few of which may emerge from this story.

It is time perhaps for some precision.

Fag hags are supposed to come in two basic varieties: the beginners model and the *deluxe* model. But, I can tell you privately, the beginners model is not really a fag hag at all; she is actually a vastly superior version of the "sweet young thing"; she is clever and cute and has a turn for camp humor and loves to cook for people. She is too bright to risk doing this for heterosexual men, who always exploit good cooks; and she has enough native political nouse to know that most women would rather talk than cook and slightly despise those that don't. So she hangs around with gay men, and usually has rather a good time. Straight men and—I'm sorry to have to say—some straight women, like to think and, especially like to say, that she is "afraid of her sexuality," but this isn't quite true. She's not afraid of it exactly, she is just a bit puzzled about where she left it last Friday evening and how to ask for and identify it in the lost property office. She is very sweet and deserves a better reputation than she gets and she may or may not grow up to be a real fag hag. As a matter of fact she may or may not grow up at all. It depends.

This field guide, based on in-depth research, deals only with the second category. The real, *deluxe* high-grade, genuine fag hag is a different matter altogether.

PART 2—SPECIES IDENTIFICATION

Here is an eight-point plan allowing the interested to identify infallibly the genuine fag hag. The reasons why you might wish to do so will be examined in a further essay not yet available.

1) A real fag hag is over forty. It takes this long to develop the necessary skills and attitudes, as well as the style.

2) Fag hags are always verbally witty, usually in a self-deprecating, ironic mode. At this level there is no such thing as a stupid fag hag.

3) Fag hags are extremely good at their jobs, whatever these may be. Their necessary combination of sensitivity and bossiness, of generosity and egotism, go down very well in all sorts of enterprises. This competence also gives them an unusual degree of class mobility, which they tend to exploit.

4) Fag hags have a deficient sense of social shame. They can discuss quite intimate matters, like preferred brand of sanitary tampon, in very loud voices, on public transport, accompanied by strings of improbable endearments.

5) Fag hags are not good mothers, although they often think they are. Their own children tend to adore them, but prefer to do so from a distance. When asked about their mothers, they tend to flinch a little and say in exhausted tones, "My mother is a *very* remarkable woman."

6) Being a fag hag, for a fag hag, is a part-time occupation. She always has women friends with whom she likes to have lunch; she has political or charitable commitments (note: fag hags love be-

ing on committees, or in groups); and her work (cf. definition 3). Often she also has a husband.

7) Fag hags are surprised by their own predilections. Every now and again, usually on the tube or at Uncle William's cremation or somewhere else equally unsuitable, they will wave their hands about in the air and inquire at 987 decibels: "Oh God, sugar plum, why am I such a fag hag?" Sometimes they even give it up for Lent. But it never works. Sooner or later they will find themselves at three in the morning sitting at their kitchen table caressingly discussing the love life and emotional problems of some gay man; or they will arrive somewhere very public accompanied by a delightful male person whom their women friends will mockingly describe as "her walker"; or they will give a dinner party and realize only ten minutes before the guests arrive that they are *all* gay men.

8) And this is the clincher. Every single fag hag owns, or knows that in the platonic sense she ought to own, a full-length fur coat, preferably mink. Nowadays she may be too poor or too politically sensitive to have or to flaunt one, but still it hangs in her metaphorical wardrobe and at moments of stress she metaphorically hunches one shoulder and snuggles her chin into its soft and slinky metaphorical collar with a sweet, self-mocking little smile.

Part 3—Recent history

The 1968 legislation which decriminalized homosexuality put the classic fag hag at risk. The vital niche she had filled in the life cycle of social intercourse became semi-redundant. The early 1970s, with the emergence of women's liberation and gay liberation, weakened her position still further. Many fag hags diverted their not inconsiderable energies into feminism, which was healthy for them. Gay men learned to prefer their own company and, having hated themselves for their dependence, gladly forgot their centuries-old debt. By the middle of the next decade the fag hag, although her plight excited little attention from the ecology groups, was in serious danger of extinction. Although she still hung on in certain rarified and clos-

eted environments—one thinks of the operatic and student commu-
nities and also of the Anglican church—she did not really flourish
there. If one was a Darwinian gradualist one could point to her
evolutionary failure and see her, like the dinosaur, as being non-
adaptable and consequently on her way out.

But I am not a Darwinian. When it comes to evolution I am a
catastrophe theorist: catastrophe theory does not accept the traditional gradualist mutation, adaptation or extinction. It posits instead
sudden environmental catastrophes, which so change the ecological
situation that while some species abruptly become extinct, others are
enabled to make fast evolutionary leaps forward, ensuring their survival and rapid development. In the middle of the 1980s such a
catastrophe occurred within the ecosystem of the fag hag which created an environment highly favorable to this declining species; and
with certain adaptations she has flourished again in the last five
years.

The catastrophe I refer to is HIV/AIDS. It is more or less impossible
to say this with anything approaching the boundaries of good taste,
but the fag hag is doing terrifically well in this situation. It is not
just that they are great at raising funds, and giving time and energy.
There is a quality in their relationships with people who have AIDS
which is symbiotic, invaluable to both parties. And I don't just
mean the business of turning up in hospital wards in glamorous hats
and smelling of Paco Rabanne *eau de calandre,* though that should
not be minimized.

I mean something about need.

PART 4—AN ANECDOTAL CASE HISTORY

Well, you may be feeling somewhat uneasy with all of this. You may
be wondering quite how, as a feminist, I can go into this pseudo-
scientific, objective mode and how I can appear to put down other
women, my sisters, in this unkind way. The thing is, darlings, there
is nothing objective about this study: I am a fag hag. See points one
through eight above. I even have a coat, which, while not mink, does

have an enormous soft fun-fur-fabric collar, chin-snuggling for the purpose of.

So I thought I would tell you a story, a case history, a hymn of praise to fag hags in a time of catastrophe.

Like all good fag hags I have a range of male gay friends. Older gentle ones, who aren't very out, and quite like me to do their camping-it-up for them. Gay men in couples who come to dinner with my husband and me and we all discuss mortgages and pretend that—and discipline ourselves to act as though—our marital relationship isn't poisonously privileged over theirs. Gay priests with whom I discuss ecclesiological politics and spirituality, and pretend that—and discipline ourselves to act as though—their gender and ordination doesn't poisonously privilege them over me. But honesty obliges me to admit that my own particular fag-hag specialty—that is the gay men who bring out most strongly that complex fag-hag element of my complex personality—are nearly always left-wing, outrageous, pretty and young—not too young or they aren't companionable, and *definitely* not young enough to be my sons. Say between twenty-five and thirty.

I have a favorite model at the moment. He's bliss. He has very blue eyes, very nice manners, and very strong radical commitments. We met because we were involved in the same AIDS charity—he was working for them professionally, and I, being a good fag hag, was on the fund-raising committee. We flounced out together because we couldn't get along with their politics. This enabled a great deal of late-night bitchy gossip, subterranean plotting and gigglish conspiracy. Then we were friends. It made me happy. It still does.

And because of him, early one morning, late last summer, I kissed my somewhat recalcitrant small son goodbye, and caught the North London Line from Dalston Junction to Hampstead Heath. It was, like so many mornings that summer, stunningly bright and golden. The pupils of Sainte Union Roman Catholic Girls' Comprehensive were on their way to school wearing their maidenly kilts; from the north, St. Pancras Station looked even more like a fairy-tale palace than it does coming down the hill from the Angel. The passing mixture of domestic and light industrial buildings of inner

North London seemed particularly charming; and flowers as well as brick walls sprouted beside the train tracks.

We were going to the Royal Free Hospital, for him to have the HIV test. This was not a panicked response to a passing fear; he is, naturally me being me, well informed and has known and lived with the risks for years. He had decided to have the test because the U.S. AZT trial results meant that for the first time there was some medical reason for knowing: there was some hope for prophylactic intervention. He said he sort of rather expected to test positive. I believed him.

I was touched to have been asked. Well a little more than that frankly, I was thrilled to have been asked. I was excited of course (or nervous if that sounds more appropriate) both at my own reactions and at my ability to meet his needs. I was curious about the whole process. I wanted to be useful to him. I thought I could be. In short, I was in my element.

The counseling session made me want to laugh. They asked, indeed they pressed, to know why I wasn't testing if he was. They assumed we must be lovers and I loved it. It was summer so I didn't have a fur collar on—a pity really as it would have been the perfect moment for a little coy chin-snuggling.

We had seven hours between when he gave them his blood sample and when we were invited to return for the results. We had cream cakes and coffee in Louis, Pâtisserie, a famous Hampstead bakery and café where the cakes come from heaven via Vienna. We went for a walk on the Heath; he showed me where he had picked up trade among the trees and underbrush just down the hill from the bus stop, and I showed him where I had lost my virginity a quarter of a century ago and where I had taught my son to ride a bicycle. We had a long and alcoholic lunch at The Dôme Café. We looked in the shop windows and bought some books. I nobly resisted the temptation to force upon him a silk shirt of stunning loveliness and outrageous price tag.

We talked. Sometimes we talked about why we were there, and sometimes we talked about other things. Once, as he seemed a little shaky, I asked him directly, "Are you OK, poppet?"

He replied, "I'll live."

This made us laugh, slightly hysterically.

I touched and hugged him constantly. For my own sake as much as his. He touched and hugged me slightly less than he usually does. I wasn't his lover, of course, so he didn't have to.

And in the meantime, in my head, I was rearranging our house so that he would have a lovely place to die. Could we, I thought, fit in another bathroom so that he could have one of his own? Would he prefer that? Could I persuade my husband that this would be an acceptable notion? I could bring him breakfast in bed (all fag hags love taking gay men breakfast in bed, but unless they are ill it is so tacky that one has to resist it). I could cook him tiny but nourishing meals, so tastefully garnished that they would tempt his failing appetite. I could hold him in the night and reassure him as he sweated and sweated, or coughed and coughed. I could hold his hand and remind him that though death was a tricky bastard there was no need to be frightened. I could have long, sad, tender chats with his friends. I could cheer him up with fun gossip and withdraw discreetly, understandingly, when his ex-lovers came to visit. At first he would look very lovely and later he wouldn't and it wouldn't make any difference to me. I could buy him primrose yellow silk pajamas and a Japanese kimono. I could be just *wonderful.*

And at the same time, throughout the course of the day, I admired him more and more—for his openness, self-knowledge and courage; for his self-mockery and his refusal to minimize what was happening. To my deep, if maternal, affection for him, which was strong enough already, I added a depth of respect, of love which will never go away.

We went back to the hospital at the appointed hour and after a not unreasonable, but unbearable, wait we were summoned to the inner sanctum where he was informed that his test had been negative.

He said later that his first reaction was one of disbelief. Mine was simpler. What I felt was joy; not happiness, or relief, but a great bubble of disinterested, pure joy.

All the crap disappeared, at least for that brief moment; all the self-indulgence and exhibitionism and fantasy. I rejoiced and was glad because he was well. That is what he gave me—a moment of purity in a wicked world. I believe now I would have had the same purity of grief if it had been otherwise. What I gave him was the special quality of relationship, detached enough, irresponsible enough, intimate enough, for him to give that to me at a time when he needed to give somebody something. There is nothing derogatory about the relationship between a fag hag and her friend.

For Christmas I gave him a Japanese kimono anyway: it is a very suitable present for a fag hag to give her fag, but I did hold back on the primrose yellow silk pajamas.

This story was written for my friend Sebastian Sandys.

The Tale of The Beautiful
Princess Kalito

Once upon a time, long, long ago and far, far away—if that makes it any easier—there lived The Beautiful Princess Kalito.

The Beautiful Princess Kalito really was very beautiful: she had skin the color of pure strained honey waiting warm and soft in the sunshine—golden with hints of darkness, but smooth and cool and glowing like the skin of a ripe cherry. She had soft black eyes, painted smoothly onto her cheeks with a disciplined, apparently casual brush stroke and her mouth was little and round and pink. Her fringe of hair lay on her forehead like mulberry silk, dyed black with all the skills of the northern dyers. She had a little round soft body. She had very tiny feet and no name. None of this is surprising.

She had always been beautiful, even as a little child; moreover she had then had feet which, while pretty of course, had been of a perfectly ordinary and uninteresting size, suitable in every way for a pretty, active and rich little princess. She had also had a name then, although she was now not always able to remember what it had been. She had abandoned it on marriage. The Beautiful Princess Kalito, understandably, was not her name, but a title indicating that she was her husband's wife.

The Beautiful Princess Kalito, as well as having a very important and highly placed husband, had also had an extensive palace: at least she understood that it was extensive, because an extensive palace is one of the things that The Beautiful Princess Kalito had every right to expect, along with not having a name and having very tiny feet. She had not of course seen much of it, but what she had seen was, like herself, precious and beautiful. There were gardens of intricate delicacy, where water-wheels turned musically and lotus flowers—blood red and milk white—flowered immaculate, and waterlilies floated serenely on ponds deep with golden fish. And the gardens changed magically, gently, into pagodas and terraces of wrought wood, where birds in cages sang tunes of entrancing loveliness. And the terraces, too, dissolved through trellises and archways into rooms where more lotus flowers—redder than blood and whiter than milk—flowered on the walls with an even finer perfection than those in the gardens; where golden fishes swam forever across walls of waterlilies; where at every turn huntsmen on horses, with long spears and dogs, chased deer of slenderness and grace around pagodas more intricate and refined than those in the garden—and did so without the noise and the sweat and the disturbance that her husband complained of on those few occasions when he could bring himself to leave those disagreeable pursuits and spend an evening of perfect joy, "in heaven, beloved, in heaven" with her.

The Beautiful Princess Kalito also had three sons, who had once been golden tumbling bundles of delight with little thatched lids of black hair, and shiny black eyes who had played and giggled around her feet when their nurses brought them in to her. They had once climbed on to her lap and stood with their arms round her neck and gazed levelly into her eyes with glorious smiles of pure devotion, but who now had gone away and when they appeared at all it was to look at her with nervous scorn through hard black lenses. The Beautiful Princess Kalito did not have any daughters; but she did have piles of silk cushions which exuded a warm rich smell, and cases of jewels which glowed and stabbed at the darkness when her maidservant opened the caskets and selected the appropriate items for The Beautiful Princess Kalito to wear. And she had porcelain bowls so fine that the light filtered through them in colors strange and rich—blues and crimson and flame. And she had horses of bronze and clay which stood with a military stiffness and an interesting greenish tinge. And she had jade palanquins carved far away and so fragile in their perfection that breath could shatter them. And she had gold ornaments so fine as to need no purpose, or use, or explanation. And she had a carved wall of pink stone and white stone with plants growing from it here and there, which kept her and all her husband's other treasures safe from all eyes. What more could any beautiful princess wish for?

The Beautiful Princess Kalito had, moreover, memories. She could remember when her sons were a delight and a refuge for her. She could remember before that, when her servants looked at her with admiration and envy. She could remember when her husband spent time with her in joy. On golden sunlit evenings when the blossom of her trees cast a special light in the garden, she could even remember how it was when she could run and dance and live without pain. And in the late watches of the night, when the huge fierce stars gaped coldly at her, she could, just sometimes, remember the day when all simplicity of joy had ended.

Although The Beautiful Princess Kalito had little to do all day and nothing to do most nights, three times a week, at the very least, she had an important and private engagement. Then they would bring to her very inner and most private room great bowls of warm scented water and herbs and unguents and oils, all strongly redolent and heady in their sweetness like overblown hyacinths. The richness of their savor would creep up her little curved nostrils and weave about in her brain until she nearly fainted with the excess of their beauty. And there, alone and unattended, The Beautiful Princess Kalito would ceremoniously take off her clean-every-morning knitted white cotton oversocks and start to unwrap and clean her feet. As she ritually unbound the bandages a new smell would start to contend with the giddy scents of her room. They were at war with each other: the perfumes of the master perfumers of the Great Empire and the stink of the rotting, unaired, dead flesh of The Beautiful Princess Kalito's tiny feet.

When the last bandage was off and the nakedness of her feet exposed, the stench from them would overwhelm the room. Then taking the dead flesh in her hands, The Beautiful Princess Kalito would lower the inanimate hunks into the warm scented water. She would prize the hooked claw of the big toe with its soft spongy nail away from the petal-like mass of where her other toes had once been and scoop out the new white dead matter from the space. She would tenderly scrape the freshly putrefied gunge from around her heels and pry into the crevasses of the rounded slug which made up the middle part of that glob. Each object was only four inches long and still it would take her over an hour to wash and re-perfume them. Then, finally satisfied, taking up the new pile of white bandages, the new pots of sweet scented oils and creams, she would re-bandage them. There was a point at the center of this process when she would be tempted to despair; when it seemed impossible that even the softest bleached wool, even the incense of the whole world, would be able to cover over that stink of putrefaction. But always, by the end, she would have won, would have ordered all things aright, and pulling on the delicately knitted oversocks, she would toddle back into her world; her feet, the lotus flowers of her husband's heart, restored, perfect.

Her husband too, incidentally, had fine feet; long and straight with a high delicate arch. Each toe, to her early amusement and delighted fascination, was separated and could be flexed individually. When she was first married she had very much wanted to touch them as he did hers. "Ah, my love," he would say, "ah, my beautiful princess." He would hold those tiny, tender, white as mountain snows little socks, each in the palm of his hand, squeezing them, caressing them; leaning over her, folding her soft little body almost in half, he would place each immaculate little cotton bundle against the soft golden skin above his brown nipples, just where the secret hiddenness of his underarm met the bold openness of his chest and seem almost to swoon with joy. Recovering physically, he would press down on her, now almost out of his mind with passion, so that the weight on her never-exercised muscles hurt—but what was the hurt compared with the pleasure that she could give him, the amount that he loved her? "Ah, my lotus flower, ah, pearl of all my riches, ah, see these perfect . . ." he could scarcely even speak for his entrancement, "for me, for me. Oh I will love you always and always, because my precious can never run away. See each little mouse, hiding in its scented hole, that is what my beautiful little princess is for me. See these feet, so tiny, so perfect, that my love could dance on a lotus flower and not bend or crush one petal of it." But as, in fact, The Beautiful Princess Kalito could not dance at all, he would have to call in dancing girls to inspire his erotic imagination further and they would lie together watching the dancing girls disrobe, while she tried neither to giggle nor to weep and he fondled and turned and twisted and hurt The Beautiful Princess Kalito's beautiful little lotus-flower feet.

And after all it was precisely for this that her mother, weeping, had called her in from her games with her brothers one day when she was seven years old. Weeping, laughing, she had told her daughter that she was now old enough to become a woman. Tickling, teasing, she had wrapped the first soft bandages, sung the first binding songs, trying through her tears to tell her daughter the old stories. How the Emperor had bound the feet of his favorite dancing girl, long, long ago and far, far away, so that she could dance for him on a lotus flower and not bend nor crush one petal of it. How, despite the pain, one day, when her little daughter lay so soft and sweet with her tiny feet against the chest of her lover and her lord, just where the secret hiddenness of his armpit met the bold openness of his chest, she would sing and praise the tiny feet which bound her lover to her with a tighter binding than any which might now seem to hurt her. And together they laughed and the bandages were made tighter and tighter. But The Beautiful Princess Kalito—although then of course she was no such thing, but a pretty little girl who played in the rich acres of her noble father's cherry trees—The Beautiful Princess Kalito was allowed to sit with her mother and her aunts and her grandmother all day and be counted by them as a grown-up, as a woman. So that it was not until some days later that she discovered that she could no longer run down to the stream and dabble her toes in its icy coldness until each individually they wriggled up, rearing away from the water until she laughed and had pity on them.

That night when the little girl was unable to settle down to sleep because of the unaccustomed tightness—too extreme yet to call it pain, although there would be nights and nights to come when pain would be a gentle and kindly word for what that child was to endure—she was surprised to hear her mother sobbing and sobbing in the next room. Her mother, who was a great lady and the wife of a great warrior prince, sobbing so loudly, so inelegantly. Then she heard her aunt come toddling in on her tiny feet and sit beside her sister and mutter sweetly, softly as women do with each other when there is great grief and nothing to be done about it. The child heard one remark only with any clarity; the aunt said to the mother, "Sweet, you know what they say, if we love our daughters we cannot love their feet." A pause, and then moving from the old proverb to her own sharp merry tone, the aunt laughed loudly, though not very happily, and said, "We love the daughters, the men love their feet . . . it all works out I suppose."

And indeed her aunt was right, because her husband did love her feet. As described earlier and so on and so on. She loved his feet too, as it happened, but once she had tried to take them in her hands—or rather to take one of them, for her sweet little hands could not encompass even one of his fine-boned feet. At the time, which was quite soon after they were married, he was lying back in that joyful exhaustion she could never understand. The silk cushions were piled around him and he was beautiful and he loved her and he had given her a palace and he spent every evening with her. She was filled with a new and restless feeling which she did not recognize, growing perhaps from somewhere near the base of her smooth golden belly. She sat up giggling with her legs crossed under her, and she did of course look sweet and enchanting and very young and innocent, as well as beautiful. She picked up one of his feet and, bending forward, inserted her little tongue into the space between his largest toe and the one next to it. They had a strong flavor of salt and a smell of grass and goats. She turned the foot back at the ankle and her tongue went exploring the stiff firm arc of his instep, while her fingers felt the powerful tension in his tendon, running up from heel to leg and then, perhaps, on upwards. He lay back sighing and she let her mouth wander on in the enchanted valleys and the mountain ranges and the forests of his foot. And the restless feeling ran up from the base of her stomach to her tongue and back again like a silk cord that tightened and tightened and also somehow spread outwards so that her fingers and her back too were caught in the cord, were part of the cord, and she toppled forward and lay out beside him, her fine silk shift rumpled up on her soft honey-colored thighs which were unable any longer to remain still, and she sucked and groped at his feet and knew that something was going to happen.

And something did. He changed from liquid delight into iron. He sat up. He said, "That's quite enough." He pulled his foot away. He got up and left the room, his back expressing displeasure.

And after that, although she never repeated the experiment; although she never asked, not even herself, what the purpose and meaning of that strange tight cord might be; although his sons grew in her body and were born with little round bodies and flabby squashed feet just like hers; although they grew up with straight fine bodies and tough strong feet just like his; although she was beautiful and sat in her beautiful palace; although she allowed him, whenever he wanted, to take her little lotus-flower cotton socks in his hands and croon to them; although she was as good as the gold she both resembled and was adorned with—still he came less and less often to her part of the extensive palace and from the pitying looks and half heard gossip of her servants she knew that he was keeping concubines—neither as well born nor as beautiful as she, but able to please him without challenge, without questions.

So there she was, The Beautiful Princess Kalito, and time went by. And what with dressing up in the morning and again in the evening, and washing her feet three times a week, and wondering if her husband would come and visit her in the evenings, she probably had as much to do as was good for any beautiful princess in a story.

But one day something new happened. She was toddling around the extensive palace and quite by chance she found a new room. It was a pretty little room, high up in the palace and hung with the most exquisite silk paintings. It had obviously been the favorite room of some other Beautiful Princess Kalito before her and the idea of this tenuous link appealed to her somehow and she took to sitting there sometimes on her silken cushions to sip her tea. And after another little while she discovered that her pretty little room had a little window and that the windows looked out over the filigree wall of pink and white stone and into an orchard of fruit trees very like the one she had played in with her brothers many, many years before. And she grew to like to look out of the window at the orchard, and with a caution quite unbecoming to a beautiful princess, she never mentioned to her husband that she sometimes sat in this little room, and sometimes looked out of the window. But then, he really did not come very often, and when he did they really had far more important things to be doing and thinking of than in which of her many rooms the princess liked to sit and drink her tea.

So, gradually, as she heard that her sons had married in their turns beautiful princesses with soft painted eyes, tiny feet and no names either; and as she met these younger women and was forced to know that she was no longer quite as beautiful as she had been; and as she discovered again the joy of plump babies in her grandsons and discovered again that they grew up and vanished; as time passed she spent more and more of it in this pretty little room. And more and more of the time she spent there she used looking out of the window at the orchard and remembering how it was when she was a little girl.

One year, spring came again as usual, and the white frothy flowers leapt onto the branches of the orchard trees and were suddenly, surprisingly much more lovely than the perfect blossoms painted on the silk on the walls of the little room. By this spring The Beautiful Princess Kalito was spending so much time in her little room that she could not fail to notice the peasant women who came to work in the orchard. Tall young women with dirty yellow faces, not little and beautiful at all, with eyes heavy and dark as though their craftsmen had used his thumb instead of a paintbrush. The young women came to the orchard on long strong legs with hard bare feet. Some of them carried their babies on their backs and laughed and sang to them while they cut the bright spring grass which was sprouting energetically around the trunks of the trees in the orchard. As they worked they sang—sometimes loud rough songs and sometimes sad songs, or one of them would cry or shout and the others would tease or comfort her according to rules which The Beautiful Princess Kalito could not understand. Sometimes their roughness and abuse, or the anger with which they slapped at their babies' fat legs appalled her, and sometimes their energetic cruelty made her giggle. But whether or not she could understand, whether or not she liked what she saw, she still hung against the window of the little room and watched and watched them. And when she saw their strong muddy feet with proud straight toes moving naked across the grass; when she saw one of them wrap a strong arm round another or heard them break into song again, she would feel that strange cord which she had almost forgotten tighten again, not in her stomach now but round her throat and her heart, but gradually as strong and tight as ever before. And as though the cord were pulling her together she started thinking new thoughts—about poverty and luxury and herself and the other women, thoughts that she hardly knew how to think. One day she went to her jewel chests and reaching in with her fist drew out a handful of gems. The cord was tight and almost hurting her and she scuttled and toddled as fast as she could and threw the jewels out of the window to the women below. But the singing stopped abruptly and they looked up askance, fearful, mute. The jewels were still lying there, bright and beautiful, when the women went silently home. Then The Beautiful Princess Kalito realized that it would have been better, safer, wiser, to have thrown them down food, bread and fruit, which would need no explanation, but she found she had none to throw and she did not dare to ask for any. And the cord in her throat grew tighter.

The blossoms fell from the trees and instead they were green with a sweeter, more translucent green than any of the paints on the walls of the palace: a green that was never flat and smooth like the green jade bijouterie in the beautiful rooms, but soft and musical in its changes. And then from where the blossom had fallen the cherries sprang—first green too, then the color of cream and finally turning to a richer red than the mouth of The Beautiful Princess Kalito had ever been, even in the first days of her marriage when it had been stung to fire by the passion of her husband's teeth. Then the women came back for the harvest and worked all through the day and into the night, when they would light lanterns that glowed like benign stars. Though the women shouted of their tiredness and moved sometimes with a slow weariness that hurt, they still worked on their long feet and they still sang and joked to one another. And the cord tightened and tightened again inside The Beautiful Princess Kalito until she knew that something was going to happen.

And something did. Afterwards of course they said it was the Woman Madness, the lost craziness that comes to women when their blood is no longer drawn off once a month but stays inside them to rot and fester their minds. They said that seeing herself old and wrinkled was too much for her to bear. They said that her sons' wives had not always been kind. They said there had always been bad air in that little room and that she should have been warned. They said her maids had not been loyal to their master, her husband. They said that it just went to show. One day as The Beautiful Princess Kalito watched the women and their beautiful feet busy at the cherry harvest she could stand it no longer. She left the window and tottered back to the silk cushions. She sank down on them. She looked at her tiny white feet with loathing, and tore off the white knitted oversocks. Then she ripped away at the bandages. And although the stench was as strong as ever and the room had not been filled in advance with unguents and the sweet smell of herbs, The Beautiful Princess Kalito did not even notice the evil rottenness— from the orchard came the odor of sunshine, of ripe cherries and of women's sweat. She threw the bandages behind her without even looking and as the women outside began to sing a bright brave song The Beautiful Princess Kalito, a child again, clambered to her feet to run in a renewed freedom back to her window.

When she had taken perhaps two paces the pain began. There was always some pain in walking—a dull ache which she had grown so used to over the years that she did not even know it was pain. But this was totally different: her unbound feet were exposed to a pressure which they had never experienced before; the rotted flesh, the ruined muscles, the distorted tendons could not carry even the delicate weight of the shriveled old Beautiful Princess Kalito. After four paces she knew she would never reach the window even though the room was a small one and softly carpeted. After five paces she began to scream. She could not see the women in the orchard and she could not stop the screams. There, halfway between the memories of sunlit orchards with the tough reality of the women who worked there and the pile of putrefied bandages The Beautiful Princess Kalito was suspended, screaming, screaming, screaming.

The screams detached themselves from her captured body and took embodiment from the air. They arrested the women in the orchard, swooping around their ears, careening out above the trees and preventing the work from continuing. The screams smashed down the corridors and spaces of the extensive palace, reverberating against the delicate jade, staining the painted walls, dumbing the musical gardens. Even when The Beautiful Princess Kalito fell to the ground in her pretty little room the screams did not cease; even when they rushed in and found her there, broken, unconscious, the screams did not finish . . . and they have not finished yet. I told you it was long, long ago and far, far away, but that might not make it any easier.

Maybe a Love Poem for My Friend

My friend has greying hair, a dangerous temper and tea breaks when she's working.

My friend has two sons and a secret man she keeps in a drawer and lets me peek at sometimes.

My friend writes poems that are witty, fierce and sometimes soppy.

My friend has funny jokes, a stream of gossip and standards so high that I need crampons.

My friend is the only person in the whole world that I am prepared not to smoke around, in the long term and without being asked. My friend wheezes sometimes, which is alarming. She keeps a private space to disappear in and never prods at mine.

My friend and I wrote a book together. A quite different intimacy from lovers, and rarer.

My friend came round one day and saw my baby, so new that the birth-dust brought from his star-traveling was still fresh on him. It is a time when women have their families about them and she was mine.

My friend says, "You should write poetry." I answer, "Does this count?"

Heart Throb

Darkness.

A drum roll, distant, muffled within that darkness.

Then half bars of strange music, unformed lost notes, discordant, chaotic, but gentle, solemn, sweet: music from before the dawn of order, pre-creation music. A steady soft drumbeat, the pulsing heart of life; but so quiet, so soft that the brain itself must be quieted to hear it. Three beautiful clear notes of a triangle and the darkness begins to shift as colored smoke wafts dreamily. The high flat mountain comes into focus as pale and far away as the dawn and at the foot of the mountain Kalubini sits, the jewels of his turban catching the refractions of light within the swirling smoke. His face is still, timeless, serious. His knees are flat on the ground while his thighs support his feet in the eternal lotus posture; his palms on his knees are turned outwards and his thumb and index finger form a soft circle within which all the powers of the gods are held.

When there is enough light he begins to move, to gyrate smoothly in strange godlike movements, beyond the power of earthbound, material bodies. He is snake in its litheness; he is pool of water in its rippled calm; he is frog in its alert stillness; he is palm tree in its mighty growth; he is power of mind and matter brought together. These are no vulgar contortions, they are the thoughts of a god awakening at dawn in the mystical east and bringing first himself and then the world to light and life.

The music becomes more orderly, fitting itself around the deep heartbeat that holds all things together: Kalubini is the heart of the universe. His gentle remote expression never changes as he rises to his feet and moves forwards. He looks around, mildly curious, and then smiles. With his smile the light increases. He picks up a small earthenware bowl, plain reddish clay shaped into the inevitable full curve. He holds it between his two long hands, turning it this way and that, peering into its empty roundness. He smiles still, and then murmurs to the bowl. A white dove suddenly, almost shockingly, flies out of it. His expression does not change. He murmurs again. Another dove, very white in the still drifting colored smoke. The pace of the music quickens almost imperceptibly, and suddenly there are more and more doves, they flow like a waterfall out of the small round bowl; they rest on Kalubini's turban, on his silken cloak; they peck on the ground. Then all at once in a moment of pure flight they take off together, circle and alight in a small flowering tree which becomes a living rustle of movement, bird and flower together, serene and vital.

Kalubini seems hardly to notice. He fixes his solemn attention on the bowl again and from it now flows, flashing gold and green, a shoal of tiny fish, which he pours gently but steadily into an ornate glass tank near his left hand. When the tank is apparently fuller than it can hold with dancing fish he looks down at his bowl again. For the first time his face assumes an identifiable expression—a wry and amused disappointment. He tosses the bowl aside carelessly and shards of clay tinkle on the ground. He finds another, larger bowl and appears contented with it. Again he turns it slowly in his arms, examining its smooth glazed surface inside and out with apparent disinterest. But when he murmurs to it a cat, pure white and sleek, erupts from the empty space, alights briefly on his shoulder and vanishes. A black dog follows, slim and delicate as a greyhound, tiny as a terrier. It jumps down and curls contentedly at his feet. Kalubini does not smile now but looks infinitely sad. He puts the bowl down on the ground. He whips off his silk cloak and crumples it into the bowl, folding it down until the bowl seems full with it, and then he turns away. Suddenly the heart throb of the drumbeat stirs, the silk ripples as though touched by a breeze and begins to rise. From the curved interior of the bowl which did not seem large enough to hold even the little dog a woman emerges, stunningly lovely. Kalubini turns back again and his face is wreathed in delight. He beckons to her and she steps out of the bowl towards him. He raises his right hand imperiously and she starts to dance, her veils parting just enough to show the glittering jewel in her navel and the bright scarlet caste mark on her forehead. Her legs are long and bare, her torso breathtaking, her feet elegant beyond dreaming, her face with its long sloped eyes and perfect mouth is fixed on him and she dances a slow swaying dance of the eternal feminine from the ancient civilizations far over the seas.

The music quickens now and her dance becomes wilder and wilder. She turns from him, dancing away, her eyes fixed on the outside world, on the morning and the space of the universe. It becomes almost a coquettish dance as she realizes that there is a whole world to enchant and not just him. Kalubini is furious, he reaches for her but she slips away. He cannot bear it—she has insulted and rejected a god. He leaps upon her, tossing her into the air as though her weight were nothing and his strength infinite. She arches upwards and falls back into his arms, where she lies laughing at him. His anger is the fountain of the world; the calm has vanished from his face and has become replaced by a terror, an awfulness. She realizes this and becomes frightened, but he remains stern. He throws her down on a small platform worked with mysterious cabalistic designs. He covers her again with his cloak and then slams over her a great lacquered lid which he wields as though it were made of straw.

The music stops abruptly. But still he is not content. His fury is manifest in his agitated pacing, in his grinding teeth and in his flashing eyes. With a shocking suddenness he whips out a huge curved sword. He brandishes it wildly, and it slices through the leaves of the tree, fluttering the roosting birds; it slices through the sleeve of his own flowing garment and the shorn silk droops sadly to the ground. After a moment's hesitation he slashes at the lacquered lid and the sword carves through it; then he is hacking, stabbing, chopping in his wrath. From inside comes one painful moan, and a small bleeding hand drops over the edge of the platform. He hurls bits of the lid, bits of his own silk cloak, bits of her veiling across the ground. He is gleeful now and triumphant. He leaps and dances, prances and cavorts in his victory over her.

Abruptly he ceases. He hears a few bars of the music which she had danced to. Suddenly the tiny dog, who has lain peacefully throughout the devastation, lifts up its head and howls. Kalubini is struck; he bends to stroke the dog tenderly and when he raises his head he is weeping. Crystal tears pour from his eyes, but as they fall they turn into jewels, diamonds and pearls, which he gathers in his hands and throws away disgusted. Slowly, sadly, he starts to collect the pieces of his love from where they have fallen. He picks up the little hand and kisses it sorrowfully. He places all the fragments in his bowl. The music starts again. The little dog trots over to the bowl and sits beside it, his head cocked hopefully. Kalubini stands by the bowl murmuring quietly and gently. The colored smoke begins to move again, the music to settle down, the throbbing of the drum to find its previous rhythm. There is a blinding flash of lightning, a great drum roll of thunder, and there she is! Whole and beautiful as ever. She casts herself into his arms with ecstatic delight. He catches her to his breast and rains godlike kisses upon her. The music reaches a crescendo of excitement; the drum throb, strong and clear now, celebrates the power of life and love. Leaping with joy, tossing her high with easy virility, he carries her away; his face is like a little boy's who got what he wanted for his birthday after all. Vibrant with delight, with no eyes for anything except each other, the couple disappear and only the drumbeat continues for another few moments.

It is a terrific act though I say so myself. He's a very skilled illusionist and between us we've managed to pack in almost everything a modern variety audience wants—oriental mysticism, suspense, a coherent scenario, some effective stunts, a touch of pathos and a bit of implied nooky without passing the boundaries. Managements like it because it doesn't need a cast of thousands and almost every damn theater in the world can scrape up a mountain scene drop—with our lighting we can pretty much get away with an alpine set if we have to. And, well, I'll tell you what it is, the act has a certain something that really goes over: "most romantic act in town," some newspaper called it the other day. . . . It's what's between the two of us really; whenever we go on, it's there, like a third person in the act, our relationship with each other, and that comes over, a kind of romantic excitement. Neither of us had it before; well, I know I didn't, and I don't think he can have, because as far as the tricks go he hasn't learned anything from me; he is very good; but he never really made it big. We met two years ago on the West Coast: I was doing a spot of "exotic dancing"—well, to be frank I was a call girl in a honky-tonk with a little specialty number. He was working what was basically a parlor act: neat tricks, pretty—especially with the pigeons and the goldfish, a suave evening-dress conjurer with pretensions to class. Not bad. Funny we ever got together really; we met fooling around at somebody's place one night, and it just came to us both, the whole thing. We put the act together on the road coming east. It went pretty well in Chicago, though it wasn't all fixed then and we were still having trouble with the music—before we thought of the drum heartbeat to hold it all together. But by Philadelphia we knew we were on to something big and managements started knowing it too, and we were getting good billings and agents after us and that stuff and New York was just wonderful. We played Keith's six months straight and we were hot.

Then with the war ending and that let's-go-to-Europe fever everywhere, and we were both pretty pleased with ourselves and thought, "Why not? Let's give it a go." Berlin, Amsterdam, Paris, London. Two months we've been playing the Oxford and we don't see much sign of it coming off yet. So you could say, I would say, that things were pretty good. In fact there are only two flies in the ointment. One of them is him and the other is me.

The snag with him is that he's beginning to believe it all: I think it was that yoga thing we put in for the opening, and that crazed teacher he went to, who gave him all this bit about mystical meditation and oneness with the universe and the power of the will in harmony with matter and that stuff. I mean, it is quite impressive when he puts his ankles over his neck or folds his rib cage into accordion pleats, but it's not the key to the universe, frankly. It doesn't make him a god; it doesn't even make him a real oriental Indian, for heaven's sake. I mean, the fact that he believes it may help the act, but he can't lay it down when we come off. I should have put my foot down when he first started wearing that damn turban off stage, in public, on the ship coming over, but he told me "publicity" and "image" and things, and it was like music to my ears, quite honestly. And where did it leave me? I mean, here I was, for the first time in my life, able to afford a few decent things, and we were in Europe, really classy things I mean, but no, because if he's going to be an Indian then of course I have to be one too, don't I? And Indian women don't go out in public, and Indian women wear saris and veils and keep their mouths shut and just adore their men. And if I argue with him he goes blank on me, his eyes narrow up and his face goes cold and I . . .

Well, I told you there was a snag about me too, and the damn stupid thing is that I've fallen for him. I mean really, the big thing. It's too pathetic, actually: I'm thirty-two years old and I've been around and I wasn't brought up sentimental either. My ma was a tough lady and she always warned me against love and told me straight out what it could do to a woman. And here I am, I'm like a little kid about him. Well, no, not exactly like a little kid, but . . . I don't know how to put it, quite: I never had much schooling and I don't read all the stuff that he reads or know all those lovely words, but he makes me feel. Just that, not good or bad, not happy or sad, but he does make me feel. So much that the feeling is for itself, it doesn't seem to matter what it is. So when his face goes cold or he turns away from me and won't listen or look or touch, then something in me dies. And when he comes back then I'm so happy and grateful that I do anything he wants, anything, anything.

So what with him thinking he's a god, and me thinking he's a god, it's not surprising that three-quarters of the punters end up thinking he's a god too; but for them, of course, it's also just a turn—a classy twenty minutes in the middle of a good variety show and them all snuggled down in the lovely plush seats and afterwards they can just go home.

Well, we go home too, of course, but it doesn't always end there. Of course we were lovers right from the start. Why pay for two beds when you need only pay for one? I said, all bright and brassy, the first week we were on the road. To be honest, he wasn't much into it then, I was the one who knew what we were doing, or meant to be doing, just like I was the one pushing the act, shaping it up, you know, because although he's skillful at his own trade he doesn't—or he didn't, anyway—have that feel for a good act that I do. I mean, even when I was just one more little exotic dancer selling something else, I knew, I knew how to put it over. It was when we got the sword trick going, when he got to slash me into little bits twice a night, six nights a week, that things changed. He loved it, he really loved it. And he was wonderful—you could see what it did to him. He took on a new something, a new power with it. And he brought that home to us. He started to change, to take more—to take the lead more, I suppose. And it was wonderful at first. His hands so clever and his body so flexible and I melted for him, I couldn't get enough. He was strong and fit and suddenly he knew exactly what he was doing, and if some of that went a little further than I had expected, well, I found that quite exciting too. He was focused on me, only me: only I could meet that need in him. We have to be a bit careful, of course, because the costume doesn't cover all that much; but there are things and places, he sucks my blood like a vampire and he needs me to feed him; as he eats me I am eaten by him, I become part of him and . . . Well, of course he would stop if I asked him to, I'm sure he would, I'm pretty nearly damn certain he would; but I don't want him to. And when he's started, of course, it would make him angry if I made him stop, and it would not be fair, because I did lead him on, sexually I mean, I was the one who started it. I need him so much, I need him to stay with me and love me. He's like a god to me, he created me, I owe him so much—I was just a little tart in some San

Francisco joint whose mother had been a hooker and who was going nowhere fast. He made me alive, he made me feel, and all that feeling is for him.

Of course sometimes when he's out I remember just how bloody stupid it is. What's the point of being halfway across the world if you have to stay in your room the whole time? What's the point of getting top billing and making a fortune if you never see a cent of it? But he comes in and he wants me to be happy and waiting and ready for him, and if I'm not he's so disappointed and knotted up and sad that he can't control himself. It's because he loves me and wants me so much that he gets so angry. I've set his feelings free, he says: before he met me he was all cold, screwed up tight and ungiving, because his mother was a frigid bitch who never gave him any loving, but now I've set all his feelings free, all of them, his loving and his anger and his sadness and his danger, and I must accept them all. Together, he says, we have crashed the barriers of dreary old morality; together we have been set free to understand and enjoy the utter, unutterable beauty of experience. And I know, I know it's true because he has done that for me too. So how can I spit out all my old childish loneliness and jealousy and spite at him, when he takes me in his arms and my belly moves and sings for him, and for him alone? When I know that what we play-act twice nightly before an audience of thousands is true: he took me out of nothing, he destroyed my old life, the old me, he chopped it up in little bits and threw them all away and then he remade me all himself. I do not exist without him. He made me, he can destroy me, that's his right, and it is all right with me.

I don't mind him going out so much, anyway. I don't even like the friends he has now, I don't know them or understand them and they probably wouldn't like me. They're all so fine and fancy, and clever and smart. When we were still in America we went out a lot, especially in New York—we had fun together and good friends. Mostly vaudeville people, and we were all doing well and there was champagne and parties and a car and decent restaurants and pretty clothes. They were all just people like us, who were suddenly pleased with ourselves and finding the good time after quite a long lot of looking, in some cases. It was lovely, actually; everyone knew who you were really so they didn't mind you pretending to be better than you were, and they were pretending with you.

But after we got to Berlin he started changing. He was an Indian all the time, and he wanted me to be one too. He read mad books at night and started saying he could see the future, started telling me about his powers. He became a stranger and only in bed could I bring him back to me, and only then if I was willing to follow him wherever he wanted to go. He went out late at night drinking absinthe with young men who weren't like us at all. Wild hairy young students and they could talk up a storm. It was quite exciting to listen to at first. I was heady with it, and by all the words they knew and how they treated us—well him, and me with him—as their equals. And they knew so much stuff: poets and thinkers and political writers and strings and strings of wonderful crazy words. They seemed wonderfully romantic to me, though silly too and often rather sweet, though I knew better already than to tell them so. They thought they were so dangerous and splendid. They were delightfully against morality, and I didn't like to tell them they were saying nothing that every pro on the waterfront has known for too long and wants to forget. They told him that experience was beautiful, only experience was pure, pure for its own sake. They thought they should prepare themselves for pure experience, for its fullness and its richness, by giving up all the old rules, morality and manners and conventions and stuff; that nothing mattered, that all those things got in the way. I could smile thinking of him and me together in our bed and how that was true and how exciting it was to have thrown away the rules and be in Berlin pretending to be an Indian and getting rich. But I couldn't take them seriously.

Then one night they started asking him about India and his god and his vision of the world and how they could purify themselves and master their emotions through sacrifice and yoga like he did. I started to giggle and he was furious. I thought he would think it was funny, but he didn't see the joke. That's the sort of thing I meant when I said he was starting to believe his whole act. He told me truth was one more convention that had to be set aside, and so was my mockery for the emergence of his true personality. He told me that he was a great master and that lower beings might need truth but he did not. And he meant it. I was really frightened for a bit—I thought maybe he was cracking up. But the act went on being good, he never put a finger wrong. I should have put my foot down, then and there, but he was so happy and so nice when I agreed with him and so fierce when I didn't. So I didn't. But on the other occasions he would talk of his own friends with so much scorn, so coldly; he would laugh at them and say they were dross for his use, silly fools with words but no wisdom. But they were only foolish little boys.

In Paris, wonderful Paris that I had dreamed of, Paris where I bought lovely dresses and hats that he would not let me wear, in Paris it was more of the same, but different somehow. More spinning words and too much booze, but his friends there took drugs and he did too. And he started to sleep with other women and come home to me and boast about it to me. And worse, somehow, the way he spoke about those women, the way he would mock and jeer at them, talk filth about them to me, foul, disgusting sneering at the poor things. Then he wanted me to sleep with other men and tell him about them; he wanted me to do things with other men, and other women, and have him watch us. When I said it was wrong he hit me—not for fun, not for sex, but hard cold in anger; it was the first time he had ever done that. He knocked me to the floor and stood over me and said there was slave morality and master morality and if I chose to be a slave he would treat me like one, but if I wanted to be a free spirit I must obey him. I told him I couldn't help my natural feelings and he stood over me, tall and beautiful, and he said, and I can remember it clearly, he said natural feelings were only there to challenge the striving soul. "I am showing you the Superman," he said sternly. "Natural man is something that can be overcome, that must be surpassed." And I was so frightened and so crazy for him and he was so completely filled up with his own power that I said I wanted to be his slave, the slave girl of the new Superman, and he smiled. I thought about running away then, when I said it, and bloody well should have too. After that it was too late. Once I had accepted his smile, consented to it and to what followed that smile; once I had learned how far he was prepared to go with my body and how I was prepared to follow him there, how I could love what he did to me and cry out for more, then there was no place to run. He was my whole world. Without him I did not exist. I love him most terribly.

And here in London, well, I don't see him much after the show. Late at night, in the early foggy mornings of London city, he comes in wild and hectic. I wait for him, sometimes all night, long past any desire to sleep, I wait for his hands and his teeth and his tongue to come to me and make me alive again, to take away the fear and the loneliness, to make me real, to make me feel. Occasionally his friends will come to the dressing room between the shows. Last night a long thin woman came; and she bowed low over his hand and called him Master and Guru. He smiled at her with infinite cold distance. I suppose I should have been glad of the distance. She petted me like I pet our little dog. She told me I was lucky to share my life with the life of the greatest spiritual master of our generation, but she was not speaking to me. She was speaking to him. He smiled. She smiled. As she left she reminded him, with caressing veneration, that she would see him later and was looking forward to a further display of his mystic powers. But that time she was talking to me and not to him.

And after she had gone I was glad that he hit me, that he beat me carefully and systematically where it hurt most and showed least, because it still meant that he needed me for something, just like I needed him.

Last night he raged on about the Superman. He told me that to find greatness a man must commit himself completely to his worldly goals, that he must be prepared to sacrifice life itself for them, and that out of the rubble, the ashes, the chaos of that destruction, that sacrifice, the Superman, the new all-powerful master of the universe, would arise. Then he went out and did not return all night.

And suddenly I knew what I had in fact known all along, known ever since we came to Europe. I will be the sacrifice. One day, one evening, under the glow of the stage lights he will cover me with the cloak and the lacquer lid and he will, in front of a breathless audience, a doting venerating crowd, he will cut me up into little bits with his long curved sword. He will be ecstatic while he does it. And the funny thing is, so will I. I won't roll away off the little table as I'm meant to do, slipping out under the concealed flap and dropping the dummy hand as I go. I'll take it, proud and happy and sexy. It will be wonderful. He will be the most powerful man in the world for that moment. He'll be the big star of the season. Their horror will be his ultimate reward and mine too. I'm the showman of this team and I always have been. It will be an unforgettable night at the theater, I can tell you. And I don't mind too much, to tell the truth, because there is not much else left for me, and because I'm the only woman in the world he could do that to. I just want to let everyone else know first, because there's a bit of me, brought up to be a competent and capable hooker, who knows perfectly well that the whole thing is bloody stupid.

I don't know which night it will be. That's part of the magic.

But it will happen, one night.

I know. He knows I know. We have both known for quite a long time.

That is the extraordinary extra something that goes on stage with us each night. That's why the papers call it the "most romantic act in town."

It's a terrific act, though I say so myself.

Daphne

There were laurel bushes along the drive in the house where I lived as a child: laurel bushes with dark, dark shiny leaves and little whitish waxy flowers. I did not care for them much; I preferred the great rhododendrons, whose leaves looked much the same, but whose flowers, pink, red, purple, shimmering white, were like ladies' Sunday hats. My mother taught me that gardens will grow either rhododendrons and azaleas or roses, but not both and the only sensible thing to do was to consent.

I did not then care for the laurels which seemed boring compared to the other delights of my mother's garden. Now they are among my favorite plants and although my present garden is much better at roses and I have no rhododendrons or azaleas growing in it, I still maintain a couple of laurel bushes despite the fact that they are unfashionable and take up rather more space than I can spare for them.

My mother had a lovely shabby garden, like her lovely shabby house. I do not quite know why, when my father took himself off before I was two years old, she decided to settle in that beautiful but cut off little world of western Galloway, but it may well have had something to do with the garden. Because of the curious journeyings of the Gulf Stream that flows steadily from the Caribbean, northeastwards across the Atlantic, around the north coast of Ireland and then swoops down towards the Solway, that part of the world enjoys a curiously mild climate; almost frost free. This makes for gardens like Eden and hers was one of them.

I must have been about ten or eleven when my mother first told me this story. I had been complaining yet again about my name—

"Daphne! Mummy, how could you?"

"I think it's a lovely name, what's wrong with it?"

"It's an old lady name."

"Are you an old lady?"

Pause.

"Well then. You are not an old lady. Daphne is your name. So, 'Daphne' is not an old lady name."

"Oh Mummy."

Now I have children of my own I can hear that patient exasperation in their voices too.

She turned back to the kitchen table. It is my strongest visual memory of her; twenty or thirty times a day all the days of my childhood I must have seen my mother turn so, and bend slightly over the wooden table, working with her back to me as she talked, her long thin neck curving downwards, away from me.

"There's not much I can do about it now anyway, perhaps you will like it more when you are older. I hope so. You were named after someone very special."

I could tell from the way her voice smoothed out, deepened, that she was going to tell me a story. My mother was a wonderful story-teller; not the kind who enfolded you on her lap and gave the story directly to you, and only to you, like a gift. She would tell her stories as she worked, sometimes she would wander through to the larder or the garden in the middle and you would have to follow after her if you wanted to hear it. She told stories as though for her own delight, and for mine or anyone's if they wanted to share hers. She never looked at you while she was telling a story; it was as though she made the story and left it lying around and it was up to you if you picked it up or not. It was never your story, even when she had told it to you; it remained her story and everyone's story.

She was a nymph, the first Daphne, an immortal. They had them then, the Greeks. It was almost as though they could not decide; they found human beings so beautiful that they could not quite agree to having gods. They muddled things up. Someone could start as a person and then be changed: changed into a god or a mountain or a whole constellation of stars. You could be half and half; half a horse and half a human like the centaurs; half a human and half a god like many of the heroes. And their gods were like people because they found the people were like gods.

And so too there were immortals; not gods, not humans, immortals. Immortals belonged not to the world of civility and the City, where people belonged. Immortals did not belong either to the world of Olympus and the supernatural like the high gods; nor to the shadow, the dark caves of dangerous truths where the sibyls and the prophetesses sang. But to the land, the hard bright land of river and mountain and forest and sea. Perhaps you have to go there to understand and one day I will take you and you will see how blue and how green and how tan-brown and how gold a landscape can be; and how suddenly a mountain can leap out of the sea, or plunge down into it again, so that the bird and the fish are just different moments of the same movement.

So Daphne was an immortal. Her father was the river Ladon, rushing from rocky mountain to salt sea in a wild movement of foam and energy, and her mother was Gaea, was the earth herself, the most ancient of the great gods, first born from Chaos and Night. Before those bright brothers, Zeus and Poseidon and Pluto, came to divide the dark from the light, the wet from the dry, the good from the evil, Gaea was there with her hundred breasts, feeding everything, shaping everything, holding everything. And even when the boys finally came to manhood and destroyed their father Saturn, they could not destroy Gaea, their grandmother, and she remained, mother of all the gods, the first and the last. So Daphne had more than a noble inheritance, she had a strong one: wherever she walked or swam or slept her mother's arms were around her, held her safe, rocked her, nourished and sustained her.

Daphne was Gaea's daughter.

She grew up in the deep clefts of the valleys, in the high reaches of her father's water. Her mother sang her lullaby each night; the soft song of growing things, of leaf opening, of petal falling, of dog fox on silent pad through moon-silvered underbrush, of badger whisker and deer antler shaping themselves towards the morning. And the low dark tune of the earth itself, of the deep bass of the drifting continents, of the liquid chuckle of the lava flows forcing themselves up between the floating dishonest plates of the earth's surface, of whole forests crashing and petrifying into coal seams, and the grinding groaning rhythm of carbon escaping from methane and being crushed into diamonds.

And when she woke from such sleeping, such dreaming, her father sang a morning song for her, lovely and sparkling bright, the song of an active young stream that knows it will become a great river eventually, but for the moment is content with its youthfulness; a playful song, jumping and laughing over rocks, eddying and spurting, and whirlpooling and giggling, cutting down hard and greedily into the steep valleys, with miniature rapids and dark gold pools, singing swiftly foamily downwards.

To grow so and in such joy. To grow up there wide-eyed, her ears filled with the fierce bubbling, the free laughter of the mountain river; her eyes filled with all the fertile tricks of her mother's trade. Of course Daphne was beautiful, of course she was strong and well and took no fever, and her dark, dark hair shone glossy in the mottled sunlight of the beech groves where she played.

And so of course Apollo desired her. Apollo, the burning sun-god, the most beautiful of all the Olympians. For Apollo then desire was a little thing, for this was before he had met Hyacinth and learned about love and loss. Easy-come easy-go, and he was a god and had world enough and time and still little patience for such coyness. He was cultured and handsome and powerful; and a god of course, which helps a lot in sexual adventurings. When he came hunting for

Daphne in the steep ravines of her homeland he had had little experience of rejection. In fact he did not believe in it. What, after all, were women for? And they always seemed to enjoy it well enough. And, Oh, by all the powers of Olympus, Daphne was lovely. She was lucky indeed that he would be the first, and she would not be bungled about by some cack-handed woodsman.

Down from the heights of Olympus he came, smiling a little at his own generosity and Daphne's good fortune. It was a bright and cheerful morning as he crossed the moorland and approached her steep-sided wooded valley. It was lovely as he went down, and his pleasure mounted; in the shade of the trees it was very quiet, very peaceful, and below him the river sang its gurgling song. At the bottom, beside the river, he burst into open laughter, grinned, smoothed back his golden curls, and went hunting downstream.

He found her in an ilex grove, those sacred silvery evergreen holm-oak trees, which filtered the bright light above down into hush and solitude. She was kneeling, very still, watching a red vixen give a first hunting lesson to her three black-nosed cubs. He unslung his golden harp and rippled out a little tune.

"Shhh," she said crossly, and without looking round, which rather annoyed him. He might have done well to remember that she had been rocked asleep and awoken by music that Orpheus himself had never dared to play. But it was too late, the vixen turned, panicked, summoned her cubs on the swift feet of their fear, and all four disappeared, vanished into the shadows of the grove. Then Daphne turned and saw, not a god, but a noisy and brash young man who had disturbed her friends with his loud and tinny lyre.

A more sensitive youth might have realized that this was hardly an auspicious beginning for a morning's dalliance, but if you had been a god, if you had built the walls of Troy and introduced the laws and the musical harmonies to all the peoples of the Mediterranean, if you had held in check the fierce stallions of the sun and forced them to pull the great burning chariot across the whole sky from the cream-colored Courts of Morning to the deep indigo Ocean of the Night, you too might well be lacking in sensitivity and modesty.

There followed a half-hour of chat, in which Apollo was charming and Daphne civil. Then he laid one elegant bronzed hand on her naked shoulder. She took it off again quite calmly and said perhaps she should be going. He laughed and put his hand back again. She smiled politely and, quite clearly so that every tree in the grove should hear her, said, "No, thank you."

Even he could not persuade himself that this was maidenly reticence. Even he could not convince himself that this was the practiced shyness of a courtesan, that this "no" meant "yes" or, at very worst, "maybe." Even he could not believe for one moment that this was moral qualm or prudish withdrawal; this, even in his self-loving ears, was the simple "no" of a woman who was simply not interested.

He was both baffled and embarrassed. And then he was angry. He was angry because he was ashamed. His anger was the tantrum of a spoiled child denied a pleasure that he had thought he had the right to expect. But his power was the power of a god.

He said, with a crooked smile, "I never take 'no' for an answer."

"How inconvenient for you," she remarked coolly. And then she looked up into his face and was terrified. Although she had lived innocent and free, she knew what she was seeing in his eyes, and swift as the fox bitch, the mother vixen, she was on her feet and running.

Along the side of the hill, weaving through the ilex trees, grateful to them that they did not encourage underbrush, she ran and heard without wishing to, the heavy sounds of his pursuit. She thought at first that she might outpace him, that she was on her home ground, that he did not know the contours and curves of the forest. But she heard too the dogged anger of his pursuit, that there was no hiding place from which he would not snatch her, there was no safety, no earth in which she could, like the foxes, take refuge.

Fear. She could taste the flavor of fear in her mouth, catching at her breath, squeezing it.

Fear and outrage. She could hear her own heart beating, dragging at her footsteps, and still behind her among the trees she could hear him coming, hear the obscenities that he was mouthing, hear the weight, the heavy weight of him pressing on her grove that would soon be pressing on her flesh.

Fear. Fear did not instruct her, but made her clumsy and stupid. At the end of the grove, where the rough bracken reestablished itself and the ilex trees gave way to scrubbier elder and ash, she turned downhill, down towards her father, towards the river at the bottom. The sides of the valley here were steep, she slithered, caught her foot on a root, stumbled, fell, struggled for balance, and still he was behind her, nearer now, nearer and he was still coming after her and there was no escape.

Fear. Terror. She broke out of the rough wood at the river's very edge. There was a small patch of grass, very green, and over on the other side of the river the beech trees rose indifferent and silent with their carpet of fallen leaves and masts a deep copper color in the still morning. The river here formed a deeper pool at the foot of a small waterfall; small but too high for her to climb it and he was behind her and there was no hope no hope no hope and she turned now like a deer at bay and he came crashing down after her his whole face contorted by the chase by his excitement his anger his own awareness of his power and her danger and there was nothing she could do and as his hands reached for her she cried out in a loud voice, "Mother!"

And then there is a moment, a poised moment when the sounds and the lights disappear, when the sun flickers, when the turning of all nine planets and their many moons pauses, when the song breaks up, when the balance between flight and stillness is so precisely held; when the words for finger, elbow, mouth, tendon, pancreas, cervix, hypothalamus, corpus callosum, larynx, pyloric sphincter, capillaries, and the acoustic nerve stretch out their sound and sense further and thinner than can be contained and the inner rhythm of osmosis, photosynthesis, hydrocarbonization, oxygen exhalation, mineral absorption, pollination, shoot, bud, leaf, blossom, rise up, take over, destroy the words and replace them in wordlessness and peace . . . a catastrophic instant, an unmeasured, unmeasurable moment of change. And then there is a sweet patch of green grass beside a laughing river, there is a hot Aegean morning with the sky blue above the pale green beech leaves, and there is a laurel bush with dark, dark shiny leaves and little whitish waxy flowers, there is a furious young god, golden and baffled, and there is no more Daphne.

And my mother gathered up the pastry she had been so patiently rolling and prepared to carry it to the cooler back-kitchen in order to give it a chance to relax.

I sort of hopped after her.

"Did her mother turn her into a laurel bush for*ever?*"

"Oh yes."

"Poor Daphne."

"On the contrary," said my mother with a smile, " 'I think that I will never see a woman lovelier than a tree.' "

"What? I don't understand."

"You probably will one day."

Of course this is not exactly how my mother told the story to her eleven year old. She told stories as though for her own delight, and for mine or anyone's if they wanted to share hers. She never looked at you while she was telling a story; it was as though she made the story and left it lying around and it was up to you if you picked it up or not. But this one, she tossed it down and I picked it up. It is not my story, even though she gave it to me; it remained her story and everyone's story. I have remembered and reworked the story for my-self, but always with her smooth deep voice lying behind mine, and the strong visual image of her thin back bending over and her hands rolling the pastry.

My mother died the winter I was twenty. At that point I still didn't understand. Later, mainly because it had my name in it, I discovered Andrew Marvell's poem "The Garden":

> *Apollo hunted Daphne so,*
> *Only that she might Laurel grow . . .*
>
> *Meanwhile the mind, from pleasure less,*
> *Withdraws into its happiness:*

The mind, that ocean where each kind
Does straight its own resemblance find;
Yet it creates, transcending these,
Far other worlds, and other seas;
Annihilating all that's made
To a green thought in a green shade.

Then I began to understand a little; to grow laurel bushes in my own garden and to appreciate my own name.

The Loveliness of the Long-Distance Runner

I sit at my desk and make a list of all the things I am not going to think about for the next four and a half hours. Although it is still early the day is conducive to laziness—hot and golden. I am determined that I will not be lazy. The list reads:

1) My lover is running in an organized marathon race. I hate it.
2) Pheidippides, the Greek who ran the first Marathon, dropped dead at the end of it. And his marathon was four miles shorter than hers is going to be. There is also heatstroke, torn Achilles tendons, shin splints and cramp. Any and all of which, including the first option, will serve her right. And will also break my heart.
3) The women who are going to support her, love her, pour water down her back and drinks down her throat are not me. I am jealous of them.
4) Marathon running is a goddamn competitive, sexist, lousy thing to do.
5) My lover has the most beautiful body in the world. Because she runs.

I fell in love with her because she had the most beautiful body I had ever seen. What, when it comes down to it, is the difference between my devouring of her as a sex-object and her competitive running? Anyway she says that she does not run competitively. Anyway I say that I do not any longer love her just because she has the most beautiful body.

Now she will be doing her warm-up exercises. I know these well, as she does them every day. She was doing them the first time I saw her. I had gone to the country to stay the weekend with her sister, who's a lawyer colleague of mine and a good friend. We were doing some work together. We were sitting in her living room and she was feeding her baby and Jane came in, in running shorts, T-shirt and yards and yards of leg. Katy had often joked about her sister who was a games mistress in an all-girls' school, and I assumed that this was she. Standing by the front door, with the sun on her hair, she started these amazing exercises. She stretched herself from the waist and put her hands flat on the floor; she took her slender foot in her hand and bent over backwards. The blue shorts strained slightly; there was nothing spare on her, just miles and miles of tight, hard, thin muscle. And as she exhibited all this peerless flesh she chatted casually of this and that—how's the baby, and where she was going to run. She disappeared through the door. I said to Katy, "Does she know I'm gay?" Katy grinned and said, "Oh, yes." "I feel set up." "That's what they're called—setting-up exercises." I felt very angry. Katy laughed and said, "She is too." "Is what?" I asked. "Gay." I melted into a pool of desire.

It's better to have started. The pre-race excitement makes me feel a little sick. Tension. But also . . . people punching the air and shouting "Let's go, let's go." Psyching themselves up. Casing each other out. Who's better than who? Don't like it. Don't want to do it. Wish I hadn't worn this T-shirt. It has "I am a feminist jogger" on it. Beth and Emma gave it to me. Turns people on, though. Men. Not on to me but on to beating me. I won't care. There's a high on starting, though, crossing the line. Good to be going, good to have got here. Doesn't feel different because someone has called it a marathon, rather than a good long run. Keep it that way. But I would like to break three and a half hours. Step by step. Feel good. Fitter than I've ever been in my life, and I like it. Don't care what Sally says. Mad to despise body when she loves it so. Dualist. I like running. Like me running. Space and good feeling. Want to run clear of this crowd—too many people, too many paces. Want to find someone to run my own pace with. Have to wait. Pace; endurance; deferment of pleasure; patience; power. Sally ought to like it—likes the benefits alright. Bloke nearby wearing a T-shirt that reads, "Runners make the best lovers." He grins at me. Bastard. I'll show him: run for the Women's Movement. A trick. Keep the rules. My number one rule is "run for yourself." But I bet I can run faster than him.

Hurt myself running once, because of that. Ran a ten-mile race, years ago, with Annie, meant to be a fun-run and no sweat. There was this jock; a real pig; he kept passing us, dawdling, letting us pass him, passing again. And every time these remarks—the Vaseline stains from our nipples, or women getting him too turned on to run. Stuff like that; and finally he runs off, all sprightly and tough, patronizing. We ran on. Came into the last mile or so and there he was in front of us, tiring. I could see he was tired. "Shall we?" I said to Annie, but she was tired too. "Go on then," she was laughing at me, and I did. Hitched up a gear or two, felt great, zoomed down the hill after him, cruised alongside, made it look easy, said, "Hello, sweetheart, you look tired" and sailed on. Grinned back over my shoulder, he had to know who it was, and pulled a muscle in my neck. Didn't care—he was really pissed off. Glided over the finishing line and felt great for twenty minutes. Then I felt bad; should have known better—my neck hurt like hell, my legs cramped from over-running. But it wasn't just physical. Felt bad mentally. Playing those games.

Not today. Just run and feel good. Run into your own body and feel it. Feel road meeting foot, one by one, a good feeling. Wish Sally knew why I do it. Pray she'll come and see me finish. She won't. Stubborn bitch. Won't think about that. Just check leg muscles and pace and watch your ankles. Run.

If she likes to run that much of course I don't mind. It's nice some evenings when she goes out, and comes back and lies in the bath. A good salty woman. A flavor that I like. But I can't accept this marathon business: who wants to run 26 miles and 385 yards, in a competitive race? Jane does. For the last three months at least our lives have been taken over by those 26 miles, what we eat, what we do, where we go, and I have learned to hate every one of them. I've tried,

"Why?" I've asked over and over again; but she just says things like, "because it's there, the ultimate." Or "Just once, Sally, I'll never do it again." I *bet,* I think viciously. Sometimes she rationalizes: women have to do it. Or, it's important to the women she teaches. Or, it has to be a race because nowhere else is set up for it: you need the other runners, the solidarity, the motivation. "Call it sisterhood. You can't do it alone. You need . . ." And I interrupt and say, "You need the competition; you need people to beat. Can't you see?" And she says, "You're wrong. You're also talking about something you know nothing about. So shut up. You'll just have to believe me: you need the other runners and mostly they need you and want you to finish. And the crowd wants you to finish, they say. I want to experience that solidarity, of other people wanting you to do what you want to do." Which is a slap in the face for me, because I don't want her to do what she wants to do.

And yet—I love the leanness of her, which is a gift to me from marathon training. I love what her body is and what it can do, and go on doing and not be tired by doing. She has the most beautiful legs, hard, stripped down, with no wastage and her Achilles tendons are like flexible rock. Running does that for her. And then I think, damn, damn, damn. I will not love her for those reasons; but I will love her because she is tough and enduring and wryly ironic. Because she is clear about what she wants and prepared to go through great pain to get it; and because her mind is clear, careful and still open to complexity. She wants to stop being a Phys. Ed. teacher because now that women are getting as much money for athletic programs the authorities suddenly demand that they should get into competition, winning trips. Whereas when she started it was fun for her and for women being together as women, doing the things they had been laughed at for, as children.

She says I'm a dualist and she laughs at me. She says I want to separate body and soul while she runs them together. When she runs she thinks: not ABC like I think with my tidy well-trained mind, but in flashes—she'll trot out with some problem and run 12 or 15 miles and come home with the kinks smoothed out. She says that after eight or ten miles she hits a euphoric high—grows free—like meditation or something, but better. She tells me that I get steamed up through a combination of tension and inactivity. She can run out that stress and be perfectly relaxed while perfectly active. She comes clean. Ten or twelve miles at about eight minutes per mile: about where she'll be getting to now.

I have spent another half hour thinking about the things I was not going to think about. Tension and inactivity. I cannot concentrate the mind.

When I bend my head forward and Emma squeezes the sponge onto my neck, I can feel each separate drop of water flow down my back or over my shoulders and down between my breasts. I listen to my heartbeat and it seems strong and sturdy. As I turn Emma's wrist to see her watch her blue veins seem translucent and fine. Mine seem like strong wires conducting energy. I don't want to drink and have it lying there in my stomach, but I know I should. Obedient, giving over to Emma, I suck the bottle. Tell myself I owe it to her. Her parents did not want her to spend a hot Saturday afternoon nursing her games teacher. When I'm back in rhythm I feel the benefits of the drink. Emma is a good kid. Her parents' unnamed suspicions are correct. I was in love with a games teacher once. She was a big strong woman, full of energy. I pretended to share what the others thought and mocked her. We called her Tarzan and how I loved her. In secret dreams I wanted to be with her. "You Tarzan, me Jane," I would mutter, contemplating her badly-shaved underarms, and would fly with her through green trees, swing on lianas of delight. She was my first love; she helped make me a strong woman. The beauty, the immensity of her. When we swam she would hover over the side of the pool and as I looked up through the broken, sparkly water there she would be hauling me through with her strength.

Like Sally hauls me through bad dreams, looming over me in the night as I breathe up through the broken darkness. She hauls me through muddle with her sparkly mind. Her mind floats, green with sequined points of fire. Sally's mind. Lovely. My mind wears Nike running shoes with the neat white flash curling back on itself. It fits well and leaves room for my toes to flex. If I weren't a games teacher I could be a feminist chiropodist—or a midwife. Teach other women the contours of their own bodies—show them the new places where their bodies can take them. Sally doesn't want to be taken—only in the head. Sex of course is hardly in her head. In the heart? My heart beats nearly 20 pulses a minute slower than hers: we test them together lying in the darkness, together. "You'll die, you shit," I want to yell at her. "You'll die and leave me. Your heart isn't strong enough." I never say it. Nice if your hearts matched. The Zulu warrior women could run fifty miles a day and fight at the end of it. Fifty miles together, perfectly in step, so the veldt drummed with it. Did their hearts beat as one? My heart can beat with theirs, slow and strong and efficient—pumping energy.

Jane de Chantal, after whom I was named, must have been a jogger. She first saw the Sacred Heart—how else could she have known that slow, rich stroke which is at the heart of everything? Especially back then when the idea of heart meant only emotions. But she was right. The body, the heart at the heart of it all: no brain, no clitoris without that strong slow heart. Thesis: was a seventeenth-century nun the first jogger? Come on; this is rubbish. Think about footstrike and stride length. Not this garbage. Only one Swedish garbage collector, in the whole history of Swedish municipal rubbish collection, has ever worked through to retirement age—what perseverance, endurance. What a man. Person. Say garbage person. Sally says so. Love her. Damn her. She is my princess. I'm the younger son (say person) in the fairy story. But running is my wise animal. If I'm nice to my running it will give me good advice on how to win the princess. Float with it. Love it. Love her. There has to be a clue.

Emma is here again. Car? Bicycle? She can't have run it. She and Beth come out and give me another drink, wipe my face. Lovely hands. I come down and look around. After twenty miles they say there are two sorts of smiles among runners—the smiles of those who are suffering and the smiles of those who aren't. "You're running too fast," says Beth, "You're too high. Pace yourself, you silly twit. You're going to hurt." "No," I say, "I'm feeling good." But I know she's right. Discipline counts. Self-discipline, but Beth will help with that. "We need you to finish," says Emma. "Of course she'll finish," says Beth. I love them and I run away from them, my mouth feeling good with orange juice and soda water. Ought to have been Sally, though. Source of sweetness. How could she do this to me? How could she leave me? Desert me in the desert. Make a desert. This is my quest—my princess should be here. Princess: she'd hate that. I hate that. Running is disgusting; makes you think those thoughts. I hurt. I hurt and I am tired. They have lots of advice for this point in a marathon. They say think of all the months that are wasted if you stop now. But not wasted because I enjoyed them. They say, whoever wanted it to be easy? I did. They say, think of that man who runs marathons with only one leg. And that's meant to be inspirational. He's mad. We're all mad. There's no reason but pride. Well, pride then. Pride and the thought of Sally suppressing her gloating if I go home and say it hurt too much. I need a good reason to run into and through this tiredness.

Something stabs my eyes with orange. Nothing really hurt before but now it hurts. Takes me all of three paces to locate the hurt: cramp in the upper thighs. Sally's fault; I think of her and tense up. Ridiculous. But I'll be damned if I quit now. Run into the pain; I know it will go away and I don't believe it. Keep breathing steadily. It hurts. I know it hurts, shut up, shut up, shut up. Who cares if it hurts? I do. Don't do this. Seek out a shirt in front of you and look at the number. Keep looking at the number. 297. Do some sums with that. Can't think of any. Not divisible by 2, or 3, or 5. Nor 7.9? 9 into 29 goes 3.3 and carry 2. 9 into 27. Always works. If you can divide by something the cramp goes away. Is that where women go in childbirth— into the place of charms? All gay women should run marathons—gives them solidarity with their laboring sisters. I feel sick instead. I look ahead and there is nothing but the long hill. Heartbreaking. I cannot.

Shirt 297 belongs to a woman, a little older than me perhaps. I run beside her, she is tired too. I feel better and we run together. We exchange a smile. Ignore the fact that catching up with her gives me a lift. We exchange another smile. She is slowing. She grins and deliberately reduces her pace so that I can go ahead without feeling bad. That's love. I love her. I want to turn around, jog back and say, "I will leave my lover for you." "Dear Sally," I will write, "I am leaving you for a lady who" (and Sally's mental red pencil will correct to "whom") "I met during the marathon and unlike you she was nice and generous to me." Alternative letter, "Dear Sally, I have quit because long-distance running brings you up against difficulties and cramps and I cannot take the pain." Perseverance, endurance, patience and accepting love are part of running a marathon. She won't see it. Damn her.

Must be getting near now because there's a crowd watching. They'll laugh at me. "Use the crowd," say those who've been here before. "They want you to finish. Use that." Lies. Sally doesn't want me to finish. What sort of princess doesn't want the quest finished? Wants things cool and easy? Well pardon me, your Royal Highness. Royal Highness: the marathon is 26 miles and 385 yards long because some princess wanted to see the start of the 1908 Olympic Marathon from Windsor Palace and the finish from her box in the White City Stadium. Two miles longer than before. Now standardized. By appointment. Damn the Royal Princess. Damn Sally.

Finally I accept that I'm not going to do any work today. It takes me several more minutes to accept what that means—that I'm involved in that bloody race. People tend, I notice, to equate accepting with liking—but it's not that simple. I don't like it. But, accepting, I get the car out and drive to the shops and buy the most expensive bath oil I can find. It's so expensive that the box is perfectly modest—no advertising, no half-naked women. I like half-naked women as a matter of fact, but there are such things as principles. Impulsively I also buy some matching lotion, thinking that I will rub it on her feet tonight. Jane's long slender feet are one part of her body that owe nothing to running. This fact alone is enough to turn me into a foot fetishist.

After I have bought the stuff and slavered a bit over the thought of rubbing it into her poor battered feet (I worked it out once. Each foot hits the ground about 800 times per mile. The force of the impact is three times her weight. 122 pounds times 800 times 26 miles. It does not bear thinking about). I realize the implications of rubbing sweet ointment into the tired feet of the beloved person. At first I am embarassed and then I think, well Mary Magdalen is one way through the sex-object, true-love dichotomy. Endurance, perseverance, love. She must have thought the crucifixion a bit mad too. Having got this far in acceptance I think that I might as well go down to the finish and make her happy. We've come a long way together. So I get back into the car and do just that.

It is true, actually. In the last few miles the crowd holds you together. This is not the noble hero against the world. Did I want that? But this is better. A little kid ducked under the rope and gave me a half-eaten ice-lolly—raspberry flavor. Didn't want it. Couldn't refuse such an act of love. Took it. Felt fine. Smiled. She smiled back. It was a joy. Thank you sister. The people roar for you, hold you through the sweat and the tears. They have no faces. The finishing line just is. Is there. You are meant to raise your arms and shout, "Rejoice, we conquer" as you cross it. Like Pheidippides did when he entered Athens and history. And death. But all I think is "Christ, I've let my anti-gravity muscles get tight." They hurt. Sally is here. I don't believe it. Beth drapes a towel over my shoulders without making me stop moving. Emma appears, squeaking, "Three hours, 26 and a half. That's great. That's bloody great." I don't care. Sally has cool soft arms. I look for them. They hold me. "This is a sentimental ending," I try to say. I'm dry. Beth gives me a beer. I cannot pour it properly. It flows over my chin, soft and cold, blissfully cold. I manage a grin and it spreads all over me. I feel great. I lean against Sally again. I say, "Never, never again." She grins back and, not without irony, says, "Rejoice, we conquer."

Better Safe than Sorry

When she first felt the tingling in her toes she was not entirely surprised. The baby had begun to move inside her. It was about ten inches long and very active, heavy enough to press now and again on the complex nervous system that allows the lower spine and the legs to communicate with each other: it was normal enough to experience abnormal cramps and pins-and-needles when you were five months pregnant. Of course everything was fine.

When she had first watched the peony bud open and seen inside, instead of the bright red crumpled tissue paper petals, the bleeding organs of a dead child and the evil little devil grinning with blood-stained lips, she was not entirely surprised. If you don't use pesticides in your garden you must expect the occasional deformation—ants were partial to peony buds and their depredations caused odd effects. It was normal enough to have abnormal fears and fantasies when you were five months pregnant. Of course everything was fine.

When she woke up in the night and saw the wicked crone at the foot of her bed laughing demonically she was startled. Her feet were so hot that she threw off the covers and then had to lie and watch her hands and feet twitching and shaking independently. The witch laughed and her toes and fingers danced. But she pulled herself together, got out of bed and went downstairs to make herself a sandwich. Of course everything was fine.

She sat in the kitchen chewing the dark bread that she had baked herself the day before, and took herself sternly in hand. Everything was fine. It was perfectly normal to be worried. It said so in the mother-and-baby book that lay even now beside her bed. Many women experience almost obsessive fears and heightened fantasies in the middle months of pregnancy. There you are. It said so in the book. Everything was fine.

Everything would be fine because this time she had been so careful. She had learned the hard way. Two years ago her other baby had died *in utero* five weeks before it was due to be born. The doctors had said there was no reason, no clear reason, that this happened sometimes and that they did not always know why.

But on the day the baby should have been born, she had read about lysisteria and her mouth was filled to choking with the memory of the picnic in the garden. The creamy brie, ripe, spilling out of its peach soft skin, oozing lusciously onto the plate. She had lavished it on white crusty French bread; she had sat in the sunshine full of love and joy and greed, and stuffed herself with its richness and she had killed her baby.

In the kitchen the dark was paling towards an early summer morning. The crone stood across the table and laughed at her, cackling maliciously. Suddenly her hand jerked wildly, the slice of bread flew across the room; the tingling and the heat were too much, she was burning alive. Once upon a time the witch had burned too; long long ago the witch had burned, punished for destroying babies. The witch had cast a glamour on her and would destroy her baby.

She gasped a little, appalled at herself. She clasped her hands firmly against her stomach, calming them and warming her child. She noticed that under each of her fingernails there was a little black new moon. She couldn't remember how she had got them so dirty, but she must wash them well. One couldn't be too careful.

She had been so careful that her friends thought she was mad. Six months before getting pregnant this time she had stopped smoking and drinking. She had checked with the proposed baby's proposed father. He had never taken steroids, he had never dropped acid and he had never worked at Selafield. She reckoned he was teratogen free. He had ceased to be amused and had departed a few weeks after the baby was safely conceived. It was a pity, but she at least had the courage to face the danger.

There was poison in the roots of the world. There was poison in the depths of the well. No wonder the witch sniggered. No wonder the little demon licked its lips. Now it was dancing on her belly swaying and grinning in time to the dancing of her hands and feet, the dancing of her baby in her womb.

Perhaps her friends were right and she was going mad. But she had kept a sense of proportion. The discovery that, although 75 percent of cars could run on lead-free gas, only 20 percent of drivers had bothered to make the change, had made her furiously angry, but it had not confined her to the house or reduced her to wearing a mask. Of course she wasn't going mad. But forewarned is forearmed. So everything was fine.

She pulled herself together and walked around the kitchen table, straight through the mirage of the witch who vanished in a puff of smoke, leaving her fingers stained black. She turned to the sideboard and cut herself a new slice of bread. Although her fidgeting hands made carving difficult, the loaf pleased her. It was slightly heavy, but hard and chewy outside, black and soft inside, studded through with wholesome germ, with fiber, with strength and wellness for her child. It had become her lifeline, this bread she made daily from organically grown mixed grain; healthy, filling, safe.

There wasn't, after all, much else she could eat. She had given up meat long before they started worrying about mad cow disease, but even so she would wake at night from dreams of her baby's head metamorphosing into a huge soggy bath sponge, yellow and pitted. Two little horns jutted from the front of the sponge. They were the cow's horns as it stumbled and twitched, as it lowered its head and charged. They were the demon's horns, and the larger holes in the face of the sponge grinned like the demon did.

Eggs were obviously out of the question, and she knew for herself the dangers of dairy products. There was a bloom of death floating on the surface of the oceans and the fresh water rivers were scummed with deadly toxins.

Even vegetables. One third of all vegetables, she discovered with alarm, were contaminated by Lindane. The pesticide Lindane, relatively harmless to adults, causes fetal cancer. There was nothing unbalanced about trying to keep your baby safe from cancer. You just had to be careful. She had been careful. She bought the flour from the whole food shop and baked it herself. Of course everything was fine.

Her feet were burning and twitching. Her hands were dancing and leaping. Leaping to the rhythm of the baby inside her, who was going to catch fire, because she was so hot. Her feet were black, they were burning, smoldering, turning to ash before her very eyes. The crescents of black under her nails were growing as the moon waxes, into full circles at the tips of each finger.

The mother-and-baby book was upstairs, beside her bed. If she climbed upstairs and got it, it would tell her that it was perfectly normal for your feet to turn black and your hands to catch fire. For your limbs to dance wildly in time with the wild dancing of your fetal child. That it was perfectly normal for the child to crash and batter at your stomach wall, to pound against your diaphragm so that you could hardly breathe.

In a minute she would go upstairs and find the book and read that it was perfectly normal in the middle months of pregnancy for the loaf of bread to jeer at you and for the pot plants to go transparent so that you could see their blood flowing through their leaves. For the room to refuse to stand still, but dance and toss you about. It was perfectly normal to have a witch stand across the table and laugh at your gyrating limbs; to have a demon with horns butt at your rounded belly till it was pierced with pain. It was perfectly normal for your hands and feet to burn and burn until they turned black.

It was perfectly normal. In a minute she would go upstairs and read about it. But just not yet. Because she was feeling so very peculiar. Not that anything could be wrong, because she had been careful. Of course everything was fine.

But everything was not fine. No book in the world could persuade her that the glee on the witch's face, the triumph in the demon's grin, the baby's panicked convulsions, the gripping pain and the slow red pool that was seeping out of her body onto the floor were normal.

❧

Ergot is a mold that grows on grains, particularly rye. Ergotism, the disease caused by eating ergot, was common in the Middle Ages. It was known as St. Anthony's Fire because of the burning sensations and black dry gangrene that its victims suffered, and because the supposed cure was to visit the saint's shrine at La Motte in France. Other symptoms include spontaneous convulsions of the extremities and violent hallucinations. Ergot is a powerful abortifacient. Although the increased use of pesticides and a better understanding of the disease have made it relatively rare there was a mass outbreak of ergotism in France in the 1950s. The organism is still alive and well.

The Eighth Planet

We see the eighth planet as Columbus saw America from the shores of Spain. Its movements have been felt, trembling along the far reaching line of our analysis, with a certainty hardly inferior to that of ocular demonstration.

> *John Herschel, President of the British Association, son of*
> *William Herschel, musician and astronomer.*
> 10 September 1846

In the end he said, quite calmly, at breakfast one morning, that he thought he would go back to London later that afternoon: he did not mean for a trip or even a visit, he meant for good, he meant goodbye and possibly even, Thank you for having me.

I said nothing; I just looked at him and realized with some deep and abiding sadness that my main emotion was of relief. He finished his coffee and went upstairs to start packing. I put on my Wellington boots—black, I would like to say, not green—and walked down to the shop to get the newspaper, and, ah God, it was a lovely, lovely morning. It was bright and clean as some days in late March can be, the sky pale blue and the branches of the hedgerow trees apparently getting fatter, pregnant with buds that are not yet even palest green, and the larch wood across the hillside was pink with promise and, despite my best efforts to tell myself that he was a bastard and my great love affair had come to a nasty end and everything was tragic, all I felt was a heart-lifting joy in the sparkly dew drops and a sweet pleasure at the thought of being alone again.

Even now I don't really understand why it turned out so horrendous. We went in with such high hopes, the hopes, we thought, of maturity and good sense, no adolescent romantics we; two people with meshing needs and a deep sense of sexual attraction. And for the first couple of months it was wonderful; we even reached the point of talking about selling both our houses and finding somewhere that would be ours. Once in the middle of a snowy night just before Christmas when we had been out, muffled up like children, we had even mentioned the possibility of having a baby—or rather, to be precise, he had said, "Let's build a snowman. I need to get in practice for when we have a child." We had started to roll one of those progressive balls that get larger and larger and leave neat black lines weaving about the lawn, but in the end we had gone to bed instead.

And then quite unexpectedly we had gone into a place of hell; of meanness and hatefulness. Never, never have I felt for anyone the hatred, the irresistible hatred, that I felt for him and he for me: a hatred that could not permit a decent withdrawal, that could not even confine itself to scathing, hurtful arguments but erupted into appalling violence that was mutual and savage and unlovely. But was also completely engaging, an eyeball-to-eyeball clash of the whole of two people, locked together like the lovers in Dante's *Inferno*. I, I who had always loathed romanticism, that "all for love and the world well lost" stuff, I who preferred relationships to be domestic and comfortable and not distracting, who liked my sex civilized and preferred to do the crossword puzzle anyway. So, on top of everything else, there was this deep shame in both of us, and more simply embarrassment that we should see ourselves and each other like this. And for me at least, a complete loss of identity; quite literally I did not know who I was and I had done no work all winter and could not imagine how I thought I was going to pay for that.

And after some months of that it suddenly went away. There was a great calm after the storm and we looked at each other more in amazement than in anything else; a sort of terrified surprise, a kind of Who *is* this, who can have reduced me to such depths? And we were courteous and civil with each other and there was simply nothing there. We even made love with a tenderness and concern for the other's pleasure, and had long and sincere conversations about where and what each of us might do next, and he fixed new shelves for my kitchen and I knitted him a huge Aran sweater, with elaborate and elegant cables up back and front. And now, when we had so to speak completed our rest cure, it was time for him to go back to London.

I walked back from the village shop with the newspaper under my arm and a couple of packets of cigarettes in my pocket and recognized that I was making new plans, plans for work and plans for the vegetable garden, even plans for a summer holiday. And that felt so good. I put the newspaper on the kitchen table and called up the stairs to him, and then I went into the garden to pick him some daffodils to take back to his cold flat in London, just as I would have done for any weekend guest. And indeed I started thinking about weekend guests and friends that I had not seen for months, and I could feel something in my lower neck relax, and my feet spread themselves out inside my spacious Wellington boots. I went inside and dumped the flowers in a bucket in the back kitchen, took off my boots and padded in my socks to my pinboard to find the train timetable.

While I was standing there he came downstairs and I noticed with an abstract pleasure how beautiful he still was, conscious that I had not noticed this for weeks, even months. He had been one of the most beautiful undergraduates of our year when I had first known him twenty years ago. A wild glamour that had somehow never gone away, not even now he was cleaner and tidier and richer than any of us could ever have dreamed of. Whereas I, it would have to be said, had not aged so well, and indeed was sloppier, dirtier and cozier than I would have dared to be then, when even my uniform jeans had about them a circumspection and a willingness to be checked out and inspected by anyone who cared. We had been in one of those Trotskyite groupings, those joyfully puritanical, fragmenting, shifting, passionate student groups in the late sixties; not the guitars and marijuana sorts, although actually we did lots of both of those, more the beer and theory until three in the morning, our radical paths crisscrossing for a while, an alliance forming between us, then a friendship. And anything was possible in those giddy optimistic times when the mornings had edges so sharp that you could cut yourself on the daylight. I had even slept with him a couple of times, before other things intervened.

Later I had got married and divorced and I met him again last year at one of those dinner parties in London where people envy each other their success while feeling slightly guilty about their own; friendship networks so old and intimate that the difficulties and differences can collapse into wild mirth at an instant, or can flare into fights which, however vicious at the time, will not actually change anything nor prevent the same people coming together again pretty soon, at an identical but different pine kitchen table where everyone tries to keep secret to themselves that they wished the wine was a little better. Property prices and psychoanalysis are mentioned shyly as perhaps our parents mentioned sex, but once on the table so to speak it turns out that we are all enormously knowledgeable. And I do not wish to sound so mean, because they are my friends and indeed I am one of them and would not be otherwise. And we are all anti-Thatcherites and those that have them struggle desperately to keep their children within the state school system, and see the all-too-frequent failures of others to succeed as being somehow like a rather nasty disease—compassion and sorrow the appropriate response rather than that clear bell-like anger we could all touch so easily once upon a time.

It was actually quite odd that he and I had not met in this way at any time before. We had that night, I remember, a conversation about who had actually believed in 1969 that The Revolution was real and immediate, and half-sheepishly both of us admitted a complete and profound faith, and had smiled wryly at each other, though whether at our once naïvete or our failure to live up to so fine and pure a commitment was not so totally obvious. But it had been, you must understand, a credo, a way of living, which had after all been sincere and which had also been expensive to abandon and left us fretful still. Later I drove him home, since Hackney is basically on the way to Ipswich, and since he does not own a car and it was late. And outside his charming Victorian terraced artisan's cottage (through lounge, 2 beds, kitchen/diner, bathroom, gas-fired central heating, tastefully refurbished preserving many period features. I know how mean and catty I am and to punish myself have to admit that my cottage has a thatched roof) we encountered one of those odd surges of pure desire that are entirely mutual and he said to me, "We have unfinished business, you and I." And whatever that had been, it was now at least well and truly finished.

So I could smile at his beauty and, indeed, at him, not without some considerable pleasure when he came down the stairs into my kitchen. He had the newspaper in his hand and an apologetic grin on his face.

He asked, "What time is the late train?"

I inspected the timetable and told him. "Why?" I asked.

"We could see Neptune tonight. With the telescope." He flapped the paper gently.

He would not ask to stay another night. I would have resented it bitterly if he had. But he would very much like to see Neptune with the telescope. It was an odd thing about the telescope. It had belonged to the uncle of mine who had left me the cottage and had been waiting along with other treasures when I arrived. I had kept it only because it was a very beautiful object, with lovely brass bits and pieces: there is something extraordinarily lovely to me in Victorian scientific instruments, along with clocks and musical boxes, where the desire that something should work perfectly is not made a reason for not having it look wonderfully wrought. Properly speaking, it is probably, like the crinoline, merely an example of conspicuous consumption, a public way of saying, Look how much I can afford to spend, but in its presence I could never focus on that but only on the pleasure that looking at it gave me. I never used it for anything, indeed found it well-nigh impossible to see anything through it, even the larch trees across the hill, but he loved it functionally. At the golden beginning of our relationship when we had first come down to the cottage he had fallen on it with joy and arrived the next time with a small pile of star charts and books. Back in the autumn he had spent hours looking through it, while I had curled on the sofa enjoying the anticipation of lust, the mounting excitement of waiting. He would try to show me what he was looking at sometimes, but proximity and darkness were usually too much for us. I had not proved myself an adept at amateur astronomy.

"Is that special?" I asked him now.

"Special enough for the late train." After a short pause he said, "Please."

"All right then," I said, "I can drive you to the station after that."

Much later, when we had had tea and were waiting for the darkness, he said, "I'll tell you something about Neptune that you may not like. It disproves the whole thing about learning coming from experience, theory being grounded on what actually is. They discovered it by pure theory."

I asked him what he meant.

"In 1781 William Herschel became the first person in history to discover a planet, Uranus. He discovered it as you might expect, as most things are discovered, by well informed accident and good luck, by looking, just by looking at everything through his telescope, which he had made himself because he couldn't afford to buy one. He looked and looked and thought about what he saw and he discovered a planet—planets don't twinkle, you see, and under sufficient magnification they show a disk not a point of light. Well, after he had found it, other astronomers tried reasonably enough to plot its orbit, but wherever they thought it ought to be it wasn't. So they worked out in total abstract that it was being pulled out of its expected orbit by the gravity of another invisible planet, somewhere out there, somewhere beyond the known limits of the sun's cosmic system. Somewhere so far out that you could not see it with the naked eye. And in principle it should be possible to work out exactly where it was. So this young mathematician called John Couch Adams did just that in 1845. Sort of typical academe, he could not get anyone to look for it for him. Some Frenchman called Urbain Leverrier worked it out too. So they knew it was there; they knew it was there, and exactly where theoretically before they found it."

I may not need to mention that he was a teacher of extraordinary verve and energy, whose lectures were well attended and whose books, given their academic abstraction, sold remarkably well. He loved to impart information like this.

And I, I loved being told stories like this. He had known that too when he had said I might not like it. That was a tease, because he knew I was a sucker when it came to this sort of incident. I pushed him for all the details he knew; I imagined poor John Adams trekking around the astronomers of Britain saying, "There it is, there it is, look, look, it's your job to look," and no one believing him enough to bother to get into their observatories and look for it. I find it odd how little people ever seem to want to detect things they're meant to detect. Like the Yorkshire Ripper, for example. How on the available evidence could they have failed to find Sutcliffe? You collect all the evidence and then you almost willfully fail to act on it. Only amateurs, lovers, in their chambers on Baker Street, half sozzled with cocaine, actually want to solve mysteries. So I said, "Tell me, tell me."

And sitting by the fireplace in my little cottage with a big mug of tea between his hands and his lovely high-boned face turned away from me and towards the flames, he told me more things.

He told me that Neptune has two moons: one is tiny and called Miranda, and the other is huge and called Triton; and Triton is the only object in the cosmic universe that revolves in the opposite direction. Of all the planets and all their satellites, only Triton has the imagination to spin backwards. He told me that Neptune has not rings, like Saturn and Jupiter and Uranus but arcs, little bits of broken-up ring, material all that way away striving to turn itself from a strip into a clump—matter that desires to be a satellite. He told me that Neptune is a liquid planet, its surface entirely covered by water. He told me that at the bottom of this ocean, which functions as a blanket, it is so hot and so compressed that the methane at its core is perhaps breaking up into carbon atoms and hydrogen atoms and the carbon is being pressed into diamond crystals. Far away, beyond the furthest seeing of the naked eye, there is the jewel-encrusted underwater cavern that the ancients dreamed of for their sea god, Neptune.

And this they knew from pure theory alone. Even Voyager 2 has not yet traveled long enough or far enough to see Neptune in any detail.

And in the freezing night we turned off the lights and he looked through the telescope, referring at first to the newspaper and then to his huge space atlas. And suddenly he gave a tiny shiver of pleasure and I knew he had found it. He looked for a moment and then fixed the telescope, twiddling one of the elegant brass knobs effortlessly and without taking his eye away from the lens.

"Come and see," he said, stretching out one arm and tucking me into the fold of his body, as I had so many times been tucked before. But his energy was flowing not towards me but towards the whole dense sky. I put my eye against the optic and at first I could see nothing, then I could see too much, a million too many stars, a great war in heaven, and I was almost terrified. And keeping his arm round me, warm and gentle, he told me very quietly what to look for, how to find Neptune and suddenly there it was: a tiny distant pale bluish disk floating out there. It did not twinkle or waver. I was amazed. Even if I never saw him again, he would have given me this gift, this sight of a new world known, discovered and created by theory.

"Thank you," I said with real pleasure.

"No, thank you," he said, and I turned within his arms and we exchanged a kiss so pure and tender that I have never known anything like it.

It was so perfect a moment that it became immediately imperative that he should catch the train. He pushed the lens cover over the telescope and took the stairs two at a time in his energetic determination to get his bags down and into the car. I helped him, not even bothering to say we had plenty of time. There was a sort of panic and unreasonableness about our haste which seemed appropriate to us both; but as soon as we were both in the car I realized that I had forgotten to give him the flowers I had picked that morning. I leapt out again and ran back into the empty cottage. When I saw the telescope still standing on its tripod at the window I knew I had to give it to him—not the flowers after all, but that. I folded it up and packed it into its leather box. He came to the door, impatient to be gone, and saw what I was doing. He didn't even question me, it was so right. He said thank you once again and then came over and squatting together on the floor we did up the leather straps and brass buckles with infinite and delicate care. Then together we carried it out to the car and laid it on the back seat. Then we both scrambled back into the car and belted off; I knew I was over-revving the engine, and that it was foolish to take the bend by the old mill stream at such a pace, but there was a desperate compulsion about it. I wanted him out of my life, right then and there. And I could feel him beside me wanting the same thing.

The silence in the car felt painfully oppressive. I heard myself jabbering suddenly, endless words pumping out. I said, "Now I'll tell you a story, or at least a thought, about Neptune. If it was discovered in 1846 there is a wild appropriateness about that: just two years, enough time for it to sneak into public consciousness, before 1848; and Neptune was the god of revolutions, of storms, of raising new worlds out of the ocean deeps. Homer says that when Neptune issued from the sea and crossed the earth in three strides, the mountains and the forests trembled. He was the god who was always restless and invented the horse as a symbol of war and slaughter. So maybe there really is something in astrology."

He laughed. I drove slower. The twistings of the country lane had, almost without our noticing it, imposed some sort of calmness on my driving. The desperate urgency evaporated, flowing off into the dark night around us.

I asked him, "How did you get into stars, anyway? It does seem a rather improbable hobby for the bright young scientific socialist."

"Oh well," he replied, apparently laughing, "scientific socialism got all buggered up. You bloody feminists did that, punched holes right through the middle of the fabric of the thing, didn't you? Where else is there for a scientific Marxist to go but off to explore new worlds and the further away the better? Like the Levellers after the collapse of the Commonwealth. You take your mysticism to the country and bury it in the mud; I take my science to the skies and bury it in darkness."

I glanced at him and his beautiful face was tense not just with anger but with pain.

I said, "You may not believe this, but underneath it all, and I don't know how the hell to go about it and I don't live it on the flesh of experience as I said we ought to and I'm a fat cat and will greet the Revolution, if it comes, with tears for what I'm losing, rather than the more traditional dancing in the streets, but . . . but I still do believe that the overthrow of capitalism is The Project."

And he said, "I know you do. The question is, do I?"

And after a little while longer I said, "It is sad. I somehow cannot escape the feeling that we all, all of us, all our generation of people, deserved better than we got. And yet we got so much."

"Sic transit gloria mundi," he said a little peevishly.

"No," I said, "that's not what I mean."

"No," he said, "I know it isn't, but I'm bloody well not going to say thank you again. More like the Transit of f***ing Venus or something."

And that was enough of that. So we talked inconsequentially of this and that, friends and acquaintances, gossip and memories. Suddenly he started to tell me about Neptune again. I thought I didn't really want to hear that, but it was better than nothing and we were still a considerable distance from the train station. I half listened as he talked about densities, and gravities, and mass versus size. And suddenly I heard something in his voice, a sharpening, a precision, perhaps even a kind of nervousness, and I knew he was telling me something that was infinitely precious to him. He was telling me about Neptune's vast moon, Triton, whom from his previous description I had assumed to be something of the joker in the pack, eternally revolving backwards against all possible odds. And yes, yes, that was part of it, obviously; but also infinitely no. There's some astronomer in Haiti who spent a great deal of time speculating—both looking at and guessing about—on Triton. Now he said to me, in the apparently enclosed world of the car rushing through the countryside, he said, "It is a world of chilly oceans, whole oceans of liquid nitrogen.

Away out there, those icy oceans colored red, vivid crimson, by organic matter that we do not yet understand, rocked with tides beyond our moon space, infinitely pulled by a different, extenuated, frail force of gravity, and riding majestic those great rollers, silent because there is no breaking shore, there is no hearer for their thunder, riding the crimson oceans are the stately blue white icebergs of another place."

He said all that and I, to my own surprise, said, "Frozen methane."

You probably understand by now that we had been trying all these months to be together—it had been an investment of great importance to us both, had taken us both into a new place of self-knowing—and now, too late to be of any use, in that extraordinary and almost casual reversal—my science, his poetry—we almost succeeded. If I had been able, just then, to take both hands off the steering wheel and show him how I had, once, a world away, oh hell, a cosmos away almost, in a small ship, seen the dignified and blue-white icebergs of our own planet, bobbing too gigantic for the word itself, seen them break themselves with a deep gonging sound off the master ice, the glacier ice, and swan, white as their own chosen style, down the great green—oh *so* green—drift waters of the Arctic Ocean, I think we might even have gone home and tried again. You know, that is the magic of incongruence, where two pieces of the apparently seamless garment of social reality do not quite fit together, and through the unknown gap comes seeping—well, what can I call it? the unexpected, the redemptive, the bizarre but also the welcome—oh well, comes seeping Joy. Like lava from between the dense, heavy, immeasurably shifting and dishonest plates of the earth's surface. But you know how it is really too—I was driving; I had responsibilities; there was a sharp bend, concentration-requiring; and then it was too late, or not appropriate, or something. That's the way it goes, all randomly and inexplicably.

As it was we were both delighted. And we damn nearly missed that train.

Triptych

HAGAR

In the desert it is hot. It is hot and she is thirsty.

It is hot in the desert and she is thirsty.

The child is thirsty, the child cries, and she cannot bear to see the wasted water as it flows down his cheeks. She licks the tears as they fall and the child laughs, but they are salt and bitter in her mouth. She is too bitter to weep, her tears would scald the flesh, cutting down like the empty gullies of the desert, scald down to the rocks of her bones. She is stripped of flesh and too bitter for tears.

The child is almost too heavy to carry and almost too weak to walk. It is hot. The sun beats and burns on her black hair, because she was too bitter and too proud to accept a head cloth from Sarah's hand. And so she is still, and so she will die. There are things that cannot be changed, not when the desert dogs come out in the desolate cold night and gnaw her bones.

But at sunset, when the child seems feverish and drifts in and out of unkind dreams, and the winds hiss across the sand dunes and the shadows lengthen evil and menacing, then she wonders about pride and bitterness, then she weakens and shakes with fear and longing. But she does not weep.

Before now she has received everything from the hand of Sarah her mistress, from the hand of Sarah her mother, from the hand of Sarah her friend. In the long cold of the night she sets herself to remember; the memories come and go as restless as the child who lies against her shaking and burning through the cold night.

She had been eight years old when Sarah had taken her from Egypt. There had been somewhere before Egypt, somewhere higher, somewhere . . . mother, father, home . . . it is gone and she will never have it back. But it had not mattered because there had been Sarah. Now it mattered because she had to find some place to take the child.

"Little one," Sarah would laugh in the long trek across the desert, "little one, you are my immoral earnings. What encouragement is that for a woman to live honestly?" She had still been confused then, only eight years old and brought up in the palaces of the great Pharaoh, a valuable ornament to his court, so black and charming with her fuzzy hair and little pink palms. She had been given to Abraham in exchange for his sister's favors. But Sarah had not been his sister, only pretending, pretending because Abraham was afraid, pretending because Abraham was greedy, pretending because in those far-off days Abraham and Sarah had played a lot, laughing, teasing, joyous. Sarah the beautiful, Sarah the great princess from the noble house of Ur, far far north in the Chaldees. She, Hagar, had never been there, only heard Sarah on long evenings tell stories about the greatest city in the world, about the high walls and flowering gardens, the gold-strewn, ancient city that made Egypt look new and brash and extravagant, the ancient City of Wisdom where it was better to be an astronomer and a magician than a warrior; the oldest city at the very center of the world where silk and spices flowed in at the east gate and iron and salt and grain flowed in at the west gate and in the center was the market and the great tower whence the wise could watch the heavens and prophesy not useful but magical things. And there Sarah was a great princess and she had left it all with a laugh to travel God-knows-where with a tough little man whose eyes lit up with a vision and who swore that he had seen in the stars an inheritance for him born like dust out of the desert. And off they had gone trekking the world for fifty years to find that land, that nation, that place they believed they had been promised: that Garden of Eden, that land flowing with milk and honey, that home prepared for them before the flood. And still from her early childhood Hagar could remember, could not forget, the cool loveliness of Sarah, her ready laugh, her carefree calm, and the huge bouncing energy of Abraham, still young, still abounding in hope and merriment and conviction. And they had traveled one year down to Egypt, clear across the desert by the coastal route, because there had been a drought and a shortage in their own land and neither of them saw any cause to go short. And they had pretended that the two of them were brother and sister so that the great lords in Egypt would pay Abraham a bride price for Sarah rather than kill him to marry his wife. The tents on their journey home again rang with merriment at the skill and success of their joke, and she had been a part of the bride price. The little black slave girl who had played on Sarah's couch on golden mornings to amuse the Pharaoh's new mistress.

But . . . Sarah's hands had been warm and gentle. Her eyes laughed but her hands were kind, always, always, till they held out a head covering that she would not take; hard lined hands, old cruel hands, hands that after so many years had betrayed the promise made all those years ago in the land of the Nile. Her hands had been soft and pale then; they had lain on Hagar's naked shoulder as she had whispered to her that she would ask the Pharaoh for her as a gift, and the child had nodded, nodded, nodded, her absurd little braids bobbing with delight, because she had never known kindness before. And Sarah had said that it was good and the child would be safe and would be hers and would be with her always.

Memories of Sarah; Sarah's hands braiding gold threads and complex patterns into her hair. Sarah's arms around her, holding her in the night, in the women's tent, holding her against both their fears. Sarah's hands, strong and commanding, under her own armpits, Sarah's knees, steady and firm either side of her waist. Sarah's breasts soft and warm against her head and shoulders, Sarah's voice gentle and determined: breathe push relax push push breathe breathe down the baby, said Sarah's voice, breathe out the baby strong strong and gentle and steady and Ishmael suddenly rushing down on the strength of her muscles and Sarah's sweet calm. Sarah's hands untiring, loving, washing her with a soft cloth after the labor, washing tenderly and happily, all over, hands like cool honey all over her, mother, friend, lover. Sarah.

She re-calls her memory to her, summoning her spirit back from the cluster of tents, the sheep cropping the sparse hillside grass, the fires glowing and whispering, the night boys moving among the folds with quiet greetings, Sarah's merry laugh, the little comings and goings of an encampment hard beside its well. Back to here, to the cold here of deep desert night, stars huge and distant, uncaringly bright, and the silence so enormous that it stretches forever, vast and all-embracing. She is thirty years old; she is black as the night itself; she has a feverish three-year-old boy child whose skin is paler than hers, who scarcely looks like her; she is a slave; and she, with the child, is going to die in the desert night and the wind will blow the sand over her bones until it will be as though she had never been. And it will be a loss to no one but herself, she who had thought herself so rich in love.

There has to be a moment of turning, a moment so subtle that one does not notice it, but so perfect that the consequences are inevitable, a moment when everything changes and what is possible before it is impossible afterwards and the unimaginable becomes the normal. Somewhere, at some well side, by some oasis, under some fierce moon, they had all changed: that what had been vision became obsession, that what had been faith became mockery, that what had been love became ownership, and yet still the shadow of what they had been, of what they believed, of their own bright hope and conviction, the shadow of their old selves, hung over those new things unseen, unacknowledged, souring what could be a richer and easier joy. Neither of them, not Sarah not Abraham, oh not herself either, could admit, would admit, that they could no longer believe. Sarah became cynical, an edge in the bubbling laughter, an edge turned against herself so that when her child was finally born she called it Isaac— "God has laughed." And Abraham had become . . . crazy; receiving ever more bizarre commands from his invisible God, inflicting his ideas upon them with ever more fervor. He had come home once from a half-moon of roaming, staggering into the encampment scarcely able to walk; blood had flowed from under his robe. For a moment Hagar had been carried back to the slave quarters of childhood when the prettiest boys had been made into eunuchs, brutally and publicly; when the loveliest girls had been sent down to the aged crone who lurked, honored and hated, in the bottom of the gardens of the palace to have their soft inner flesh sliced away with the little bronze knife, so that they might not be tempted to infidelity or desire, and might work out their lives fully attentive to their lord's service, fully complacent to his usage. She had been struck with terror, standing there, the water jar slipping from her hands, slipping and breaking into little sharp shards while Abraham called all the men of the camp to him—all of them, even her child, and told them that his God had given him a covenant of promise and would winnow the deserts in the night, but would spare the household of Abraham and make his seed like the desert sands. And all they had to do to be worthy, worthy of this great inheritance, was to cut off their foreskins so that his God would know them in that night. Not Ishmael, not her boy child, her joyful bubbling baby then hardly weaned from the breast. Oh let him, Sarah had said, it could be something worse. It could be us. For, years ago, when Hagar had been approaching puberty, Sarah had woken her from recurrent nightmares in which the little bronze knife cut away her tongue, or her breasts or her . . . and Sarah had held her in her arms and promised, promised, promised that never never never would she let that happen to her and the child Hagar had been comforted. Now she said, it will not hurt, it will not hurt, Abraham would do nothing, never, that would hurt his precious manhood; and she had led Hagar away gently into the depths of the tent and covered her with a blanket and kissed her ears and eyes and mouth and genitals so that she would not have to hear the screams of her mutilated child. And as so often, Sarah was right, and within hours Ishmael was bumbling and buzzing again, but why had Sarah not spoken, why had Sarah kept silent in the tent, smothering Hagar with kisses rather than challenging the madness that grew in Abraham, rather than telling him that there was no God that would seek to damage the children of the promise? Was that the moment when they had changed? When they had given up, when they had realized that Abraham would if he thought fit sacrifice his own flesh and blood to please his deranged and unreasonable God who grew, with each passing year, more and more like Abraham himself.

Or was it when Sarah started returning from his tent not laughing and full breasted, but irritable and sore? When her monthly blood-letting ceased and her skin wrinkled not just along the lines of her smile, but sagging away from her cheeks and lying in dead folds around her neck. Her husband's desire was no longer toward her, but only toward an ever more desperate pumping of his seed into her barren sack, more demanding, more cantankerous, more fanatical as her hope faded and her beauty dimmed. She who had left Ur for him, whose wisdom and beauty and calm steadiness had kept them safe for half a century of adventuring. And he turned his lust towards her own maidservant, her child and her friend. No, she had said, no. And Hagar, steadied by Sarah's firmness, had said no, too; though actually there was something about his eagerness and his conviction. Then, after too long and when any possible pleasure had gone out of it, Sarah had changed her mind; oh do it, Hagar, for God's sake. Get the old goat off both our backs. We need a child in the tents, an end to sheep girls' mockery of me, an end to this obsession. Let him give us some peace. The two of them had lain together in the women's tent and Sarah had urged her, urged her, urged her to consent to him. She had said and said that it was Sarah that she loved, Sarah that she served, that she whored for no married men, and Sarah in a sudden fury told her that she was the mistress, that Hagar was hers, hers to do as she willed with, and if she chose to use her to get children for her old age then that was just Hagar's bad luck. From the day she had received into her own hands Hagar's seal of ownership Sarah had never, ever, not once, mentioned the relationship between them until that night. Hagar had pushed Sarah away from her, stood up, stripped naked and in front of Sarah had oiled her body, flaunting the long curves of her buttocks and thighs, asked Sarah with impudence how her husband liked it best, how he would respond to virgin flesh, tight and sweet, after years of aged flesh, and with her mouth tasting of vomit she had gone out into the night and did not return for six days; and when she returned it was with a haughty knowledge and a wide sneer.

They had made up, delighted in the pregnancy, together in the birth, they had fondled and loved and embraced, but something had changed; had changed because Sarah who had called her daughter, called her beloved, called her friend, had now also called her slave and used that power over her; had changed because she let Sarah do so, because she had acted on Sarah's commanding against her own heart, because she had, named and hurt, accepted the naming, she had acted like a slave. She would never do so again. But they had together set the scene for their own betrayal of each other. And the roads of a woman's life lead clearly, straightly forwards; the seed that is sown will be the grain that is reaped, and in choices made in anger, made in pain, made in loss, the future is forged more certainly than the smith at her fire can temper the iron.

They were happy for two years, happy in their child. Hagar and Sarah's boy-child made both his mothers happy. Hagar tries, with the child dying in her arms, to hold on to that sweetness, but it is not enough. She who had no mother and no lover has lost her mother and her lover, and in the darkness of the night she knows that she will lose the child too.

But they had not chosen, and could not have chosen, and by then would not have chosen, either of them, Sarah's pregnancy. It was Abraham's victory and he strutted it before the whole encampment while Sarah was sick, stomach sick and heart sick for nine long months, embittered, sour, cross, frightened and ill. Hagar knew that, knew those things, but could not move out to her, could not understand, would not understand. When Sarah's child was due Hagar took her son and ran away into the desert; she knew the love with which Sarah had held her through that dark country in which a woman must travel searching for her child and bringing it back strong and well. Sarah had been, on that hard journey, her strength and her stay, but she could not give it back again. She could not and she did not know why she could not. It was not seemly that flesh so old should be fruitful; it was not seemly that the woman who had held her so lovingly in her arms should hold another child there. For ten days she had roamed, and it should have been a foretaste but was not, because that which is chosen, that which can be re-chosen, is different, is totally different from that which is forced upon one. She had been oddly happy those ten days away from the encampment, away from Sarah's bitterness and Abraham's obsession—the two of them had marked her life, marked it with joy and grief, but marked it beyond the reasonable; they were neither her parents nor not-her-parents; they had both been her lovers, the parents of her children. Her household, both chosen and given. For ten days she had been a free woman. Then she had gone back. Sarah was trying to suckle an obdurate, large-nosed, cheerless baby; a night screamer and day whiner, a fretful unsettled baby, not like her golden boy. "What's his name?" she had asked. "Isaac, that is 'God laughed,' " said Sarah, without laughter.

And the rest was perhaps inevitable. She, Hagar, could not bend the neck that Sarah had taught her to hold so stiff. She, Sarah, could not bend the neck that Hagar had allowed her to hold so high. Isaac grew, Ishmael grew, in stature and in love of their mothers. But his birth, too late, and in an unexpected moment, did not allay Abraham's fears. Isaac was not reared in the women's tents but in the courts of the men. She and Sarah found it hard to talk, to meet, to kiss, to be together.

There was a long week when she did not see Sarah, when Sarah was in Abraham's tent. Once she heard Sarah cry, cry out in pain and in loss, but she did not go there, they were the courts of the masters and if Sarah chose to be there that was her matter, not Hagar's. She would not ask for entrance, knowing that it would be forbidden to her. And where now were all the brave promises, the bright and childhood faith in the covenant, in the invisible and unknowable Lord who held all people in equality, for which they had gone out from their lands, from their known places, from their certainties?

"Sarah feels that it is not right that the son of Abraham should play with the seed of slaves," said Abraham.

"He is the son of Abraham," she muttered. But when he said he could not hear her she did not repeat it, she did not dare.

"Sarah says that you set yourself up against her in a manner unbecoming to a slave girl," said Abraham, and now Hagar did not know what they were saying. Abraham in that week they had been together had venerated the purple blackness of her breasts, had been amazed and delighted by the different colors flowing over her body: plum, indigo, black, crimson, pink, scarlet, nut, ash, honey, ochre, cream. The rainbow sign, he said as he stroked her, and she had believed him. The rainbow sign, the sign of hope and promise. The old lecher.

"Sarah has asked me to have you leave the camp."

She looked at Sarah once, and Sarah first lowered her eyes and then raised them and in them was a mute appeal, so beaten, so defeated, so unbearable, that she did not look again.

"You want her to go, don't you, Sarah?"

There was a silence. Both of them had pleaded for her. Surely she had the power. Even now, even in the great darkness of the desert, to believe that she could not have defied him was more painful, was even more painful than to believe that she could have and did not.

The silence stretched. Every man in the encampment, every man who had known how they loved each other and had not liked it, every woman who had known and who had seen it as a sign of hope, had waited.

Wielding his power, the power they had all given him, freely and in love, over fifty years, he said, "Don't you, Sarah?" And Hagar could feel the force of his will, the depth of his desire and need that Sarah should say it.

The desert wind hushed to hear her answer, it seemed in that encampment that the sheep themselves, the sheep the final arbitrators of their being, the lining and basis of their wealth, of their survival, paused to hear that whisper in the air: paused to hear Sarah say, "Yes."

And Hagar could not afford to see the black bruises round Sarah's eyes and neck; because dear God, she would rather, she would rather die here in the desert than acknowledge that Sarah could not have said otherwise.

Abraham, satisfied, took the child and set it on her shoulder and gave her a water skin, filled, and a sack of bread ready baked, both of which she accepted, and she turned from the camp and set out upon her lonely journey, and when Sarah came to her and offered her a head cloth, against the sun, against the sun of the desert, she had looked at her with dignity and said, "If my son were to starve before the first well I would not accept any gift from your hand. You took me as nothing out of your charity and you can dispose of me as nothing. I am yours to command."

She saw the tears spring in Sarah's eyes, and Sarah's tears sprang from deeper in her than any woman she had ever known, but tears were salt and would not comfort her child or her soul when the sun beat down on them. Sarah had chosen. Understanding was pointless, was too expensive, was unaffordable, when you were the black slave girl and she was the wife. In bitterness she said, "I am yours to command." It was the only insult available to her after so many years of love.

And now she was in the desert and pride was a bitter fruit, born from an evil root, and she wished she had been a woman who could beg and plead, and she was not; and she was not because Sarah had been her mother. There, there, was the pain; there was the unbearable, unsustainable truth. That Sarah, who had taken her from the land of the Pharaoh and told her she was lovable, who had touched her black skin and found it lovely, found in it the source and power of resistance and had given back to Hagar that strength which she had drawn from her, that it was Sarah, that it was love, which had betrayed her, which had given her child over to the desert dogs to maul in the darkness. That the name of Sarah, the name of love, that was the taste of tears, of bitterness and of thirst in her mouth, the tears that made her child smile even as he choked on them.

The dawn comes, the sun leaping up garish and sudden, no moment of grace between intense cold dark and blinding hot light. And with the morning comes despair. So she takes her child and lays him in what little shade she can find, under a scrubby tenacious bush, clinging against all odds to life in that bright wilderness. He is weaker now, bleating occasionally like an animal, and fretfully curling and uncurling his fingers. She knows he is dying and she cannot bear it, so she crawls away, moaning, and sits down about a bowshot's distance where she cannot hear his whimpers, where she will not see the moment of his death. She cannot watch him die. She seeks no shade for herself but sits cross-legged, upright, and the sun rises over her head. And by mid-morning she is half-crazed with grief and heat, and still she sits not looking at her child, looking instead straight into the sunlight which crashes against her eyes. The only black thing in that burning gold space.

And then, the world flickers . . . the whole world quivers . . . the world turns, shifts, the stars crash against each other . . . and then the world moves deep under her and the sun stands still . . . stands over her head. And then . . . and then . . . tongues cannot tell nor words proclaim what things have been prepared for those whom God loves. There is a shadow, a great cool shadow, and at the heart of the shadow is perfect darkness, blackness so thick and soft, as black and soft as her mother's breast in her high homeland of Cush, and she can taste the sweetness of the milk from those black breasts, which are like Sarah's breasts, and in the heart of the blackness are black flames which purge, burn, reduce all things to black ash, to the purity of darkness and beauty. And the great black God caresses her, arms as strong as kind as Sarah's arms, arms as fierce and tender as her mother's arms a thousand miles a thousand years ago in the mountain place where all people are black. To be touched by so much beauty where she has not been used to see any is aweful to her and she tries to cover her eyes, but she would not accept a head cloth from Sarah's hand so she has nothing to cover her face with. And God takes her by the chin and raises her head and says, "Look, look, look at me." And God says to her, soft, loud; wrapped within the God she hears Her speak and She says, "What troubles you, Hagar? Do not be afraid for God has heard the voice of your silence. Get up and give the child a drink of water, for I will make you mother of many nations." And God strips her of her clothes and caresses her, kisses her sweeter than dreaming, and the great black smile of God makes her laugh a laugh as merry and dark as Sarah's laugh once was. And God grins delightedly and is gone.

And here is Hagar, dancing, dancing naked on the desert dancing floor, leaping and singing and laughing, the long curves of her body absorbing the bright sunlight and turning it into the darkness of God, refracting, consuming, kaleidoscoping blackness, a new thing born of a brave moment. And Hagar leaping sees, sees that no distance away there is a spring, a spring of black water, sweet and wholesome, and she fetches the child a drink, and takes him by the hand and leads him over to the spring and together they built a sand heap, knowing and laughing that the wind will blow it away almost before they have completed it, but it is an altar in their own honor, and Hagar smiles and says, "Here, here I will mark the place because here I have surely seen Her who sees me. I have seen God and lived."

*A*nd they travel safely. Although it is hot and thirsty in the desert, they travel safely, south and west, until they come to the shores of the Red Sea, and there, not bothering to ask God to part the waters for them, they take passage of an Arabian dhow and so come at last to the beaches of Hagar's homeland. And she is full of joy.

SARAH

In the tent it is cool. It is cool but she is sweating.

It is cool in the tent but she is sweating.

For years I have heard Sarah's voice; for years I have strained my ears to hear it, identified with it. Not just I think the sharing of names, though that should not be discounted. It is easy for a woman like me to hear the voice of a woman like her; two women, of different time, place, space, race, but two women of privilege, articulate, sophisticated, adept, self-controlled. Women, even, of power, by class, education, marriage, status. I hear her voice too easily, Hagar's too furtively. But now . . . it is cool in the tent but she is sweating.

She is sweating with shame and confusion. Sarah is blushing—a deep hot flush that she thought she had finished with ages ago. She is blushing, sweating, ashamed. For herself. She does not like it.

For no matter how I context it, Sarah's laugh in the tent, by the oaks of Mamre, rings uncomfortably in the ear. Sarah the beautiful whom kings have desired. Sarah the courageous who followed her adventurous husband throughout the whole world. Sarah the charming, who has created and sustained a loving and fruitful relationship of great complexity and delicacy for so long. Sarah the gracious, laughing in the tent curtain and trying to deny it so that her husband's guests will not be embarrassed. Sarah the old and barren.

Why is she laughing? What are the echoes and the vibrations of her laughter? That uncomfortable, stifled laughter will not quench Hagar's thirst in the hot desert. She is laughing because it is too late. To be pregnant now will be a final twist of fate by a God who has ignored her for too long. Once, she used to pray to Him, begging Him for the child who would cement her crazy husband to her, and later praying for the child to fill the gap that seems enormous to her now that she knows that she cannot love the man she left her lovely homeplace for. Once she prayed with the same zeal and faith as he does still. Then she learned that this God of his was not hers. Everything she knew of now belonged to Abraham: the sheep, the servants, the tents, herself. And his God, too. That it is not so somewhere else, far away, in the scented courts of her childhood, is little or no comfort to her. She left them proudly, she cannot return. Abraham's God does not listen to a word she says to Him. After a while she stopped believing that her prayers would be answered; after a little longer she stopped praying.

Hagar, however, is young and lovely. Sarah despises Abraham for fancying her. She is lovely, but she is neither wise nor beautiful as Sarah was. The Pharaoh of Egypt has desired Sarah, to this she holds when there is little else to hold to. But, nonetheless, Hagar is lovely, and young. Sarah loves her: she loves Sarah. Neither of them love Abraham who pesters Hagar with his hot, but old, hands. With a slave's sensitivity to what is and is not permissible Hagar tells Sarah that Abraham fancies her; she does not tell Sarah that the old man disgusts her. With a wife's sensitivity Sarah knows this anyway and decides it will be best for all concerned if she ignores it.

Sarah is a woman of great dignity. She is not prepared to have her husband touching up slave girls behind the tents. She is not going to have Hagar, her maidservant and friend, made a byword for sheep boys. She loves Hagar: the energy that she once directed towards her husband is now redirected. Some evening when Hagar is brushing her hair, tenderly back away from her face, brushing it admiringly up from the nape of Sarah's still glorious neck, sending shivers of plea- sure down Sarah's spine, Sarah reaches up a single hand and touches the younger woman's wrist, or she leans back so that her head rests on the pliant stomach of her friend. Hagar is young enough to be her daughter; she has won this lovely daughter for herself. She decides she will let it be easy, and from then on it is easy. She lures the two of them to bed, teasing and encouraging Hagar, binding Abraham more subtly to her will. Hagar's baby is therefore her baby; she created the relationship that conceived him. Ishmael is her delight, her son: she had achieved him by the use of all the power and skill that she holds in her own two hands.

"Ishmael, Ishmael," she calls, and he comes, crawling, staggering, then running, from Hagar to Sarah and back again. Sarah is not jealous, at this time, of Hagar. She and Hagar are good friends. They share the child, they share the relief, never quite named, that Abra- ham, now satisfied in his obsession, bothers them both less. They feel free to concentrate on their son. Sarah is, for now, perfectly happy; for now she is a mother twice over. A mother to Hagar whose man she chose with truly maternal care, whose back she supported through the long night while the child was pushed laboriously towards life, that great and mighty work, that costly and rewarding labor. A mother to Ishmael, because she called him into being, not by lust but by intelligence. Moreover she no longer has to endure the embraces of that senile goat whom she used to love, and for whom she sold her own life and thought it a bargain.

She stifles her laugh in the curtains of the tent, because it is not a very nice laugh. She does not now want Abraham's child: she already has her own children. This is a last trick by Abraham's God. Although she does not believe that Abraham's God listens to her or cares about her, she has no doubt at all that He exists, and that her husband and his God plot together to get the best of all possible worlds for Abraham.

She thought she had outwitted them and now her puny body is going to betray her.

There is no more faith possible.

"Why are you laughing?" Abraham and his God's messenger say.

"Laughing? Me? I wasn't laughing."

"You were laughing. Don't you believe that you are going to have my son? Don't you believe that my God can do anything He wants to?"

Her laughter turns to racking sobs, but the men do not hear them. The sobs continue painful, unending, for nine months. Isaac is born. Her body is too old for this and it takes its toll. She hates Isaac. He is not her son, because she did not consent to him. Instead she consents to her own degradation. She lets Abraham make her say it, she lets Hagar be sent away. Isaac looks like his father from birth. He is not beautiful and spoiled like Ishmael; he is sturdy and clever and arrogant. She weeps and weeps. Hagar and Ishmael are sent away. She is defeated and she punishes the only person she can punish. Abraham wants Hagar out, and Sarah consents. Punishing Hagar she is punishing herself, and she feels Hagar's hatred and is, for a brief moment, glad of it. She cannot talk to anyone; nor can she forgive herself. Hagar and Ishmael have to go; they must not be allowed to confuse the issue, to detract from Abraham's real son. As the mother of his son he loves Sarah again, and she hates him for that too. Abraham hears her anguish; he says that Sarah is jealous of Hagar and Ishmael, and that this will spoil her milk. Ishmael sucked at her empty breasts for the simple pleasure of it, but Isaac will not feed from her at all. Her breasts are huge, swollen, revolting, but her son will not feed from her at all. The milk will not flow, her tears flow instead. She wishes she were dead and that will not help. She does not want Isaac, she wants the children of her heart and mind, not this child of her gut, so she condemns them to die of thirst in the desert. She knows that she will not ever be forgiven.

When she hears the messenger speak, down by the oaks of Mamre, she knows that she, who has plotted and schemed so carefully for so long, has been outwitted. The joke, subtle and tortuous, is—like all the best jokes—a matter of timing. She is a sophisticated woman. Of course she laughs.

She laughs at herself and all her plotting. It is best to laugh at foolish women who think they can get their own way in a world where even God is a man and on the other side.

ABRAHAM

I thought, I really did, in all sincerity, that I would write Abraham's story too. I thought I would write it here, like the others, trying to recreate it, enter in to it, understand it; tell it.

But I'm not going to.

Not because I think I couldn't do it. On good days I have immense faith in the power of my own imagination (and other people's too of course). If I want to do that sort of story I can, and will. I even have now and again, though not often. (Whether men can do women's stories is another question, one that feminist literary discourse asks often; but it is certain that the oppressed develop insights about their oppressors to a greater degree than the other way about because they need them in order to survive—a sort of natural selection, like Darwinian evolution.) So, no, it is not because I don't think I could not do Abraham's story, but because I can't be bothered.

Anyway, almost everyone knows it already. If you really don't, and you really want to, here's what you should do. Sneak into almost any second-rate hotel (there are hotels both too grand and too grotty for this to work, but a decent old-fashioned railway hotel, for instance, will do nicely, and so will one of those vast international chains where every branch looks identical, like a Holiday Inn). Open the drawers of the bedside cabinets, and in one of them you will find—sometimes accompanied by adverts for local car-hire firms etc.—a fairly bulky hard-covered book. This is entitled *The Holy Bible* and has been placed there by a charitable organization which holds Abraham's version of this story dearer to its heart than I hold it to mine. This *Holy Bible* is not a single coherent text and should not be read as such. It is rather a curious, and very beautiful anthology— poems, stories, philosophy, helpful maxims, ethics, diet advice and mythology all jumbled up, a sort of *Commonplace Book of Western Culture* (no I haven't forgotten the Greeks) put together by a slightly crazed editor. Never mind all this: the first—and from a reader's point of view one of the best—section of this anthology is called *Genesis,* which is itself an anthology. Chapters 12 to 25 deal with Abraham's story. Chapters 16, 17, part of 18 and 21 deal particularly with his relationships, if such they may be called, with Hagar and Sarah.

(The rest of 18 and 19 will introduce you to a nasty little tale of homophobia and misogyny. Don't miss it. Ask yourself rather how it fits in here.)

So now you know Abraham's story; the story of the first patriarch. I could not have told it better myself. So instead of telling it again I am going to put on my theological hat and give you a few brief notes from the *S. L. Maitland Biblical Commentary.*

i) From a literary aesthetic point of view the whole thing is chaotic, clumsily narrated, muddled and repetitious. Incidents, clearly garnered from different sources, are confused, conflated, reused but not integrated. This reflects the extraordinary skill of the compilers: only by lulling the reader half asleep with tedium and confusion can they hope to slip past her some intolerable sets of attitudes, some moral turpitude of such depth that normal concepts of ethics cannot even address the material and at the same time manage to persuade three thousand years' worth of readers from diverse cultures, philosophies and social contexts that is the wellspring of God's will towards justice, of decency, of normality.

ii) Father Abraham is, frankly, a real bastard. Among other things, he lives off his wife's immoral earnings (cf. chapter 12 verses 10-20 *et al.*); he is prepared to bump off his supposedly beloved son in order to please his boss and gain material advantages (chapter 22). He is almost certainly insane and demonstrably selfish, autocratic, lecherous, cowardly, violent and megalomaniacal. All these things are renamed "virtue." This is called patriarchy.

iii) Here we see, perhaps for the first time in recorded history, one of the classic devices used by men against women. Sarah, the wife, gets blamed but not punished. Hagar, the mistress, gets punished but not blamed. Abraham gets neither; he has his cake and eats it too. This is neat.

iv) The compilers, despite what has to be seen as a first-class job, make two very serious errors. First, in the face of their best efforts, they dismally fail to write out, or suppress, the abiding emotional reality of Sarah and Hagar. At their every appearance the text vibrates, leaping, shining, buoyant, alive. It is there, it is undeniably there—Hagar praising in the wilderness, Sarah laughing in her tent. Their vitality searing the pages across the long silences.

Second, and even more serious, the compilers failed to edit out an extraordinarily and revealing fact. There is only one person in the *whole* of this weird and wonderful book who "Sees God and Lives." And she is Hagar, slave, foreigner, unmarried mother; the woman expelled from the protection of the encampment, driven out of the book, the woman who sojourns in the desert, the outcast, the stranger. And there she is, singing, dancing, rejoicing. How can we not rejoice with her? Whatever were they thinking of, those priestly, juridical editors, that they let her dance undamaged in the mid-day sun?

You probably don't like the tone of this bit of the story. I don't blame you, I don't really like it much myself—edgy, cranky, cynical; it is not even "proper fiction." Let us get back to the mythic, the lyrically imaginative, as quickly as possible. Let us bring that hyped-up prose, that imaginative understanding, that poetic psychoanalysis, to bear on that poor crazed old man; let us explore, illuminate, perhaps even beautify those dark corners of his driving obsession.

I do wish I could. But it is too soon and too late. To understand all is to forgive all. And I do not want to forgive. I cannot forgive. I am Hagar who is driven into the desert. I am Sarah who betrays her friend. This nasty cynicism which destroys joy, hope, transformation, magic, truth, love, it is still necessary, still—as always—a useful mutation, an adaptation vital to the survival of the species. As we dance, dance on the hot sands and rejoice, as we laugh, laugh in the cool tents and weep, we must remember and give thanks for that too, alas.

Apple Picking

Classic Baked Apple

4 large apples
8 tbsp jam
1 oz butter
4 tbsp sugar
4 tbsp castor sugar

1) Wash, dry and core apples.
2) Place in a greased ovenproof dish and fill each apple with jam. Add a small knob of butter to each.
3) Put water in the bottom of dish, then bake at 375° F, (190° C) for 25 minutes. Serve sprinkled with sugar and cream if desired.

Of course I loved the baby. Of course I did. That was the point. It was because I loved the baby. My breasts would ache with loving that baby. Sometimes I would lie in the bath, soaking deep, deep in hot water, toe tips, tummy, nipples and neck—with head and curly hair looped up into an elastic band on the top—sticking out, like little pink coral islands in ocean of warmth. And I would soak there staring at the islands of my breasts, and watching that magical marbling of the water where the milk flowed invisibly out. Sweet fine food for my lovely milky baby.

Mother Angela, her skin as fine as tissue paper, her smile as bright as morning, places her almost transparent hand on her little novice's head. It is a touch gentle and loving, but it is also a judgment and a reprimand. Sister Juliana puts down the cup. She wants to say, "But Mother I am thirsty." Mother Angela knows that she wants to say so, and knows too that she herself wants to reply, "Child, so am I. I have been thirsty from matins until vespers for forty-two years, and I am still thirsty. Let us, just this once as no one is watching us, drink and drink; even plants need watering and so do we; let us let the cold sweet water dribble down our chins and cool our necks." And deep in her is again and still a sense of the profound unfairness of God. Their Blessed Sister Catherine in Siena, who was only a tertiary, who was not even a nun, was freed by Christ from hunger, she felt no hunger, she felt only repulsion. And yet she herself, fifty years on, would still wake in the night her stomach churning with hunger—not even for the exotic food of her noble childhood, but for something as simple as a little piece of bread, the piece her old nurse used to give her, broken in the morning from the end of the loaf, crusty and cool. And this little one, this secret favorite of all her novices, of all her daughters—what mother does not wish to nourish the child that comes to her in hunger and thirst? What mother does not desire to open her dress and let the little one suck and suck?

But Sister Juliana is not a child; Sister Juliana is not a baby. Sister Juliana, fifteen years old and beautiful, is a woman. The time has come for her to put away childish things. What Mother does not desire for her child the sight of the living God, the salvation prepared for her before the dawn of time, the robes of glory like a bride with which the angels will clothe her?

She says only, "Dear Sister, Christ thirsted on the cross and no one gave him fresh water, and yet he has promised that he will give you the water of life, and then you will never be thirsty again. Come." And she rests her ancient hand on Sister Juliana's arm, pretending to need support, and leads her away across the cloister, away from the well, away from temptation. Later she will speak to the Sisters in Chapter, speak with that sweetness and wit which have made her renowned, which bring Bishops and rulers to her cloister door seeking advice, which bring lovely children to the novitiate so that she will have to undertake the responsibility of seeing their tired and hungry faces in the refectory, of hearing the strange swish and thud sound that twenty women together taking the discipline in their cells make Friday after Friday. She is tired now herself, but later she will remind them that their brothers train themselves, discipline themselves and starve themselves just for the week of festival so that they can outrun one another in races and leap up the palazzo steps to claim their garlands and prizes. The Blessed Apostle Paul had told them they must run the race so as to win it; the garland that Christ will put on their heads will be of flowers that never fade, the prize will be the beauty of God's glory forever, the sweetness of his presence everlasting. They were God's athletes: would they be other than in training?

Oh I loved the baby. I know a lot of women who hate those night feeds, but not me; I remember those as peaceful and happy times. On the sofa in our living room, cushions piled around both of us, a throne of warmth and comfort, a book, a box of those wonderful dark Bentick chocolates, and the pale, scrambled-egg-colored dawns, thickening visibly out of the grey times at the end of the darkness. And the autumn sun rising apricot gold and the baby, softly furred as a peach, warm as toast, buttery and cuddly, laid sweetly across my soft belly and sucking, sucking, sucking at my breasts. A land of milk and honey for my sweet child. Tiny joyful grunts and squeaks. My own little suckling pig with my apple in its mouth. Loved? I adored the baby. Don't look at me like that.

Anyway it isn't my fault. You can't understand. You never knew my mother. No, I'm not blaming her, I'm not saying a word against her, now or ever, but you do have to understand. She had a hard life, I mean a hard childhood. You look around you now, at the flat and at me and at Tony, and it is too easy to forget that we have done most of this ourselves. I'm not lazy, I have worked hard. Like my mother. She was born in 1922, in Sunderland, the oldest of six children; one a year for six years, they were good Catholics my grandparents. Her father worked in the docks, he was a good man, a good man and a good hard-working docker. I remember Pa—we all called him Pa; now Nan I don't remember, she died when I was little, I hardly ever saw her, Sunderland was a very long way from Bristol when I was growing up. But my mother remembered her, talked about her, made us know her—a big strong Wearside woman, and you had to be to bring six children through the Depression, up there then.

When my mother was growing up there wasn't enough to eat. As simple as that. In 1934 my mother's little sister, the next one down from her, died. You can't say she died of starvation. My mother always said she died of the measles, but people don't die of the measles if they're well fed, if they're strong and healthy. I had the measles, I expect you had the measles, everyone has the measles. Well my would-have-been aunt died of the measles when my mother was twelve years old. That's bound to affect someone, isn't it? No, I don't blame her. I'm just trying to explain.

She did well in school, all things considered, and Pa and Nan supported her in that. She got to the grammar school, and they were proud of her—sturdy Geordie Labour Party they were both of them, and they believed in education, even for the girls. My mother always said she would have gone into local government, as a secretary, been a civil servant, something like that, a long way up for a docker's daughter in the thirties. Then the war came. My mother had a "good war" as it's called. She was sent to India. She loved it—well it wasn't Tyne and Wear in the Depression for one thing. She got promoted and she ended up a sergeant. She liked India too, it was hot and colorful; when she talked about it you could always see her glow a bit. She was demobilized in 1946. She once told me she was scared then; scared to go back home to all that poverty and waste and greyness and the outside loo. She met my father in London on her de-mob leave, and they got married six months later. He was a school-teacher and became headmaster of a small primary school in Bristol. It was a long way up and a long way away from the Sunderland docks. It was the 1950s, the "you've never had it so good" years, and for her that was true. She had me in 1950 and my sister in 1953 and my little brother in 1958. She was happy, fulfilled and con-tented, but she didn't forget anything. When I was two I won a "bouncing baby" competition. She was so proud. She kept that photograph of sweet chubby me and a huge cup right out on the front room mantelpiece. And I know why: she could feed her children. She loved to feed us. She used to bake us biscuits. I'd come in from school and there would be this warm, rich smell; little round hot biscuits with crunchy brown sugar on top. And cinnamon toast, nursery toast we used to call it; even now the smell of hot cinnamon and butter makes me drool. Sunday lunch, shoulder of lamb and gravy, roast potatoes, little and crispy, and then baked apples with cloves stuck in and custard, or apple crumble. Those sorts of things. Roast chicken with little bacon rolls on your birthday, and mashed potatoes silky smooth, and suet pudding with golden syrup on the top sinking in and trickling down the sides like those little hill villages in Umbria, and pork chops, and something called cheese dreams, we used to have them for tea on Sundays, baked slowly in the oven, the only meal in the world that justifies those dreadful Kraft processed cheese slices, and you can't make them right with anything else.

She was immensely understanding. Later on, when I was about ten or twelve I suppose, I started doing something that was really quite naughty; if my father had known he would have half-killed me I expect: though talking it over now with friends I think that almost all children do it at some time or another—I used to take money from her purse, or steal small change if she sent me on errands. I used to buy cream buns from the baker: doughnuts stuffed with that fake cream which now I couldn't swallow if I had to. I don't know why; it wasn't hunger, it was the utter delightful wickedness of it I think. Hiding round the back until you had finished, wiping your mouth very very carefully, checking your front for crumbs—they were the best tasting doughnuts I have ever sampled. The point is that my mother knew—she told me so years later—and decided to let me keep my secret. She never said a word. I think she was proud in a way that she had enough money for it not to be a disaster if her children nicked the odd small change, but I think more than that she understood, understood wisely and deeply the need for secrecy, the need for secret feeding and special treats. It was love for her and it was food and she was happy, and so were we.

Krapfen

2 eggs
3 fl oz beer
4 oz plain flour
pinch of salt
1½ lb dessert apples
oil for frying
sugar and cinnamon

1) Separate eggs. Beat yolks, beer, flour and salt to a smooth batter. In another bowl beat the egg whites till stiff, then fold into the batter.
2) Peel and grate the apples, then mix into the batter.
3) Heat the oil for frying to 360° F (180° C) in a deep fryer.
4) Slide spoonfuls of the apples and batter mixture into the hot oil and fry for about 2 minutes, or until crisp.
5) When cooked, remove from pan on slotted spoon, drain well, roll krapfen in castor sugar and cinnamon mixed. Serve hot.

In her stall in the dim chapel Mother Angela excoriates herself for the sin of envy; her conscience scalds her. Deep under the folds of her habit her hands twitch distressfully. She stills them, but she cannot still either her envy or her conscience. Who is she to envy the graces that God sees fit to offer the deserving? Who is she to envy Sister Catherine the peace of not feeling hunger? God does with each soul what is proper for it. Who is she to question that the hunger, the daily suffering from it, is not itself a grace from God, allowing her to be ever more united with the suffering humanity of her savior on the cross. She does not, she tells herself sternly, she does not need ecstasy, she does not need visions, God has dealt graciously with her. She needs no spiritual gymnastics when daily, daily, she can receive the physical humanity of God in the Sacrament.

Yet I, least of all souls,
Take Him in my hand.

Eat Him and drink Him
And do with Him what I will.
Why then should I trouble myself
As to what the angels experience?

Not her own words, alas, even that joy she has never been given. No joys, no graces, no ecstatic visions, no angelic experiences. Just a long, long life. "Take me home," she wants to demand of her God, she has after all demanded more of Kings. She banishes the thought. Her nagging hunger replaces it. Under her habit her hands clench suddenly in an attack of physical rage, that fades almost immediately into irritation and then guilt.

For God's sake don't look at me like that. If there's one thing I can't stand it's that sort of puritanism about food. I can't abide it. It's bloody unfeminist as well. There's no morality in skinniness you know. Fat is a feminist issue. I'm not going to reconstruct my whole body to give pleasure to some dictatorial fashion bosses. Tony isn't complaining. Wasn't. He liked it. It's not as though I was obese; well . . . well I admit at the moment that I'm not in great shape, but I did have a baby less than six months ago you know. I can take it off any time I want to. It's interesting how deep that dualism goes, isn't it? That real hatred of the body and the flesh; the more the worse. Funny that the '60s set sex free for those who want it; now if you're not fucking like a bunny rabbit you must be neurotic, but food goes on being wicked, yes wicked. Naughty but nice. There's nothing wrong with a little bit of hedonism. Pleasure is an important principle. Look at all those poor little kids with anorexia and bulimia and all those other eating disorders—it is exactly, it's exactly that expression of yours that has done that to them. Yes I feel guilty, of course I bloody feel guilty, but I hope you do too.

Oh God . . .

All right if I'm honest I have to admit that the whole thing was getting out of control, I mean years ago.

I'll tell you a story. We laugh about it quite often, me and my friends, Tony and others. Well, we used to; I don't suppose anyone will laugh about it again. When I was an undergraduate I went on a holiday to Italy—to Tuscany and Umbria mostly, we toured around a lot. It was great fun. We had this little battered car and there were four of us and we traveled about, just looking and enjoying; sitting in bar-cafés and drinking cappuccini and eating those wonderful little sweet pastries, and fruit, and big rough bowls of wonderful pasta. What's your favorite? Mine's cappelletti in brodo I think; when that ricotta and spinach stuffing sort of explodes into your mouth. And the sun hot, hot, hot and those wonderful peaches. In Venice they have little blood oranges and in Florence that unbelievable *gelato limone* that you can just buy from quite ordinary ice-cream stands in the street. And I still say that when it comes to cheap wine—I'm not talking about real claret or anything, I just mean plonk, that there is nothing to touch some of those rural white wines from central Italy. Good imported Orvieto, secco of course, isn't bad at the moment, but it doesn't have that almost flowery taste that you can get if you're lucky in some little taverna off the main road, and you can sit in the shade all afternoon, and drink and eat those stunning great fat peaches, all dribbly until the wasps come. And that was the first time I'd ever been. We go most years now of course, Tony and I. It was the first time and I was overwhelmed by it, even though I didn't really know then what to look for and often would take the *menu turistico* and look round at local people and wonder how you could order the things they were eating. Zucchini flowers for instance: you know, you'd see them in the greengrocers and think "how odd." When someone showed me how to dip them in flour and deep fry them I thought I had learned what the angels eat in heaven.

Anyway there we were, and the people I was with were lovely and we had a lot of fun. But the point is, we went one day to Gubbio, which—and I've been back so I know—is the most enchanting town. Very dark and troubled under its mountain. Well we arrived in Gubbio at about mid-morning, and then we split up. Different people wanted to do different things—they make nice pottery there and Clare wanted to look for some and there are a couple of museums and the cathedral right at the top. When we got back at the appointed hour, the other three were all full of their cultural delights and they asked me what I had been doing and it turned out that I had spent the whole two hours looking for a restaurant for us to have lunch in. I had inspected every damn eating place in the town I should think, for money value and for food value. It was mean of them to laugh, because they liked the food too: I had found a gem, where we had some cold veal with cream and caper sauce. I can still remember, and they appreciated it. But they always laugh about it now and call me the woman who prefers menus to the renaissance.

It isn't fair really, because they all like coming to dinner still, and I cook better than almost anyone I know. Clare came only a month or so ago, to meet the baby. She's one of those people that when you go to dinner there you arrive at eight and you know she hasn't even started cooking, she may not even have decided what she's going to cook and she laughs and calls it pot luck, and then everyone has to drink for hours while she messes about; and by then you're too drunk to enjoy it, even if it were to be enjoyable food, which it usually isn't. I do think that is rude. It seems to me that if you ask people to eat with you you do owe them something halfway decent. And when she comes here she eats like a pig. It's all right for them to be so high-minded about a bit of Italian culture, but she never turns down decent food if someone else will make it for her. Speaking of which, would you like something to eat? I've got some quite OK apple cake in the kitchen. All right. You think this is in bad taste don't you. What do you expect me to do? Starve myself to death? It's not just my fault. It's not just my fault. I'm sorry. Ohh . . . oh God. Oh God . . .

Hot apple flan with calvados

    8 oz sweet flan pastry as preferred
    1½ lbs cooking apples
    2 oz butter
    5 oz icing sugar
    3 tbsp calvados

1) Bake pastry blind in 8-inch flan ring.
2) While pastry is cooking, peel and core apples, and cut into quarters or eighths depending on size.
3) Melt butter in saucepan, add apples and cook over high heat until they are light brown.
4) Add 4 oz icing sugar and 2 tbsp calvados and cook gently until apples are tender.
5) Spoon apples and some of the juice into the warm cooked flan case. Sprinkle sieved icing sugar over and place in warm oven until needed.
6) To serve: warm remaining calvados in a ladle. Light and pour over flan immediately. Take, flaming, to table, and serve with whipped cream.

Weariness, for Mother Angela, is one more thing that must be put aside. She rises from her stall and goes to the refectory. Her daughters rise and bow. She takes her place and sings a blessing. In front of each sister there is a small cube of bread, and a glass of water. The water is drawn at dawn and set in the sun; now it is warm and a little dusty. In a row along the center of the table are set bowls of olives. They have been there for several days and their skins are shriveling. Every sister is free to eat them: very few of them do. Mother Angela observes them with pleasure, her huge shining eyes full of love and holiness. She notices that Sister Maria is crumbling her bread needlessly; later Mother Angela will tell her that it is as much a discipline to eat what you are given as it is to fast. Christ gives them himself in the form of bread, bread is sacred, not to be sprinkled under the table secretly, but eaten and rejoiced in. Did they not come to this place to imitate the poverty of Christ: the poor do not scatter good bread on the floor. Sister Maria will be sulky, as she too often is, but Mother Angela wants no hysterical excitement in her house; no manifestations of the miraculous, and no dying young women, she has seen that too often and loves them all too much. She wants love and prayer, prayer and love: when Sister Maria learns to smile Mother Angela will let her fast further. She looks down at her own cube of bread and takes a hold of herself so that she does not cream it into her mouth, salivating and munching, but treats it as the holy thing it is. There must be courtesy here at the bare table, courtesy greater than that displayed in the Courts of Princes, out of respect for the bread, out of love for the giver and out of charity for the company. But she is so hungry. And when she is hungry the bread tastes so sweet; she tries to hold it in her mouth to prolong her pleasure, but her throat and stomach demand it. She swallows and rejoices. She overcomes a spontaneous desire to help herself to one of the olives. She imagines the moment of stillness that would descend on the refectory if she were to do so, and she laughs internally.

I got my degree in 1972. And you remember how exciting everything was then. There was feminism, which was and still is immensely important to me, I felt we were on the edge of something huge and real; the old standards were being desecrated and profaned. I gave up being a Catholic, I stripped myself of all those old guilts, it seemed summer all the time and I was very happy. I went to London and started working for a libertarian magazine; I wanted to be a political journalist then, but for various reasons I started doing a series of restaurant reviews for them—kind of adding it on to my editorial duties; it was rather fun and there were lots of new places opening up and lots of old places that people hadn't heard of. And I was good at it. Then we added a cooking column, it was meant to be magically radical somehow: how to put hash into chocolate-chip cookies and where to find free-range eggs, but I started to believe then, what I certainly believe now: that a great deal too much fuss has been made about those sorts of things, and that the most radical thing you can do around food issues is to enjoy things. More and more my column was about enjoying cooking, enjoying food. You can make wonderful meals very cheaply if you want to, if you bother to think about it.

It's not just conspicuous consumption you know. In the early seventies there was a great deal of puritanism about those sorts of things, but the women's movement has grown up now. We used to be so stern with each other, all that endless brown rice and lentils— though actually you can do some pretty neat things with lentils if you put your mind to it, but you know what I mean. So when I was offered the job at *You and Yours* I jumped at it. Some people were a bit dubious—it is after all hardly a hotbed of the revolution, but I thought that it was important that women did get those big jobs, I didn't want to be part of a ghetto, I wanted to take feminism into the real world: no one bitched when other women went to work for the *Guardian* and so on. It is true that the sort of writing I do now is rather more gourmet, but we've all grown up and got richer, and despite all the mockery I don't see anything much wrong with being a foodie. And the television program was a lot of fun you have to admit. The job I liked best of all actually was the time I spent with the supermarket chain, introducing women—via those little cards— to things they wouldn't have known how to cook before.

And then I met Tony, and fell in love. Yes, he is very rich, and of course I like that, I'm not going to pretend I don't. Wouldn't you? Are you jealous? And he is an old Tory. But, well you can't control love can you, and he certainly doesn't bully me. I mean I haven't changed my politics because of him. Oh for God's sake; yes, it is true I voted SDP. I'm sick and tired of the Labour Party if you really want to know—what real support has it ever given to women?

Look, do you want me to tell you about the baby or not? OK. I got pregnant. I was really pleased, I was so happy I can't even tell you. I was over the moon. You know how it feels, something valuable and special tucked inside you, growing there, filling you up, ripening secretly. My truffle, I used to think, my precious underground peanut. You know. When the baby moved I could feel it like a fish; my lovely troutling I would sing to my stomach. There was the baby rising perfectly like a soufflé: I have some really pretty Edwardian soufflé dishes, individual soufflé dishes, you know the little ones with sides a bit higher than ramekins; they are fluted and hand-painted, with gilded rims. They are rather valuable and very beautiful—and that was what I felt like. I read somewhere that when West Indian teenagers go out all dressed up and walk in that lordly way they have down the streets, showing off, they call it "strutting your stuff"; well when I was pregnant I wanted to strut my stuff all round the world, and at the same time it was secret and dark in there where I was cooking up my delicious baby: it used to make me laugh, just thinking that happy thought. You know when a soufflé is cooking you aren't meant to crash things around, and you aren't meant to look in the oven. Actually that's a bit of a myth now because with thermostat-controlled ovens the whole soufflé business is a doddle—but so is pregnancy, or it was for me so perhaps the analogy holds. When I had my amniocentesis they said they could tell me what sex the baby was going to be but I did not want to know—I felt it would be like peeking at a soufflé rather than waiting just longer than you think you should, and then snatching it out with the top edges just splitting open and browning perfectly and everyone saying "ooh" and "ahhh" and "oh, aren't you clever?" and that extraordinary mixture of sweet and savory that a good dessert soufflé gives you; it's one of the few very hot things that really do melt in the mouth.

In fact I cooked quite a lot of soufflés while I was expecting the baby. They were wonderful to eat, light and nourishing and fun and I had this little private joke about being a soufflé dish, which made me giggle more and more as my tummy swelled.

And the birth was good too. Not quick or easy particularly, but emotionally rich, darker than I had expected. But down there in the depths of the darkness there is a great rich place, tasting of chocolate fudge cake, a warm place in the bottom of the pain. Tony was wonderful. He was simply there for me, and also there between me and the world, so that no one could interfere with that dark rich center. I had not expected it quite honestly, not expected to be given so much of him. He had remembered everything, Buxton water on a sponge to suck, ice in a tidy thermos, and afterwards, before the slightly shocked eyes of the midwife and doctor, he stood there in the labor ward and mixed the best Bloody Mary I have ever tasted, and abracadabra out of his briefcase like a conjurer he produced pâté de foie gras and little biscuits and made the hospital people eat them with us, and then strawberries in a real punnet instead of a plastic container. The two of us were laughing, and the baby so perfectly sweet and delightful was sucking and sleeping. Oh I was so happy.

Mother Angela goes to her cell, still biting down on her hunger and tiredness, still full of rejoicing. Of one thing at least she is certain and that is that God prefers a loving heart to a bleeding back. Christ's back bled and his hands and feet and side were pierced because he loved us. Not to force himself into love, but because he already loved. Love first, then the disciplines of loving.

Just training, she tells herself, as she has told three generations of novices. Just sharing with him what he shared with us. In unity. In unity, she murmurs. If you do not love the body there is no purpose to disciplining it. When we learn to read, held in our mother's arms, taken from our toys, we do not imagine that we hate the intelligence, but we must train it, train it. When we struggle out of bed to pray we do not imagine that we hate the soul, no we love the soul and train it up the way it, of its true nature, desires to go. We have been given a way, we may unite ourselves with God, through discipline. Surely it is worth it. That it works she has no doubt; she has not doubted since that strange spring forty years ago when she and Francis had been tempted, when she had been overwhelmed with desire, when her body made its own demands although her head and her heart and her spirit had no desire to leave her lovely convent, the sweet company of her sisters, to bring on him and herself both shame and unhappiness. But she had learned, as the little novices learn now, to subdue the flesh, to keep it in its place, and now she is old and honored and happy.

She is trying, she realizes, to persuade herself; to silence the other self who says you are over seventy years old and you have earned a rest. One olive cannot do an old lady any harm. The olives will still be sitting on the table, one shriveled olive, not even especially sweet, just one. She wavers. Then she lies down on her pallet. "Get thee behind me, Satan," she says and fixes her eyes on the image of Mary holding the sweet child. She gives thanks that she has resisted the temptation to eat, even though she cannot believe that Mary will appreciate how real the temptation is. She lies quietly waiting for sleep.

Mary says to her quite clearly and not in the ears of her mind, but in the ears of her flesh, Mary says, "Dear Child, you have nourished so many; now nourish my son." And Mary places the infant Jesus in Mother Angela's arms. It is over fifty years since Mother Angela has held a baby, and she takes the Christ Child tentatively, but her breasts, her ancient saggy breasts with nipples as wrinkled as the olives, respond, and his warm sleepy little hand curves up, petting her. Milk and love flow from her into him, and she can scarcely bear the happiness he gives her. She feeds him for a while until he seems to sleep and then, with a gracious word of thanks, she returns him to his mother. She is weeping with delight and humility, almost she wonders whether Mary can really know of her weakness and her temptation. She is not worthy. Mary says, "There is no worthiness, but that God has called you worthy." The two women smile over the sleeping baby.

And then with a trumpet blast and surrounded by angels, the great Ruler of the Creation comes to her; the five wounds glow with fire and the whole universe is a tiny jewel in his crown. "Blessed," sing the angels, "blessed are they who hunger and thirst after righteousness for they shall be satisfied." And he takes her in the power of his arms and opens the dazzling raiment and feeds her at his breast and the milk is sweeter than wine and smells of distant honey. The angels sing, "Oh taste and see the sweetness of the Lord," and she suckles and suckles, a little child again in the arms of love, a young woman again in the arms of her lover, an old old lady who had not dared to hope to be given such glory.

Alsatian apple tart

Pastry	Filling
8 oz plain flour	4 Golden Delicious apples
4 oz butter	2¹/₂ oz castor sugar
2 tbsp castor sugar	¹/₂ pint double cream
1 egg	2 eggs
white wine to mix	2 oz vanilla sugar
	1 lemon

1) Mix pastry and cool for 30 mins. Then roll on lightly floured surface to line 9-inch flan dish. Bake blind at 400° F (200° C) for 20 minutes.

2) Peel apples, cut in half and remove cores. Arrange on pastry, round side up; sprinkle lightly with sugar and bake for 10 minutes.

3) Meanwhile, whip cream and beat in eggs, vanilla sugar, grated rind of lemon and castor sugar until creamy. Spread creamed mixture over apples. Reduce heat to 350° F (180° C) and cook tart for 20 minutes. Serve warm.

Yes, I am getting to the point. I'm trying to anyway. It is hard to talk about the baby. She was completely lovely. She was so soft and dimpled and silly and funny and loving and warm and strong and sweet. She was almost totally bald when she was born but her ears had a fringe of adorable fair hair along the top of them, like a pixie, surprisingly long. If you held her up to the sunlight her ears would glow pink and her ear-fringe would shine like spun gold. It made Tony and me giggle.

And then one night I got up to feed her. She was crying so I got up to feed her. When I went to her crib she was yelling but as soon as she saw me she smiled, a great wide welcoming grin and immediately I was happy to be up with her, and I carried her into the living room and fed her. She sucked and sucked, and I smiled and teased her, called her a greedy little thing, but gently, and night was thinning out into morning, and when she had finished and dozed off, I was ravenously hungry. I shifted her onto my shoulder and went into the kitchen to find something to eat and there was practically nothing; certainly nothing you could prepare one-handed with a baby on your shoulder. No, not nothing, I had forgotten. There was a small piece of dolcelatte. I remember now, because I looked at it and thought how like my breast it was, soft and creamy with those delicate veins. And I ate it and I was still famished, starving and a bit cross with Tony for being so selfish and eating all the leftovers even the ginger biscuits. I thought I would put the baby back to bed and then cook something. I carried her into her room and started to change her nappy. She was still pretty much asleep, with her arms tucked in close against her body, so I didn't put the ceiling light on, just the soft glow from the night light. She was wearing one of those sleep suits that you are supposed to be able to change a nappy without taking off, but it was soaking. I was irritated and I almost didn't bother; you can just slip a clean nappy on and let it go if you want to. I wish I had. But I wanted her to sleep comfortably, so that I could too later in the morning when I was full of whatever it was I was going to cook myself. So I stripped her right off, even her vest once I had got started; she had those little vests that cross over and tie in the front because she never seemed to like having things pulled over her head. And then she was naked and sleepy and fat and sweet and I was tired and hungry and I reached for a clean vest and she rolled over and there was her beautiful little rump stuck up in the air and those wonderful ears just catching the gentle light, and I knew exactly what I was doing and I knew I shouldn't and I couldn't resist it. It was as simple as that, I couldn't resist it. Just one bite I said to myself, one bite won't hurt her. She tasted heavenly. After the first bite I couldn't stop. A delicate cross between chicken and veal I would say; I thought of salt and perhaps paprika, but I didn't have them to hand, and I couldn't stop to go and get them. I ate my baby, à la tartare. It was the best meal I had ever had. Simply delicious. I loved her. I loved her and I ate her.

After considerable thought, and consultation with her confessor, Mother Angela told no one of the gift she had been given. She wanted no hysterical excitements and manifestations of the miraculous in her house. Nor does she want her daughters to grow up believing that penance and training and love are in order to gain spiritual prowess. But she was contented. Even when the glorious vision faded she was left with another, a lighter gift, and as she goes about her convent, from dim chapel to bright garden, from austere cell to airy refectory, over and over again she sees Eve pause.

Eve must have paused just before she bit into the apple, either then or just before she plucked it from the tree. She paused, but this was Eden, this was the original sinless apple, round and smooth and smelling of the first long perfect summer in all creation. She was overwhelmed with longing. She ate the apple. Genesis got it wrong. It wasn't pride, it wasn't desire for knowledge, it wasn't even competition with God. It was greed. The apple beguiled her and she ate.

So though Mother Angela's skin is finer than tissue paper, her smile is far brighter than the morning, and she goes on her way rejoicing.

This story comes with special thanks to Ros Hunt who helped me with the theology and Carol Fry who helped me with the cookery.

The Wicked Stepmother's Lament

The wife of a rich man fell sick, and as she felt that her end was drawing near, she called her only daughter to her bedside and said, "Dear child, be good and pious, and then the good God will always protect you, and I will look down from heaven and be near you." Thereupon she closed her eyes and departed. Every day the maiden went out to her mother's grave and wept, and she remained pious and good. When winter came the snow spread a white sheet over the grave and by the time the spring sun had drawn it off again the man had taken another wife. . . .

Now began a bad time for the poor step-child. . . . They took her pretty clothes away, put an old grey bedgown on her and gave her wooden shoes. . . . She had to do hard work from morning to night, get up before daybreak, carry water, light fires, cook and wash. . . . In the evening when she had worked until she was weary she had no bed to go to but had to sleep by the hearth in the cinders. And as on that account she always looked dusty and dirty, they called her Cinderella.

You know the rest I expect. Almost everyone does.

I'm not exactly looking for self-justification. There's this thing going on at the moment where women tell all the old stories again and turn them inside-out and back-to-front—so the characters you always thought were the goodies turn out to be the baddies, and vice versa, and a whole lot of guilt is laid to rest: or that at least is the theory. I'm not sure myself that the guilt isn't just passed on to the next person, *in tacta,* so to speak. Certainly I want to carry and cope with my own guilt, because I want to carry and cope with my own virtue and I really don't see that you can have one without the other. Anyway, it would be hard to find a version of this story where I would come out a shiny new-style heroine: no true version, anyway. All I want to say is that it's more complicated, more complex, than it's told, and the reasons why it's told the way it is are complex too.

But I'm not willing to be a victim. I was not innocent, and I have grown out of innocence now and even out of wanting to be thought innocent. Living is a harsh business, as no one warned us when we were young and carefree under the apple bough, and I feel the weight of that ancient harshness and I want to embrace it, and not opt for some washed-out aseptic, hand-wringing, Disneyland garbage. (Though come to think of it he went none-too-easy on stepmothers, did he? Snow White's scared the socks off me the first time I saw the film—and partly of course because I recognized myself. But I digress.)

Look. It was like this. Or rather it was more like this, or parts of it were like this, or this is one part of it.

She was dead pretty in a Pears soap sort of way, and, honestly, terribly sweet and good. At first all I wanted her to do was concentrate. Concentration is the key to power. You have to concentrate on what is real. Concentration is not good or bad necessarily, but it is powerful. Enough power to change the world, that's all I wanted. (I was younger then, of course; but actually they're starving and killing whales and forests and each other out there; shutting your eyes and pretending they're not doesn't change anything. It does matter.) And what she was not was powerful. She wouldn't look out for herself. She was so sweet and so hopeful; so full of faith and forgiveness and love. You have to touch anger somewhere, rage even; you have to spit and roar and bite and scream and know it before you can be safe. And she never bloody would.

When I first married her father I thought she was so lovely, so good and so sad. And so like her mother. I knew her mother very well, you see; we grew up together. I loved her mother. Really. With so much hope and fondness and awareness of her worth. But—and I don't know how to explain this without sounding like an embittered old bitch, which I probably am—she was too good. Too giving. She gave herself away, indiscriminately. She didn't even give herself as a precious gift. She gave herself away as though she wasn't worth hanging on to. Generous to a fault, they said, when she was young, but no one acted as though it were a fault, so she never learned. "Free with Kellogg's Corn Flakes" was her motto. She equated loving with suffering, I thought at one time, but that wasn't right, it was worse, she equated loving with being; as though she did not exist unless she was denying her existence. I mean, he was not a bad bloke, her husband, indeed I'm married to him myself, and I like him and we have good times together, but he wasn't worth it—no one is—not what she gave him, which was her whole self with no price tag on.

And it was just the same with that child. Yes, yes, one can understand: she had difficulty getting pregnant actually, she had difficulties carrying those babies to term too. Even I can guess how that might hurt. But her little girl was her great reward for suffering, and at the same time was also her handle on a whole new world of self-giving. And yes, of course she looked so lovely, who could have resisted her, propped up in her bed with that tiny lovely child sucking, sucking, sucking? The mother who denied her little one nothing, the good mother, the one we all longed for, pouring herself out into the child. Well, I'll tell you, I've done it too, it is hell caring for a tiny daughter, I know. Everything, everything drags you into hell: the fact that you love and desire her, the fact that she's so needy and vulnerable, the fact that she never leaves you alone until your dreams are smashed in little piles and shabby with neglect, the fact that pleasure and guilt come so precisely together, as so seldom happens, working towards the same end and sucking your very selfhood out of you. It is a perilous time for a woman, that nursing of a daughter, and you can only survive it if you cling to yourself with a fierce and passionate love, *and* you back that up with a trained and militant lust for justice *and* you scream at the people around you to meet your needs and desires *and* you do not let them off, *and* when all is said and done you sit back and laugh at yourself with a well-timed and not unmalicious irony. Well, she could not, of course she could not, so she did not survive. She was never angry, she never asked, she took resignation—that tragic so-called virtue—as a ninth-rate alternative to reality and never even realized she had been short-changed.

So when I first married my husband I only meant to tease her a little, to rile her, to make her fight back. I couldn't bear it, that she was so like her mother and would go the same way. My girls were more like me, less agreeable to have about the house, but tough as old boots and capable of getting what they needed and not worrying too much about what they wanted or oughted, so to speak. I didn't have to worry about them. I just could not believe the sweetness of that little girl and her wide-eyed belief that I would be happy and love her if she would just deny herself and follow me. So of course I exploited her a bit, pushed and tested it, if you understand, because I couldn't believe it. Then I just wanted her to *see,* to see that life is not all sweetness and light, that people are not automatically to be trusted, that fairy godmothers are unreliable and damned thin on the ground, and that even the most silvery of princes soon goes out hunting and fighting and drinking and whoring, and doesn't give one tuppenny-ha'penny curse more for you than you give for yourself. Well, she could have looked at her father and known. He hardly proved himself to be the great romantic lover of all time, even at an age when that would have been appropriate, never mind later. He had after all replaced darling Mummy with me, and pretty damned quick too, and so long as he was getting his end off and his supper on the table he wasn't going to exert himself on her behalf, as I pointed out to her, by no means kindly.

(And, I should like to add, I still don't understand about that. I couldn't believe how little the bastard finally cared when it came to the point. Perhaps he was bored to tears by goodness, perhaps he was too lazy. He was a sentimental old fart about her, of course, his eyes could fill with nostalgic tears every time he looked at her and thought of her dead mother; but he never *did* anything; or even asked me to stop doing anything. She never asked, and he never had eyes to see, or energy or . . . God knows what went on in his head about her and as far as I'm concerned God's welcome. She loved him and trusted him and served him and he never even bloody noticed. Which sort of makes my point actually because he would never treat me like that, and yet he and I get on very well now; like each other and have good times in bed and out of it. Of course I'd never have let him tell me how to behave, but he might have tried, at least just once.)

Anyway, no, she would not see. She would not blame her father. She would not blame her mother, not even for dying, which is the ultimate outrage from someone you love. And she would not blame me. She just smiled and accepted, smiled and invented castles in the air to which someone, though never herself, would come and take her one day, smiled and loved me. No matter what I did to her, she just smiled.

So, yes, in the end I was cruel. I don't know how to explain it and I do not attempt to justify it. Her *wetness* infuriated me. I could not shake her good will, her hopefulness, her capacity to love and love and love such a pointless and even dangerous object. I could not make her hate me. Not even for a moment. I could not make her hate me. And I cannot explain what that frustration did to me. I hated her insane dog-like devotion where it was so undeserved. She treated me as her mother had treated him. I think I hated her stupidity most of all. I can hear myself almost blaming her for my belly-deep madness; I don't want to do that; I don't want to get into blaming the victim and she was my victim. I was older than her, and stronger than her, and had more power than her; and there was no excuse. No excuse, I thought the first time I ever hit her, but there was an excuse and it was my wild need, and it escalated.

So in the end—and yes I have examined all the motives and

reasons why one woman should be cruel to another and I do not find them explanatory—so in the end I was cruel to her. I goaded and humiliated and pushed and bullied her. I used all my powers, my superior strength, my superior age, my superior intelligence, against her. I beat her, in the end, systematically and severely; but more than that I used her and worked her and denied her pleasures and gave her pain. I violated her space, her dignity, her integrity, her privacy, even her humanity and perhaps her physical safety. There was an insane urge in me, not simply to hurt her, but to have her admit that I had hurt her. I would lie awake at night appalled, and scald myself with contempt, with anger and with self-disgust, but I had only to see her in the morning for my temper to rise and I would start again, start again at her with an unreasonable savagery that seemed to upset me more than it upset her. Picking, picking and pecking, endlessly. She tried my patience as no one else had ever done and finally I gave up the struggle and threw it away and entered into the horrible game with all my considerable capacity for concentration.

And nothing worked. I could not make her angry. I could not make her hate me. I could not stop her loving me with a depth and a generosity and a forgivingness that were the final blow. Nothing moved her to more than a simper. Nothing penetrated the fantasies and daydreams with which her head was stuffed so full I'm surprised she didn't slur her consonants. She was locked into perpetual passivity and gratitude and love. Even when she was beaten she covered her bruises to protect me; even when she was hungry she would not take food from my cupboards to feed herself; even when I mocked her she smiled at me tenderly.

All I wanted was for her to grow up, to grow up and realize that life was not a bed of roses and that she had to take some responsibility for her own life, to take some action on her own behalf, instead of waiting and waiting and waiting for something or someone to come shining out of the dark and force safety on her as I forced pain. What Someone? Another like her father who had done nothing, nothing whatever, to help her and never would? Another like him whom she could love generously and hopelessly and serve touchingly and givingly until weariness and pain killed her too. I couldn't understand it. Even when I beat her, even as I beat her, she loved me, she just loved and smiled and hoped and waited, daydreamed and night-dreamed, and waited and waited and waited. She was untouchable and infantile. I couldn't save her and I couldn't damage her. God knows, I tried.

And now of course it's just an ancient habit. It has lost its sharp edges, lost the passion in both of us to see it out in conflict, between dream and reality, between hope and cynicism. There is a great weariness in me, and I cannot summon up the fire of conviction. I do not concentrate anymore, I do not have enough concentration, enough energy, enough power. Perhaps she has won, because she drained that out of me years and years ago. Sometimes I despair, which wastes still more concentration. We plod on together, because we always have. Sweetly she keeps at it, smile, smile, dream, hope, wait, love, forgive, smile, smile, bloody smile. Tiredly, I keep at it too: "Sweep that grate." "Tidy your room." "Do your homework." "What can you see in that nerd?" "Take out those damn earphones and pay attention." "Life doesn't come free, you have to work on it." "Wake up, hurry up, stop daydreaming, no you can't, yes you must, get a move on, don't be so stupid." And "You're not going to the ball, or party, or disco, or over your Nan's, dressed like *that*."

She calls it nagging.

She calls me Mummy.

Cassandra

Section of the interhemispheric tracts (commissurotomy) to control epilepsy has been found to eliminate much of the normal integration of sensory information. . . . For instance commissurotomized subjects cannot put words to music, or music to words. Subjects could identify by pointing to stimuli seen in the left field and by naming stimuli simultaneously seen in the right field. They could not explain the discrepancy and they gave no indication that they had seen either stimulus as other than complete and regular. The recognition and memory of faces—a skill of the "minor" (right) hemisphere—cannot be articulated in language—a skill of the "major" (left) hemisphere. Catastrophic reactions and feelings of guilt and depression were common after left-hemisphere anesthetization; while feelings of euphoria often followed right-side anesthetization. Commissurotomized patients reacted strongly with blushing and giggling to the presentation of pictures of nudes in the left visual field, even when the "major" hemisphere showed by its verbalizations that it had no idea why this was happen-

ing. The right hemisphere outperformed the left in accurate perception and memory of stimuli that have no
verbal label or are too complex or too similar to express
the words, but only the left hemisphere can give language to these memories.

There is a gap and she knows there is a gap between what she sees
and what she says. She cannot, she cannot leap the gap. It is lonely. It
is cold. There are too many feelings of depression and guilt and
euphoria. She feels entirely alone, and the horizon still glows with
the burning of the towers of Ilium.

The severing of the *corpus callosum,* the hard bond of
nerves that connects the left and right hemispheres of
the brain, has been found to eliminate the normal integration of sensory information.

He watches her unhappily as she stands in the prow of the boat; she
looks huddled and cold. The usual scars, bruises and scratches on her
face seem to stand out. She seems small and frail. Her beauty is not
diminished, indeed it is undeniable, overwhelming, but suddenly it
is the beauty of a child, not of a woman. A child, and a sad lost child
at that. He draws in a breath, racked with a new pain. He, Agamemnon, King of Argos, commander of the victorious forces of Greece, is
in pain; and the pain is inflicted on him by a little hunched child
who rides the prow of his boat with an unreadable expression. It is
called compassion, that is the name of his pain, and he is not used to
feeling it. They say, the Greek warriors, that he struck a poor bargain
in the taking of the spoils; that he chose the mad woman, the crazy
one, when he could have chosen the voluptuous courtesans of Troy,
any of the women of the city who flocked in defeat about his feet and
begged to be his portion. He knows, fretfully, that he made the best
bargain of his life, that just to have her, have her here, untouchable
and untouched, to have her ride the prow of his ship and gaze at the
sea with her dark eyes, that this is enough. And if he is gentle, gentle
and patient as a fisherman, strong and unmoving as the sea, she will

come to him and tell him, tell him what it is, what happens in her head, what happened in the beginning to make her so different from other women, so alone, so powerful, so frail. But the pain of patience irks him and he paces the boat half-irritated.

He is wrong. She will not tell him. She will not tell him any of it. At one moment she is riding the ship, mourning the city of her childhood, mourning the bright princes who were her brothers, mourning the gallant stupidity with which they died. "Hector," she murmurs, but even as she says his name his face disappears from her mind, and when she finds the face again she does not know whose face it is. She likes Agamemnon. She has a knowing that he will not . . . that he will wait . . . that he will . . . she does not know the word for what it is she fears, for what it is she knows he will not do. Then the next minute it is gone, it is all gone; there is a clear, familiar, strange sensation which begins in the middle finger of her left hand and spreads through her body, a feeling of intense stillness and power that reaches out from inside her to the whole sea; and the bright islands of the Aegean dance on the water, totally vital, totally still. A transparent moment, turning from gold to green. Everything is green. Green. She feels quite clearly the spittle forming on her lips, she hears her own mouth open with a strange birdlike noise, she feels her whole body lurch forward, her shoulders smashing down, the heel of the God forcing her face into the wooden deck.

He runs along the ship, suddenly shaken into movement. He feels immediately the compassion of the crew, but his fear is that she will fall into the sea. He forces her mouth open, inserts the leather scabbard of his dagger between her teeth, wipes the foam from the side of her mouth, tries to hold her firmly but gently, and is amazed at the extraordinary strength of her convulsions. It does not last long; as suddenly as it started she flops against him, limp, washed out like a soft cloth. She opens her eyes and smiles at him.

"She will kill you," she says, "in water. Not in the sea, which can wash away the blood. She will kill you. There will be a lot of blood. I can see it."

"It's all right," he says, "it's all right, don't worry. I'm here, I won't let anyone hurt you."

"Not me. You. It's the swan's eggs; there was too much blood, there in the laying of the eggs, too much blood and yours will be there."

"Don't worry," he says again desperately. Is the look in her eyes consent or despair? Quite suddenly she seems very sleepy. He gathers her up in his arms and carries her like a little child below decks and there on his own bunk, surrounded by the outward signs of his military prestige—sword, helmet, trophies from Troy—she sleeps, curled round; the scab of blood on her lip looking like the traces of a child's sweetmeat. She seems innocent and open, but she is closed off from him. Asleep, this feels forgivable, although with a sigh he knows he would forgive her anyway. He tries to focus on what she said. He had killed his own daughter for a prophecy; he believes in prophecy. "She will kill you." The first time she had said it it had been with urgency, with commitment. It was only the repetition that had sounded crazed. As he tries to concentrate he sees the speckled foam from her mouth still clinging to his left sleeve, he remembers the power of her body racked by the convulsions. She was raving. He shrugs his shoulders. Of course she was raving, he tells himself. Standing up he feels his tunic wet against his stomach. She had lost control of her bladder and he had carried her closely: he does not know why he is touched instead of revolted. Checking surreptitiously that she is truly asleep he strips and changes. He wants to promise the world to her; he wants, against his own self-knowledge, to swear that he will never use his power against her, that he will keep her safe, that he will never do anything she does not like. But she is asleep, uninterested in his professions, in his promises.

She dreams. But even she does not know what she dreams.

Troy burns. The flames are high and hot. She has fled from the broken city to a sanctuary. But the Greeks come there and all women are spoils of war. She is spoiled, despoiled, raped. There is no end to it; the flames in her eyes and in her belly. Her vagina broken, the secret places smashed into. She could have suffered this in the beginning, and then all would have been well.

Hector's body is dragged around the walls of the city. She sees Helen smile faintly, uncaring. She sees the eyes of Paris, her favorite brother, light up with jealousy relieved. Paris has hated Hector for years. Hector, the bravest of the Trojans, the hero without blemish, is dragged round the walls of Troy and her sad, old father has to beg his enemies for the return of the battered flesh.

Agamemnon who has rescued her is chopped up with an axe. Undignified, struggling to pull on a tunic whose armholes have been sewn together. An infantile prank turned deadly. And everything she sees, she sees over and over and over again. Again and again in the still, pure moment before the God stamps on her shoulders and flattens her to the ground, she sees. She sees what will happen and she tells it and no one can believe her. She cannot believe herself; in each bitter instant Cassandra hears her own truths as spittle and crazed foaming. There is a gap and she knows there is a gap between what she sees and what she says. She cannot, she cannot leap that gap. She cannot fit the words to music, nor music to words. She cannot remember faces and names at the same time. It is very lonely.

> Commissurotomy—the severing of the *corpus callosum,* the tissue which provides the connection between the two functionally asymmetric hemispheres of the brain—has been found to eliminate the normal integration of sensory information. The left hemisphere thus receives detailed information about visual stimuli only if they fall in the right visual half-field and about some aesthetic stimuli only if they contact the right side of the body. The same is obviously true for the right hemisphere. The two hemispheres process information differently; the left hemisphere being superior in terms of language function while the right is superior when required to perform a spatial transformation on sensory input. Moreover there is competition between the left and right hemispheres of commissurotomized patients for control of motor output; and this leads to further, complicated distortions in motor-dependent communication.

She is a very beautiful woman. No one ever questioned this, even with the inevitable cuts and bruises to her face and hands; and her frequently bizarre and inappropriate expressions. She had been, though, a radiant child. Loving, laughing, lovely. Cassandra. Now there is, inside her own ears, a hissing and a writhing in her name; but then there had been a musical giggle.

Apollo had desired her. No, Apollo had loved her. But this she does not remember. She remembers nothing about this at all. It is all burned away. She sees the future, but she does not see the past. She does not remember, recall, recollect.

But Apollo, the burning sun-god, the most beautiful, most vital of the Olympians, loved her. Before there was time for confusion, before there was time for anyone else, he came to her. Just post-menarche, still joyful in her own power, still untried, untouched. Too much love for one so simple. His desire left him insensitive to his love. He would not be stayed. The horses of the sun champed on their bits while he spoke with her; she was blinded, confused by his brightness. Perhaps she did not even know what he was talking about. It was the first time. The first time that every inch of her flesh reached out greedy, greedy and needy. There was no past, no future; no family, no friends. He offered her anything, anything that she wanted; he was a god and his godliness rose up between his legs just to watch her considering the offer, halfway between greedy spoiled child and greedy sexy woman. He felt his power and prepared to produce for her castles made of ice that would not melt although the sun shone day and night upon them. He prepared to unsling his own lute from his shoulders and give her authority over all the music in the world. He prepared to summon Pegasus so that she might ride on the great winged horse and bestride the mountains and the oceans to the stabling place of the golden sun chariot and the eight great stallions that pulled it. His power to give her what she wanted delighted him. And she asked him for a spiral shell that was pink inside and without a chip missing. She and her sisters had a collection of shells; they would walk with their handmaids beside the sea and gather up beautiful shells from the beautiful beaches of Ilium and carry them home; but none of them had ever found an unflawed, perfect, spiraled horn with the silvery pink lining. The request struck his pride, and in his anger he laughed at her and she was humiliated. She spoke as a child and was exposed as a child, and in the shadow of his mockery she became a woman, a woman who knew her power over men and gods. She said, "Give me the power to tell the future, give me the power to know what will happen. Make me a prophetess and a seer and a soothsayer and an oracle. If you can."

There was a flicker, a flicker in the sunlight by the river. There are things that are not permitted, even to the most golden and potent of young gods. The sunlight flickered, and the flickering was the shadow of his doubt. She sat, not caring, as happy to dabble her toes in the river and smile as she was to be given this thing. But she clearly sensed her own desirability, and she pulled in her cheeks and pouted and looked little and cross and his heart melted with . . . with what? With lust, with amusement, with tenderness, with the desire to show off? She was old enough to seduce and not old enough to know what it meant. He knew then that he did not have the right; that he could give her presents and affection, and love, but he did not have the right to take her, to own her, to possess her whole lovely sweet virginal body. And he was ashamed, and angry and greedy. So he did not restrain himself from using all his power.

"If I do that for you, what will you do for me?"

"What do you want?"

She became sly, the slyness of curiosity, because she wanted to know, wanted to know what this feeling was, both the feeling of power and the feeling of reaching towards, wanting, wanting, wanting.

"I want you to be my lover."

She laughed. It seemed so little a thing, of course she would love someone who gave her what she wanted; and the words brought a feeling to her arms and her high hard little breasts; the tickling rising feeling in her nipples and the soft sinking feeling in the pit of her belly, and she wanted suddenly to cover his golden body with honey all over and lick it off slowly, slowly in the sunshine. She wanted to spread her legs and . . . and she knew not what, but she consented to the bargain.

And now he was haughty and calm. He spat neatly on his finger, and crouched down beside her on the grass. He touched quite gently her lips, and then her eyes, and last her ears, and when he touched her ears she saw the first high flames leap above the topless towers of Troy and felt the great grief of loss and pain and the great chasm of fear, but before she could think about it he took his finger and laid it on her right nipple and the darkness vanished and she reached up with the innocence of a child and the passion of a woman and put her arms around him and gave his neck a long kiss. They stayed there a minute and her desire mounted. Then he took his hand away from her breast and placed it under her chin and compelled her mouth towards his. The sun shone and she was full of joy and curiosity and excitement.

Then he kissed her.

She responded to his kiss with an eagerness, a voluptuous enthusiasm, receiving his tongue deep in her mouth and working her own with happy little wriggles along the inside of his lip. And he pushed her gently backwards and kissed her deeper, harder, more demandingly, reaching with his free hand for her white thigh. And suddenly she could not.

It was too much, too much feeling, too much closeness, there was no Cassandra, no princess there, but only flesh and burning flesh and she could not. She was frightened. He did not feel her fear, he could not give her space, he was not willing to wait. She pushed at him and there was no escape, and she hit out at his face with her hands, and she bent her head back strangely and banged it, banged it on a rock. She was outside herself and unable to think, unable to breathe, and there was too much feeling and he was too close and she would not survive it, and she could not bear it, and she could not, she could not, she could not. Her whole self went cold, because it was too much. Too much feeling, and she would be lost in it, lost if she let him nearer to her own darkness and let him illuminate it with light. And she beat at him and herself, fluttering like a bird, not like a little chicken bird but like a trapped eagle.

"I can't," she cried. "Stop it, let me go. I can't."

"You must," he said. "You like it."

"I know. Yes. No. No I don't like it. I won't. I can't." And she scratched at him, and at herself, her nails tearing her own face and his. He thought at first it was her passion and he was excited, but she beat and fought, lost, lost, lost, in a strange place and insanely she muttered and banged and struggled.

He could not speak to her, she had gone away. He was almost frightened, but more angry. He could not for some time get her back to him, get her conscious. She was shaking and deranged. She was mute and broken.

"You have to," he said, "you promised. We made a bargain."

"I don't care. I cannot." Now she was sulking like a baby, her face turned away. She knew only that it would kill her if she did, that the explosion in her would kill her if she let him bring that golden pleasure any nearer. He could kill her by some other means if he wanted to, she was not going there. She was shaking with fear.

"I don't want it. I don't want your present. I don't want to know the future. I was only joking."

He has made love to mortals before and they have delighted in him; who is she, this child, to make mock of a god's desire? Who is she to shame him and despise him? And seeing her as a child, he is more ashamed than ever. And like white heat his anger rises, rises to replace the rising of his genitals, which are withered by her rejection.

"We gods don't take back our gifts. But I will punish you."

"Yes," she sighs, "yes, do that." The punishment will obliterate the dangerous joy; she will not go to that perilous place, the punishment will take away the memory of the pleasure. "Please."

He is vengeful because he is baffled and embarrassed. He is vengeful because he is ashamed. She does not look radiant now, but little and shriveled.

"I won't take back my gift," he tells her, "but I shall make it so that you will always know the future but no credit or reliance will ever be placed on anything you say. Ever. Even by you. Since you make a gap between me and my desire I shall make one between your seeing and your saying. You can never leap that gap. You will never leap that gap. It will be a very lonely place."

He stood her up. He held her by the shoulders and he looked at her. She felt the desire rise again and with it the fear. The desire, the fear, the pain. She cannot. But now he does not let her go. His hands are very hard; they shift from her shoulders to her upper arms, which he grips tightly.

"You're hurting me," she says, trying to wriggle free.

"I know," he says, without compassion. He puts his tongue on her lips, but now there is no desire, his tongue is like a knife, he runs it up the narrow crevice above her upper lip, very slowly, very coldly. She feels his saliva on her like a snail's trail; straight up the middle of her nose and forehead. With the force of his chin he bows her head and runs his hard cutting tongue right across the center of her crown, and she feels the sharp blade cut into her cranium, and into the depths of her brain, a single even slicing and there is intolerable pain, intolerable confusion. Her mind is severed. She is severed. There is a gap between her seeing and her saying. It is a very lonely place. It is very cold. The words and the music separate: she feels them pulling apart, stretching out, out, till the song collapses into chaos and she will never sing again. She feels catastrophic reactions of guilt and depression and euphoria. She remembers faces and names but she cannot associate them with each other. The normal integration of sensory knowledge is destroyed. She faints.

When she becomes conscious, she does not remember. They do not understand the long scratches on her face, nor the bruising on her head until she starts having fits. In her fits she murmurs dreadful and dangerous things, lost perceptions that make no sense but are discouraging and not to be encouraged. Although she is very beautiful they conclude that she is mad. She is often placed under restraint, because of the complicated distortions in all her forms of communication. She likes men still, but she will not let anyone touch her. She will never let anyone touch her, although she is not able to say why.

She says over and over again that Troy will be destroyed.

The city will burn, she tells them. The flames will be high and bright. As bright as a god, she says. But she also says as bright as lentils, or as bright as three days ago, or as bright as stag's antlers so they do not understand. They place no credit or reliance on anything she ever says, and she does not know why.

When she wakes up in Agamemnon's bunk she does not remember what has happened. He comes down again into the cabin and smiles at her. She smiles back, warm and sleepy. He is overwhelmed again with tenderness. He will not hurry, he must not hurry, he will be patient, patient and kind, because she moves him so, as no woman has ever done.

"Feeling better?" He fills the hatchway and for a moment cuts off the light. They rock together in the dark movement of the ship's belly.

"I feel fine," she replies, then as he moves the light floods back into the small space, she smiles radiantly and says, "She'll kill you. With an axe. So don't change your tunic. In the bath."

He thinks it is a joke; that perhaps she was awake when he changed his tunic before, and is teasing him.

"All right," he says, "that's all right."

"I know," she says, giggling because his smile in the half-light is so sweet. "By the way, she'll kill me too." They both laugh and the ship sails gently on towards Argos and Clytemnestra who will indeed kill both of them.

> Despite its effectiveness in the control of certain forms of epilepsy, commissurotomy (section of the *corpus callosum*—the interhemispheric tract) is no longer used as a surgical treatment. Since the discovery of multiple functional asymmetries favoring the right as well as the left hemisphere, it is generally recognized that the therapeutic value of this intervention is outweighed by the fact that it has been found to eliminate much of the normal integration of sensory information.

The information on hemispheric section comes principally from Robert Nebes's article in Marcel Kinsbourbe (ed.) *Asymmetrical Function of the Brain* (Cambridge University Press, 1978), to whom thanks.

The Tale of the Valiant Demoiselle

I fingered the winterkilled grass, looping it round the tip of my finger like hair, ruffling its tips with my palms. Another year has twined away, unrolled and dropped across nowhere like a flung banner painted in gibberish. There is death in the pot for the living's food, fly-blown meat, muddy salt and plucked herbs bitter as squill. If you can get it. How many people have prayed for their daily bread and famished? In a winter famine, desperate Algonquian Indians ate broth made of smoke, snow and buckskin, and the rash of pellagra appeared like tattooed flowers on their emaciated bodies—the roses of starvation; and those who died, died covered in roses. Is this beauty, these gratuitous roses, or a mere display of force? Or is beauty itself an intricately fashioned lure, the cruellest hoax of all?

Annie Dillard, *Pilgrim at Tinker's Creek*

"Mummy, Billy says I can't play soldiers with him because I'm a girl."

"Well, don't play soldiers then; it's a silly game."

"Mummy." Exasperation, frustration, an answer not good enough.

"Well then, tell him not to be so silly, tell him you're Thérèse Figueur."

"Who's she?"

"She was a soldier in the freedom army of the French Revolution. And later the great General Bonaparte himself gave her a medal."

(But don't tell her because eight is too young to know, don't tell her that on campaign in 1799 the Piedmontese peasants demanded that she should be given over to them, to be burned as a witch. And her comrades in arms consented.)

"Mummy, Billy says I can't be Robinson Crusoe 'cause he was a man; I have to be Man Friday all the time."

"That doesn't make sense."

Yes it does, of course. Her own son. Oh, Christ.

"Tell him that there was a woman castaway over a century before Alexander Selkirk—he was the true man that Defoe made up Robinson Crusoe from. She was called Marguerite de la Rocque, and she was so brave that the Queen of Navarre put her into one of the first books of stories that was ever written in France."

(But don't tell her, because eight is too young to know, that Marguerite of Navarre, sister of Francis the First, the most sophisticated, intelligent and virtuous woman in all Europe, had to lie, had to change the story, had to make it respectable, and had to present her whole courage as coming from her love of a man.)

"Mummy, tell me that story."

Over four hundred years ago Columbus sailed across the Atlantic and discovered America. Then the Spanish and the Portuguese went there and they brought back lots of exciting stories and lots of gold.

(And they killed and raped the Indians and destroyed their culture, and paid for their gold with measles and syphilis; but don't tell her that bit because she is too young to have to know.)

So then the people in England and France got a bit jealous and they thought they'd like to find some new countries too, and gold and spices and silk and adventures, so they built ships and set out. And one of the first to set out was a sailor from St-Malo, in Brittany, and his name was Jacques Cartier. He made two voyages, wild and difficult journeys beyond the end of the world. You must understand how brave you had to be to go to the strange countries across the Atlantic which might not even exist: a few fishermen had gone before to fish on the Great Banks where the cod ran so fat and plentiful that they could be pulled up for the asking if you could make the crossing; but Cartier went beyond that, he sailed his little ship into a new sea, a new ocean, and he thought he had found the way across the top of the world and through to China. Actually, though, he'd found the Gulf of St. Lawrence which leads into the Canadian interior. Some Indians he met told him that if he could travel up the great river he would come to a magic land called Saguenay, where there was gold and jewels and strange beautiful things, and people with one leg, and unicorns and spice trees. He spent one winter up the St. Lawrence river, where Quebec is now, and no one from Europe had ever seen such cold, so much snow, such hard frosts; and they got scurvy and other diseases and the river was full of rapids; so he realized that if they were going to explore this new country and find Saguenay they would have to build a base, found a colony there on the river as a sort of launching pad for the interior. So he went home and asked the King of France to give him money and ships and people to go and found a city in New France. The King thought this was a very good idea, but he was a bit of a snob and he didn't think that Cartier, who was just a master mariner and captain, was the right person to be in charge of a new country. So he appointed another man, who was a nobleman called Jean François de la Rocque, Sieur de Roberval, to be Lieutenant General and in charge of everything. But of course Cartier knew more about it all and was better at getting organized than Roberval, so he set out first with about half the people and equipment they needed, and he built the fort and spent another freezing, depressing winter in Canada; but at the end of the winter Roberval still hadn't turned up, and they thought he wasn't coming, and so many of the company had died and they were all fed up, so Cartier decided to go home.

In the meantime Roberval had finally got his act together, but I don't think he really had very much idea about what exploring was really like, because he took a very strange expedition, including lots of ladies and gentlemen who were friends of his, as well as sailors and soldiers and working people. And for the grand people it was all like an exciting adventure, a picnic almost; they didn't have the least idea about how dangerous and wild Canada really was. And one of the ladies who went was his own niece, a pretty young woman, about eighteen, called Marguerite, which means both a daisy and a pearl in French.

Imagine it; they sailed out of La Rochelle harbor in the spring winds of April, three ships with their square sails set and their high castles at the front and back. There were three hundred soldiers, sixty masons and carpenters, ten priests, three doctors, and all sorts of necessary stuff, like pre-fab carts to put together when they got there, and mills and ironware. And all the crowds of La Rochelle stood on the harbor and cheered and sang to see such a brave expedition going off under the King's Lieutenant General to discover and conquer a New World. They had a safe and sunny crossing of the huge Atlantic and arrived in the harbor at Newfoundland; and they must all have felt very happy and confident.

But then, while they were resting in the harbor and in such high spirits, Cartier sailed in and told them that it would be impossible to defend themselves against the cold and the Indians, and that he for one was going home to France; his crew wouldn't face another Canadian winter and it was all Roberval's fault for not arriving when he had said he would. Roberval was really the commander officially, but Cartier was older and more experienced, and it was probably difficult for him to take orders from Roberval. Because, when Roberval ordered him to stay and return to the St. Lawrence, Cartier took his three ships and stole away at night and sailed back to France.

I expect that everyone in Roberval's expedition was really upset by this, and probably a bit frightened as well. They had come all this way thinking that Canada would be a rich country littered with gold and jewels for them to pick up and have some good adventures on the way, but they must all have known that Cartier was the most knowledgeable sailor and explorer in all France and if he said it was impossible then . . .

Then the excitement and the tension would have mounted. The mutterings, fear and anger, and their dreadful, dreadful dependence on Roberval, now not the golden young lord from Picardy who had friends at court and wit and charm, but an iron man, a despotic, arrogant young man who could not take advice from anyone. And wanting comfort, wanting fun, wanting reassurance . . . and he was so pretty, so gallant and young and fine, and his wife was so far away and perhaps they would never go home, perhaps they would freeze to death and die here in the strange country. And it was high spring and the bright salty air filled with sea birds in the May sunshine.

Perhaps they would never go home because they had come to the New World beyond the dangerous ocean, where the old harsh laws did not apply and they were young and beautiful. Of course she had an affair with him, sneaking down among the bales and goods in the lower hold, sneaking away with him across the rocky beaches where the sea birds were nesting too. His face so salty under his beard and her legs so white under her petticoats. To make love in the New World where even the stars were different. And when the company sailed on again, how could they stop? Roberval's gentlemen volunteers were a young and brave band, unconventional, high-spirited. Their lines of decorum shifting, what was and what was not allowed. And, dear God, how she wanted him; couldn't keep her hands to herself, in those cramped close quarters and nowhere to get away. Just to see him toss his curls, his earrings dancing, made such shivers in her belly. She had to touch him. And when she touched him it was not enough, and there was no retreat. The sweetness of first love. She was crazy about him, greedy for him, lost her good sense, lost her good name, and three-quarters of the below-decks crew must know about it, the Governor's own niece, because there was so little space and it could not be kept secret.

So probably everyone was a little nervous and edgy when they sailed on. They went up the coast of Newfoundland and into the Gulf of St. Lawrence through the Strait of Belle Isle. In the summertime it is stunningly beautiful—flocks of sea birds, great plunging gannets, little funny puffins, and seals disporting themselves under the cliffs of little rocky islands and to the north the low flat lands of Labrador and Quebec stretching away away endlessly into the unknown places. We don't exactly know what happened, but Marguerite did something that upset Roberval very badly and he refused to have her on his ship any longer. They were passing some little islands at the time—they're called the Harrington Islands now, they're quite little but luckily for her they have some fresh water—and he put her on one of them and sailed on.

Why could he not forgive her? Dear God, she had wept and sought forgiveness, crawled on her knees to him. She knew, she knew damn well, he was a Calvinist, a hard man wedded to his Bible, but . . . but he was willing to forgive her lover, and that hurt. It was she, she alone, who was damned; had gone outside his and his God's forgiveness. In the July sunshine the island looked pretty enough; it was not that. She could not read the meaning on her uncle's face. He could not forgive her, and he said it was God's judgment. He said they sailed with God and he would keep no blighting Jonah on his ship, no whores. He needed to show his power over them all. He could not stomach her beauty, her joy; she was radiant with her love, love flowered her flesh rosy and the sun and the sea flowered it golden. She was too beautiful for him to forgive her. He would, he said, have no befouling lust on his ship; but he was willing to keep her lover. It was woman flesh that stuck in his craw. She was the Gateway to Hell, and his gallant young men must not risk her corruption. A whore, a slut, a witch out of hell.

So he gave her few provisions and sailed on westwards towards central Canada.

He gave her a gun, he gave her a flintbox, he gave her a Bible.

Cartier had made a list, a list of the minimum supplies necessary to survive—276 men, including apothecaries, tailors, carpenters, masons, blacksmiths, men-at-arms. He had written his list for the King saying they would need windmills, boats, anvils, food supplies, bales of woollen cloth, artillery, domestic animals and hens, geese, seeds, grain, cooking utensils and pig iron. They had all known the list and laughed at some of the meticulous details, and they had felt safe because Cartier knew his job.

He gave her a gun, a tinderbox and a Bible.

He wanted her dead.

He didn't want her blood on his hands.

He said if she was so damn free she could taste the freedom of the savages.

She had asked him for sugar and he had hit her in the face.

She did not know how to use the gun. He gave ammunition and powder, but he knew she did not know how to use the gun. One of the sailors putting her ashore gave her his own knife. It was a kindness, but when he slipped it to her he was careful not to let his hand touch hers. He set his mouth in silent embarrassment. The whole ship's company was embarrassed, but silent. No one raised a murmur for her. One of the priests had raised his hand to bless her and thought better of it. She was in mortal sin. She did not repent.

But just as the ship was sailing away her . . . her boyfriend leapt over the side and came swimming to the shore; he had decided to stay and help her.

The silly fool. The silly beautiful fool; his arms so long and white, cutting the smooth surface of the bay. His grin irrepressible, his body glorious. She went down into the water to welcome him as he swam towards her, standing almost to her waist in the soft sea, her arms stretched out. And there, in the sight of the ship's company, they fell into each other's arms giggling, laughing. For those few moments she had felt so bereft, she had felt the taste of loneliness and death and he had leapt into the sea to come to her. Holding hands they ran up the shingle, dripping wet, her dress clinging to her legs, his shirt clamped on his chest revealing his nipples. This was their paradise; they could fuck all day. Morality had abandoned them, they were free. Outrageous, bold, untrammeled, they waved handkerchiefs to the departing boat, laughing.

Then they lived very happily for a while. They built a hut out of the pine trees, out of logs, and they made furniture for it and got it all as cozy as they could, just like in *Robinson Crusoe* and *Swiss Family Robinson*—well, almost like; it couldn't have been so good, because they didn't have those handy wrecks the others had to get supplies off—they didn't have nails for instance, so the hut can't have been very secure. And an island in the Gulf of St. Lawrence is rather a different thing from a warm sunny one in the Caribbean. But luckily Marguerite was very clever and creative, and she sewed and carved and made fishing lines by unraveling her petticoats; and her boyfriend shot and fished and they ate berries and fruit and stuff like that. It was hard work, but they did have a lot of fun.

At first. It was their paradise. Each morning she woke snuggled in the curve of his armpit. They played and teased and laughed and made love through a long golden summer, and at night the stars were heavy and golden; bigger brighter newer stars than they had ever seen, and they named new constellations in the honor of their loving. And she knew she was going to have his baby. It was their paradise and they giggled together and swore they would never eat the apple of civilization again; and that when Roberval came back to rescue them they would laugh in his face and tell him to sail away wherever he wanted for they were content. The sun shone warmly and she grew lean and fit and free in her limbs as she had never been since childhood, and they wandered their kingdom naked and unashamed as the savages were said to do.

But. Except. There was an undertow. A darkening shadow. The sex was not as good as it had been on shipboard: there was nothing else to do, nothing to hide, nothing to plot, no planning, no scheming, no exciting delays. And he: he thought he had been so wonderful, so heroic and generous and romantic, leaping off the ship for her. He acted, just, at moments, hardly hinted, barely noticed in the delight of sunshine, he acted as though she owed him something.

But Roberval would have forgiven him, would have kept him on the ship. Sometimes she thought that he, somehow, somewhere, agreed with Roberval—and yet what had she done that he had not? He thought that by forgiving her he had earned her love. She would give it to him as a gift, but not as a debt. But she did not like to say these things and intrude on their happy laughter. And when the evenings began to be cooler and longer she found that his conversation was not very interesting to her, and she started even to read the Bible to amuse herself, and he resented it and she felt guilty.

In Canada, you know, the autumns are extraordinary. They had never seen anything like it, that wild extravagance of color; none of that soft mournful wet decline that we have here in Europe but golds and yellows and crimsons and scarlets after the first frost. There's a time they call the Indian Summer, St. Martin's Summer, late in October, when the winds die down and the days are hot and hazy, and they must both have felt that all was well with them and that the rumors about the winter had been a mistake, a silly joke. Perhaps they played that they were a king and queen who had ordered one of the new Italian artists to come and decorate their palace for them, in the bright, brave, gaudy colors of that time.

And then the winter came.

Cold. She had not known what the word meant. They had been warned and like children they had not heard the warning, because they had no knowledge or experience to measure the warning against. Early one dawn the calm had been broken by a whirring noise, a low murmur with an inner beat, an unearthly sound. The heavy skeins of geese were passing, straight as arrows, running south and pulling the darkness of winter down on their strong pinion feathers from the north. She thought of the baby and she was frightened. And they went, innocent and ignorant as children, into the maelstrom of winter. Hell would not be hot, but cold and everlasting as that Canadian winter: and the weight of the snow drift, drift, drifting forever, or borne on the storm winds, battering out of the north; the bay rearing up against them, iced spume far flung; the great reefs of ice riming up along the shore, shifting and moaning like hellish harps at first, but as the cold locked down tighter there came an ominous and enormous silence in which there was no noise at all but the relentless wind. How could she help thinking about the baby and being frightened? The fear moved in, gnawing as fierce as the cold, and there was no escape from either. And the hut itself a feeble joke before the cold and the wind and the terror. Hunger. Thirst. Tedium and the smoky darkness of their frail shelter. The immense heartbreaking effort that the simplest task of survival used up. The weariness. And above and beneath and within all things, the numbing, bemusing, battering cold. And in the hut with nothing to do they tried to keep warm, clinging together not for delight, or for tenderness, or even for consolation, but for need—a need more gripping and impelling than the need of their lust in the far away and almost forgotten springtime. And the bitterness of the need crept in between them and wedged itself there and there was nothing, nothing left at all of the golden loving but a bitter, cringing hatred and a bitterer and more cringing need.

And then I'm sorry to say, that winter her boyfriend died.

She killed him. She was both whore and murderess. The bitterness had eaten them up and they snapped and snarled still locked together against the cold. Like bears in a den. Fire in them both, fires flaring for no reason, and violent savage sex afterwards that used energy and did not restore affection. And when he hit her, when he started hitting her, she groveled before him, begging, pleading with him to stop, apologizing for things she had never done and of which he had not even accused her, cradling her belly and her head, rolling on the ground, crawling before him on hands and knees, begging, beseeching, pleading. She hated him more for reducing her to that humility than she hated him for hitting her. She hated him and herself and they had come to a great black place from which neither could escape.

    Finally she had turned, turned on him for no real reason beyond the cold and her sordid humiliation. She had half broken the hut apart in the cataclysm of her fury, hurling abuse and objects and spit and spite: savage, animal, rodent, vicious. And where was the young and tender girl who had stood on the deck of the ship out of La Rochelle and longed to see the glories of the New World? She drove him in her mad anger out of the hut and into the wind. He was weak, confused by the cold and by her raving. He slipped. He gashed his leg. Hours later, frozen and blue-lipped, he crawled back into the hut. It had not seemed a bad wound at first, though quite deep, about two inches above his ankle. She resented him; resented shredding yet more of her inadequate clothing to bind the wound. She resented his clumsiness and the extra burden it laid on her. She resented her own guilt and the skill with which he had punished her. A few days later when she took off the bandage to re-dress the wound, she noticed that it was opening up, high and proud, and that the flesh above was puffy, greenish. He could put no weight on the foot. It was not getting better. A sweet, sticky smell pervaded the hut. Two nights later she heard the foxes howling outside and in the morning their marks were around the door. The skin above the bandage turned black. He had a fever, muttering through the night while the wild beasts howled. In his fever he said dreadful things, about her, about himself and about Hell. She knew that he was telling the truth. It took him three weeks to die.

She tried to dig him a grave, but the ground was too hard. She dragged his body into a snowdrift and it took all the strength she had. In the night she heard the foxes again, excited, with greedy snufflings and snarls. When she went out they were like white ghosts pawing and pulling at his corpse. She frightened them away and knew they would return. She dragged the body back into the hut and collapsed beside it. All night long she held him in her arms, rocking him and herself in a fever of passion. God how she loved him, how beautiful he was, how long and strong in the shadows, his skin so soft and sweet. She had loved him and sacrificed her life for him. He had betrayed her and deserted her. He had run away and left her, dishonored and pregnant, cast out from society, alone in the wilderness, pregnant, alone and bitter. It was an old boring story, a woman's story, and she had thought herself to be above it. God how she hated him, and there was no love so sweet as this loathing, a hatred so strong that it warmed her at last. It enflamed her, she kissed his body all over, everywhere, long hard kisses, and she buried her lips in his gangrenous wound, tasting and probing the putrid flesh. He was dead. She was alone.

All that winter she guarded his body in the hut. She no longer minded the smell. The white foxes still came at night, waiting, waiting, waiting their chance. When she did not hear their shrill barking, she heard the deep and dreadful howling of the wind, tearing across the water, across the ice. Beating against the hut, seeking access, seeking her flesh with a wild lust that would not be tamed by her. And in the ghastly screaming of the wind, she heard a voice she could not hear, words she did not know. The hut was too small; she could not step away from him; his body bloated up, his lips pulled away from his blackened gums into a grin of malevolent triumph. He swelled larger and larger and she did too. But he was dead and she was alive. She ceased to care.

At last there came a day which felt different, though she could not tell what the difference was; an ending, a beginning, a changing. Outside it was as cold as ever, but along the rim of the horizon far away as she could see there was a separation: between slate-grey water and slate-grey sky there was a rim of pale pink. She gathered snow and melted it. She stripped off her clothes and washed herself. She covered his face with a rag: there were things that no man, alive or dead, should see.

She was in labor for thirty-three hours and there was no one to wipe the sweat from her face; it clogged her eyes, matted her hair and trickled salty into her mouth, and when night came she was wrapped in a shroud of ice. She screamed and heard in her own howls the echoes of the waiting foxes. She was animal. She crawled on the hut floor and chewed pieces of wood. She smashed at her own body. The pain threw her around the hut and shook her as a dog shakes a rat, and in the teeth of the pain she became a rat and snarled like a rat. And she screamed to him for help and he could not help her because she had killed him. She was far away from the places where there are other people. Then later she was weary, weary, weary with the pain and the loneliness, and there was no one to bring her vinegar on a sponge.

Just before the spring came she had her baby, all on her own in that little hut. It's very hard work for a woman to have a baby, and you really need to have people with you to help you and hold on to you. She must have been terribly brave to go through that all on her own.

Out beyond the place of courage, of choice, of free will, she came at last to chasm, enormous and black, and she knew that it could not be endured any longer and she lay down on the floor almost quietly to await the end. She knew her body would be ripped apart by the devil flesh in it, and particles of her would be caught in the evil wind and hurled in flayed fragments across the island, out on to the icecap, and lost forever in the great white desert. And then, miraculously, she found a new strong rhythm, and she leaned on the rhythm and recognized in it some of the rhythm of her desire and it was the sweet rhythm of passion which had brought her to this last place. But it was a new place too, a new command, a new power, a new dignity. And she pushed down, bracing herself firmly against the wall of the hut. She was no longer herself, but a new strong woman, and not cold, nor hunger, nor death itself could stop her in the power of her striding. She would walk the great white plains beyond the ocean, beyond the sunset, and give birth to a child in the New World. And in the first shadow turning of the morning her daughter was born, tiny, white, bloody and screaming defiance and joy and life. And never, never, since the dawn of days, had anything been more beautiful and she was no longer alone and the spring would come with the child and they would blossom and flourish like the bay tree. She wrapped her tiny daughter as warmly as she could and they lay together watching the light creep into the hut, creep into the world, and she was filled with a fierce triumphant joy.

But sadly the baby died.

There wasn't any milk. The baby sucked and sucked and sucked. White and little and eager. At first it seemed to grow and strengthen, responding to the promise of spring and to her enormous, welcoming love. Soon, soon, the spring would come, the snow would melt and there would be growing things and she would stop bleeding and go out and hunt and put on weight and both the land and her breasts would flow with milk and wild honey, and the child would be the first daughter of freedom. But there was no milk. And she was too tired, too tired, too tired. So for six weeks she watched the baby die, its huge wise eyes uncomplaining, its tiny mouth still trusting, still hoping, still sucking. It shrank, shriveled away just as the snow was doing, and suddenly in the middle of one night she knew that it was dead.

It could have hung on a little longer, just a little longer. Just a few days later from far away on the mainland she heard the gonging of the breaking ice and very soon she was able to bury them together, and with the burial it was springtime, and small white flowers blossomed among the rocks and the sea birds laid their eggs casually in the crevices of the cliffs. Then the great geese flocks pulled the warm weather with them as they flew northwards overhead to their nesting grounds. They passed so thickly that using the gun for the first time she was able to have roast goose for supper every night for weeks and the fat ran down her chin sweet and oily. She could not bear to think about her little white baby, so she did not. She had survived and the sun came out sweetly and warmed the cold marrow in the depths of her bones.

So that when the spring came she was all on her own and she must have felt that she would never get off the island. She could see other islands not too far away and on clear days probably the mainland too low in the distance, but she had no way of getting that far; probably she did not even know how to swim, because rich girls in those days weren't taught that sort of thing, but even if she could, why should she leave what little she had to go to another deserted island? That corner of eastern Quebec is, even today, one of the most godforsaken places in the world; there are still no towns, no roads, no nothing, just spruce trees and silver birches and scrub and rocky land for miles and miles and miles northwards until you get to the Arctic. Southwards was the great sea, reaching as far as she could see, and for all she knew it went on forever.

And perhaps this was really the time when her courage was most tested, when she was bravest of all. Because now she had no one depending on her, no one needing her like her baby did, no reason at all for keeping going. And she knew what it was really like; she knew there would be another winter, and another winter, and another winter, and she must often have wondered why she bothered at all. She must have been dreadfully lonely and desperate and miserable sometimes, but she kept struggling on.

She had to learn how to do all sorts of new things—things that no woman she had ever heard of had done. She must have learned to shoot and fish and hunt, and build fires and find eggs, and chop wood. She even shot a couple of bears.

And in a different way that second year was worse than the first had been, partly because she wasn't so strong and well as she had been the year before. She really wasn't getting enough to eat, and especially not enough vegetables and greens, and she had had the baby which must have worn her down. But also something very scary began to happen to her: she was attacked by demons. Well, I expect really they were just in her head, and perhaps she was going a little crazy or something from being on her own for so long and not knowing if she would ever see another human being in her whole life; and because of the sad sad things that had happened to her. But she believed in them all right, and all through her second winter on the island they tormented her, howling round her little hut and scaring her out of her mind. She even tried to shoot them with her gun, but that didn't work at all.

Busy. Busy. It was essential to keep busy. To wake up in the morning and make plans, and then to carry them out. Be organized. Be efficient. Today I will find grasses and mosses and stuff the cracks in the hut walls; today I will walk across the island and watch the seals playing; today I will check the lines and lay them for fish.

In the spring she shot a bear; a big, rough, brown bear. She never knew where it had come from; she walked through the spruce trees one day and there it was, its back to her, grazing. Almost without thinking she shot it dead, and realized with a deep joy that she would have a warm cover for the next winter. The bear meat made her sick, she did not eat it; but she had skinned the fur off, hacking bloodily, excitedly through a whole day, the warm fur, the warm blood and the distant memories of the pig-killings at the childhood farm in Picardy. And she stretched the skin and dried it and salted it and scraped it and it was a great victory. She danced for herself on the green grass and thought that she was the only French lady in the whole world who had killed a bear and stretched its fur for a blanket. There were so many little joys. She had to think about them and keep busy. She danced for hours before she felt silly and naked and self-conscious. Naked, bloody and dancing like a savage; if she were not careful she would forget how to be a decent Christian; she added reading the Bible to her daily tasks.

That summer she thought she was happy. She did not let herself think about the things that made her unhappy. She did not sleep much for when she was asleep dreams came to her and they did not make her happy. She stayed up through the nights and watched the heavy stars and thought about nothing and sang little snatches of old songs, and of new ones that she made up for herself. And as autumn came she noticed with amusement that like the animals her hair was turning white for the winter.

What changed? It changed the day she shot the second bear.

She saw them from her hut, the great swimming bears, white and strong, churning up the channel to her little cove. A huge white bear, creamy and immense, black nose and mighty forelegs. And with it two bear cubs; half grown, snowier. She sat still by her hut and watched them enchanted. The mother bear stretched out and the little ones curled against her great wet flank and they dozed a little on the pebbles. Then the cubs woke up and they played, such joyful play, and so like children, rolling and cuffing and delighting, nose to nose the two cubs and heaving up over their mother's body while she stirred in her sleep and pushed them off with those great fierce paws made gentle in mother-love; and they nuzzled her and rollicked in the autumn sunshine while the sea reflected a soft, playful approval. She wanted desperately to go and play with them, rolling and smothering in that density of white fur, that warm and vital softness. And she knew that if she moved, if she coughed or stirred, they would be gone, back on a sudden into the sea and she would be alone again.

Then she knew in all her being that her baby was dead and that she was alone and the realization broke her heart. And in a great anger of jealousy for the bear mother, of jealousy and spite, she glided, crafty, graceful—oh, yes, premeditated; made—not wild and manic in her jealousy—but mean, mean. She got her gun and she stood at the door of her hateful hopeless little hut and she shot one of the bear cubs. At the explosion the mother bear leapt up on to her hind legs and roared; and she thought for one glorious moment that the bear would come, terrible as the Lord on Judgment Day, and kill her dead, and she could go where her daughter had gone and be silent as stone for always and forevermore. And even as she thought that she was reloading her gun, ready, determined.

The mother bear looked at her baby, poked it with her nose, and then she and the other cub took to the sea, a great slither of white fur and hard muscle and they were gone. From the rocks beyond the cove she thought she could hear the wail of ursine grief, the great screams of a loving mother whose child has been stolen away by death. Slowly she went down the beach, slowly with her bare foot she touched the baby bear. It was not dead, it turned to her, its eyes pleading love. It was bigger than her baby, but white, white as an egg, and it had the same dark, puzzled, huge, wise eyes. Unthinking, she bunched her fist and put it on the cub's muzzle, and the bear sucked it firmly for a moment and then it died. She pulled it on to her lap. Sadly she stroked the thick white fur and she wept.

The soul of her daughter who had longed to live had traveled forth into the body of a bear cub because the thick soft fur would protect her from the cold. She had killed the mother bear's child and she had killed her own child. Everything that she touched she killed; his violence had not been in him, it had been in her. She had killed him. She had killed her daughter, and her daughter's soul had gone into the body of the bear, into the great rich womb of the mother bear and had come out safely again; her child's soul had found at last a real, a good, a mighty mother, but she had killed her child again.

So when the winter frosts came again she lay broken under the brown bear's fur, cuddling and caressing the fur of the small white bear, her daughter whom she had killed twice. And when the winds came the demons came too. She let them come. She gave them power. She let them come because with the white fur in her arms she could not refuse all the memories anymore. For three weeks he had lain dying and she had hated him; she had killed him and she had hated him. For thirty-three hours she had labored for her daughter, but it was not enough. The child had died and she had been there and had done nothing. She had not been able to save her. Slowly, cunningly she had crept into the hut, and taken the gun, and killed the snow-white bear, for no reason, no reason but spite and jealousy and greed for power.

The mother bear sent the demons.

The mother bear had come to the island to be her friend and guard, to let her burrow into that thick fur, to let her pass the winter curled up against the store of sweet fishy fat. And she had killed the mother's cub. The mother's child, her own child. So the mother bear had sent the demons.

No. The mother bear was a demon. She had come on the shoulder of the snowstorm to torture her with memories.

God had sent the demons to punish her, because she had killed another woman's child, for spite.

God did not exist. God had abandoned her. God could not endure the hellish cold. Here, in this land, she had gone beyond the power of God. She had come into the power of demons. God who had hung on the cross had given her, in his weakness, over to the strength of the demons.

The demons came in from the sea as the mother had come. They came riding the wind, triumphant and screeching. They came on the driving eddies of the snowstorm. They howled about her house, shaking the timbers and trying to get in.

Last winter she had known there were voices in the wind, but she had not heard their words. Now she could hear. Now she was open to them. Now she could not escape them.

Whore, they said, whore, slut, cunt, bitch. Adulterer, murderer, blasphemer. Whore, slut, cunt, witch.

They stripped her down to the bare bone.

The wages of sin are death. This is judgment. Yea, though you flee to the uttermost parts of the sea, we will find you. The wages of lust are death. There is no escape. The sweetness of your white skin in his arms; the sweet smell of putrefaction.

Whore, slut, cunt, bitch. Death is too easy for you. We bide our time. You hear our voices in the foxes singing for their carrion flesh. You stink of sin; they will not need to wait until you are dead.

You birthed us in the power you birthed your baby. You thought, you slut, that you were strong and free; in the maw of your stinking belly you gave birth to use. Your daughter is our mother. Her soul fled howling and angry to the north places and she bred us there. The daughter of sin, the child of adultery, bred demons and witches out of her tiny cunt. Monsters. We are your children.

Hairy, the Devil is hairy. Your gash is hairy. You let him put his foul, hairy member into yours. You encouraged him. You kissed the arse of the Devil and bound yourself to the demons. We are better lovers than he. You groveled to him to tickle your slit. We will slit you, and you will grovel to us, beg, plead, whimper. Witch. Your uncle knew. A wise young man. Upright. Holy. Beloved of God. He was given the gift of discernment. He could smell your corruption and he rooted you out. He gave you to us because you deserved it. Whore.

They burn witches. The marketplaces of Picardy are sweet with the smell of cooked flesh. We are burning you, burning you to the bone with cold and grief.

Humble yourself, daughter of pride. Grovel. Beg. Beg us. You begged him and we are stronger. Much stronger. Grovel to us or we will break you. We will break your body. We will break your mind.

Calmer moments: the bright freezing nights, when the rocking and the pounding of the hut remitted. She would step outside to

breathe, and the sky would be illuminated with the strange cold
fireworks from the north, a spectacle making nonsense of the night
and of the winter and of her puny littleness in the whole great void
beyond the west of the world. And then they would come again, the
demons, whispering, singing sweet and low, women's voices, kind
and gentle, luring her to a more secret doom: You can escape, once
and for all, you can get away, sweetly, easily. Walk away from the
hut, walk out into the snow, out into the sea and all will be well.
They promised her insanity and suicide and made it a gift. They
whispered on the brittle air that there was a place without pain,
without sense or meaning, a place where dark and light, good and
bad, cold and warmth were all the same and all indifferent. And even
the shapes and sounds of words collapsed inwards, imploding, shaken
in their fabric, breaking down, down, down into a warm place inside
which there was no effort, no end, no beginning.

Come down, they murmured across the shapelessness of the flat
sea, come down, come in, come closer. Come, come, come. A small
step, an infinite drop, down, away, and the cold as sweet as a blanket
and sleep, sleep, sleeeep. Dream a new time. A time before. Before
there was anything; before the voice of God called the word of law
across the void. When there was only the shapeless, wordless
swirling. We can give you that, that formless, wordless rocking. We
can give you that, if you submit. Let go. Submit. Bow down and
worship us. Consent. You have only to consent. To let go.

And in the darkness she would cling to the frail hut, physically
hold it, bite her own hands, hug the white fur until her ribs ached.
She would remember, she would try to remember that the cold was a
killer, that she must not leave the fireside. That spring came after
winter, that order came out of chaos; and out of order came pattern
and out of pattern history and life and herself. She did not consent.
She did not submit. She was alive. She was still alive.

And then roaring again. Enormous. Fierce broken roaring. The
noise so great it would break her ears open and her brains would
strew the shore red on white. Slut. Whore. Cunt. SLUT. WHORE.
CUNT. SSLLUUTTWWHHOORREECCUUNNTT. Finished. You

are finished, whore. We have the power here, cunt. We have the power and we will break you, slut. You are damned, whore; you are damned for all eternity. Damned, damned, Damned.

And on and on and on and on and on and on and on andon andon andon on on on on on on on on o n o n o n o n o n o nnnnnnnn oooooonnnnnnnn.

Until she cannot stand it any longer; and in a fury of destruction, anything, anything to silence their voices, she took the gun and shot at the wind through the roof, shoving in the shot, blasting wildly, great holes in the roof and powder burns on her arms and face. Bang, bang, bang. Enormous explosion—the wonderful great crashing of the gun at her behest silencing all other sounds, for a glorious and powerful time.

When the fury left her she saw she had used all her powder; there was none left. She had reached the end. She would die. And she lay on the floor of the hut, and their voices came again, no words now because she was as the animals are, just roaring and grunting and squealing and howling. How she had been in his arms. How she had been in her anger against him. How she had birthed her daughter. Pig grunts, and fox howls, and mewlings on her knees before his violence. And enormous growling, snarling, screeching and never never leaving her. And it was the end and all things were finished. And . . .

And no, she did not consent.

"I do not consent," she said, and her own words echoed in the hut with a magnificent reality.

Words. Words at least were better. She seized the Bible. Grateful, even and suddenly, to Roberval who had given her nothing, but had not deprived her of human words, human contact.

> Out of the depths I have called unto you, O Lord; Lord
> hear my prayer. Oh let your ears consider well the voice
> of my complaint. If you, Lord, will be extreme to mark
> what is done amiss, Lord, who may endure it; but there
> is mercy with you and therefore shalt thou be feared.

And again louder. But their voices were louder still. WHORE. CUNT. SLUT. FOULNESS. ADULTERER.

> Then he said to the woman taken in adultery, Go in peace and sin no more. He said, Do not be afraid, be of good cheer, for behold I am with you always.

WITCH. SLUT. ANIMAL. IN THE SILENCE WE WILL KILL YOU. YOU ARE DAMNED.

> And the Word was made flesh and dwelt among us.

WHORE. SLUT. WHORE.

> And he blessed her saying, Much will be forgiven her, because she loved much.

BELIEVE THAT, FOOL, AND YOU'LL BELIEVE ANYTHING.

> And when they had mocked him they stripped him. And they led him out to crucify him.

Whore. Slut. Cunt. Starving bag of bones, careened in the desert, lost, lost, hopeless.

> It is when you are weak that you are strong.
> God chose what is foolish in the world to shame the wise.
> God chose what is weak in the world to shame the strong.

Witch. Slut. Whore. Your uncle deserted you, drove you out from the camps of men, gave you over to us.

And the Spirit drove him out into the wilderness. And he was in the wilderness forty days, fasting, tempted of Satan. He was with the wild beasts and the angels ministered to him.

Cunt.   Bitch.   whore.

He was with the wild beasts and the angels ministered to him. Do not be afraid, be of good cheer.
The word was made flesh.

We have power.

He was in the wilderness, fasting, and tempted of Satan. He was with the wild beasts and the angels ministered to him.
Do not be afraid. Be of good cheer. For lo, I am with you always, even to the ends of the world.
I tell you, her sins which were many are forgiven, because she loved much.
I come that you may have life, and life more abundantly.
He was with the wild beasts and the angels ministered unto him.

silence.

The world was made flesh; and she wrapped him in swaddling bands and laid him in a manger because there was no room for them at the inn.

silence.

The word was made flesh and dwelt among us.

silence.

there was silence. And in the silence there was a turning of the year and in herself.

My soul magnifies the Lord, and my spirit rejoices in God my savior;
God who is mighty has magnified me, and holy is His name.
And all generations shall call me blessed.
He has put down the mighty from their seats and exalted the humble and meek. He has filled the hungry with good and sent the rich away empty.

It was an old song, a woman's song, a song of victory.

The winter was over. Naked, bloody, battered. Starving. She opened the door of the hut and fell forwards into the sunshine. The blood of battle stained her face. Emaciated, hanging on to life by a thin thread, the soft generosity of the white bear skin still in her arms. The roses of starvation flowering fresh on her back. She lay there, spread out. A deep and everlasting peace. To go so near to death that you have tasted its sweetness and decided against it. Decided for life. Hell had been harrowed, she had walked the unknown pathway and found the road home. Death had no more dominion.

Blessed are those who going through the valley of misery use it for a well, and the pools are filled with water.
They will go from strength to strength and unto the God of Gods appeareth every one of them in Zion.

It actually wouldn't matter if she died now.

But I shall not die, I shall live and praise my God.

She had been in the wilderness, fasting and tempted of Satan. But there were words spoken, fur coverings chanced upon, and a sunrise, a victory, a triumph. The silence in her head was perfect and perfectly peaceful.

And by amazing luck, after that winter was over, some Portuguese fishermen, driven in from the Great Banks, saw her fire smoke and came and rescued her. They took her back to France and she went home. Later she told her story to Jean Alfonce, who had been Roberval's pilot, and he told it to his friend and patroness Marguerite of Navarre, and she put it in her story book called the *Heptameron* and that's how we know about her.

"Mummy, what happened next?"

"She stayed in Picardy and taught school for the rest of her life."

"Oh. Mummy?"

"Yes, darling."

"Can I have a chocolate biscuit now?"

Seal-Self

In Cleveland it was well known that any wild goose which flew over Whitby would instantly drop dead; and that to catch a seal it was first necessary to dress as a woman.

Keith Thomas, *Man and the Natural World*

It is cold when he wakes, stirred from forgotten dreams by the deep whirring in the air. The goose flocks are driving north again. It is cold and still dark, too dark to see the great wide arrowheads, spread wide, not yet regathered since they had split up to avoid Whitby, but he can hear them and he shivers. They stir his blood each equinox with their coming and going, up there, out there, beyond. He does not know where and he could not imagine. Last week he had seen the falling stars, the serene and magic performance of the heavens to celebrate the turning of the year. And after the falling stars the wild geese, uncountable also, will pass over along the pale coastline. For the next week they will appear, from the south, at dawn and at dusk, through the night watches and in the morning, as swift as falling stars flighting northwards towards the cold wind. And after the wild geese have passed, the seal mothers will surge up from the icy water and lay their pups on the great flat sands below. And he . . . but he does not want to think about it.

He twisted into himself seeking what warmth there still might be in the bed, wrapping his arms around himself, deliberately seeking the safety of sleep, but the deep whirring noise over the cottage roof continued unabated until it was fully dawn.

*H*is world is shaped by the stripes. Green stripe. Yellow-gold stripe. Lead-colored stripe. Blue stripe. Across the stripes, at right angles to them, ran another stripe, invisible but every bit as tangible; the fierce east wind that rushed in from far away across the ocean, coming at him, vicious and greedy, coming in a straight and evil line, down the sky, the sea, the sand, the fields. May God have mercy on his soul. He crosses himself, half scared, half scornful, for this is old women's thinking, and he is ashamed; and men now do not cross themselves, for times have changed, and his mouth curls in scorn of his mother and her fussing ways, for he is a man, and when the goose flocks are passed over and the seals come to play on the beaches, he will prove he is a man.

For the next ten days the wild geese pass over. He knows they are watching him, his friends, the geese, even the rising sun. His mother. In the village when he passes across the square the young women look at him, curious and questioning. The tawny maiden from the high farmstead eyes him, direct and challenging. She is taller than he is, and her legs run up under her skirt, legs so slender and long that they must lead somewhere good. She tosses her head in the pale April sunshine and diamonds scatter from her hair. He is bewitched by her long cool stare. As he carries the milk pail she passes by, almost brushing against him, and her clear voice bells sweetly to her friend. "They say the first of the seal mothers are come to the sand dunes. I would love a sealskin cloak this year." He hates her suddenly and brilliantly, bright as the April sunshine, but his penis stirs and he watches her breasts. She smiles at him, promising him. And if not her then another. They all promise him together.

Last year he could not bring himself to do it. It is not the killing;

he has cut pigs' throats, catapulted birds out of the sky, snared hares, wrung chicken necks, drowned kittens, baited bears, put his evil-snouted ferret to the rabbits' warrens. It is the other. They do not understand. His mother had smiled last year when he had tried to tell her. She had laid out the apparel for him even. His stomach feels sick to think about it. His dreams fill with it. And it must be this spring, for by next year his beard will be upon him. Now is the time. He knows it. He is frightened. For it is well known that to catch a seal it is first necessary to dress as a woman.

He wakes again in the darkness as before, and there is silence; the whirring of the goose flocks has vanished northwards, and though it is still cold there is a new softness in the air. His fear is very present to him. He strips off his clothes and stands naked. He pulls on his mother's skirt and arranges it at his waist, it falls lumpenly, ugly, and his hairy feet appearing at the bottom strike him as ungainly and ludicrous. He knows, blindingly as dawn, what his fear is. It is pleasure. It is pleasure and desire. He tiptoes to his mother's kist, and takes for himself her boned corsets, her linen hose, her full Sunday petticoats, her best bonnet.

Before he is half-dressed his hands are wet with his own juices: his fingers tangled with bodice ribbons and semen, his mind with delight and shame. But after that he knows that it must be done well and fully. He takes great care, padding his hips with fleece, tightening the corset with gentle concern. The skirt hangs better so. He chooses for himself breasts not too large, too heavy, but high and delicate like the tawny maiden from the high farm. He smiles for himself that smile of veiled promise that she gave him in the village square. Then when everything is ready he realizes that it will not do. He takes off the petticoats and skirt again; he takes a hair-ribbon, soft satin smooth, the same rich rose color as the chaffinch's breast, that his mother brought home from the Whitby Fairings; she never wore it, it was too fine for her, she said, she wanted it only because it was a pretty thing and no one bought her pretty things anymore. He ties it now gently round his penis, which is soft and pleased and sleepy, and draws it back between his legs, folding his testicles carefully. He feels the flat firm skin behind them and knows that there should be a hole, a place of darkness and wet that he will never know. It cannot be helped. He attaches the other end of the ribbon firmly to the bottom hole in the back of the corset. Now when he pulls on yet again the skirt and petticoat he knows that it is almost right. Shoes he must do without, for he will not mar his own loveliness with cloggy boots but none of his mother's will fit him. But stockinged feet are charming for a maid out in the fields at daydawn.

As he passes the parlor he sees in the half light himself in the mirror glass, gold curls fluffing out under the sweet bonnet with its delicately ruched and pleated inner brim. How pretty she is, he thinks, so much prettier than the tawny maid from the high farmstead. He smiles. How pretty I am, she thinks, and she raises the latch craftily and skips out, silent and dainty, into the waiting springtime.

The preparation has taken longer than was planned. Now it is dawn already; the great stripes of the countryside have already divided themselves, though not yet into colors, only into different greys. But there is a ribbon, laid tidily between the grey stripe of sea and the paler grey stripe of sky, a rose pink ribbon holding the world in shape, the day spring whence the sun will be born.

She shivers in the cold dawn and wishes that she had a sealskin cloak to snuggle in, a cloak made from the softness of baby seal, white and thick and dappled. A sealskin cloak trimmed and fastened with rose pink ribbons, she thinks, and then she laughs at herself for her vanity. Nor would she wear one if he gave it to her, for seals are friends to honest women, and she is going now to meet her friend Seal Woman and greet the new Seal Child who will have been carried in the deep waters all through the winter, wrapped in thick sweet blubber and rocked in a secret bay between the promontories of her mother's pubic bones, safe within the greater ocean. And who would now be pupped in the soft golden sand, clumsy and enchanting, pug-faced, soft-furred, playful and unafraid. No woman of sense or worth would accept a sealskin cloak, not from the King himself were he to come to the cold coastland north of Whitby and hear the wind rush in from far across the ocean; nor would she wear one and mock the mourning of Seal Woman for her child.

So she laughs, though kindly, at herself and her vanity and walks across the grey meadows towards the seaside; and as she walks the light seeps gently into the air and the grass turns towards green and the birds begin to sing and the sea sedge and saxifrage are pale pinky mauve and the celandines are yellow. The pink ribbon beyond the sea widens and pales and the broad sweep of the sky overhead is almost as white and pure as the frothed edges of her petticoats, bleached out with love and joy.

Closer to, the line, which from the cottage seems so precisely drawn between grass and sea, is blurred, indefinite, hesitant. First there is grass and woolly sheep still huddled against the night, then there are scrubby plants mixed in with bare patches of earth, of sand, then there is mostly sand with the occasional bold push or outcrop of reedy grass, and then almost unnoticeably there is only sand, great reaches of it in rolling hills, swirled into fantastic shapes by the long-drawn wind from the sunrise side of the ocean. And finally the hillocks settle, flattened out by the waves, and there is a wide wet beach changing constantly with the long pushes and tugs of the tide.

And when she comes at last to the very end of the dunes, to the edge of the tide beach, she heaves a great sigh of relief, coming home, united in her belly with the pushes and pulls of the tide, of the moon, of the great spaces of the sea. Quietly and easily she folds her legs, her skirt ballooning softly around her and sits in silence watching the long waves roll in, smooth and strong from out there, out beyond her eye view, and each wave is different and each wave is exactly the same forever and ever and she feels calmed, rocked, soothed, contented.

And as she sits there, waiting for the sun to rise, the seals begin to emerge. Some from the sea where they had gone at her approaching, and some from the dunes where they had slept. Now they flop, heavy and clumsy, on the shining golden sand by the waterline. Some are still gravid, ponderous and careful, and some have already pupped and their tiny young lurch around them or frolic idiotically in the wave edges. Not thirty yards from the shore a mother seal floats on her back, her tail flapping balance against the wave tossings, her little white pup held, flipper-fast, against her breast to suckle. So water-graceful, land-clumsy; so strong, so tender; so like and so unlike herself. She forgot the reason and the manner of her coming and waited only on the movement of the tide and the rising of the sun.

"Good morning, my dear," says Seal Woman, "and welcome."

She springs to her feet to curtsy.

"Hello," says Seal Child. "I'm new."

And new she certainly is, but already with bright black eyes that look and see, and with flourished whiskers, moustaching out from her black nose, and dappled white-grey fur fluffed in the sun. Barely two feet long, neatly constructed for an environment that cannot sustain her, at home in no element, timeless, lovable, perfect and preposterous. She smiles and reaches out a hand to touch Seal Child's nose.

And now, now he is meant now to take a stone and smash it down on Seal Child's head, blanking out the shiny eyes forever and carrying off the soft skin to the tawny maiden from the high homestead to wear as her victor's spoils, and to prove to the village that he has become a man, but she has forgotten this, lost in the wide free space of air and ocean, lost in the wide loving gaze of Seal Woman.

There is no need to talk much, or to talk of anything in particular. She sits, Seal Woman sprawls, and Seal Child suckles unhindered, occasionally wriggling or squeaking in delight. And all across the wet beach there are a hundred other seal mothers suckling, snoozing, sprawling, and now the gulls come swooping, wailing, to join them, and out on the breakers the older pups play and beyond that the sea pours in, in, in, a long solemn, musical procession, ancient and careful. And, quite suddenly, the sun rises.

Seal Child waggles her flippers in delight, tosses her tail, gambols a little. Seal Child says, "Will you play with me?"

"Yes," she says, "yes, please."

"Mother, come too," begs Seal Child.

"Of course," says Seal Woman.

So together the three of them go down to the seashore and plunge in. And suddenly she is not woman to woman with Seal Woman, but child to child with Seal Child. In the water it is a new Seal Child, graceful, strong, rhythmic; suddenly no longer little and sweet but powerful, fast, the fur no longer soft and fluffy but streamlined, completed. Together she and Seal Child splash and paddle in the breaking water, dance in and out of the foam, going deeper, deeper, deeper in. The waves mount around her, lifting her skirts gently up and down, until they are soaked through and dragging at her legs; her balance fails and she falls into the next wave, is lifted by it, raised up, brought down, and left as it runs on in towards the sparkling sands. When she realizes that her feet will not touch the bottom again she is, for a moment, scared and then it does not matter because she too can swim like a seal, strong and shapely, powerful in the water as never on the land. And deep new places opening in her lungs so that she can go down and under and be there unafraid.

And now they swim and swim; the dark cold waters are the breeding grounds of fishes who move in vast shoals hard to see. But flipping over and rising upwards the surface is a great starry sky, brighter and fiercer than the terrestrial constellations; where the water meets the air there is a barrier, a great spangled ceiling, chandeliered with light, with air, water, sun-fire sparkled. And turning downwards, down, down into the dark there is the everlasting silence, the great underwater drifts and waves and forces of currents unlit by the sunshine, and great still mountains, cliffs, ranges, beflowered in dark growths whose shadows deepen the green darkness and whose rhythms are from before the beginning of air breathing, and Seal Woman flows between her two children, guarding them, hovering over them, around them, protecting them, remembering them in the forgotten places. And there is no weight, no gravity, no memory, and deep, deep below there is the ocean floor whence they all came and whither they do not choose to go and they are carried above it joyfully, on the strength of their own limbs, wings, fins. And Seal Child, using flippers and nose, pulls away the ties on the sweet little bonnet and it floats a moment in the water, like a dark jellyfish, and is gone.

Then, on another shared thought, they all turn and shoot upwards, breaking the surface into sprinkled jewels, whooshing into sunlight, their lungs pulling in new fresh air, bobbing upon the surface and laughing together. And Seal Child, using tail and teeth, strips off the knitted hose and chases them playfully across the wave tops till they drift away.

They swim far north to the gathering and gossiping grounds of the salmon, under the shelter of the great ice pack, where the waters teem with microscopic life, and are greener than the grass. They swim among the mating places of the wild geese and see the cold slopes where the white swans winter. They watch the dignified icebergs sail regally out towards their death, glittering bravely in the bright sunlight, and they dine without effort on the herring shoals that drift on unseen currents across the sub-polar waters. And Seal Child, using nose and mouth, nuzzles off the skirt and petticoats, the bodice and sleeves, and lazily they float away to provide refuge for some weary tern in some other distant sea.

And then they turn and drift slowly southwards, following the cold current that finds its way along the eastern coast of Scotland, leisurely riding the water and watching the ships in the distance break the tidy line of the horizon. And the sun comforts those bits of them that break the surface of the cold sea, so they turn on their backs and let their tummies feel the gentle spring warmth in the morning light. And they play in the rocky pools off Lindisfarne, the Holy Island; and watch the great gannets drop sixty vertical feet through the air, white streaks of power; and they tease the gaudy puffins who bob and wimble under those serene cliffs. And Seal Child, using tail and flippers and mouth and nose, unties the corset cords and pulls the garment off and with a weary sigh it sinks down and down to amuse poor drowned sailors from years and years ago.

And as they come back to their own golden beach to the north of Whitby, the end of the rose-pink ribbon, which she had tied to the corset and which had worked its way in between her buttocks, floats loose and drifts like the colorful seaweed in a coral lagoon two thousand miles away to the south and west. Seal Child plays with it as it dangles and they all laugh, riding in on the breakers and coming to rest at last on the sunny wet sand in the first early hours of the day.

And Seal Woman and she lounge on the beach and talk of those things that women talk of when they have had good physical exercise and are met in magic places, while Sea Child frolics around them playing with the ends of the pink ribbon and with her penis.

Seal Child says, "I love you."

She says, "I love you too." All three of them grin peacefully. And it is simply true.

Seal Child is still very young. Love means warmth and cuddling and feeding. Seal Child scrambles up on to her body and tries to suckle from her, not finding flat breasts, small nipples or a soft furred chest anything out of the usual. She holds Seal Child under the front flippers to steady her, feeling with great pleasure the softness of wet fur against her own belly. Seal Child's whiskers and soft mouth tickle, she giggles and rolls over with her; mother child; child puppy; child child; happy. Seal Child tries again to suckle, her mouth is round and pink, her lips firm and sweet against the nipple. And suddenly the soft and floppy penis, still bedecked with rose pink ribbon, springs up, awakened. She rolls over on to Seal Child who wriggles in the sand. Suddenly he looks up. Seal Woman is looking at him, not just with anger, but with great sadness and greater amazement. He springs to his feet, the ribbon still dangling.

"I'm sorry," he says to Seal Woman.

"Come and play some more," says Seal Child.

"No," says Seal Mother.

Seal Child looks puzzled. She is about to start whining. She flops to her mother and finds there the milky sweetness she had been seeking; with enthusiasm she begins to feed.

"I'm sorry," he says again.

"I have never been fooled before," says Seal Woman. "Why is it?"

"I was naked," he says, beginning to be annoyed. "You could have seen. You must have known."

"That's not what counts," says Seal Woman.

They are still. They both look out at the sea, where the waves break still. They both look at Seal Child sucking. For a last moment they both share equally the desire to protect the baby at all costs.

Feeling their attention on her, Seal Child breaks her sucking and grins. She flops affectionately over to him and for a moment Seal Woman just watches them. Seal Child tugs at the wet pink ribbon. His penis swells again.

"You must go now," says Seal Woman sadly.

Seal Child, silky wet, rubs her flat face across his belly.

"I could cut it off," he offers; and for a sweet moment of fear, excitement, desire, loss, he means it. Seal Child's snout snuffles downwards, nibble-mumbling his soft hair; her whiskers tickle him. His penis stirs, Seal Child and he giggle.

"No, that's not what counts," says Seal Woman.

"No," says Seal Child.

"No," he agrees.

"Please," he says.

Now, he thinks, now I should take up this heavy stone, that is here, by good fortune, here just beside me, here at hand, and bash in her head and strip out her blubber guts and carry home her soft sweet fur and have her forever and be a man. This is what I came for, he thinks, and his penis stirs again.

"Please," he says, "please let me stay."

And if they will just do what he says, wants, needs, he thinks he will not have to hurt them.

"No," says Seal Woman. She knows his thoughts but she is not afraid. She is angry-sad, sad-angry. "No."

They vanish.

They have taken from him even a moment of choice. The stone is there, round, heavy, fitted to his hand, but he had not decided. Round the very base of his penis, tangled in his golden pubic hair, is one long whisker caught underneath the rose pink ribbon, but he had not decided. He will never know what he would have decided.

It is full morning, suddenly, bright beyond bearing. On the golden stripe of the beach there is nothing but his golden body. Out in the leaden-colored stripe he sees their leaden-colored heads bob, spaniel-eyed, sad and smiling.

He goes home. He crosses out of the golden stripe and into the green one. No one sees his solemn, naked procession.

Later he says, "It is well known that any wild goose which flies over Whitby will instantly drop dead; and that to catch a seal it is first necessary to dress as a woman."

Later he says, "I caught a seal, but then I let her go." He does not know if they believe him; he does not know if he is a man.

Blessed Are Those Who Mourn

Then at his fated hour, Scyld the Brave departed to go into the keeping of the Lord. His loving friends carried him to the seashore as he himself had asked. There at the landing place the ring-prowed vessel lay, the prince's ship, rimed with ice, but eager to start. They laid their beloved chieftain on the ship's bosum, glorious by the mast. They brought many valuable treasures, ornaments from distant lands. I have never heard of a ship more fairly fitted out with war weapons and battle raiment, swords and coats of mail. On his chest lay a mound of treasures which were to travel with him far out into the power of the sea. They also set a golden standard high above his head and then they let the sea bear him—gave him to the ocean.

I had a late "spontaneous abortion"—miscarriage to most of us—at twenty weeks.

"By the twentieth week of pregnancy (measured from the first day of the last period, that is about fourteen days before conception) the fetus is clearly human. Its skin is no longer transparent and it is covered with fine downy hair over the whole body. The eyelids are still fused but the internal organs are becoming mature. It is now about ten inches long and weighs about eleven ounces. It is very active in its weightless condition within the amniotic sac; and the mother will be feeling the movements within the uterus."

Or: The embryonic group of unconfirmed, indefinable cells which I wanted to get rid of only a couple of months ago has become for me (for this is a subjective definition) my child; the child I had come to love and want.

That is my baby I am mourning and am not allowed to mourn.

"There's no need to feel guilty." But what does need have to do with guilt? Of course I feel guilty. I never made her welcome, I did not treat her well. Perhaps she found her conditions unacceptable, perhaps she could not endure it in my womb. They are forever telling us what lack of maternal love can do to a small child; how do they know that a fetus can't be affected in the same way? It's no use saying of course it can't: I know it can't, but how do I know, how can I be sure? That's what neurotic guilt is. What I do know is that I did not want her. Yes, her. I've seen her now, lying in my bread bowl. I rang the Doctor and said, "Please, I'm bleeding, please do something. I'm bleeding heavily and sort of lumpily, I've got strange pains in the pit of my gut, please help me."

And he said, "Oh dear; look, go to bed, lie still. There's very little we can do. Either you will miscarry or you won't. I'll come round as soon as I can. If the pain gets very bad ring the hospital, otherwise you'll probably be happier at home. Oh yes, and keep the products of conception will you."

"The what?"

" 'The products of conception.' That's what we call what you're losing, the blood and everything in it. We have to check them you see."

What I think I'm losing is my baby; I do not say so, though. The products of conception. A week ago I went to see him at the ante-natal clinic. He called her Mr. Bump. I felt that was nauseating enough, but she was a person to him then, only a few days ago. He was telling me about some of the things she would be needing and how without a man-about-the-house he could arrange for me and her to stay longer at the hospital, to give us a chance to get used to each other. But she was alive there. We were laughing together, the Doctor and I, because I said that her tiny fluttery movements inside tickled me. He told me how his daughter had kicked so hard that it tickled him in the night; he could feel her feet distinctly between his ribs. When I left he'd said, "I'll see the two of you next month then."

Now it was "the products of conception" . . . at the beginning when I'd talked to him about abortion, or rather demanded that he should talk to me about abortion, he had not talked like he's doing now. He was a good liberal, of course, if I really wanted, he did understand, but he was not convinced. I might mourn afterwards, he did not like to use the word guilt, but grieving for what might have been was a very common syndrome, particularly from my Catholic background, if the need or the desire wasn't clear cut. Life was not impossible nowadays, not easy of course but a challenge, possible in my social position, assistance was available. My need and desire had not been clear, I'd felt grateful to him, he had understood that; it's easy enough not to be sure what would be the best thing, especially as he said, for us ex-Catholics, it hangs around that feeling, more than a feeling in my case, a definite desire, a sense of wrong. Illogical if you like, but I felt it. I decided then to be pregnant, to have the baby. What do decisions decide? I'd felt close to the Doctor then, but now . . .

"Perhaps, all things considered, it's the best thing that could have happened, in the long run." He liked the long run, my nice liberal Doctor, that long run like the long range weather forecast, you can always change it, no one can hold it against you. In the long run, he had said, I think you might find having an abortion even more traumatic than carrying the baby to term; after that you could think about the future; successful motherhood means a surprising amount about how you feel about yourself, you identify, you know; you must take a gamble on yourself and your sex; a very satisfying experience in the long run. Well, isobars drift off course, depressions and highs come and go. The Next Ice Age and a prolonged warmer period are both confidently predicted for Northern Europe, in the long run.

"Please," I said to the telephone receiver, "can we leave prophecy for a moment, please, my baby is dying. I know my baby is dying."

"Take some of the Valium I gave you for the morning sickness."

"Doctor, my baby is falling out of me, she's going to die, I don't want her to die, not now, now I want her to live, I've wanted her to live for some time now and she's dying. Doctor, please."

I can feel him getting embarrassed; I can feel him remembering that he can't use his old palliatives, better luck next time, you can always have another, if the worst comes to the worst. I advise you to get pregnant again as soon as possible. You can't say those things to an unmarried mother. Poor Doctor. I can feel him shake his shoulders, long for a cup of coffee and long not to have to think what to say. "Come on, you mustn't hang on here talking, I want you in bed, now. I'll be round as soon as possible."

My feet are cold. The pain is bad, I agree, prepare to hang up. Then he said, "Look, one thing, if you do miscarry, you mustn't feel guilty or inadequate. A single miscarriage, even at this late stage, is no *proof* of inadequacy, nothing wrong with you as a woman, if you see what I mean."

I did not see what he meant. I had not even thought of it. I did not want assurance about my psychological welfare. I wanted him to do something to stop my child from dying.

> With faces smeared with blood, breasts bared and garments rent the hired mourners groaned, wailed and recalled the virtues of the dead man. In his lengthy funeral procession servants carried cakes and flowers, pottery and stone vases, figurines and tools. A second group bore normal articles of furniture; and a third was responsible for personal effects like clothes and writing equipment. The sarcophagus itself was hidden beneath an elaborate catafalque drawn by a pair of cows; it was mounted on a boat flanked by statues of Isis and Nephys, the boat itself being mounted on a sledge. The procession made its elaborate way, which included a ritual crossing of the Nile, to the tomb. The dead man's

colleagues walked soberly, discussing their friend and his tastes and making standardized observations on the blows of fate and the brevity and uncertainty of human life. His wife made her prescribed formal laments. After much ritual activity, including censings, purifications, laments and the arrangement of immense quantities of equipment the dead man would need for his resuscitation and life in the next world, the priests and assistants were free to withdraw and the mason walled up the tomb's doorway. The friends and relatives however would gather in the tomb's lobby and eat and drink and sing before making their way back to the town as noisily as possible.

Afterwards the Doctor had the grace to say that he was sorry, so sorry, that if he had realized I was alone he would have done something about it, if he had realized how serious and heavy the bleeding was he would have acted more promptly, he would have done something. I do not blame him, if I had thought about it I too could have done something. There were plenty of friends I could have asked. I could not bear the thought of them: they might have grieved for her. So when she was born, miscarried, appeared, put in her brief appearance—I do not know the appropriate term—I was alone. I was glad, though. If there had been anyone else there I could not have done what I did. I could not have spent time with her. Their embarrassment, and indeed my own, would have prevented it. I would have had to have been strong and sensible and good and not put anyone out.

I could feel, quite distinctly, her being born; it was not in itself painful, and totally separate from the pain, the gripping pain in the womb itself. Probably she was too small, but right there I lost all faith I might have had in "painless childbirth"; if my womb could hurt like this for her, so tiny and unresistant, what could it be like trying to expel a full-sized, real baby . . . or perhaps they want to be born, perhaps their participation makes it easier. I don't know. I'm avoiding the point: it seemed so right at the time; simple and necessary and good, I must trust that; already it seems strange and awkward and embarrassing. When she was ejected I was able, being alone, to pick her up, cradle her, not in my arms she was too small, but in my hands, examine, inspect her; discover she was not, as I had half-imagined, an It, but so clearly a She. Tiny but perfect, although skinny and wrinkled. A few beginning bits of hair on her head, but almost furry on her shoulders and back. You could see the blood vessels through her skin. Her eyes were shut. I wanted to force them open but it was not possible, they were sealed, no split at all between the lids. Her hands covered her face, I thought at first to stop me seeing her expression, but when I pushed them back I realized that she really had no expression, just a blank look, nearer to resignation, but not that. She had fingernails, they were transparent too and not fully grown, softer than my own.

My worst fear was that she might be alive and I would not know what to do about it. If she was, though, I did not have to detect it. I was as gentle with her as I knew how to be. But I had to look, I had to know. I slid her back into the bread bowl, after a while. The blood received her, she seemed to wiggle like a fish. In Medieval Europe scarlet was sometimes used as a mourning color for the very great and important. Jesus washed us in his blood, but she drowned in mine. I don't understand why she should wait until I cared. It seems so fatuous, so deliberately cruel. If she was not set on living, why ever start, or why not give up earlier. So short a time ago she could have vanished and I would never even have missed her, never even known. Later she could have died and I would have been glad. Or would I? Perhaps I never got the abortion because I never wanted to; I could have overcome the obstacles, in this town, with the money accessible—I could even have asked her father. Perhaps if I'd had her aborted I would have felt just as bad. I don't believe that, though; it is only just in the couple of weeks, if that, in the last few days that I believed in her, really believed that I was going to have her, that she was going to be my baby. Now I do believe and I do care; as soon as I begin to love her, she leaves me. The very stuff of romantic fiction, for this little fishlike person. I love you, how can you leave me, don't go, love me back, love me please; I don't understand, I don't understand.

Steady. Steady. Why doesn't the Doctor come? Why doesn't somebody come, please. I shall go mad. No, it's a perfectly normal reaction to miscarriage and especially late miscarriage, to feel both grief and guilt; and owing to hormonal factors, similar to those experienced after normal birth, these two feelings may develop into clinically treatable depression. So there, I'm perfectly normal. Or not, because my book goes on to say that it is of vital importance to talk over these feelings with your husband . . . well I can only hope that the book is wrong, unless they mean vital for him, because I haven't got one. At one point I even crawled to the telephone to ring her father. Darling, I could say, do you want to see your daughter? She's very beautiful, though she can't look at you, and she's swimming in my bread bowl, the one you used to get such pleasure out of because seeing me kneading wholemeal loaves made me seem like a real woman to you. Well, now the bowl contains another mark of the real woman: the ability to conceive—alas, inadequately fulfilled, but you, better than most, know my difficulties in this direction. Also in the bowl, my dear, is some blood and some leftover bits from what is meant to be one of the best designed life-support systems ever devised; which can support a human being for forty weeks in conditions exactly duplicating those in space, providing oxygen, nutrients and the disposal of waste products for the astronaut who floats freely in the weightless environment. This is better than male technology has managed to do so far. Unfortunately in this case the system has collapsed. Or, in other words, I have killed your child. The one you did not even know you had begotten. You would point out that male technology made fewer errors than women's natural systems; and inquire with earnest interest what the difference might be between male chauvinism and female chauvinism. These are the reasons why I did not ring him. I did not want him.

I was confused. I was not feeling so good. The pain was getting worse all the time, although I had supposed it would stop once she had come out. I didn't ring him, I don't think. I did telephone the

Registrar of Births and Deaths. I had to talk to someone and it seemed as though one way or another it ought to be his business. It wasn't. I think he got worried while I was talking to him; he kept asking my name and address and if I was alone. I was worried too, because he did not seem able to help me. A fetus before the twenty-eighth week is no concern of his. It doesn't have to be registered with him in either of his capacities. It was never born so it can't have died. It has been born, I tried to explain, she is in my bread bowl, now, what shall I do with her? The law does not want to know if she died by accident, only if I killed her myself, deliberately. I don't understand I said to the man on the telephone; I could not help it if he was sounding desperate. You haven't seen her, I told him, of course she had been born, she's a person, like a spaceman whose spaceship has broken down. I don't understand. I think he tried to explain. It's simple enough if I can remember it rightly: if I kill her, especially now she's getting big, it's abortion or feticide, and the latter is a category of child murder. But if she dies of her own accord she never was a person in the first place. What is one to do? I felt bereft. The space between me and the world was beginning to be filled with baby, literally, physically, and it is suddenly empty and what was there, they say, never existed. Nothing, nothing.

> After the embalming her body was enclosed in a leaden wrapping, and laid in a coffin covered with a blue velvet pall. Her daughters and son came to pray beside her and attended Mass every day. . . . The gentlemen of her household carried the coffin to the funeral car, which was drawn by six black chargers draped with black velvet; a golden pall replaced her blue covering. The chief mourners were met by one hundred pensioners in black gowns and hoods carrying tapers, an ecclesiastical dignitary carrying a cross, and the bulk of the mourners.
>
> The next morning two low Masses were said followed by the Solemn Requiem Mass in the afternoon. Then the coffin was lowered to its last resting place, the officers of the household broke their white staves and

with great weeping and lamentation threw them into
the grave. After that a funeral feast was provided for all
the mourners.

I was brought up as a Roman Catholic. I have done nothing about
this for a number of years, but it remains a part of me. It is quite
possibly the reason why finally, despite indecisions, rationalizations,
explanations, I did not have her aborted. The rites and rituals returned through the darkness and the pain. "Hail Mary full of Grace,
the Lord is with Thee, blessed art thou among women and blessed is
the fruit of thy womb . . ." While the fruit of my womb lies bobbing gently in the bread bowl. Did she have these fears, or did the
assurances she had received keep her safe from panic and fright. "The
desert shall blossom like a rose." A few weeks ago my child was
flowerlike, an unspecified grouping of cells with infinite potential.
Already she is beginning to make up her mind; she should have
inclined towards life not death. Death is contaminating, it might
prove infectious. The Children of God, the Israelites knew: "This is
the law when a man dies in a tent: everyone who comes into the tent
and everyone who is in the tent shall be unclean for seven days.
Everyone who in the field touches a man who is slain by a sword, or a
dead body, or the bone of a man or a grave shall be unclean." Our
Lady, then, would never have prodded the fetus, she would not even
have touched the bread bowl, for that is my daughter's grave. She
will not get another. No grave, no monument, no memorial. Miscarried children cannot be given Christian burial, they cannot be baptized. But she had a complete soul, that was why she had a right to
live, why I was not allowed to harm her. Is she to go to hell because I
had a congenital weakness of the cervix? She is innocent, innocent.
We must believe she was innocent; or did she want to die, did she
commit a moral suicide, suicide in the will? Did she have a will?
Deeds she certainly had, a whole biography. I have produced perhaps
180 ova in my life, one a month for fourteen years, but hers was the
only one to make the long journey, to be impregnated, empowered,
and break forth into generation. And then what adventures she had
endured: daily changes in her conditions, both physical and mental,

threatened with murder, conspired against, surviving, finding love, cherished, and now evicted from her home. I could not hurt her because God loved her, and now I cannot even pray for her. There is nothing that Mother Church can do for her; forget it, flush it away.

Holy Mother Church is embarrassed because I want to weep for my daughter. The unwept tears clog our eyes. I know why children cry when they're born: it is for all the crying they won't be allowed to do later. Cry at birth before they have a chance to say, "don't cry, look on the bright side, don't think about it, trust God."

I was wrong, it is not death but grief which is the infectious disease; avoid it like the plague, it might creep out from between the sealed eyelids and contaminate our silences, it might remind us that we too will have to mourn, don't be morbid, don't talk about it. I learned recently that ostriches don't really hide their heads in the sand . . . but small children do something like that. I have been watching small children lately. I saw a child, wearing green shorts and no top; her shoulder bones like wings, so delicate and mobile. She ran down the street and leaned against the wall, her face pressed to the bricks and shouted, "Say, 'Where's me?' Say, 'Where's me?' " And her obliging grown-up pretended it could not see the child, "Where are you? Where are you?" Did the child really think it was hidden, or invisible, or was it a game?

I will bury her myself. I won't need a shroud because her nakedness is unashamed. Or, if sin is in the conception, she can use the red shroud she is lying in. And even now I catch myself thinking that I cannot spare the bread bowl, because nothing is simple for me anymore. I shall bury her in the back garden. I read somewhere that the stretched skin over the belly of a pregnant woman becomes permeable to light, so that the baby does not grow in the dark, but in a translucent dome, bathed in light. But I think my child is too young for that. She would prefer the quiet dark of a grave to the bright light of cremation. But as she has swum so freely and gracefully all her life, perhaps I should take their advice and flush her away. It is not for her, but for myself that I want some dignity, some humanity to adorn the process. You can buy a dignified burial space for your pet dog, but not for your fetal child. You cannot buy a gravestone for your loving sentiments. I could write her an epitaph: Here lies my daughter who grew in grace from embryo to fetus but died on account of her mother's laxity. No and no. I will not return to the guilt. I feel cold and tired. I wanted to want my baby, that is the best I can do. That will have to be her epitaph.

In the end the Doctor came, of course. His hands were strong and firm, although his conversation was embarrassed. When I felt better and recovered from the loss of blood and the shock I was of course happy to learn that the Doctor had poured the products of my unfortunate conception into a plastic bag, and scrubbed out the bread bowl and left it to drain beside the sink, and carried the plastic bag off to the hospital incinerator.

> To one's own dead one displayed extreme respect and care. As soon as the last hour was presumed to be approaching the dying person was put in a special hut, and when the spirit had departed the hut was burned down. Dressed in his best clothes the corpse was laid out for public view, while the survivors, with green wreaths on their heads, made deep gashes on their breasts and broke into long shouts of dismay, which alternated with dirges and speeches in honor of the dead. The corpse was wrapped in a mat and placed on a platform in the crowns of the trees. After the burial there was a big celebration, and food and other gifts were distributed to the sorrowing guests.

The funeral rites described in the extracts are i) Anglo Saxon; ii) Ancient Egyptian; iii) Medieval English; and iv) South West African contemporary.

Andromeda

My mother would say that it was wrong to call one's husband a thief. Mine is. Thief, thief, thief, I scream at him silently.

My mother would say that it was worse than wrong to hate one's husband, to stay awake through the night and pray for his death. I do. Die, die. I curse him while he sleeps.

My mother would say it was the worst crime to loathe one's children and wish they had never been born. I do that too.

My mother was a great queen, a beautiful woman and a loving mother. She fed me at her own royal breast until I was over five years old. I can remember the sweet whiteness and warmth of her cradling me. Like a queen bee in a hive I was fed on royal jelly. I slept in her bed with her until I was nearly grown up. If I woke in the night she would stroke me and soothe me back into gentle dreams, holding me close against her own softness.

My father was a king, a true hero; he sailed with the Argonauts on the last great adventure of the golden age. He was away for most of my childhood, but he was always devoted to my mother and me.

My husband is a thief, a bastard and a patricide.

Perseus the golden, son of Zeus, the slayer of the Gorgon, the savior of Andromeda, the founder of Mycenae. Ha.

They don't know I'm mad. No one knows I'm mad. It's my own secret. I guard it closer than I guard my life. It's mine, mine, the only thing of my own that he has left me. I will die before I let him take that too. My madness and my hatred: fed on the milk I would not feed my children, nursed on the breast where I would not nurse my sons.

Perseus' queen walks gently through the court, a model wife, calm but busy, her eyes lowered, veiled by her long dark lashes, an example to all young women in her modesty, her humility, the love and duty that she shows her husband. She seldom raises her eyes except to smile benignly on her husband's subjects or sweetly, gratefully at him.

But Andromeda is mad, mad, mad, and no one knows. In the night she roams the palace, nursing the famous dagger with which her husband killed the Gorgon, planning her thrusts, in and out, in and out; blows of vengeance that would make her more famous even than he is. He claims Pallas Athena gave him her helmet to make him invisible. I need no helmet; no one is more invisible than his good, gentle, devoted wife. That is more than helmet, it is a whole armor of invisibility, which the mad woman wears all day and is safe. Mercifully he is also a fool. There are days when I sit beside him at the table, eating my meal and watching him through my meek, humble eyes, watching him shovel his food between his thick red lips, watching his coarse mouth masticate and his throat heave as he swallows it down, and wishing that each mouthful was snake's venom. And I think, How can he be so stupid? How can he not feel the waves of poison pour out of me and into his food, thrusting down and into his innards, as he has thrust his poison into mine? And then he will turn to me and say in his silly sickly smiling voice, "My Andromeda, aren't you hungry? Don't you like this food? You eat like a bird, my little chicken." And he may pick up some revolting morsel and try to feed me with his own sweaty, blood-stained hands.

*W*hen I was a child I sat on the laps of my mother's Eunuchs and they would feed me sweets and peaches, their soft rounded fingers caressing my hair, and I would hop like a hummingbird from silky nest to silky nest, or come to rest against my mother's naked arms and she would reach for a grape for me; or I would bury my face in her warm sweet-smelling stomach and taste the softness of her for a dark moment.

*H*e bangs and crashes, leaping up from the table, calling for more wine, shouting at his friends, bantering crudely, challenging someone to some absurd contest, stripping off his tunic, yelling for his horse, his slave, his hounds, his spear. Pausing only to stroke the golden hairs on his chest with a little tender gesture, he dashes outside and for hours I have to hear the wild shouts and confused arguing from the gymnasium or the arena. Then he comes puffing in again, victorious, performing to me, crying out, "Admire Me, Admire Me." It is not an appeal, it is an expression of his conviction that I, and everyone else in the world must share his admiration of himself. He believes I admire him, because he completely believes he is admirable. He notices nothing; not even the fact that his subjects and so-called friends always let him win every game, being sensible men and as aware as I am which way survival lies; and certainly not that the golden hairs he strokes are fading and yellowish, or that the famous manly chest is slipping slowly lower. Yes, he's a fool my husband as well as a thief.

$\mathcal{B}$ut sometimes I do envy him his perfect unshakeable arrogance and blindness. He can see everything exactly as he wants it to be. His loving devoted wife. His fine sons, his chaste daughter. His enthusiastic subjects. And above all his heroic, wonderful self. I tell you seriously, he sincerely believes he is the son of Zeus. His mother's family were very strict, and she was kept permanently under guard to keep her chaste. It didn't work, she became pregnant from "a shower of gold" as popular idiom has it. The only thing anyone knows about my husband's father is that he was rich enough to bribe the guards. But Perseus has chosen from childhood to believe it literally. His mother was imprisoned, but beloved of the Gods and Zeus disguised himself as a shower of gold in order to impregnate her. We got on rather well his mother and I; we shared something in common, we had both been driven mad by him—she through devotion and I through hatred—mad to the point that we could see through him. We never spoke of it, but just occasionally we would exchange tiny glances of amusement, of complicity, from beneath our chastely lowered lashes.

$\mathcal{W}$e all have to hear the story of his birth even more frequently since, in a fit of showing off at some public games, he managed to kill off his grandfather. Now of course he was fated by destiny from the beginning of time to do this. That is why his mother was in the tower, that is why, under the influence of predetermined Fate, Zeus had to be his father. Or, in more simple words, like everything else that goes wrong in his life: It Wasn't His Fault. Because he is perfect.

*S*ometimes I really cannot believe that a grown man can accept this self-created delusion as a historical fact, but if you start from an unassailable assumption that you are perfect anything and everything becomes perfectly logical. The great advantage of being a King is that you can deal very effectively with anyone who is foolish enough to express a contrary opinion. Which is one of the reasons why I keep quiet. I am going to live to see him dead. With my own wifely hands I shall perform my ritual office. I am disgusted, I say publicly, by those queens who hire professional substitutes. "How brave, how devoted, how good our queen is," they murmur. With my own hands I am going to wipe that smug smile off his face, gently and with such joy I am going to close those pretty blue eyes, and then when he is no longer watching me, I shall spit in his face and laugh. I shall wear the full, heavy, royal mourning veil when we process to his mausoleum; I shall wear it so that no one will see the unholy glee on my face when they seal up that body for the worms to devour. Yes, yes, I shall long to see you then, Perseus the golden, the favorite of the Gods, with the worms boring and thrusting down into your bloated flesh and growing fat on your decay. They are on my side, King of Mycenae. Everything you have stolen from me they will steal back again, strip away the layers of beauty and complacency, and expose what I have known from the very beginning, the stinking putrifying foulness of your inner being, my dear husband, my own sweet royal lord. You thief, you fat arrogant hog of a petty thief. They hang men like you daily in the courtyard and I lean out the window, secretly, and imagine it is you, rotting, with the birds picking out your eyes. I laugh and laugh, mighty slayer of the Gorgon, to think how little those snaky tresses will help you then.

*W*hen I was a child they called me their little bird, as I pecked and chirped and sang through the palace. I long and desire to chirp as I peck at your dead eyes, and sing as the worms destroy your proud manhood.

His pride is at the root of him. He is that and nothing more. It is easy to understand; yes, I can be understanding too, I can say how hard it must be to be a landless child, a fatherless son at the mercy of a whim of charity from foreigners, cast away unwanted and unrecognized by his own family. I can understand what that lack would do to a pretty, able child and to a passionate headstrong adolescent. I can understand how the lust to say "Mine," to own to possess to lay claim to everything would grow in a person from that background. Understand yes. Forgive, tolerate, even care. No. No, because it is not right, but no even more because I am one of the things possessed, taken over, made into his. His, His, Everything has to be His. "It was love at first sight." He says of me. "As soon as I saw her I knew that I would run any risk, dare any venture, if I could make her my own. Don't believe anyone who says there is no such thing as Love at first sight. We know better don't we, my own?"

*L*ove at first sight. It was jealousy at first sight. He was passing through Ethiopia and found that someone else was the hero of the moment. That was the intolerable thing, that someone else, not him, had laid claim to a moment of history. That he could not endure. If love was the price of grabbing one more chance of being the great hero he was more than willing to pay it. But for me it was my moment. The moment that I chose, that I had dedicated to myself; my one chance, the one time when I had a choice and could offer myself, as something more than the little princess, their bird, their darling; I was to be the pure, the chosen symbol of my mother's love for her people. The only acceptable sacrifice, the only freely offered gift. Can you understand? When the sea monster raged up from the deep, my happy homeland was turned overnight into a place of despair. And only I could save them. I offered myself as a sacrifice for my city. The perfect sacrifice has to be offered voluntarily. I offered. What were my motives? Love I say, my one true impulse of love. Perhaps there were other things in it too; things that were less pure, dark poisoned things. But it was my decision for my life; my own moment of choice and I chose it. The mixture of joy and grief that greeted my offer confirmed me. They all needed me in a way that is very rarely offered to women.

*H*ow can I describe it? There was a hysteria in me and in the whole city for the week of the ritual purification. Was it here that the seeds of my madness were sown? I know that is possible, but if things had fallen out as they were meant to, what would my madness or sanity have mattered. The rituals are complex and, to the uninitiate, uninteresting—the important factor is the growing separateness of the chosen person. I had to move from the palace to a special appointed room inside the temple; the day before the last day my mother came to say goodbye to me, she was the last person allowed to do so, I had not seen my father since the second day, after this farewell she would not be allowed to touch me or even speak to me. I lay in her arms, neither of us weeping, just close and tender. She petted me, kissed and embraced me. Her last words were, "My sweetheart, I'm heartbroken, but for myself, not for you. I almost envy you, I'm glad, I love you so much, I could never have borne losing you. I always wanted this, to be able to keep you pure and safe, and free from so much. And now you'll never have to know. O treasure, sweet heart. A bride of the sea, the sweet clean gentle sea. O my beloved. Be strong." For the last time I buried myself in her softness, the two of us twined together, our lips against each other. But when she went I felt only a growing excitement and certainty.

*I*n the morning the priestesses came to dress me. The soft white dress felt like my mother's last caress, but the scent of the flowers was almost overwhelming, sweet and cloying; a marked contrast to the bitter rich smell of the incense which was now burning everywhere. My head began to swim and my stomach contract in nervous, thrilling spasms. The hands of the priestesses seemed to dance over my body. I wanted to rush into the sea now, to have it round me, embracing me, cool but strong. We set in slow procession for the half-mile to the shore. The jewel green, sheep-cropped sea grass seemed as buoyant as waves, and the sea daisies almost blindingly white. The sun warmed the back of my neck as it rose over the city and through the thin white robe I could feel the breeze with my whole body. Where the grass comes to an end and the firm sand beach begins we stopped. About fifty yards away, where the water begins, there is a jagged outcrop of rock, on the seaward side of which I would wait, invisible from the land, totally exposed to the sea. The priestess bent down and cut my sandal thongs so that I could step out of them. I raised my arms and cried my intention to the sea, that I came freely to be given to the sea by my people, in love and in duty. Then the priestess cut the bands that held my hair, and the back of my neck felt suddenly cool where it was protected from the sun. Again I called out that without ties and freely I offered myself to the sea. Then finally the priestess cut through the girdle of my dress and it fell gently down my body. I stepped out of it and naked began to walk along the marked path to the rock. The solemn Lament for the Maiden began and to its beautiful notes I walked round the rock and out of life.

The waves lapped my feet and the sea was very bright. I remember quite clearly hearing the sound of the lament, feeling the wine cool dampness of the rock behind me and enjoying a moment of contentment and joyous expectation. Then the sun seemed to quiver, followed by a moment of unnatural stillness, and four huge waves lashed out at me, beating me down onto the rock, the hot strong waves of the monster's breath; I fought to receive the full impact of them, embracing their thrust and feeling them soak right into me; I caught a sort of glance, hardly that, a physical sensation of the golden lion who hunts with his mane as the waves, I don't know, don't remember, can't describe. I leaned longingly towards that hot mouth that would finish all things with its welcome. And sweaty and muscle-bound He ripped me from my triumph.

*W*ith the help of that serpented profanity of his he stole my moment and made it his. I didn't know at once what had happened, but I did know heartbreakingly that something had gone absolutely and forever wrong. He could not allow anyone else so much as a single instant of courage or generosity. He stole it, he stole my moment, robbed me of my own choice, violated my sacrifice. He stole the one thing I had; stole it and possessed it and made it his own.

*W*hat else he and his snake friend stole from me I do not like to think of.

*W*ell, in the eyes of the world, I have been a good wife to him. I never saw that I had any choice; he stole my moment from me and I was never granted another. But my husband is a thief and in those depths of me which even he can never ravage, I revile him.

Dragon Dreams

The Palace,
The Kingdom

Wednesday, 23 April 1989

Dearest Dragon,

You will probably think I shouldn't write to you like this. Perhaps you would be right. You will think it a terrible impertinence
maybe, especially after everything and then leaving it for so long.
But there is no one else. There is no one else I can write to; there is
no one I can talk to. At least you'll be able to think "I told you so!"
and get something out of it anyway.

If indeed you bother to read this at all, you will almost certainly
begin by thinking, Why *now*? Why now after all these centuries of
silence? And of course there are lots of reasons, but it does seem to
me a sensible question, and I will try and tell you one reason, something that happened to me some years ago.

We took a small cottage in Umbria that summer—George and I
and our beautiful frail son, almost translucent by then, and looking
the more fey because all the chemotherapy had made him entirely
bald, and who was fairly obviously going to die; as indeed he did the

following winter. We, George and I, probably knew already that our marriage was not going to survive that fall from heaven, weighted as it was with rage and guilt and too many years of not-fun. Already then we were treating each other with a polite and solemn tenderness, shot through with the murderous emotion of pity. In short, as you will notice it was almost an exact return to the feelings we had for each other when we first met in your company.

It's probably cheating to begin a letter to someone who is by now a virtual stranger like that. It demands too much sympathy. "My child died" I write, and then anything I choose to say must be forgiven. And why should you, of all creatures, have to drum up sympathy for me? So it is only fair to tell you that George has got married again, to a really sweet woman, and they have two sturdy little children called George and Georgina, which is rather charming, and after all, originality never was his strong point. They always invite me to come for Christmas dinner, although I do not do so: but that is my own fault of course. I do know that. And I too am getting by in my own way.

But I am getting off the point a little; something you and George both used to complain about, if you remember. There we were in Italy, near Orvieto, that dreamlike and peerless city, which, as you may know, sits up high on its own tufa block, plugging the hole to the ancient volcano and surrounded by a tight circle of hills. It was on one of those sharp crags that our cottage sat, an ancient Umbrian farmhouse restored for the summer letting trade. I spent most of the days lying under a sun umbrella beside the pool with my tiny son flopped on top of me, watching the butterflies, telling him fairy stories, or just lolling there together. I don't know if he knew he was dying; it is mercifully hard to tell with such small children. He was old enough to mind about having no hair though, and so he liked it in that house, where there was no one to see him, and where wearing a white cotton sun hat was a normal recourse when we went, as we occasionally did, to the towns or villages about us. It is quite primitive in those hills; the peasant farmer who came to service the pool and bring the new Calor gas cylinders seemed to act as though my rather skimpy bikini was a damn sight odder looking than my emaciated son's shining head and he knew that and it helped him relax I believe. He liked the old man and would sometimes clamber off me and go trudge round behind the guy trying to help or copy, and he was always received with a natural courtesy which gave him pleasure.

Of course, as you can imagine, this was all a bit too peaceful for George, who having been persuaded to leave his clients was feeling both virtuous and frustrated. He hasn't changed at all over the centuries; he's a social worker now, and in London there is no shortage of maidens in need of rescuing, and hideous young frogs whom he can convince himself need only an expertly applied professional kiss to turn into charming princes. The fact that the maidens laugh at him and the frogs spit saddens but does not depress him. Well, after a couple of days of such floppy idleness he was chafing at the bit, and most mornings he leapt into the white Fiat we had hired and roared off to collect culture, and delicious things to eat which he would bring home and cook for me in the evenings. I think our son's dying was very difficult for him because he could not accept that there was nothing he could do except enjoy each day. Death was a dragon mightier than any he had had to face before and he did not like that. But he meant well.

Anyway despite the long dozy days, or perhaps because of them, I had a great deal of difficulty sleeping on that holiday. George and I would drink ourselves into a semi-stupor each evening after we had put the little one to bed. The white wine was dry and cheap, heady for such hard-working and virtuous types as we were then. And later we would go to bed implying to each other that of course we would make love if it were not quite so hot, or if the mosquitoes were not quite so vicious, or if we weren't both aware that our son might need us in the darkness. And at that point I would fall headlong into sleep, crashing down through the dark tunnels of sweat and tiredness, down into a black pit where I did not dream good dreams. And then towards five o'clock or so in the morning I would fight desperately up to consciousness and lie there in the paling light, giddy and sick with a sense of escape. Knowing it impossible to sleep again, I would lie there for a while and listen to the silence of their sleep throughout the house. Then I would get up, half cross to be awake when other people were still sleeping and half pleased with the intensity of quiet and peace. Downstairs I would make myself a cup of coffee and carry it out onto the patio and drink it at a table, smoke a guilt-ridden cigarette, and watch the coming of the dawn. Then sometimes I would read and sometimes I would go and swim all on my own, the water slightly cooler after the night, swallowing me into itself and the darkness retreating before the splashes of my arms and legs. Now the sky would begin to change from grey to silver gilt, then peach, but still the sun would not rise. After swimming I would feel thoroughly alive and glad to be awake and to have this time of my own, free from both the steady ache of attention that I gave the boy, or the steady ache of grateful irritation that I gave George. At this moment, this moment of the day alone, I could give way to tears or to anger, without responsibility to anyone. On the tears mornings I would lie beside the pool and weep and weep, as silently as I could, but in the certain indulgence that neither of them would hear me. On the anger mornings I would often go for a walk.

One morning, despite the peaceful and immeasurable beauty of the Umbrian dawn, I was shaken with such an anger that even now I remember it with shame; a fury that boiled up from a place deeper than any depression, a great lava-hot core of rage, immense anger against whatever it was that was slowly and irresistibly killing everything I loved, killing love itself in me. A great growling ferocity, more like an animal, a monster, than like a gentle and liberal-minded woman. Terrified I rushed inside for shoes and shorts and a T-shirt. I was too dangerously angry even to go check on my sleeping child. I left him to George's more well regulated mercies and fled the house, stomping up the short driveway and out onto the road.

But one thing about that part of Italy is that it is all very hilly; you cannot, if you are an unfit smoker like me, rush very far in espadrilles without being brought to a panting pause. After a very few minutes I was forced to slow down and look around me. I was charging up the road beside a field of sunflowers, and although the sun had not yet risen I could sense the whole field turning away from me and each flower raising its face towards the eastern hills over which the sun would shortly leap. I felt the whole silent movement of that field, each straining golden head, instinctively, blindly, passionately turning towards the light. And instinctively, blindly, passionately I turned with them, leaving the road and taking a cart track along the upper side of the field. Above me the fields rose steeply, rough grass and scattered olive trees, which in that light looked unmoveably ancient and grotesque. Below me the muttering sunflowers continued the ghostly and invisible movement. The track was rough, I had to look at my feet in order not to fall, but I went on. Suddenly, the track fell away sharply, in front of my feet, and I felt rather than saw the expanded horizon. I looked up; like the sunflowers I was facing right into the heart of the brightness which preceded the sun. The eastern mountains looked black and shapely, silhouetted against that great apricot-colored fire. I was on the very edge of the steep hills which surround the basin in which Orvieto sits; and the basin itself was alive and moving, swirling with smoke, with smoky white mists which filled it almost to the brim. Then and there the sun rose abruptly and I could see the city, bright and sunlit, floating on the mists, like the magic cities of medieval romances, where we have both been before. The great cathedral dominated the city, like the spines along your back, and the rest of it lay in a rough sprawl, basking in the first rays of the sun and oblivious to the dangerous mist below that might suck it in before it could wake up and take wing against the now blue blue sky. That sleeping peaceful beauty was too much for me, it crashed against my anger too painfully. Only a few moments before I had thought my anger enormous, the most huge and violent thing in the world, and now it seemed like a puny little tantrum in the face of this great silent loveliness. I turned abruptly away, to my right, westwards.

The steep slope which had risen above me as I had walked down the track had retreated perhaps twenty yards, leaving behind it a tiny enclosed plateau, walled in by a broken cliff, facing out to the sharp escarpment which looked towards the distant city. In the rough rock face were deep shadows, indents, caves perhaps. At the foot of the rocks, almost directly in front of the deepest looking cave was a small pool. Its presence had kept the grass on the plateau bright green, unlike the crusty brownness of the hills around it. Nestled in the green carpet there was a tapestry of tiny flowers, yellow and white, casually scattered; among them the early morning bees and butter-flies were just stirring. Far away, only emphasizing the silence, a cock crowed, shrill and certain. Perhaps it was just the rising mist, the last effusion of the night, kept trapped longer here than elsewhere be-cause of the still water in the pond, but it seemed to me as though from the cavelike shadows there came a faint wisp of smoke, blowing gently across that magical, sweet-scented, quiet place.

Then of course I remembered. I had been here before. It was here, it was this very place, that you and George and I had been together all those years ago. It was here that you and he had fought and I had watched. It was here that your thick green blood, more shiny than the emeralds of my engagement ring, had flowed over the grass and George had waved his green stained sword above his head and the cheers from the distant city had been blown towards us both by the early morning breeze. I had forgotten. For centuries I had forgotten and now it all came back to me as bright as the morning was becom-ing, and I felt the gentle stir of the wind, heard the olive leaves bustle softly against each other, and when I raised my hand to wipe my blurry eyes I found that they were full of tears.

There is something mysterious about memory, recapturing mem-ories revives one. Oh who needs this abstract sentiment. . . . All I'm trying to say is that in that glowing moment of morning some-thing was restored to me, a part of myself, that I needed and that I clung to. And also what was restored was you, and all the old passion and excitement.

"But," you will say with justice, "but all that must have been at least five years ago. Why have you waited so long? Why are you writing *now*?" Well, at first I was so busy. Even that morning I had to hasten back to my child. Though there, beside that swimming pool, and over and over again after we had returned to London, I refreshed the memory by telling him the story. By telling him about your deep mysterious cave, where you had once led me down into the dark and illuminated it with your breath; about the great stalactites hovering over your hoard and exchanging flash for flash the beauty of water and the beauty of diamonds; by telling him about the astonishing strength of your wings, and the stunning moment when I first saw your silhouette dance against the sunset and knew that you were coming for me; by telling him about the great fight and the brilliance of his father's sword play on the green grass before your lair. I think these things comforted him against the coming of the dark; they certainly comforted me, though they could not keep the dark at bay. He was in so much pain before the end that I thought it would shake his tiny body to pieces, and yet it was so hard to take him finally to the hospital where indeed they could stop the pain, but had to stop everything else as well. I could feel him going away, turning to another place and not even waiting to say goodbye, just slipping off one wintery evening, as casually as though he were running round the block to visit his friend.

And when I had reeled away from that business I had to deal with the business between me and George, which took up a lot of my time and energy, as you can imagine. In the end I was relieved rather than desperate when he found his lovely new wife, who suits him so much better than I ever did.

It took a long time, as such things do. Finally I have shed him like a snake its skin and a new me had emerged shiny and delicate into the sunshine; and it is a me who realizes that, all those years ago, I made a terrible mistake. I could not realize it fully until I was shot of him and free again. Although really I have known it all the time, right from the beginning, if I am honest, but you frightened me. You shouldn't go for virgins, dearest, you need a tough wily woman, honed on pain, as iron-scaled as you are. A grown-up woman who knows her desires and knows that she will not achieve them, but does not mourn and keeps searching.

When I came out to you from the city, white as milk in that first peach gold morning, I came freely, as you know, and I came loving and excited. But that was a secret. How could I say that to my weeping Mamma, to my Father who bit his lips in agony and tried to be brave for my sake? I knew what I wanted and it was you. Had I not seen your wild dance against the sunset? Had I not felt the heat from your scarlet mouth, hot against my flesh when we all ran screaming from the lake side and were warned not to go out into the

wild woods because you were loose? Had I not dreamed you at night;
the golden danger and the dark, the dark side of myself that George
would never countenance? Had I not gone with you into your deep
cave and seen the diamonds, so delighted to be yours that they bred,
crushing each other into life, littering the cave with their offspring,
baby diamonds brooded over and hatched by you? Had I not felt, in
myself, my own magic power, my strength, that could match yours
and make us a fitting couple?

And then on that sparkling morning, when the time had come, I
was afraid. I lost my nerve. If I gave myself to you, and took you into
my arms, I too would have to grow scales and wings; I would be
beautiful, but I would be a monster. All that city wanted me to be
their sweet virgin princess; they did not want me to be a fierce
dragon woman, although that was my truth. Civilized people kill
dragons to make the world safe for civilization. Through religion and
mythology and folklore they must hunt and slay the darkness of the
dragon, the unnamed, the fierce freedom. I could feel the long lance
thrust against my neck, where the scales pale to cream color and are
soft for kisses and tenderness; I could feel the fear and the hatred and
the blood lust and the death throes, and I could not face them. I
wanted safety. That fear was very real, but there was yet another, a
still greater fear; I was afraid of the dragon of me, the great ferocious
growling monster of rage and passion.

I knew, you see, I knew that I could do it, I had the power to
become a dragon, but that if I did I would never be ordinary ever
again. I would have to go out into the hot tearing desert, and live
with you in all my power and glory. My tail would sweep down a
third of the stars from heaven and cast them to the earth. The ancient
dragon in me would gobble up all the sweet little girl, and would
devour the mother and her son, and there would be no space left for
all my pettiness and silliness. At that moment when you came towards me, lizardlike, lithe and loving, I suddenly wanted only to be
the sort of ordinary princess who goes to the supermarket with a
shopping trolley and who blows smoke rings rather than fire for her
party trick. In a moment of weakness, cowardice if you like, I wanted
an ordinary boring prince to appear on a white charger and rescue

me. I summonsed poor George all by myself, and then I hurled myself into his arms, demanded that he felt for me a polite and solemn tenderness, shot through with pity and self-satisfaction. Then I let him kill you. When he appeared with all that blond hair and noble profile, and solid virtue, I should have thought "interfering bastard," but instead I thought he would keep me safe from my own desires.

Even as you bled I knew that you knew, that you let yourself be killed for me and it nearly broke my heart. Moral cowardice is a leprosy to the soul, it shrivels it up and makes the sinner small. So after that I just forgot the whole damn thing, and went proudly back to the city and married him. Lots of princesses do, we are brought up to it you know, and it is harder to change than one might think.

So that is why I am writing to you. When my child died I knew there was no safety, anywhere, and I will not sacrifice to false gods. There is no safety, but there is wildness and joy, there is love and life within the danger. I love you. I want to be with you. I want to reclaim my dragon soul and fly. I refuse to believe we only get one chance. This letter is just a start. I am going to hunt you down now in all the lovely desolate places of the world. You are my Questing Beast, like the valiant knights in olden days. Wherever there is a perfect sunrise, a dark cliff, a small pool of water, a distant city wreathed in morning mist, there I will be waiting for you. Please come.

Please come soon.

With everlasting love from,

The Princess

A Fall from Grace

Those years the children—in Brittany, Bordeaux and the Loire Valley, even as far away as the Low Countries, Andalusia and the Riviera—missed their acrobats. In the Circus the dingy wild animals, the clowns, illusionists and freaks remained, but earthbound. Gravity held the Circus, and the mud, the stench and the poverty were more evident. The magic-makers, the sequined stars that flashed and poised and flew and sparkled through the smoke above the watchers' heads, the death-defiers who snatched the Circus from the mud and turned it into flowers and frissons, were gone.

Gone away to the strange camp on the Champs de Mars, where they were needed to help Monsieur E. build his beautiful tower. Oh, the local residents might tremble in their beds with fear at the fall from heaven; intellectuals and artists might protest that "Paris is defaced by this erection." But the Circus people, the artists of body and philosophers of balance (with wild libidinous laughs at so unfortunate and accurate a turn of phrase), they understood; the acrobats—without words and with a regular fifty centimes an hour—knew. They alone could comprehend the vision. They knew in the marrow of their bones and the tissue of their muscles the precise tension—that seven million threaded rods, and two and a half million bolts could, of course, hold fifteen thousand steel girders in perfect balance.

With sinews and nerves and cartilage they did it nightly: that tension and harmony against gravity was their stock-in-trade. Their great delight was that Monsieur E., a gentleman, a scientist, knew it too, and knew that they knew and needed them to translate his vision. High above Paris they swooped and caracoled, rejoicing in the delicacy and power of that thrust, upwards, away from the pull of the ground. And so they left their Circuses, sucked towards Paris by a dream that grew real under their authority—and for two years the acrobats and trapeze artists and highwire dancers and trampolinists abandoned their musical illusions to participate in historical, scientific reality.

Eva and Louise too came to Paris. Not that they were allowed to mount up ever higher on the winches, hanging beside the cauldrons which heated the bolts white hot; not that they were permitted to balance on the great girders, shifting their weight so accurately to swing the heavy strands of lace into place. Their skill, as it happens, was not in doubt, but they were women. They drifted northwards, almost unthinkingly, with their comrades and colleagues, simply because the power of Monsieur E.'s vision was magnetic and all the acrobats were drawn inwards by it and Eva and Louise were acrobats. And they lived with the other acrobats on the Champs de Mars, poised between aspiration and reality, and the city of Paris went to their heads and they were, after a few months, no longer who they had been when they came.

Their Circus had been a disciplined nursery for such children. Born to it, they had known its rhythms, its seductions and its truths from the beginning. Precious to their parents because identical twins are good showbusiness, they were only precious inasmuch as they worked and made a show. With each lurching move of the traveling caravans they had had to re-create the magic from the mud. Only after the hours of sweat and struggle with the tent, with the law, with the unplanned irregularities of topography, and with costumes which had become muddy or damp or creased or torn—only then were they able to ascend the snaking ladders and present the New Creation, where fear and relief were held in perfect tension; where the immutable laws of nature—gravity and pendula arches, weight, matter and velocity—were apparently defied but in fact bound, utilized, respected and controlled; where hours of dreary practice, and learning the capacities and limits of self and other, where the disciplines of technique and melodrama and precision were liberated suddenly and briefly into glamour and panache. And still were only a complete part of a delicately balanced and complete whole that included the marionette man, the clowns, the seedy lions and the audience itself.

But Paris, and a Paris in which they could not do what they were trained to do, was a holiday, a field day, where the rewards were quick and detached from the labor. As the tower grew so did Eva and Louise, but the tower was anchored and they were free-floating. They learned to cross the laughing river and seek out the *boîtes* of Montmartre. Here, their white knickers and petticoats frothed easily in the hot water now available to them, they learned to dance the new dance—the Cancan. Here their muscularity, their training, their athleticism stood them in good stead. They were a hit: with the management who paid them to come and show off round bosoms, shapely legs, pink cheeks and bleached petticoats; with the clientele whose oohs and ahhs were more directly appreciative than those of any Circus audience.

Yes, the beauty and the energy of them as they danced and pranced and watched the tower grow and watched their comrades labor upwards. They walked under the spreading legs of the tower and laughed at the jokes called down to them; they ran among the tents and teased the laborers; they turned the odd trick here and there for affection and amusement, although they could get better paid across the river where the rich men lived, Monsieur E., coming each day to see how his dream was developing, soon learned their names and would stop and smile for them, and they smiled back, arms entwined with each other, but eyes open for everything that was going on in the world. And they reassured him of his beauty, his virility, his potency, all of which he was manifesting in his tower, which broke the rules of nature by the authority of science and the power of men. One day he told them, for the simple pleasure of saying it, for he knew they were simple girls and simply would not understand, that when his tower was finished it would weigh less than the column of air that contained it. The girls laughed and wanted to know why then it would not fly away, and he laughed too, indulgently, and explained, paternally, about displacement. But from then on the idea of the tower simply, ooh-la-la, flying away with them was fixed in Eva and Louise's minds and it made them laugh because of course they knew that it was impossible.

And walking in the streets and parks they learned new styles of dressing and new styles of living; and their eyes were wide and bright with delight. Having little to do all day they wandered here and there, through boulevards and over bridges. In the flower markets they were overcome by the banks of sweetness, the brilliance of colors; in the antique-shop windows they saw the bright treasures from China and Egypt, from far away and long ago; and in the cafés they smelled new smells and heard raffish conversations about things they had not even dreamed of. And everywhere they went, because they looked so alike and smiled so merrily and were always together, people came to recognize them and smile at them, and they felt loved and powerful and free as they had never felt before. All Paris was their friend and the city itself was their Paradise.

They were a hit too in the *Salons des Femmes,* where the strange rich women, who dressed like men and caressed Eva and Louise like men too, were delighted by their health and energy and innocence. And by their professional willingness to show off. Louise enjoyed these evenings when they drank tiny glasses of jewel-colored drinks and performed—dances, tumbles, stage acrobatics—and were petted and sent home in carriages. But Eva felt nervous and alarmed; and also drawn, excited, elated and it was not just the colored concoctions that made her giggle all the way back to the Champs de Mars and swear that they would not go again. In the dark warmth of the bed they shared, Eva's arms would wind round Louise as they had done every night since they were conceived, but her fingers crackled with new electricity and she wondered and wanted and did not want to know what she wanted.

And of course they did go again, because it was Paris and the Spanish chestnut flowers stood out white on the streets like candles and the air was full of the scent of them, giddy, dusty, lazy. At night the city was sparkling and golden and high above it the stars prickled, silver and witty. And Monsieur E.'s tower, taut and poised, was being raised up to join the two together. In the hot perfumed houses they were treated as servants, as artists and as puppy dogs, all together, and it confused them, turned their heads and enchanted them. One evening, watching them, the Contessa della Colubria said to her hostess, "Well, Celeste, I think they won't last long, those two. They'll become tawdry and quite spoiled. But they are very charming." "I don't know," Celeste said, "they are protected. By their work of course, but not that; it must be primal innocence to love, to be one with another person from the beginning, with no desires, no consciousness." "Innocence? Do you think so? Perhaps it is the primal sin, to want to stay a child, to want to stay inside the first embrace, the first cell." The Contessa's eyes glittered like her emeralds. "Do you think it might be interesting to find out?" Celeste turned away from her slightly, watching Eva and Louise across the salon; she said quickly, "Ah, *ma mie,* leave them be. They are altogether too young for you to bother with." The Contessa laughed, "But, Celeste, you know how beguiled I am by innocence. It attracts me."

She was mysterious, the Contessa della Colubria, strange and fascinating; not beautiful *mais très chic,* clever, witty, and fabulously wealthy. She had traveled, apparently everywhere, but now lived alone in Paris, leaving her husband in his harsh high castle in Tuscany and challenging the bourgeois gossips with her extravagance, her outré appearance and the musky sensation of decadence. Rumor followed her like a shadow, and like a shadow had no clear substance. It was known that she collected the new paintings, and Egyptian curios and Chinese statues; it is said that she also collected books which respectable people would not sully their homes with, that she paid fabulous sums to actresses for ritual performances, that she slid along the side of the pit of the unacceptable with a grace that was uncanny. But she had created a social space for herself in which the fear, the feeling, that she was not nice, not quite safe, became unimportant.

She took Eva and Louise home in her carriage that night. Sitting between them, her arms around each neck, her legs stretched out, her long narrow feet braced against the floor, her thin face bland, only her elongated ophidian eyes moving. The sharp jewel she wore on her right hand cut into Louise's neck, but she did not dare to say anything. The Contessa told them stories.

"You see the stars," she said, and they were bright above the river as the carriage crossed over it. "Long ago, long long ago, it was thought that each star was a soul, the soul of a beautiful girl, too lovely to die, too bright to be put away in the dark forever. The wild gods of those times did not think that so much beauty should be wasted, you see. Look at that star up there, that is Cassiopeia, she was a queen and so lovely that she boasted she was more beautiful than the Nereides, the sea-nymphs, and they in their coral caves were so jealous and angry that they made Neptune, their father, punish her. But the other gods were able to rescue her and throw her up to heaven and make her safe and bright.

"And those stars there, those are Ariadne's crown; it was given to her by Bacchus who was the god of wine and passion, not an orderly god, not a good god at all, but fierce and beautiful. Ariadne loved Theseus first, who was a handsome young man, and she rescued him from a terrible monster called the Minotaur who lived in a dark maze and ate people. Ariadne gave her lover a thread so he could find his way out and a sword so he could kill the monster. But he wasn't very grateful, as men so seldom are, and he left her on an island called Naxos."

"I know those ones," said Louise, pointing, breaking the soft flow of the Contessa's voice with an effort, "those ones up there, those are the Seven Sisters who preferred to be together."

"The Pleiades, yes, how clever you are. And you see that one of them is dimmer than the others. That is Meriope, and her star is faint because she married, she married a mortal, but the rest are bright and shiny."

Louise's neck hurt from the Contessa's sharp ring. She felt tired and uneasy. She wanted to sit with Eva, their arms around each other, tight and safe. She did not understand the Contessa. But Eva liked the stories, liked the arm of the Contessa resting warm against her skin, admired the sparkling of emeralds and eyes and was lulled, comfortable and snug, in the smooth carriage.

The balance shifted. They knew about this. As Eva leaned outwards and away, away from the center, then Louise had to move lower, heavier, tighter, to keep the balance. As Louise pulled inward, downward, Eva had to stretch up and away to keep the balance. On the tightrope they knew this; but it was a new thing for them. There was another way, of course; their parents had had an act based on imbalance, based on difference, based on his heavy grounding and her light flying, the meeting-place of the weighty and the floating. But they had not learned it. Even in the gravity-free place where they had first learned to dance together, in the months before they were born, it had been turning in balance, in precise sameness. It was the poise of symmetry that they knew about; the tension of balance. And it was foolhardy always to change an act without a safety net and with no rehearsals. They did not know how to discuss it. The difference was painful, a tightening, a loss of relaxation, of safety. The acrobat who was afraid of falling would fall. They knew that. But also the acrobat who could not believe in the fall would fall. They knew that too.

The Contessa took them to a smart pâtisserie on the Champs-Elysées. She bought them frothing hot chocolate, and they drank it with glee, small moustaches of creamy foam forming on their pink upper lips. They were laughing and happy. "Which of you is the older," she asked, "which was born first?" "We don't know," said Eva and giggled. "No one knows. We tumbled out together and the woman who was supposed to be with my mother was drunk and she got muddled up and no one knows." "If they did it would not matter," said Louise. "Our mother says we were born to the trade, we dived out with elegance." Eva and Louise were pleased with themselves today, with the distinction of their birth, with their own inseparability, with the sweetness of the chocolate and the lightness of the little apricot tartlets. The smart folk walked by on the pavement outside, but they were inside and as pretty as any grand lady. And in the bright spring sunlight the Contessa was not strange and dangerous, she was beautiful and glamorous, she was like something from a fairy story who had come into their lives and would grant them wishes and tell them stories.

The Contessa came in her new toy, her automobile, roaring and dangerous, to seek them out on the Champs de Mars. She was driven up in her bright new chariot, and stopped right between the legs of the tower. The acrobats swarming up and down, laboring, sweating and efficient, swung aside to make space for her, as she uncoiled herself from the seat and walked among them. And she knew Monsieur E. and gave him a kiss and congratulated him on his amazing edifice. Louise did not like to see her there, but she invited them into her car and they rode off to the admiring whistles of their friends. "In Russia," the Contessa told them, "the people ride in sleighs across the snow and the wolves howl at them, but it does not matter because they are snugly wrapped in great furs and the horses pull them through the dark, because it is dark all winter in Russia, and the motion of the sleigh is smooth and the furs are warm and they fall asleep while the horses run and the night is full of vast silences and strange noises so that they hang bells on the horses' bridles, and all the nobility speak in French, so that people will know how civilized they are, and not mistake them for the bearded warriors who live in snow houses beyond the northern stars. And even the women of these people wear high leather boots and ride with the men on short-legged, fierce horses. They ride so well up in that strange land that ordinary people have come to believe that they and their horses are one: they call them Centaurs, horses with human heads and trunks and arms. Long, long ago there were real Centaurs who roamed in Anatolia and knew strange things and would sometimes take little babies and train them in their ways and they would grow up wise and strong and fit to be rulers, because the Centaurs taught them magic, but for ordinary people the Centaurs were very dangerous because they were neither people nor animals, but monsters."

And they rode in the Contessa's car around the Bois and she took them back to her house and taught them how to sniff up a white powder through slender silver straws and then they could see green-striped tigers prowling across the Contessa's garden with eyes like stars, and butterflies ten feet across with huge velvet legs that fluttered down from the trees like falling flowers. And when they went home they found they could believe that Monsieur E.'s tower could fly, and they could fly on it, away away to a warm southern place, but they did not want to leave Paris, so they waved to the tower and they were laughed at for being drunk, and they did not tell anyone about the white powder.

One day at a party, in a new beautiful strange house where they had been invited to do a little show, the Contessa sought out Eva for one brief moment when she was alone and said, "I have a pretty present for you." "Yes, madame." "See, it is earrings." She held out her long, thin, dry hand, the palm flat and open, and there was a pair of earrings, two perfect little gold apples. "These are golden apples from the garden of the Hesperides; Juno, the queen of all the Gods, gave them to Jupiter, the king of all the Gods, for a wedding present. They grow in a magical garden beyond the edge of the world and they are guarded by the four beautiful daughters of Atlas who carries the world on his back. And around the tree they grow on lies a huge horrible dragon who never sleeps. So you see they are very precious." Eva looked at them, amused; she had little interest in their value, but liked their prettiness. "One for me and one for Louise, madame?" she asked. "No, both are for you. But you will have to come by yourself one evening to my house and collect them." "But madame, we always go together, you know that." "Eva," smiled the Contessa, "I'll tell you a little story: once there was a woman and she was expecting a baby, and she wished and wished good things for her baby and especially that it would grow up to have good manners. Well, her pregnancy went on and on, and on and on, and still the baby was not born. And none of the wise doctors could make any sense of it. And in the end, ever more pregnant, after many many years, as a very ancient lady she died of old age. So the doctors who were of course very curious opened her up and they found two little ladies, quite more than middle-aged, sitting beside the birth door saying with perfect good manners, 'After you,' and, 'No, no, my dear, after *you*.' *C'est très gentil,* but what a waste, what a waste, don't you think?" Eva giggled at the silly story, covering her mouth with her hand like a child. She did not care about the earrings but she knew that if she went to the Contessa she would find out, she would find out what it was she did not know, what it was that made her nervous and elated. She could feel too the weight of Louise, the weight of Louise inward on both of them, the weight swinging out of balance. She had to correct that inward weight with an outward one. Had to remake the balance, the inward weight with an outward one. Also she wanted to know, and if she went she would know that and something else perhaps.

"Yes, madame," she said, "yes, I will come."

And the Contessa smiled.

She did not know how to tell Louise. She could not find any words for what and why; they have never needed words before, they have not rehearsed any. Next Tuesday she would go to visit the Contessa. This week she had to find words to tell Louise. Instead she drank. Louise, who knew she was excited but could not feel why, could not understand, could not pull Eva back to her, drank too. Their comrades on the Champs de Mars thought it was funny to see the girls drunk; they plied them with brandy and wine. Drunk, Eva and Louise showed off, they performed new tricks, leaping higher, tumbling, prancing; they do not stumble or trip, they cannot stumble or trip. They are beautiful and skillful. This is their place. The men clap for them, urging them on. In the space under the tower they dance and frolic. They start to climb, swinging upwards; from each other's hands they ascend. Somersaulting, delighting, they follow the upward thrust of the tower; its tension, its balance is theirs. The voices of the men fade below. Once, as they rise above seven hundred feet, they falter. "It's your fault," says Eva, "you lean in too hard." "No," says Louise, "it is you, you are too far out." But they find their rhythm again, trusting the rhythm of the tower that Monsieur E. and their hard-worked colleagues below have structured for them. On the other side of the river they can see Paris, spread out for them now, the islands in the Seine floating on the dark water, the gay streets shining with golden lights. Above, the sky is clear: the moon a bright dying fingernail, the constellations whizzing in their glory.

The tower seems to sway, sensitive to their need. It is not quite finished, but as they approach the top they are higher than they have ever been, they are climbing and swinging and swooping upwards. Suddenly both together they call out to one another, "It was my fault, I'm sorry." The rhythm is flowing now, their wrists linked, trusting, knowing, perfect. It is their best performance ever. Down below the men still watch, although it is too dark to see. They know they will never see another show like this. They know these two are stars. They make no error. They do not fall. They fly free, suddenly, holding hands, falling stars, a moment of unity and glory.

But it is three hundred yards to the ground and afterwards no one is able to sort out which was which or how they could be separated.

True North

Far north, inside the ice circle, in the land of the long night, lived two women. One was a young woman and one was an old woman. The old woman must have known how they came to be living there, on their own, so far away from other people, but she never said. The young woman did not know—she remembered no other view than the long lifting of the snow banks and the chopped ragged ice in the sea below their home.

Because there was no one else they did not need names for each other and used none. Because they had no community they did not need to name their relationship either, and they did not do so. They never used the words mother or daughter or friend or sister or aunt, niece, cousin, lover. They just lived there together. Because there was no one to see they did not know that the young woman was very beautiful and that the old woman was not. They knew that the old woman was full of ancient knowledge and useful skills, was wise in the ways of weather and seals, and knew all the hundred words for snow. The young woman was strong and tough and could run all day, a slow steady lope across the snow, in pursuit of the moose herds, and she could crawl and slither over the ice after seals and polar bears. And in the evenings the old woman could tell stories about the Seal Queen, and the lemmings maddened by each other and the winter fever who rushed into the sea; and her gums could chew, her hands could carve and her fingers could sew and plait and skin and braid. The young woman could sing and dance and let down her beautiful long hair and comb the thick dark mess until it glowed and sparkled with strange lights. And so they lived happily for a long time.

When spring comes inside the ice circle it is not with long rains and sweet emerging greenness. Instead there is the strange sound of the deep ice crashing and gonging as it breaks up—howling at night as it shifts and moves at last. The skeins of geese overhead break the stillness of the air with the powerful rush of their homecoming; and the she-seals are fat with promise and contentment. The light begins to seep back into the air; hardly noticed at first, the blubber lamp pales and the distant ice floes take on specific shapes. Where the winter freeze humped and pressured the sea into strange designs there is a new flatness smoothing itself back into water, but slowly.

And one year, with the spring, came something new. One morning when the young woman left the warmth of the ice house she saw, far away across the whiteness a new shape she had never seen before and heard, borne on the motionless air, a new noise, a swish-swish. The shape was dark and tall and it was not silent. In fear she watched a while and the shape came nearer. She turned back into the ice house and told the old woman. And the old woman wrapped a polar fur around herself and came out. The shape had come nearer; it had a strange rising and falling gait, not the smoothness of an animal but rhythmic, lilting like the tune from a song. The shape was coming towards them directly and with purpose and both women were afraid, though for very different reasons: the young woman was afraid because she did not know what the shape was. The old woman was afraid because she did. It was a man.

He was a young man, tall and handsome. He was an ice traveler. He had spent the winter far from his village, all alone, because of a courageous but foolish error of judgment which had taken him too far to get back before the snowstorms and the darkness had come. He had wintered far from his own people and was now on his way home. He was surprised to discover this ice house; he had not known that anyone could go away and live so far from the village. Now, swishing on his wide snow shoes, swinging each leg wide of the other, his pack on his back, he came across the snow plateau and, seeing the smoke, thought of singing and company and warm meals cooked by someone not himself and of a few days rest before he went on with his endless ice traveling.

The two women stood at the door of their home. With the necessary courtesy of people who live in such cruel terrain it never occurred to them that they would not welcome him and feed him with whatever they had available and keep him in comfort until he was ready to travel again. In the pale light of the mid-morning he came towards them, slowly, swinging and swishing, and they stood there and waited for him. And when he came up they took him by the arms and led him into their home, and all three of them stood unwinding from their fur clothes in the light of the blubber oil lamp. And as she took off her seal skin jacket and pulled back her fur-rimmed hood the young woman learned at last that she was beautiful, because his eyes told her so. And as she sank to her haunches to tend the cooking the old woman knew that she was old and ugly, because his eyes did not even turn from the young woman.

Of course the young man loved the young woman; and the young woman loved the young man. Nothing else was possible with the spring crashing into life around them and both of them strangers to the other, and the young woman had never seen a man before and the young man was far from home on a courageous but foolish journey. Yes, they loved each other and the young man took the young woman to wife there in the ice house, on the fullness of the spring tides in front of the old woman and she said not a word, but squatted lower over the cooking pot and faded as the summer came. She could not hate the young woman, because she had known and lived with her for far too long and she could not hate the young man because she could see the rightness of this mating. But her sleep was disturbed by their loving and then by the dreams that came to her afterwards.

In some ways it was good to have the young man with them. With two hunters, both active and tireless and whose bodies know the curves and thoughts of each other's, there is hunting possible which cannot be done alone, and the piles of fur beside the house mounted and the young man talked of trading and possessions that the women knew nothing about—of drink that turned your head to fire and allowed you to meet the ancestors again and fight with the monsters; of fishing hooks and needles so fine and strong that they seemed magical; of colors and ribbons and beads and clothes that the women thought were parts of stories and not real though he told them over and over again. He took the old woman's skins in his hands and admired them and said that she had more skill with the knife than anyone, man or woman, he had ever seen and the skins that she handled would fetch higher prices. And he picked up the carvings she did, in bone and rock, marveling how the walrus and the bear and the fish were revealed growing there. These too they could trade and he described the things that he and the young woman could have if they sold the carvings the old woman had made. And she who had carved for delight alone, through the long winter, wanted to snatch back her animals from his hands and hide them, but she did not. She did not because the muscles on his neck stood out like the sinews of the moose, and his legs were sturdy, strong and planted firmly in the ground, and his hands were driving into her heart and gut with their strength and beauty, and because the white horn of his nails made her think of the new moon. But she did not trust him.

And she was right. One day the young woman came to her and said that they were going away. She did not think about the old woman left alone in the ice house when winter came again; she did not think about the cold wind and the wildness to be endured alone. She said that he had made a sledge for her, each runner the rib of a great he-walrus that the young man had killed for her; he had worked on the sledge secretly when the old woman thought that he was hunting or walking or fishing. She said the sledge was the most beautiful thing she had ever seen; each runner was intricately carved; the seat was lined with pale fur; the seal sinews were so strong and taut that she would ride without a jolt across the frozen wastes. He would take her to his village and buy for her beads and jewels and garments worthy of her beauty. The young woman told the old woman that her husband was going to take her away from this dreary desolation, and this empty lonely life, and bring her to a place where her beauty would be appreciated and reflect credit on him. She told the old woman also that there was a child growing in her, that she hoped for a son as lithe and fine and strong as the young man, that she would have a son and a place where her beauty could be admired.

She desired the beauty of the young woman; she desired the child of the young woman; she desired the husband of the young woman; and she had little enough to do all day except feed those desires. So that they ate into her, like the ice of the approaching autumn, creeping up the rivers of her blood. Soon the couple must be gone, because the courage and foolishness of the young man were diminished by the loveliness of his wife and his tenderness for her, and he wanted to be in his village safe and certain before the hard weather and the long night came. The time was approaching when the old woman could wait no longer. One day the young man was gone from the house, so the old woman said to the young woman that it was a long, long time since she had braided up that beautiful hair. She said that they should prepare a special feast for the young man and that the young woman must look her most beautiful. The young woman was pleased; she felt that the old woman had not entered into her joy and had withdrawn from her recently so she was happy to find that she had been mistaken. So she unpinned her long hair and sat cross-legged on the floor at the feet of the old woman. The old woman took the comb made from bone which she had carved many years ago for the young woman and began to comb her hair. And she combed and combed. She reveled for the last time in that living loveliness; the hair shone and shook in the light of the lamp and sparkled like the sea-deep does in midsummer when it is crazed by the lights of the underworld that float up and dance on the surface. The young woman told her to hurry, eager to see her beauty in the admiration of the young man. So then the old woman took the hair and began to twist and braid it into a fat rope, and she took the rope and wound it round the young woman's lovely cream-colored neck and pulled and pulled, tighter and tighter, until the young woman was dead. Then

she took her little hand knife, which she had made herself for skin-
ning, down from the wall and, using all of her immense and practiced skill, she skinned the young woman's face, not spoiling the
hair, which was both lovely and necessary, not pulling out one eye-
lash nor missing the soft curves of lip and cheek. And when the
young woman was faceless and bloody she dragged her out of the
house and buried her in the soft snow of a drift not far away. Then
she took a broom and swept the house and the snow with great
attention so that no blood and no drag lines and no mess could be
seen. Then she took a soft seal skin shift that she had made herself for
the young woman and put it on; its gentle folds caressed her skin and
everything seemed possible for her. She washed in ice water, the
coldness of it bracing her joyfully. After all that she took the skin
from the face of the young woman and with the delicate practice of
the years smoothed the young woman's face over her own. Its lovely
pliability covered the wrinkles and jutting bones of her old, ugly
face; she pulled the creamy skin of the neck down as far as it would
go, securing it with an ivory pin to the top of the soft shift; she
tugged the heavy mass of hair back over her own thinning greasy
locks and shook her head so that it fell loose again covering the seam-
lines. And then she lay on the bed that the young couple had made
themselves, and covered herself with the furs and skins under which
they lay night after night, leaving her outside. The thought of what
she had done warmed her; the thought of what was coming heated
her. She lay there waiting, ready and eager.

The young man came home. She heard the gentle rhythm of his
snowshoes; she heard him banging off the spare snow and stomping
about outside the house; she heard his muffled breath as he pulled his
skin-jacket over his head; she heard the soft whistle that he always
made when he was tired but pleased with himself. He came in. And
seeing her lying on the bed all beautiful and waiting for him, he
smiled. Where was the old one he asked. And she told him that she
had gone to the beach to look for a special stone for a special carving,
to be a present for them at their departure, a very special carving as a
bride gift and a gift for the child. The young man said that that was

good because such a carving by the old hag would fetch a good price from some white-skinned collector and he laughed. The old woman would be gone for hours on such a task. The young man tugged at his boots; then he pulled off his shift, his trousers. His chest was muscled and beautiful, his loins were leaping for his bride, he fell upon her and she, kicking back the blankets, received him in her eagerness. He plunged into her body and she responded with delight. He was so far into his joy and lust that he did not notice the changed body. He plunged and bucked like the melting of a river when the great chunks of ice are hurled suddenly into the sea; he melted into her like the full tide of spring; and she leaped up for him like a young seal taking to the water for the first time. He rode her like the porpoise schools, she held him like the ocean deep. There was a love and a knowing in them both.

He worked her like an old bull walrus and it was hot hard work and at last he was done and lifted his head and smiled down into her eyes. And the sweat from his joyful labor dripped from his forehead down the fringe of his black hair and fell onto her face. It shriveled the skin, because the old woman had not had time for proper curing. The skin of the young woman shrank and curled away from the face of the old woman. Where it was secured at the neck with the ivory pin it tore away; from around her mouth the lips peeled back revealing her thin tired gums. The bones of her cheeks broke through the tenderness of the young woman's skin. The tears that sprang in her eyes rolled away the young woman's soft velvet and uncovered the harsh wrinkles. The hairline parted under the strain—the thick hair falling backwards onto the pile of bed-skins, the forehead dissolving, shrinking, disappearing.

With his hands he completed the work his sweat had begun, scrabbling at her face, scratching her, making her bleed. She herself did not move. Still naked, still lying on her, his lower body still replete with joy, the horror came into his eyes. The young man screamed and leapt to his feet; he grabbed for his shift, his breeches and boots and rushed out into the gathering gloom. She heard him retching and gasping as he fumbled the straps of his snowshoes. She heard his heaves and moans as he gathered what was necessary from around him. At last she heard the swishing, swishing mixed with his horror, repulsion and guilt. The noises died away into the twilight, diminishing, fading and finally, after many many minutes, finally gone.

And then the old woman was alone.

"Let Us Now Praise Unknown Women and Our Mothers Who Begat Us"

It was the apples that did it.

The smell of warm apples, because in the weary muddle of the evening before she had left the bag of apples too near the radiator; and the memories, released, surged into the dark room and wrapped her as tenderly in their arms as she wrapped her baby.

No one had warned her, or rather, yes they had but she had not been able to hear any warnings. The utter exhaustion, the disorienting lack of sleep, the constancy of demand, those things she had more or less anticipated. But the debilitating draining passion of love she had not been prepared for; nor the sense of being laid too wide open, spread out too thin, her sense of personal boundaries destroyed, the confusion of self and other, the exposure of body and thought both to the use of another and not even knowing when it had become another not a part of herself. Worse, worse even than being-in-love, an experience she had always found uncomfortable and self-annihilating because the object and the source of the passion, the self-destruction and the confusion, was both utterly vulnerable to her and utterly ungiving. She had woken and slept and listened and organized and suffered physically and slaved and poured out the resources of her own body, blood and milk and time and energy, for six unrelenting weeks of service to someone who gave nothing in return, nothing at all except the physical fact of its existence. The baby took, and took and took and took, long after she had nothing left to give and still she does not hate but loves the baby, passionately, tear-jerkingly and finally, wearily, bitterly, defeatedly, and this was the third time in five hours that she had been dragging awake, her dreams smashed, fragmented, stolen, sucked down with the milk into the maw of that all-consuming, tyrannical, tiny, powerful, beautiful body.

And then she catches the smell of apples, and sitting on the dark sofa with her daughter sucking, sucking, sucking, she spins away out across the galaxies of time and memory and smells afresh apples in a warm cupboard, tastes the strange cleanness of elderflower tea, touches the soft roughness of old linen curtains, hears the clear note of a flute playing in a next-door room, sees beautiful orange dragons on delicate china cups and knows herself, long legs in shorts, bony, awkward, lost, waylaid temporarily on her certain journey through childhood. Ten or eleven years young; unkempt, not physically but emotionally, lonely, fierce, on holiday with her mother and her mother's new lover; husband and child replaced. Husband rightly, the daughter knew, but herself *wrongly,* and dangerously and what certainty can there ever be again and a great passion of anger and injustice and trying-to-be-good and sulking instead. And too much, "Why don't you go out and play, darling," and, "Go on, darling, don't mope around so, the fresh air is good for you," and, "Do go out and enjoy yourself, darling, you don't need to wait for us, we don't mind."

So she had moped around through the first half of a hot and lovely country August. To amuse herself she took to spying on other people, listening to the chatter at the counter of the village shop, lurking behind the bus stop and peering in through windows. She bought herself a notebook and filled it with mean sketches and vicious reports on all the people; and nobody liked her very much and none of the other children wanted to play with her because she was not very nice at all. She speculated for her victims' lives of dreariness and small-mindedness and believed in the objectivity of her own observations so she did not even want them to like her, because they were not very nice people anyway.

She extended her researches to the edge of the village. Up a small track there was a cottage with a lovely garden and behind the garden a wooded slope with undergrowth and one morning she decided to hide up there and see what she could see. A hot sunny morning, and the garden with rough grass, not a lawn, which ran under fruit trees and around casual flower beds down to the green back door. And after a little while a big, fat, old woman came out of the door and started weeding in the garden. She turned her back on the slope and leaned down to pull weeds, leaning from the waist with her legs apart, barely thirty feet away. And the enormousness of her bottom sticking up, the rest of her trunk and head invisible, huge and fat and disgusting, her floppy tweed skirt stretched wide and held by the huge knees, ungainly, ugly and, from the vantage point in the under-growth, splendidly ludicrous. So she whipped out her notebook and was about to sketch that enormous bottom and write some telling comments on it and its owner when, without looking up and without turning round, the gardening woman said, very loudly, "Don't you dare." And without thinking she had shoved away the notebook and said, "What?" "Don't you dare write any comments on how hideous and silly I look here." And the woman straightened up but still did not turn round, her hair was escaping wispily from its bun, and she still looked silly and ugly, her cardigan was baggy too. "Come down here."

She had been frightened then, embarrassed and scared, convinced that the woman would demand to see the notebook; but she tried not to let it show, hopped over the garden fence jauntily, and with a moderately successful assumption of effrontery strolled down the gar-den. But the woman did not demand or ask anything, she just smiled and said, "My name's Elaine, what's yours?" The smile undid her jauntiness. "Clare," she muttered, shifting from leg to leg. Elaine said, "Well, if my legs are too fat, yours are too thin. Do you like our garden?" And without touching her she showed Clare round the garden telling her the names of the flowers and pointing out interest-ing things that were happening—rose suckers and old nests and ripening fruit. She never mentioned the notebook. Emboldened, Clare finally asked, "How did you know? I mean, that I was there, and about the notebook?" "Oh, I'm a witch," said Elaine calmly. "My friend is too; and we have a cat as our familiar, which everyone thinks is called Smudge, but whose real name is Thunder-flower." She was not laughing at Clare and Clare knew it. Elaine said, "Why don't you come in and meet the others?" And they had gone quite comfortably through the green door and into the kitchen. From the front of the house she could hear a flute playing, and Elaine said, "That's Isobel but she'll finish practicing in a minute; in the meantime if you look in that cupboard you'll find three blue mugs. Could you get them out while I boil the kettle?" And while Clare was looking in the cupboard, which was full of different-colored mugs and plates, not proper sets like her mother had but different colors and sizes, some of them old and fine and some of them modern pottery and some just plastic, and getting out the three blue ones, the flute-playing stopped and Elaine put her head out of the kitchen and called, "Isobel, we've got a visitor." Isobel, who was very tall and not much older than Clare's mother, but much messier and wearing the sort of crimplene slacks that her mother would not have been seen dead in, came into the kitchen and looked at her and said, "How do you do?" Not kindly to a child, but properly. She didn't seem to be at all surprised to see a strange child in her kitchen, but smiled and said to Elaine, "I have had such a lovely practice, it was really sweet of you to go outside while I tried the frilly bits." Then she reached down a tin from a high shelf and opened it and put it, half-full of biscuits, on the kitchen table. The kettle boiled and Elaine made the tea and she had sat with them at the wobbly table and they had chatted. And the women had asked no finding-out questions, they had just let her be and join in or not as she wanted. And when she realized that it was nearly lunchtime she said that she ought to go and they took her through to the front of the house and let her out of the front door very politely. When she was halfway down the path Isobel called out, "We hope you'll be able to come again. Any time you want to, drop in. You haven't met Thunder-flower yet." And Elaine added, "We need an apprentice anyway." And when she got back to the cottage they were staying in she was not in a sulk anymore, but she did not tell her mother where she had been all morning because she wanted to keep it as her own secret. She did not want her mother going and getting friendly with them.

And for the last two weeks of her holiday she went there nearly every day. They didn't do anything very exciting; they taught her how to make jam, how to care for the garden, how to store apples, each one having its own space and not having to touch the others. They gave her homemade elderflower tea to drink, a cool taste with a sharp touch somewhere, not like anything else she'd ever tasted. Isobel played on the flute and Elaine accompanied her on the piano and taught Clare how to turn the pages. Sometimes Elaine read stories to her and Thunder-flower coiled around her shoulders when she sat in the big armchair; and what they had done, though she did not know it then, was pay exquisite attention to her in the simple assumption that she was worthy of attention, that she was a nice and clever person, not a small and ferocious animal. So she told them lots of things that she had never told anyone else, and they listened and discussed them and were interested, but not pushy. She told them about school, and her friends at home and how she did not want to go and live in a new poky flat instead of her old home; she told them about the divorce, and how her father did not talk to people and was sad and grouchy, and about Ben who was nicer than that and how that made her feel bad, and about how angry she was with her mother and how she hated her and loved her and how it all hurt so much. And telling it aloud didn't make it feel better exactly but it did help it to make sense. They listened and respected her and liked her. She was too young even to wonder why; she was just happy and useful there, with them and they were happy and useful with each other, and she could see that. It was true that they were witches and she knew it, although Isobel pretended to be a schoolteacher and Elaine pretended to be a retired schoolteacher, and Thunder-flower pretended to be a sweet little pussycat called Smudge; and if she had not known she would never have guessed that she came in from nightprowling with blood on her paws and wild green eyes. The flowers grew in their garden, the copper shone in their fireplace, the irregular weave of their curtains changed color from minute to minute and the smell of apples pervaded the whole cottage. And one day when they had all been chopping up logs in the garden and Clare had helped carry them down to the wood shed she saw their two broomsticks leaning against the shed wall and had felt a shiver of excitement. Two well-made besom brooms, one slightly thicker in the handle than the other, and their delicate fingery twigs spreading out and casting tangly clear shadows from the afternoon sun onto the dusty walls of the wood shed.

Her mother and Ben had been only too glad to have her happier and calmer and busier, so they did not ask too many questions. The weight was removed and she flourished in the freer air. Once, when her mother had planned a well-intentioned and guilt-absolving picnic on the beach and Clare had casually rejected it in favor of one more day with Elaine and Isobel, her mother exclaimed in exasperation, "Whatever do you do there all day? What's so special about two old ladies and a cat?" But Clare did not answer because she did not know. She was careful though, careful not to tell her mother they were witches, because a witches' apprentice never gives her teachers away. Sometimes they burned witches on bonfires, so she knew she had to be careful.

The holiday came to an end. She went the last day, sadly, to say goodbye to them, to try and say thank you for a gift she knew even then she had been given without knowing what it was. They had tea together, not in the blue mugs but in some beautiful delicate china cups with orange dragons on them; not at the kitchen table but in the sitting room, and although it was not cold they had lit the fire for her. There was cinnamon toast and fat fruitcake with nuts in. Isobel poured slowly, carefully, from a silver teapot. They had made tea special for her, ritualized, timeless, because she was their friend. When it was nearly time to go, Elaine had looked her straight in the eye and said, "You know, I think you should leave that notebook with us. You know we will never never read it, but we would keep it safe; furious, mean thoughts need to be kept safe. We will put a very firm, strong, good spell on it." And she had taken it out of her pocket and given it to them without a qualm. Isobel said, "Of course, we will replace it for you." They gave her another notebook, small and covered in bottle-green watered silk, and the pages were old and creamy, heavy, soft, and they had no lines, just blank so she could write and draw whatever she chose. It was ancient and beautiful. "It's a spell book," said Elaine. "You can of course put in anything you want, but try only to make strong, hopeful spells if you can. It is all right to do angry spells, but not mean ones or despairing ones. Remember—'Hope has two lovely daughters—anger and courage.' Witches always take responsibility for what they do. They are loyal and loving and hopeful."

"Have you made me a witch now?" she asked.

"No," said Elaine, "nobody can ever make anyone a witch, but you can be one any time you want to. You just have to believe it, that's all. You just say, 'I am a witch,' and you will be. You can even fly if you want to, but you have to believe in your own power. You see, it's very easy." She smiled and Clare smiled back. "Oh, and by the way, you don't need to have a broomstick, that's completely optional. All you need is to remember that you are a witch woman, full of power and strength, and then you can do anything you want. You can make things and break things and call storms and grow plants and heal people and hurt people. It's up to you."

And a little later she had gone down the path in the long light of the afternoon, leaving them standing arm in arm in their cottage doorway. She had been completely and perfectly happy, warm tea and toast in her tummy, warm love and power in her stomach. The next day she and her mother and Ben had driven away and she had gone back to school and forgotten. She had forgotten. But now, feeding her new daughter in the depths of the night, she remembered. She remembered not just the happenings of that summer, but absolutely the taste and touch and sight and smell and sound of them. She remembered her own nervous embarrassment when Elaine had called her from the garden; and how comfortable it had been with the two of them. She felt again how it was to be a perfectly and absolutely happy child, and knew again the power and goodness of being a strong woman.

So, now, she laid the sleeping baby on the sofa beside her, and wedged her in with a handy cushion, because a witch always takes responsibility for what she does, and she walked over to the window and opened it. The moon, on its wane, rode the shoulder of a cloud and illuminated its frilled edges; the air was cool and milky. She said, "I am a witch. I can make things and break things, and call storms and grow plants and babies and heal people and hurt people. I believe in my power. I can fly." In her cotton nightdress she clambered on to the windowsill and leapt out into the waiting air. After the first delighted surprise at finding that it really worked, she soared upwards, dancing upon the darkness, and testing her twists and turns. Steering was more problematic than she had imagined, but by no means impossible. She alighted briefly in the tree opposite her window to thank it for its beauty and generosity, which she did not always remember to notice, then she flew back to the window to check on the baby. She was sleeping sweetly, the fluff on her head poking upwards and her long lashes folded downwards on her cheek. So Clare turned and left her and flew over London; a strange new and magical city seen from the air—Primrose Hill a tiny paradise with little lampstands and the playground sheltering under the huge spider's web of the Bird House in Regent's Park. St. Pancras Station was a fairy-tale castle, turreting and cavorting outrageously in the moonlight, and the great dome of St. Paul's a loving and protective breast. She swooped now, moving with certainty in her new element, and rose to greet the stars, and swung low over the streets of the City, deserted and ancient and longing for her visitation. She shot out over the river and flew upwards to watch it snake its glittery way across the town. She darted from side to side, delighting; the bridges were garlands, garlands of fire, linking the two heavier masses of earth across the deep of water; and the air embraced them all. She was perfectly and absolutely happy, and knew the power and the goodness of being a strong woman.

And as she flew downstream towards the docks and Greenwich she began to sing a deep new song, and she called on all other witches everywhere to come and sing it with her, and they came. Elaine and Isobel, still smiling, and a woman who lived four doors down from her at home and whose fierce purposeful striding had always filled Clare with fear; and the middle-aged woman who guarded the changing rooms at her local swimming pool and whose shiny black skin rippled gloriously in the moonlight; and the midwife who had delivered her daughter and hauled her through the confusion of pain and emotion. And more and more women, thrusting beautiful, confident bodies through the new air and singing, singing, singing her song with her. And flying over the river more fun than she could have dreamed: Formation Flying, as funny and silly and skillful as the women on *Come Dancing;* and Free Fall, where there is no gravity but only perfect dignity; and Pairs, more sensuous and tender than terrestrial dancing can ever approach; and Exhibitionism, solo flights and stunts of daring and careening wildness and mutual admiration; and just being there, flying, dancing with crazy, immodest, hysterical, free laughter and song. "Welcome to the Coven," laughed a woman just below her and she looked down and it was her science mistress from school, who grinned and adjusted her white overall and not for the sake of decency. There were women she recognized from history books and portrait galleries and women she had never seen before, and young and old and in-between and witches' dancing-skins come in more colors than the rainbow. And the trying soreness that still irritated her vagina from where she had been stitched after the birth was soothed and healed by the soft air, so she tugged off her nightie and laughed as it floated like a tiny pale cloud down into the river beneath. Turning deftly in the air she saw her stretch marks as silvery-purple bands of strength which glowed pearly in the moonlight. And she was full of joy.

And later she flew quietly home, leaving the radiant dancers, fliers, singers; because after childbirth a witch knows she needs a certain amount of quiet and solitude so that she can learn again what are her boundaries, and a certain amount of rest because caring for a small baby is very demanding; and witches always take responsibility for what they do. She rested after her pleasing exertions in the green tree outside her home and when she felt perfectly comfortable she flew back in through the window and alighted. Her daughter was still asleep, tidily on her tummy on the sofa, and the delicate hair which fringed the rims of her ears seemed to glow in the moonlight. Clare picked her up carefully and was about to carry her safely back to her basket in the bedroom when the baby opened her eyes, awakened but not frightened by the cool softness of Clare's naked body. Four eyes very close to one another and glowing in the dark like cats'. And the baby was so quiet, so present, so softly smelling of warm milk, so beautiful, so perfect, so courageous and bold a decision against such impossibly long odds, so little and funny, that Clare could not help but smile. She murmured, "You little witch, daughter of a witch, you can be a witch too if you want to. Remember that." And in the quiet of the ending of the night, the daughter, for the very first time, smiled back.